Channah —

Thank You —

I hope you enjoy
Cat's Story

Ray Lowenstein

LOVE
BEHIND *the*
LIES
Book One of the
O'Connor Sisters Trilogy

RAJ LOWENSTEIN

Order this book online at www.trafford.com
or email orders@trafford.com

Most Trafford titles are also available at major online book retailers.

Print information available on the last page.

ISBN: 978-1-4907-8844-9 (sc)
ISBN: 978-1-4907-8843-2 (hc)
ISBN: 978-1-4907-8842-5 (e)

Library of Congress Control Number: 2018942075

Trafford rev. 04/23/2018

www.trafford.com
North America & international
toll-free: 1 888 232 4444 (USA & Canada)
fax: 812 355 4082

ACKNOWLEDGMENTS

To my dearest sister. Before we had our wonderful husbands to bolster us and love us, before we had our children to fill our hearts, we had each other. No one fills my life with so much. Thank you for being my sister! Thank you for being my friend.

Always and forever to my husband, Rick. You are continuously so patient with my quirkiness. I was lucky the day we met. Love you! R

To my cousins Terry and Jamie. Thanks for the beautiful tour of Palm Springs and all the information.

To Linda A., who is my sister/friend in real life and in the pages of my books.

Can't forget the kids and grandkids . . . Hello, my darlings!

To the cast and crew of the Desert Palm Apartments. You know who you are, and I thank you for letting me share you with my readers!

www.rajlowenstein.net

PROLOGUE

SIX MONTHS AGO

Dylan Farber was standing by the craft table. It was his first day as an intern at the studio, and his instructions had been clear: don't move, stay out of the way, watch, and learn. He was excited and doing his best not to do a little jig.

His first day and he was on the same soundstage as Cat Connors. No one would believe he was fifteen feet from where she was filming a scene in her latest movie.

Her costars were equally as famous as she, yet Dylan was the same age as Connors. She had been his first crush when she was on the Disney show *Blue Sky Hawai'i*.

The soundstage was quiet except the scene. Even though Dylan could see the cameras and crew, his focus was on the living room scene being filmed. He was mesmerized. Cat Connors as Judith Traherne in a remake of *Dark Victory* was angry at the world, in particular, her friend the Monsignor. She screamed and cursed the man and his deity. Tears flowed down her cheeks, and her nose ran.

The scene was practically too hard-hitting to watch. Dylan's heart ached for the character, while his awe of Cat Connors doubled. It wasn't pretty. It was raw, and even from the fifteen feet distance, Dylan could feel her anguish.

Cat Connors would get another Oscar nod for this scene alone.

The director yelled cut. The two dozen crew who had been frozen in their places began to move about. Instructions were called out. Lighting was adjusted. The set rearranged.

Dylan had learned from his half day of observation that it would be a half hour before they would either reshoot the scene from a different angle or shoot a new scene altogether.

"So, kid, what do you think?" the woman, someone who had come to the craft table throughout the morning, asked as she stood next to Dylan.

Dylan turned to look at the woman. She was perhaps in her fifties. Her hair was a purple bun held together with neon green chopsticks. Her black lacquered lips smiled broadly at him.

He let out his breath, not realizing he had been holding it.

"It's amazing to be on this side of the process. I'm Dylan Farber."

"Nice to meet you, Dylan." She looked around and then back to him. "Yeah, it's all great, but the glamour will fade soon enough," she commented, adjusting a stack of plates on the table.

"I don't see how." Dylan gasped. "I understood how it all works—you know, the process—but to see it firsthand is worth the seven years of college to get my degree. And to be this close to Cat Connors," he gushed, knowing he just exposed his *fanboy* persona to the older woman.

She laughed before reaching over to the craft table and getting two éclairs, handing one to Dylan. "I'm Rhoda Maehr. I'm the craft manager for this end of the studio. Been working in the industry for thirty years."

The frown and shaking of her head took Dylan back.

"It's all for the camera, the stage, her adoring fans, and the paparazzi. In real life, she's a cold fish!" she confided after glancing around to see who, if anyone, was near.

Whom was she speaking of? Definitely not the actress who had just ripped out his heart and handed it back to him. Dylan could only stare at the woman, his mouth hanging open. What she was saying wasn't possible. She was a superstar in an industry that didn't hide the flaws of the actors. The studio system days were long gone.

"That can't be true!" he defended in a harsh whisper.

"Wasn't always," Rhoda began sadly. "If you've read any of the rag mags, you know the kid from that Disney show was the first to break her heart."

"Blue Sky Song, yeah, I remember."

Rhoda continued, "Then remember that asshole Malcolm Ramsey about three years ago. He really pulled the rug out from her. She was naïve enough to fall for his handsome magnetism. It changed her. She doesn't trust anyone."

Dylan couldn't believe what she was saying. Perhaps she just didn't care for Cat Connors. He started to rebut what she was saying but was quieted with a hand.

"God knows I feel for the poor thing. Seems like she is all alone in the world. No parents or close family members."

"What about her twin? I thought they were close."

Rhoda gave him a crooked smile. "Not that I've seen, and I've been around her ever since she came back to la-la land. But to the point, she closed herself off. Doesn't associate with anyone outside the studio. It's affecting her career.

"The studios are pushing her agent to get her to take some time off, six months to a year, after they finish filming this movie. But I'm telling you, it's gonna take something major happening to her before that ice melts."

Dylan still wasn't convinced with anything the older woman had said. It just wasn't possible for a woman who lit up the screen and stage, as well as sold millions of recordings, to be this "ice princess" Rhoda was describing.

Her hand on his arm brought his attention back to her. "Watch," she said.

Dylan followed Rhoda's gaze to the approaching actress under discussion.

"Don't say a word. Just follow my lead." He was warned.

As Cat Connors approached the craft table, Rhoda greeted, "Good afternoon, Ms. Connors. Was everything to your liking in your trailer?" Rhoda's voice was warm and genuine.

Cat Connors turned to look at Rhoda. The smile she gave didn't reach her eyes. With a flat tone, she thanked her for the sparkling water and fruit that had been left in the trailer. There was no warmth, no animation in her face.

"This is Dylan Farber. He is one of the new interns," Rhoda introduced with a look in his direction.

"Nice to meet you. Have a good day," she said before turning to head back the direction she had come.

Dylan had never experienced being looked at and through at the same time. There had been nothing in her tone or manner that was rude or disrespectful. There had just been nothing.

"Oh my god!" Dylan turned to Rhoda.

"Hurts when your idols fall?" She laid a sympathetic hand on Dylan's arm.

"That bastard Ramsey did a real number on her."

"Like I said,"—Rhoda shook her head, a little of the sadness in her voice on her face—"she needs to have something happen to her so she can learn that people aren't all assholes and, sometimes, if you're lucky, you can be surrounded by people who love you just for you. I gotta go. Good luck, sweetheart." Her face lit up with a smile. "See you at the movies!"

Dylan watched the woman walk away.

"I hope you're right, Rhoda. I hope you're right!"

THE BEGINNING

I was exhausted.

For the last week, we had been doing voice-overs and shooting close-ups and exterior scenes—the characters walking on the beach, in the park, or sitting in a restaurant. It was all rather dull stuff, but the director had promised George Clooney, my costar, and me that if we busted our asses this week, we would be done on Sunday. It was technically Monday morning, as midnight had passed well over an hour ago.

We had been filming the remake of the classic 1939 Bette Davis movie *Dark Victory*. The incredible Mr. Clooney had been cast as George Brent's Dr. Frederick Steel and I as Bette Davis's tragic Judith Traherne. The supporting cast was equally outstanding, and with Ron Howard directing, it was bound to be as enjoyable as the original.

When we had finished, I had had several offers to drive me to either my Malibu home or my Beverly Hills estate. I wanted total quiet. I declined all the offers and called for a studio driver to drive me to my small Burbank apartment. I would have almost six months before I started my next project. I needed the break. I had been working steadily, going from one project to another, for the last five years.

In the middle of the six months, I had promised my agent and the recording studio I was under contract with that I would record a live album and show of standards from the likes of Ella Fitzgerald, Billy Holiday, Rosemary Clooney, Streisand, and Garland for HBO. This would be a week of rehearsal with the band and two nights, if necessary, of actually performing. When I look back on the last five years, that was nothing at all.

The midrise had been built back in the '50s. The building had nine floors with the top two floors housing four apartments each instead of the eight the first six floors contained. Mine had been bought and remodeled by a semifamous actor who had been known more for his paranoid personality and less for his acting ability. What had made this eighth-floor apartment so unique was that Ronald Edgar VanVelt had taken the master bedroom and turned it into a panic room.

The walls were one foot of reinforced concrete, with the ceiling and floor already strengthened. The room had its own ventilation system as well as air conditioner. There were no windows, but it did have a small three-piece bathroom and an equally small closet.

When I had bought it at an estate sale, my friends had been charmed by the place. Aside from the kitchen and the updated security system, I spent little money on the apartment. As a joke, I had placed cameras, tiny pinholes in the crown molding, throughout the house and had them wired into the panic room, my bedroom.

From a laptop, I could see everything that was going on in any room, including the balcony. Except for the powder rooms. On the few occasions I had a houseful of guests, many spent as much time watching the other partygoers from the small settee in my bedroom than actually participating in the event.

I had moved furniture from my father's house, things I had grown up with, to furnish it. This, more than any other property I owned, was my home. I felt comfortable, relaxed, and safe.

I turned on no lights when I entered. I wanted to get out of my shoes, open a bottle of wine, and sit out on my balcony and just melt into the night.

The balcony was wide and long, wrapping around two sides of the corner apartment. The master bedroom would have had access to it had VanVelt not remodeled. As it was now, the only access was from the large glass French doors from the living room. I made it an extension of my living space with plush lounges, side tables, a dinette that sat eight, and an outdoor kitchen. At two thirty in the morning, Burbank was quiet.

Or it should have been.

"Look, for fuck's sake! I didn't tell them anything. Planz, you know I wouldn't cross you!" A strained and frightened voice came from the other balcony. "Who told you I talked to them? I would never. Shit . . . you have to believe me."

"Oh, I believe," a cold voice replied. It was Planz, whoever the hell he was.

I sipped my wine and relished the argument. This was better than any movie or television show. I didn't know what the two men were going on about, maybe a lovers' spat. This was LA. I relaxed into the wine and the drama but was soon putting my wine down and sitting up. This was getting serious. *Maybe I should call 911*, I thought.

"Hasset, you have worked for me for almost ten years," Planz told the other man.

I stood, caught between moving inside to call the police and keeping my nose out of something that was plainly none of my business. I took a step toward the door.

"Please, I got three kids!" Hasset groaned.

"I'll make sure they are taken care of. Your family is in no way responsible for your fucking stupid behavior." Planz's voice snarled.

I heard Hasset's voice hitch as he started to say the Hail Mary.

"You should have thought about how this would end before you turned your back on me." His voice was so cold and casual it terrified me.

It wasn't loud, the slight "Pop! Pop! Pop!" Nonetheless, I knew what it was. Someone had just shot a gun with a silencer.

Without thinking, I stepped closer to the edge of the balcony. As I got to the corner, I saw the limp body of a man as it was leveraged off the railing and out into empty space.

I must have made a noise—something to catch the attention of the man who had tossed the body over the railing. He turned his cold gray eyes at me with surprise.

"Cat Connors," he said, his voice now warm and surprised, "I always wanted to meet you, but, as you can imagine, not this way. Oh, well . . ." He sighed as if he was exceedingly disappointed in an unruly child. "The best most often die young."

The gun came out of his jacket so fast. I stepped back just far enough, so there was no way for him to get a clear shot unless he leaned over onto my balcony. I ran, tripped over the threshold of the door, righted myself, and sprinted into my bedroom. I slammed the door closed, punching the bright red button that would seal me inside.

Thank you! Thank you! I chanted to the paranoid Ronald Edgar VanVelt. I didn't turn on the lights but went to the laptop. In less than a minute, I was looking out into my apartment. The tall, handsome man was tearing up my apartment. I watched as he pulled the gun out of his jacket again and shot at the door to my bedroom. The door was two-inch steel. The bullets ricocheted off the door and embedded into the opposite walls.

I watched his expression rapidly change from unconcern to astonishment to worry and to irritation. I didn't know who he was, but Planz was a dangerous man. He moved from the balcony door and stood there for a moment.

I fished my cell out of my pocket and dialed.

"911. What is your emergency?" a man calmly asked me.

I whispered even though the man outside the room couldn't have heard me. "I am Teresa O'Connor . . ." I gave

4

him my address. "I just saw a man in 8A shoot a man and then throw him off the balcony. He's in my house now," I told the operator, trying to stay calm and not doing as good of a job as I wanted. "I'm in my panic room. His name, the shooter, is Planz. I heard the other man. He was called Hasset. I heard them talking. I just thought they were having an argument. Oh, shit!"

"Ms. O'Connor, we have already dispatched several units to that address. I will advise them that you are in your apartment. My name is Farris. I'll be on the line until you are ready to hang up. OK?"

I interrupted. "He's leaving!"

"Who is leaving, Ms. O'Connor?" he asked.

"I have cameras that show me the apartment. Planz just left my apartment. He is wearing a nice suit, was tall, maybe six-two, and good looking. He is dark complexioned, but I think he is white or Hispanic. Is someone coming?"

"The police units are four minutes out. Ms. O'Connor, did you say that you heard the man, the man who shot the other man, was called Planz?"

I told him it was and that Planz had called the other man Hasset. Was I repeating myself?

After a moment of only background noise, the 911 operator came back on the line. "Ms. O'Connor, the first unit just pulled up. They will be there in a few minutes. There are also several detectives that will be following."

"I don't think I can come out," I spoke into the phone but really to myself.

"The detectives, as well as the police officers, have identification. Once they get there, you will be safe."

I focused on the computer screen and let him know that there were three uniformed officers in my apartment. "But I am not coming out, not yet."

"That's fine, Ms. O'Connor." Farris's soothing voice came over the cell. "There are also two detectives arriving soon. They will be there in about ten minutes. As soon as I have their names, I will let you know. Can you see identification if they show it to you?"

"I bought this place as a joke." I had no idea why I was telling him this. "I don't need a panic room." A sob hitched my voice. "Thank God, thank God," I chanted to the ceiling.

"Ma'am, when the detectives arrive, will you be able to see their identification?"

I shook my head to clear it. "Yes, there are cameras in each corner. They're not that easy to see. They look like black dots in the crown molding. All they have to do is find them and hold up their IDs. I will see."

He acknowledged my comment.

Farris was speaking. Just his voice helped me relax. "You doing all right?" he asked, sounding genuine.

"You know,"—I laughed—"I have had better days. Oh!" I started to cry something without a camera rolling I never do. "Hasset has three kids. I heard him tell Planz. Those poor babies." I cried softy a few more seconds before I pulled myself together.

"Farris?" I said. "I don't want anyone to freak out."

"Why are they going to freak out, Ms. O'Connor?" he asked, sounding concerned.

"Teresa O'Connor is my real name, but . . ." I looked at the screen of my laptop. There were no less than seven police officers in my house now. From one angle, I could see into the foyer off the lobby, and I saw there were more officers out there. This was going to make everything worse. "Most people"—I took a breath and continued— "know me as Cat Connors."

I heard a sudden inhalation of breath before a muffled "Holy shit!" before Farris's calm voice returned. "Ms. Conn . . . O'Connor, I will inform the detectives who are on their way and the commander who is on the scene. It will be the detectives whom you will be coming back to the station with."

After an explanation that he was getting information about the detectives, the line was quiet except for the ever-present background noise.

"Ms. O'Connor, I have the names of the detectives. Hearn and Morales should be arriving in just a moment. They have been told to show their IDs and where. Also, you can open the door when you are ready. However, Ms. O'Connor, they want to get you to safety as quickly as possible. Do you understand?"

"Yes, thank you!"

I took a few minutes to let this soak in. I had asked Farris to stay on the line, but I really hadn't anything to say. He agreed, and I heard background noise as I didn't dare remove the phone from my ear.

"Ms. O'Connor, I was just informed that Hearn and Morales are in the building. They asked me to convey to you when you are ready to open the panic room door and let them in."

I agreed, telling Farris to let the agents know that there was a camera about six feet high on the left side of the door to my bedroom, the panic room. If they found that one and showed me their IDs, I would let them in.

He agreed to relay the information, and I sat on the settee waiting.

I saw them enter the apartment. Unlike the uniformed police officers, they were in suits, rumpled and worn. I watched as one of the uniform officers approached and pointed to the corners of the apartment as well as the door to my bedroom.

After several minutes, the detectives moved to the door, pulled out their IDs, and held them, so I was able to see each.

"Ms. O'Connor, are you all right?" Farris's concern startled me as I forgot about the phone pressed to my ear.

I laughed. "The detectives are here. I will be letting them in. Thank you for your kindness, Mr. Farris." I hoped he knew I was genuine.

"Abdul, ma'am."

"Thank you, Abdul. You made a terrifying situation bearable," I said before I let him know I was hanging up the phone.

"You're welcome." The line went dead.

After taking another minute to pull myself together, allowing my Cat Connors persona to take the place of the terrified Teresa O'Connor, I took a deep breath and hit the green button under the red that would unlock the door and put the panic room protocols on hibernation. I cracked the door only enough to see them before I stepped back and let them in. I am six feet tall, and both Hearn and Morales were shorter than me by several inches. I motioned for them to have a seat as I sat back down on the settee. The men offered their IDs again for verification. I waved them off.

"How are you holding up?" Morales asked, pulling the chair closer and taking my hand.

He was trying to be comforting, how cute. With a slight smile, I replied, "I would have to say"—I looked at him and then at his partner—"this has got to be the shittiest day of my life."

Hearn seemed stunned that I used the word "shittiest," but Morales laughed, saying he would have to agree.

Morales clear his throat. Hearn took over the conversation. "When you are ready, but not too long, we are going to get you down to the parking garage." He began. "There will be four patrol cars leaving at the same time. In the back of each will be someone with a hoodie. We have a hoodie for you. The idea is to try and make sure that if we are being followed or watched, they don't know which car you are in."

Morales added, "The good thing is the station is only five minutes from here. We'll be good." He finished confidently.

I smiled politely at each of the men while thinking this was going to be a great story for my agent to sell. Lori Liebman could turn anything into great PR.

Before we were out of the underground parking garage, I was told to lie down in the backseat and stay there until I was told otherwise.

We were only out of the garage for a moment before a voice blasted from the car radio. I wasn't able to understand what was being said. However, Hearn, who was not driving, turned back to offer me a drawn smile before angrily replying to what was being said.

"This is fucking bullshit!" Hearn complained, Morales agreeing as he told Hearn to punch in the numbers.

I wasn't sure what was going on, and when I asked, I was informed that the detectives had been ordered to take me to a more secure building. I pushed for more information but was told they had none.

My mind pondered with the idea of a more secure building. Why? Was it because I was who I was? Perhaps the Burbank Police Department took special care of their VIP witnesses.

Lori Liebman was going to love this!

The ride, instead of being five minutes, had ended up being forty minutes. I was tired and wanted to sleep.

Hearn pulled into an underground parking garage. I hadn't been paying attention to the street signs, so I didn't see the name of the building or where it was. Instead of going up, we went down three levels. Hearn pulled up to a well-lit door where four men dressed in dark suits waited.

Hearn and Morales got out of the car and left me sitting. When I tried to open the back door, I found there was no way to open the doors from the inside of the vehicle.

I knocked on the window and was unequivocally ignored. *How dare they!* I fumed.

Checking my watch, it was ten minutes before Hearn and Morales went through the doors with two of the four men. The other two approached the car and opened the back door.

"What is going on?" I demanded.

The older of the two men, his face void of any expression, answered, "Ma'am, you will follow us."

The other man put his hand on my lower back and gently propelled me forward behind the man who had spoken.

Despite my constant questions, demanding to know what was going on, I received no information; nor did either man speak to me.

We took a series of elevators from the parking garage until we deposited onto the twenty-seventh floor.

In the same silent manner, I was lead to an unmarked door. The man who had led the way opened the door, while the other gently nudged me into the room. The door was closed behind me without a sound.

I tested the door, finding it locked. I turned my focus to the room. It was, perhaps, eight by ten feet. There was a metal table bolted to the floor. Four chairs, two on each side, pushed against the cold steel of the table. There were no other furnishings. Scanning where the walls met the ceiling, I found two cameras.

Nothing would happen in this room without it being watched. I was in an interrogation room.

Did they not know who I was? I wasn't usually a bitch. Quite the opposite. I was quiet and calm, never causing a fuss. This treatment, however, was not acceptable. I would definitely be reporting this behavior.

With nothing else to do, I pulled out a chair and laid my head on my folded arms.

I was awakened by the sound of a man's voice. "Ma'am, you are to follow me."

I looked up into the face of one of the two men who had left with Hearn and Morales.

"Where?"

"You are to follow me, ma'am." He repeated.

My list of complaints regarding my treatment was growing longer by the minute.

I stood up and followed him. On the same floor but around several corners, another of the men stood next to a door.

"It's clear." He informed his comrade in the same monotone.

I was ushered into a bathroom. The vanity held a bar of facial soap, facecloth, a hand towel, a new toothbrush, and toothpaste. As there had been no instructions, I first used the facilities before washing my face of the makeup I had been in for over eighteen hours and then brushing my teeth.

I left everything where I had found it and exited the bathroom.

I was returned to the room, again without any words exchanged. Once at the table, the door smartly closed behind me.

I didn't have to wait long for a knock to pull my attention back to the door. I sat and looked into the square face of a female officer. Despite the fact that she wore a gun on her hip, she was plainly nervous.

Finally, a real person. I could use this.

"Excuse me, Ms. Connor, I mean Ms. O'Connor!" the block of a woman said.

I smiled and helped her out. "Call me Cat."

After a moment, she composed herself and took on the appearance of a stern headmistress at a reform school. "I am Agent Turnbull."

Of course, you are, I thought. Yet I couldn't miss the fact she had said agent and not a detective. What the hell was going on?

She seemed to appraise me for a moment before beginning. "Cat, I cannot give you any information at this time other than to say someone will be with you soon. They will explain what is going on. However, I have to make some dental impression." Without any further explanation, she produced the required tools for the task and went about with her undertaking.

I had many dental impressions made as part of my job. A set of dentures can radically change the shape of your face, your appearance. Why would I need to change the shape of my face?

I made no arguments with the woman. When Agent Turnbull was finished, she carefully placed everything back in the small box she had brought in with her and snapped the lid shut. She was about to leave when she turned around and smiled. It changed everything about her. She was not an attractive woman, but her smile was warm and genuine.

In what could only be described as a "conspiratorial whisper," she confessed, "Normally, I would never ever do this. I am so sorry that I am doing it now, but my daughter *loves* you! Can I get your autograph for her? I understand if you say no, but I would never forgive myself if I didn't ask."

I smiled back, grateful for something ordinary. "I would love to. What is your daughter's name?"

Agent Turnbull pulled out a pen and sheet of paper. "Her name is Heather, Heather McInnis. That's my married name. God forbid she be stuck with the name Turnbull. But it works for my job." She laughed an anxious laugh. "Thank the stars she looks like her daddy."

I wrote a sweet note, saying that her mother had helped me out at the local coffee house and best wishes to her.

I handed the paper back to the agent, who held it with such care as she folded it and put it in her breast pocket.

"Cat,"—she giggled and then cleared her throat and suddenly became the headmistress again, "can I get you something from the Starbucks on the first floor?"

"Agent Turnbull, I would kill for a coffee with nonfat cream." I took a second to look at my watch again—7:49. "I haven't eaten since 6:00 p.m. yesterday. Could I get something to eat?"

"They didn't offer you any food? I'll take care of that!" She nodded in my direction and left, the door snapping shut behind her.

I waited for a beat before getting up and testing the door to see if it was locked. It was, and I wasn't sure if I was troubled or relieved.

Ten minutes later, a young male agent opened the door and, without a word, placed a triple venti nonfat latte and a bag from McDonald's before me. He left without a word.

I slowly pulled the contents of the bag out after fashioning a placemat with a few napkins. Inside the bag were a sausage, egg, cheese, and biscuit sandwich; a hot rectangular hash brown; and a small container of orange juice.

I stared at my breakfast, unable to decide what to do.

The last time I had eaten at a McDonald's was when I was thirteen or fourteen. Most often my breakfast was an egg white omelet with spinach or kale, a thin slice of organic multigrain bread, and a mug of coffee.

My food intake was as regulated and monitored as if my life depended on it.

Fresh fruit and vegetables were my snacks. Dairy, unless it was fat-free, gluten-free, and organic, was forbidden to me.

The thought of eating this delicious-smelling trio before me was so appealing and also so forbidden. Perhaps a few bites of each would be OK, as it would be my first bite of food in almost eighteen hours.

I almost wept with the first bite of the breakfast biscuit. It was too incredible to comprehend, so different from my usual fare.

I promised myself, after the last bites of biscuit and hash browns, I would have a sensible lunch after I was let go. No one had to know I had just finished off the breakfast trio from McDonald's.

After finishing my breakfast, I had glanced at my watch. It was now a few minutes after nine. Except for Agent Turnbull and the men who popped in to look at me as if I might have mysteriously disappeared, I hadn't seen anyone or received any information. I was ready to tell what I had seen and go home. I had a six-month vacation I wanted to get started on.

The unexpected knock on the door roused me from my nap. I glanced at my watch as I answered with a "Yes?" Fifteen minutes had gone by.

The door opened. A shorter Caucasian woman and a tall Asian man entered the room. The man closed the door behind him and followed the woman, who had taken a seat across from me.

"Good morning, Ms. O'Connor. I am Special Agent Soto, and this is Special Agent Rosenbaum."

I looked at the identification tags they offered.

After a moment for me to examine, Agents Jennifer Soto and Abraham Rosenbaum clipped them back to their lapels.

"When can I go home?" I demanded without acknowledging their introduction.

The man looked at the woman, who gave a slight nod.

I didn't give him the opportunity to say what he intended to say before I spoke again. "I don't mean to be rude . . ."—always a good indication that someone was about to be rude—"but I have to tell you, I think I have been treated horribly."

Soto, a woman in her forties with mousy brown hair and a tired expression on her face, smiled.

This pissed me off!

"Do you think this is fu—"

She interrupted me this time. "Ms. O'Connor, I understand this must be a very uncommon and stressful situation for you. What you need to understand and understand completely, you witnessed a drug cartel hit. You are lucky to be alive, and we are going to make sure you stay that way."

I was slack-jawed first at her tone—a tone that very few people ever used with me—and, when her words penetrated my attitude, by what she had said.

"Who are you guys?" I asked after I pulled myself together.

It was Rosenbaum who answered, "We are with the High Profile Bureau, HPB for short."

I had never heard of them and said so.

Soto smiled; this time it warmed her face. "We're a family member of the FBI that no one likes to talk about. We like to do things a little different."

"We are responsible for keeping high-profile witnesses safe. Unfortunately, as of this morning, that is you." Rosenbaum looked at me. "This is what we do."

This took another moment to sink in. "Who the hell was Planz?"

There was a knock on the door. One of the two men who had taken me to the bathroom entered with three large cups from Starbucks. He placed one of each of the cups before the two agents and set the third before me.

The label read "Non-Fat Latte." This was three times the amount of caffeine I was allowed in a day. Being jacked up on coffee was probably not a good idea.

I took a long sip before returning my attention back to Soto.

"This is what we know," Rosenbaum began. "Planz, it seems, is the second in command to a drug cartel called Los Tigres Rugientes, or the Roaring Tigers. He's in charge of the West Coast operations. Los Tigres Rugientes appears to be a small cartel but is known to be an up-and-coming group in the drug trade."

This was not good news to me, and for the second time in less than eighteen hours, I was terrified for my life.

"What's going to happen now?" I was surprised to hear my voice tremble.

"You are going into witness protection until we can get our hands on Planz and bring him to trial. You will be kept safe until that time," Soto said, trying to give me a reassuring smile.

"What? For how long? Where the hell are you going to put me? There isn't a person in the world who doesn't know who the fuck I am!" I yelled across the table. I knew they knew who I was, but this wasn't possible.

"It's what we do," Soto replied calmly.

"We are better than the FBI at keeping you safe," Rosenbaum added. "You're your life is about to take a drastic turn. We need to know if you are willing to cooperate with us to keep yourself safe, or are you going to be a prima donna about everything?"

My head snapped up at his words. I wanted to get into his face. I wanted to ask him who the hell he thought he was. Yet a small voice told me this wasn't a game. Not some script I had to follow to please my fans. This was my life. The reality of what was happening, bit by bit, was sinking in.

I knew I was going to do what I was told. Or try to anyway.

"What about my friends?" I asked, my voice again even and focused. Linda Arnold, who ran my household, and Lori Liebman, my agent?

Soto informed me that Linda had already been taken, along with her family, into protective custody. Lori Liebman had refused to be placed into protective custody but had agreed to have round-the-clock agents at her side. My homes, I was informed, would be under surveillance as well during the time I was away.

The next four hours, I told my story three times to seven different people, the final stint with a stenographer in the room. I was given the option for bathroom breaks between each of the sessions.

Soto and Rosenbaum never left the room. They were always present.

After Soto, Rosenbaum, the stenographer, and the final two additional agents left the room, Agent Turnbull entered the room.

"You look tired." She patted my shoulder with her large hand.

What I really wanted to do was sleep, I told her. She nodded her understanding but informed me sadly that was not to be the case for another few hours.

"The best I can do is feed you," she told me, pulling out several paper menus from her jacket pocket. All of the five lists of options were for hamburger joints. After my decadent breakfast, I opted for a grilled chicken salad.

The last thing I needed to do was to gain weight. The camera and the critics were cruel if you added too many pounds to your figure. I had once added forty pounds for a Broadway play, and, although I won a Tony, the press roasted me like the main course at a luau. I didn't think I was going to be in front of either a camera or the media anytime soon, but I didn't want to take the chance.

After my salad, Soto and Rosenbaum arrived again. There were more questions and answers, but, finally, I was too exhausted. "When the hell am I going to get to sleep?" I barked.

Rosenbaum laughed. "I was wondering when you were going to get fed up with us and all the questions. You will be happy to know that we are going to be moving you in about twenty minutes. We're just waiting on clearance. In about ten minutes, we're going to move you to the roof of this building. Then from there, as soon as the helicopter arrives, you will be transported to an undisclosed location."

"Can I sleep on the helicopter?" was all I wanted to know.

Soto nodded.

"Thank you," I said a bit too brightly. Even I heard the heavy sarcasm.

Ten minutes later, Rosenbaum escorted me, along with Turnbull, to the roof of the building. From there, I could see where I was in LA. I was still in the slacks, shirt, and jacket I had left the apartment in, and the wind was cold, even though we were in a protective alcove.

Ten minutes later, the helicopter arrived. It looked like one of the helicopters that studios used. No distinctive markings to designate it as official government property. In fact, I was surprised at how sleek it looked, as if it were someone's personal property.

"Let's get you into that thing!" Turnbull yelled as she pulled me toward the craft. With one hand, she held my elbow, and the other gently pushed me, so I was slightly hunched over.

She made sure I was inside and buckled safety into the harness before closing the door. She stood on the outside of the helicopter and gave me her winning smile. She mouthed the words "thank you" and patted her breast pocket.

I smiled back and nodded.

Rosenbaum came from the other side of the helicopter and, after securing the door, handed me a headset with a mic. I waited long enough to watch him put his own before following suit. It was surprisingly quiet inside the helicopter once the headset was on.

"This will allow us to communicate with each other without shouting. I think, too, that you should be able to stretch out a bit after we get going. The pilot will let us know when we can." He gave me a thumbs-up.

"Can I ask you a question?" I began.

He nodded for me to ask.

"Do I call you Agent Rosenbaum?"

He laughed. "No, as I think I am going to be one of the agents assigned to you. You can call me Akio. That will be my name if I am actually assigned to you. Akio Kajiya is my working name." He laughed again. "Basically, it is the Japanese equivalent of John Smith."

"Thank you, Akio." I was silent the ten minutes before the pilot informed us we could loosen our harnesses and get more comfortable.

Akio help me loosen the harness and stretch out on the bench seat before rigging it again to secure me if the ride got bumpy.

It was 5:00 p.m. when Akio woke me. "We're getting ready to land." He again helped with the harness and secured himself to prepare for our descent.

I looked out the window. I wasn't sure where we were or what direction we had headed when we left LA. What I could see as we descended was what looked like a compound. There were a large main house and four smaller cabins. There seemed to be a lake and many trees all within a gated area. Maybe fifteen or twenty acres in total. When I looked to the east, away from the setting sun, I saw the mountains of the Sierra Nevada range.

There was nothing else to give me any inkling of where I was. Was this a layover, the place I would be spending the next few weeks, or more?

The helicopter landed, and as soon as we disembarked, it was off. Akio motioned for me to follow him, and we walked the several hundred feet to the main house. It was a large log cabin, and the smaller lodges were replicas of the main house. I also could see as I scanned my surroundings there were armed individuals in small towers along the perimeter of the fence.

"What is this place?" I asked once I caught up with Akio.

In a hushed tone, he answered, "This is one of those places it is better not to ask."

I let it drop.

He did not knock but went right into the house. It had a rustic feel to it. Homey and comfortable. This surprised me considering the armed perimeter.

"Hello, honey, we're home!" Akio shouted out, causing me to start.

"It's about damn time." A woman's smooth alto came around the corner. She stepped out and offered her hand. "I am Louise Little Feather." She introduced herself. "Starting now, you and I are going to be best friends."

The woman was about five-six and built like an athlete. Her long dark ebony hair was pulled back into a braid. I assumed, with a name like Little Feather, she was Native American, and like many who were, she was striking, with rich copper-colored skin and chiseled high cheekbones many women in my profession paid to have.

"Nice to meet you, Agent Little Feather," I began.

"Just Louise," she said, motioning for us to follow her back into the kitchen. "Dinner will be ready soon. I have some wine to go with everything."

I wanted to cry and hug her and kiss her feet. Wine, lots of wine, was precisely what I needed before passing out into a long deep coma-like slumber.

"Then we have to get to work."

She must have noticed my crestfallen expression because she added, "I promise you we will be done and have you tucked into bed before nine tonight."

I looked at the watch on my wrist. It had only been a few minutes since we had landed.

"Louise," Akio said, nodding in my direction, "how long before dinner? Maybe she would have enough time to shower and change. Do we have anything for her to wear yet?"

I was falling a little bit in love with Akio, a.k.a. Agent Abraham Rosenbaum.

"Yep! Follow me."

Louise led me to a small bedroom with an attached three-piece bathroom. It wasn't big, but the promise of a hot shower was enough to lure me into the tiny space.

"Teresa, we have clothes coming, but for now,"—she opened a closet and pulled out a very yellow jogging suit—"this will have to do."

I didn't care. Just to put on something clean was more than enough.

"Thanks," I told her as I closed the door.

The shower washed away not only the almost two days of grime but also about seven minutes of terrified sobbing. Inside the steamy bathroom was the first place I had been alone since I had stepped out on my balcony.

It seemed like ages ago.

I was tired, but more than anything, I was petrified. For the first time in possibly my entire life, I didn't know what was going to happen to me. I didn't even know what I was having for dinner. That small detail puts everything in stark perspective. Linda, the woman and friend that ran my house, kept me on a tight leash when it came to my meals. Depending on what I was doing, Linda would adjust my diet accordingly.

I always knew what I was having for breakfast, lunch, and dinner. Linda kept me on track. Today, I had eaten things I hadn't had in ages, and the breakfast sandwiches I hadn't even known existed. My world was indeed tiny.

I had to trust that the HPB and the agents I was surrounded by would keep me safe. I had to put my life into their hands.

It was a hard thing to do.

There was a knock on the bathroom door. It was Akio. "You OK in there? Dinner is almost ready to be set on the table."

I called out, "I'll be out in a second. Tell Louise I like my wine in a Mason jar."

I heard his retreating laughter as I pulled on the jogging suit. I had no clean panties, no clean bra to wear. Again, my situation hit home.

The dinner was spaghetti with huge meatballs, a Caesar salad, and hot garlic bread. To my surprise and pleasure, Louise or Akio had poured a bottle of Coppola Cabernet into large Mason jars.

There were a few minutes of small talk as we filled our plates and sampled the food Louise, I assumed, had prepared. I thanked her through a mouthful of pasta. She lifted her own Mason jar in response.

"We," Louise began, "the HPB have located a place that is a secure and safe environment for you. We are getting a team together and in place before we move you. Tomorrow, clothes and Special Agent Johnson will be arriving to create a persona for you to live as until this is all over."

Akio took over. "Almost everyone in the world knows who you are, as you reminded us. So we have to change your looks enough to make sure no one recognizes you."

I wondered out loud, except for the dental prosthetics that they were having made for me, how the hell were they going to do that? I had been working almost steadily since I was eleven years old. I had been a brunette, a blonde, a redhead, had had my head shaved; in one movie, I had been blue with black spots. People knew who I was.

"Johnson will take care of that. He is the best on the West Coast. There is an Agent Fine on the East Coast and one more in Dallas. They are creative geniuses. I wouldn't worry." Akio nodded as if this was supposed to put me at ease.

"However," Louise added, "before you go to bed tonight, you're getting a really drastic haircut. Tomorrow, Johnson will do the color and clean up the cut."

I looked up from my spaghetti. I looked from on agent to the next. "Which one of you is cutting my hair?" I questioned in alarm.

Louise indicated it would be her with a raise of her fork.

Did I have to agree to this? "Do you have a license?" I asked.

Louise shook her head. "I'm just going to cut your hair to shoulder length."

I bulked at this.

Akio took up the conversation. "Look, Teresa, Agent Johnson is the best. He will finish what Louise will do with style. You don't need to worry."

The hell I didn't! This wasn't anything I had asked for.

As we finished the meal, I let the two agents chatter as I focused on my delicious dinner. My hair was a riot of strawberry blond curls that reached almost the middle of my back. It was one of my trademarks. The other was my eye color. They were a startlingly clear jade green, my mother's eyes. They, the hair and the splash of freckles across my peaches and cream complexion, were what helped me become at one time or another the face of Lancôme Paris®, Estée Lauder®, and a few others.

I had no idea how this was going to be possible. Again, I had to trust the agents.

As promised, I was in bed by 9:00 p.m. I was sure I would be unable to sleep, yet as soon as my head, minus sixteen inches of hair, hit the pillow, I was out.

I opened one eye to look at the nightstand. It was a few minutes before six, and I was wide awake. The night before, Louise had shown me the coffeepot and all the essentials for making coffee. I knew I was awake, so after a brief stop in the bathroom, I headed to the kitchen. It took only a few minutes to ready the coffee maker. All I had to do was wait.

I looked out the window in the kitchen and noticed already the darkness of night was becoming the light of early morning. I stood there as the coffee maker performed its task, watching the shadow of night fade.

When the coffee was ready, I poured myself a mug and decided I would go out onto the broad porch and watch the sunrise. With my mug in hand, I headed out the front door.

I stopped before the door was even halfway closed. Outside, standing in a nightgown, was Louise. She was facing east, and from her body language, it looked as if she was meditating or praying. I kept the front door from loudly closing before slowly stepping out. I didn't know if I should turn around or go back in.

It was clear that whatever was happening was something sacred and unique for the Native American agent. Nevertheless, I was too fascinated to allow her privacy.

Within a few minutes, the sunlight crept its way across the Sierra Nevadas and spilled onto the clearing. I observed with quiet reverence as Louise seemed to reach out with open hands and pull the sun's light to her face, bringing the light with open palms to her face and moving them up to her head. After several repeats of this movement, she washed her arms, chest, and legs with the same motion.

I held my breath, not wanting in any way to disturb her.

She pulled out a pouch from under her nightgown that was attached to cord around her neck. With great care and deliberation, she opened the sack and with her thumb and forefinger pulled a pinch of something out. Facing each of the four corners, north, east, south, and west, she allowed the substance, whatever was inside the pouch, to slip away in the wind. She chanted something low and with an unusual cadence as she faced each direction before, still singing, she repeated the "washing" of the sunlight on her face, head, and body.

I felt embarrassed at watching her, but the beauty and sacredness of what I was witnessing kept me glued.

"Did you bring me a cup of coffee?" Louise's voice startled me out of my thrall.

I looked at her, this time noticing she was on the porch and looking at me with a crooked smile. "I could really use one!"

After a heartbeat, I found my voice. "No, but I have a fresh pot made."

"Great! Let's make some breakfast. Akio will be out in a few, and he is really a bear before he's had his coffee." She spoke as I followed her into the cabin and toward the kitchen. "Johnson should be here at about nine o'clock. His team will be here an hour or so before to set up the room for him to do his magic."

I refreshed my mug after Louise filled hers and began to pull out the makings of a hearty breakfast from the refrigerator. *Who knew danger made one hungry all the time?* I thought as I pulled a basket of oranges from the crisper.

Even then, Louise was still working. "We need to get you a voice that is not your own. I am sure you can do any accent you want and change the tone or pitch of your voice. What we need is something that you can maintain over a long period without having to think about it. Think about it while I get showered and dressed. Be out in fifteen."

From the time I was seventeen until right after my mother had died of a stroke when I was nineteen, I had been on a Scottish TV melodrama. I had just ended almost five years living in Hawai'i and working on the Disney sitcom called *Blue Sky Hawai'i*. I had had my heart broken by my costar and had wanted to get as far away from Hawai'i and California as I could. Scotland seemed perfect.

I had lived in Glasgow with my grandparents, where the hour-long show was filmed, and I knew without a doubt I could kill at a *Glasgow patter*, or *Glaswegian*, which is the Scots dialect spoken in and around Glasgow. As I cooked breakfast and waited for Louise and Akio to return, I practiced under my breath.

In the time it took the two agents to return to the kitchen, I was ready.

"I drank all the coffee," I began. The stunned and confused looks were my confirmation to continue. "But don't worry. I'm making another pot. Also, I looked around to see if there was any black and white to go with our eggs and baked beans but couldn't find any."

"What the fuck did you say?" Akio said the same time that Louise gave a bark of laughter and commented, "That's a bit heavy but will do."

I smoothed out the accent, just a touch, and repeated myself.

"Wow!"

"Better!"

"Good, then. Breakfast is served." I smiled as I put the plate of eggs and bacon on the table.

Still in the brogue, and with my voice pitched just a bit higher than usual, I told them about my time in Scotland, knowing I could use the accent and pitch without thinking for an indefinite period.

"I will call Soto and let her know. This information will be forwarded to the three other agents that will be assigned to you."

I had a thought. "Louise, is that your real name?"

She smiled that crooked smile and replied, "As far as you are concerned, it is."

We finished our meal with a constant stream of questions and answers comments and rebuttals. I think they were trying to see if I could indeed keep up the tone and accent without thinking. The conversation was rapid and left no time for the three of us to think before speaking.

It was almost eight when we finally pushed away from the table.

Akio began cleaning up, and Louise informed me that we were going to put the color in my hair. Telling me to wait, she went off to what I assumed was her bedroom and returned with a tank top. "Put this on and come back to the table."

I did as I was instructed and returned to the kitchen, finding a towel spread out on the end of the table with the bottle of hair color, several combs, hair clips, and two Q-tips.

Louise had just applied color to my eyebrows when three men entered through the front door. Two of the men each carried a large box and nodded as they came through the kitchen and opened what I had assumed as a pantry door. From my limited view, I could see that it opened onto a stairwell that led down to a basement. The third man cleared his throat and informed Akio, who had dish soap bubbles covering his hands, that the documents he had were for him.

"Put them on the table," he said before going back to the dishes.

After giving Louise and me a glance, he placed several folders and a document tube on the far end of the table and went back outside.

As Louise adeptly applied the color to my hair, the men from the basement returned, and, together, the three made two more trips with what looked like garment bags and several suitcases.

The man who had brought in the documents pulled the door close. "Johnson will be here in about an hour. I am also supposed to tell you to watch the local entertainment show at one." He provided the name of the show and the channel. "Soto said it might help put your mind at ease, Ms. O'Connor," he finished and looked at me, giving me a smile.

Louise thanked him, and with the same brief nod he had given when he entered the house, he left.

As I waited the prescribed twenty-five minutes for the color to take hold, I watched as the two agents went over the papers that had been delivered. From my end of the table, I could not really see what was on the eight-by-eleven sheets, but the reel that was removed from the tube looked like an architectural rendering of a building.

They spoke quietly among themselves until the timer went off. I was instructed to go shower, using the conditioner provided to set the color, and then return to the table.

I took my time because again I was afraid. As I towel dried my hair, the reflection looking back from the foggy mirror was already different than it had been less than two days ago. I looked tired. With no makeup on, my freckles were in stark contrast to my complexion, and the dark circles under my eyes seemed to age me. Considering the situation, maybe that was a good thing.

After dressing back into the ugly yellow jogging suit, I steadied myself with several breaths before heading back to the kitchen.

The agents looked up as I came around the corner. I could see understanding in both their faces, and I liked and trusted them even more.

Akio started. "How are you feeling, Fiona Reid?"

So I was to be Fiona Reid?

"Mr. Kajiya," I answered in my newly established accent, "I have felt better. And you?"

"Actually," Louise added, "it will probably be Fiona Reid Park. The HPB has a specific agent in mind to be your husband. It is almost set, but they are juggling assignments. You don't really need to worry about that. The rest of the details regarding your new persona, Agent Johnson will bring with him."

"What we can tell you is where," Akio said, pointing to the drawing on the table, "and who else will be there. We also want to explain why this is a very safe place for you. We want you to be as comfortable as possible with the information and the location."

"Akio and I will be part of the team. There will be several other agents, but for the most part, you won't really deal with them on a day to day. Akio and I will be old acquaintances of you and your husband, as we all 'work'"—Louise did air quotes in the air—"for the same Tech Company."

"Come and look and see the site plans." Akio rolled out the drawings as I moved to get a closer look.

The first thing I noticed was that the building that looked like an apartment complex was on the corner of East Tamarisk and N Indian Canyon Drive. Exactly where these two streets were, I didn't know, but I soon learned it was Palm Springs, California.

Akio explained the apartment complex, Desert Sky Apartments, was originally built in the 1920s by a famous architect who meshed Mediterranean-style and Spanish Revival-style architectures together. The apartment had fallen into disrepair. About twelve years ago, a small development company bought the property and the lot behind it and completely refurbished and reconfigured the flats, building an attached thirty-car parking structure at the rear of the apartment building. The new owner also applied for recognition on the National Historic Registry.

"There are only two ways into or out of the complex." Louise took over. "Both the front gates and the parking structure are secure. Both require the tenants to use a key and a code to enter. Because it's on the National Registry, the HPB, through a shell corporation, was able to add additional security measures."

Akio sat down, continuing where Louise had paused. "The shell corporation, IFB Technologies, was able to add discreet security cameras throughout the common areas of the complex and the garage. IFB Technologies also keeps, on an open rental contract, six apartments. Whenever those apartments are occupied, the entrances are monitored 24/7, and no one, even with a key and code, can enter if they are not on the list."

I looked at the drawing. The complex was built around a public courtyard, with a pool placed at an equal distance from each of the units. The front of the complex was accessible via a massive iron gate. Opposite the front entrance at the rear of the courtyard was a gate leading to the three-story garage.

"There is a total of twenty-seven units. IFB has a contact for one of the two-bedroom apartments, four of the efficiencies, and two of the one-bedrooms. You have the two-bedroom, as you are a married woman." Louise grinned.

"I get stuck in one of the efficiencies, and Louise gets a one-bedroom. I don't get that?" Akio joked with his fellow agent.

"The owner lives in a large three-bedroom apartment at the front of the building. Every tenant had been vetted as part of the application process. We know everyone there."

This was all overwhelming. Yet I had one nagging question that seemed to float to the surface again and again.

I asked, "Am I a prisoner? Will I be able to leave the complex?"

Akio came around and took my hand, pulling me to a chair, and sat across from me. I looked at his hand holding mine and for the first time noticed the intricately designed wedding band. Black with white gold, it was inscribed with some language, possibly Japanese. *So you're married*, I thought.

"Fiona," his voice brought my attention back to his face, "you are not a prisoner. But you cannot just wander off alone. If you leave the complex, you must do so in the company of one of the three agents directly assigned to you. That's Louise, myself, and your husband." He looked over at Louise, who shuffled through the papers before informing me my husband would be named Mason Park.

"Within the complex itself,"—Louise took a seat across from us—"you are free. You can stay in your apartment, but you can go out in the common areas. The way the front gates are arranged, there is no clear visual from the outside to the courtyard."

Akio squeezed my hand. "The courtyard is lush and comfortable. The owner really has it set up to be an oasis inside the complex."

"I need to go outside for some air." I looked at the agents, waiting to be told I couldn't.

"Take all the time you need," Akio said, smiling down at me as he stood.

Louise offered me another cup of coffee, which I gladly accepted. I went out and sat on the porch swing and tried to sift through everything I had just heard.

I sipped my coffee, which I really didn't need, and thought about the last . . . how long? I needed to put this all in order. I was to play a part—be someone else. I had done this since I was eleven. If they, the HPB, gave me a script, an outline of things to know, I could do what I needed to do to keep myself safe. That was the goal, right? To be safe?

Monday, yesterday, had been pretty much a blur. Today had been easier to stay focused. I had slept. I had eaten. I hadn't been kept in the dark—well, at least this was how it seemed to me.

Something was nagging at me, though. I wasn't sure what, and the more I thought about it, the more it alluded me. It would come to me, I hoped.

I don't know how long I sat on the porch swing. Neither Louise nor Akio came to find me. I was grateful for the solitude.

Yesterday, Soto had collected my purse, diamond earrings, the diamond ring that was my gran's, my dad's mom, my Rolex, and my cell phone. She explained that the cell phone could be traced, so it would be powered off and put into a secure shielded place. As far as my purse went, it was explained that I would be issued a new driver's license and passport as well as credit cards under my new identity.

My diamond ring, earrings, and watch would be placed in a safe and returned to me when this was all over. As far as my Rolex, it was replaced with a serviceable watch. It currently sat on the nightstand for the moment. I was without any regard for the time.

I watched as a helicopter descended several hundred feet from the cabin in the same clearing we had landed yesterday. A tall African American man in casual slacks and shirt spilled out of the craft and almost doubled in half as he moved away from it toward the cabin. As soon as he was about twenty feet away from the helicopter, it took off again. He was carrying a large duffel bag and smiled as he approached.

I wondered if this was Mason Park, my husband, or Agent Johnson.

As he got closer, I recognized him. It had been almost ten years since he all but disappeared from public view, but together with his size, muscular build, and his average-looking face, he was unmistakable.

LaShaun Johnson had been a popular and successful defensive end for my father's favorite football team. He had received the Lott Trophy during his college career and earned the NFL Defensive Player of the Year five times, with the last four being awarded consecutively. With his teammates, he had won two Super Bowl rings, his last being ten years ago. A month after that win, Johnson had given a small press conference announcing his retirement. No explanation other than it was a "tough, extremely personal decision."

After fulfilling his lucrative contracts for various companies, he basically disappeared.

I stood up as he reached the porch. "You broke my dad's heart when you retired." I offered him my hand and watched it vanish in his giant paw.

"I am truly sorry to hear that," he said, leaning in. His voice was as heavy as a thunderclap. "Cat Connors, your last movie made me cry. It was very embarrassing."

I laughed.

"Fiona Reid, nice to meet you." He stepped up onto the porch, and I looked up. At six feet five inches, he was one of the few people I had met in a while that towered over me. I followed him into the cabin and down into the basement.

Once we descended the stairs, I was astonished at the bright space. It was large and, while not sterile looking, very white and clean. There was a wall of mirrors at which several barber-style chairs and counters stood, as well as a sink for washing hair.

Two clothes trolleys stood to one side, full of everything from slacks to dresses. Two medium-size suitcases were perched on stands. I could see they were unzipped but not opened. Opposite the wall of the mirrors was a small sitting area with an overstuffed love seat, two recliners, with a small refrigerator tucked in the corner.

"This," the booming voice announced from behind me, "is where I make the magic happen. I need you to go in and shower."

"I already showered," I interrupted him.

Johnson pointed to a door in the corner near the love seat and repeated himself. He pulled a plush robe from the trolley and handed it to me. Pointing to one of the suitcases, he said, "Inside are panties. They are your size. Not as fancy as I imagine Cat Connors would normally wear, but for Fiona Park, they are perfect. There are a few bras, but you will understand why soon."

As I rummaged through the suitcase for the cute but cotton panties, he continued to speak. "I have to go upstairs for about thirty minutes. When you're out of the shower, I want you to look at this folder I am going to put on the sofa."

I grunted my understanding and headed for the bathroom.

"Get your hair wet, but don't wash it."

"Yes, sir!" I barked as if he was my drill sergeant. It wasn't meant to be nice. I waited until he headed up the stairs before I stepped into the bathroom.

It only took me ten minutes to lather up and shower off. It was nice to have clean panties on again. I pulled the rope tight and went to the love seat.

The folder contained an outline and information regarding my new persona.

Fiona Reid Park
Born: Glasgow Scotland, UK.

Fiona was two years younger than my actual twenty-nine. She had married Mason Park three years earlier. She still carried a United Kingdom passport, as her husband's job required travel back and forth from the UK to America.

I, Fiona, was an only child. Like myself, her parents were both gone. I had some college but had met Mason while working at a pub in Dowanhill not far from the University of Glasgow. It seemed Mason was getting his PhD in computer engineering.

"Great! I married an übernerd," I said.

IFB Technology had sent Dr. Mason Park and Dr. Akio Kajiya to their Palm Spring headquarters to train a select group of engineers on a new technological breakthrough. Dr. Louise Little Feather was a guest lecturer at the community college on Native American religions and a part-time consultant with IFB. I was a tagalong.

As I kept reading my history, I discovered Fiona Reid Park was thirty weeks pregnant. "Really!"

"Really what?" Louise said.

"I'm almost seven months pregnant!" I told her in horror.

"Wow,"—her tone feigning shock and horror with just a hint of disgust—"you look pretty damn good to be so far along."

"Johnson should be down in a few more minutes. I wanted to see if you needed anything before he begins. He won't let anyone down here until he is finished. So there is water and a few snacks in the fridge. He knows we need to have you back up before one to watch Hollywood Entertainment, so I am assuming he will have finished his latest masterpiece." She gave me a hug and under her breath said, "Ciao, Cat!"

Ten minutes later, the magician himself returned.

"Ready?"

"Do I have a choice?"

"Not really, but I am gonna make it, so you don't need to worry about anyone recognizing you. Trust me!"

I moved to the barber chair he was standing next to and sat down. He pulled a smock around me, after securing it, pulled out the first of his tools, comb, and scissors.

I held up a hand. "LaShaun Johnson, are you as good with those scissors as you were protecting the quarterback?"

He leaned over, and his breath tickled my ear as he assured me. "Better!"

And to my joy, he was indeed.

The cut was as good as I had gotten in any Beverly Hills salon. This alone guaranteed and bolstered my trust.

After we had blown out my new hairstyle, he darkened my eyelashes to match the hair color. He explained how I was to touch up every week my roots, eyebrows, and lashes. Louise or Mason would be able to help me.

I wanted to ask who Mason Park was, knowing obviously that Mason Park wasn't his real name.

Next, he moved on to my mouth. He pulled from his duffel a case I recognized. Whenever I had worn dentures or prosthetics to cover my teeth, this was the small case they come in. Similar to the retainer case I had as a teenager, I wanted to see how they would change my jawline.

It wasn't so much that they changed the shape, although it did. I had the straightest and whitest teeth money could buy, and these undid that. I looked at the slightly crooked and uneven teeth. Not pearly white but not dirty looking either. I was surprised that so little changed so much.

Hazel contacts followed. I had trouble putting them on, but with a little coaching from Johnson, I managed after a few minutes. There were, he informed me, enough contacts and contact solution in the suitcase to last me two months.

Two months. Would I be hiding for two months?

"I have two more things to do to your face before we are done and can change the shape of your body. This might be a bit uncomfortable, but I can promise only for a short time." He reached again into his bag of tricks and pulled out a small medical-looking container. "First, I am going to place a small cylinder into each nostril. These will flair the end of your nose, changing the shape just enough. They won't come out even if you have a sneezing fit or have to blow your nose. They are that snug."

This I didn't like. Could I tell Johnson no? I didn't think so. He must have seen my thoughts on my face because he added, "You can have Mason take them out at night if you promise you will remember to put them back in before you leave the apartment."

I filed that for later and offered him my nose. The two cylinders fit snuggly just inside my nostrils. I looked in the mirror, and like the dentures, these two small objects completely changed the shape of my nose. Johnson explained the process of installing and removing the cylinders. They made me want to sneeze, but the feeling lasted only a few seconds.

"Finally, and I am sure you are not going to like this. I am going to give you a port-wine stain over half of your face. The dye I am going to use will not wash off but will fade over several weeks. The color, like your color for your hair, will need to be touched up every week. You are going to have to get into the routine of this without delay.

"I need you to sit in this chair." He indicated the other salon chair. It reclined all the way back, so I was almost entirely horizontal.

He continued, "Turn your head away from me, close your eyes, and do not open them. The dye will not damage your eye if it gets into them, but it will sting. I am going to start now. This will tingle, but it shouldn't be too bad."

I felt the wetness of a sponge as he began to apply the color to my left cheek. The dampness continued down my neck, my entire left ear into the hairline, and, finally, the side of my nose and my eyelid and the surrounding skin. The sensation of fine needles dancing over my skin was bearable, but I was silently praying it wouldn't last long.

"How long before the stinging ends?" I asked after the application had finished and I could no longer feel the dampness of the sponge on my face.

"About two minutes total." He was back at my side informing me he would be setting the chair back up. "I have some makeup you will be able to use to cover the stain. It's made for covering this type of birthmark. You will not be able to wash your face or apply any makeup for forty-eight hours. After that time, you will be able to tend to your normal facial routine without fear that the color will come off. Also, when you reapply the color, there will be only an hour wait before you can apply your makeup, and the stinging will be almost nothing."

I could hear Johnson as he moved around the room. He made small talk but continued to remind me to keep my eyes closed until he told me otherwise. I heard what sounded like blinds being pulled down from in front of me and the sound of a zipper either being opened or closed from somewhere near the hanging clothes.

"OK, you can open your eyes."

I did and discovered that shades had been pulled down over the mirrors.

I looked at him questioningly. "A port-wine stain can be extremely shocking. I want you to think about it. Use your imagination. When we are finished with the rest of the work here, I will show you your new self."

He again motioned me to come to where he stood and told me to drop the robe.

At this, I balked.

He smiled. "Fiona, I have seen women's breast before, and as sure as I am that yours are particularly beautiful, I am working and could care less."

I wasn't sure if I should be insulted or not. I took a deep breath and let the robe drop. As an actor and model, I have often stood around in less to let wardrobe and makeup do their thing. This, I supposed, was no different.

He produced what looked like a bathing suit but with a distinct baby bulge in front. Johnson offered me the prosthetic and told me to step into it. I did as I was told and found that, like a bathing suit, it fit snug and tight. The top was like a bra that also seemed to increase the size of my breasts.

It was heavier than I had anticipated for as light as it looked. The weight seemed to be concentrated in the center of the belly and also in the lower part of my back. I tugged at the fabric and found that it gave almost imperceptibly.

"There are snaps in the crotch to make it easy to use in the bathroom without taking the entire thing off. It's snug, and if you touch the belly, it will give just like a real pregnant belly would. That is critical." He moved to me and patted my fake stomach. "Remember there is nothing more appealing than a pregnant woman. People will want to touch your belly. As an additional element of realism, there is a small device inside the belly that will simulate the movements, kicks and feet and hands from the inside. A long-lasting set of lithium batteries are inside, so you don't need to recharge or, worse yet, to forget to charge it."

I laughed at his words. "This is absolute bullshit! Is this really necessary?" How could it possibly be anything but an additional bother?

I began to pull it off.

Johnson's hands reached out and stilled my attempt to remove the body suit. "Cat,"—his tone was enough to get my full attention—"the idea is to have you look as different as possible from Cat Connors. Yes, I have to admit it is almost too much. However, putting it all together is going to make you more distinctly Fiona Park. That's the goal. That is going to keep you safe and under the radar."

I looked back at him, speechless. I wasn't sure how to respond.

"If someone is rubbing your stomach, sensors will detect the motion and will randomly select a movement." He took my hand and demonstrated.

I looked at him in complete shock. Was this really necessary? I choked.

"Fiona," Johnson said, squeezing my hand and nodded, "your life depends on how realistic everything about your new persona is. Since you are pregnant and will be surrounded by all the people who live in the complex, even your movements must appear natural. That is another reason for the weight in the back. It will change your center of gravity, so you move more like a woman who is seven months pregnant."

Realism, he'd said.

I nodded, not being able to find my voice.

As I was pulling on crisp white capri pants to go with the mint-green maternity blouse I had already picked, Akio's voice called down from the stairs. "Fifteen minutes."

I turned to face Johnson and noticed him turning the wedding band on his left hand. It matched the one that Abraham Rosenbaum wore.

He noticed me watching him and started to speak.

I interrupted. "I know you're about to introduce me to Fiona Reid Park, but I need a minute." He nodded his understanding.

"Why did you leave at the height of your career?" I asked.

He looked at me, measuring me in a way I hadn't experienced in a long time before saying quietly, "I wanted a life."

"There are many married football players."

"Yes, I suppose there are. But I didn't want my personal life and the life of my family caught up in the limelight. I was never about that." He moved away from me and pulled two bottles of water from the mini-fridge.

"How long have you and Abraham been married?"

He didn't answer but handed me the water and then a handful of tissues. Walking over to the mirrors, he pulled the blinds up.

Had I been making a movie and the makeup team had performed these changes for a role, I would have applauded and been awed at the brilliant and realistic transformation they had created.

I began to sob.

Before me stood Fiona Reid Park. I didn't recognize anything about her that was me. The burgundy color of the port-wine stain seemed to steal the focus from every other thing except my pregnant belly.

LaShaun Johnson came up behind me and placed his hands on my shoulders. "This beautiful woman who is looking back at you is going to keep you safe and secure.

She also might give you something you might not have had in your entire life. Anonymity."

He again took my hand and rubbed my belly. I felt what seemed to be a small fist jab and retreat. My knees went weak, and had it not been for the man behind me, I might have fallen to the floor.

His breath again tickled my ear when he whispered, "Abe and I have been married for eleven years. We have four beautiful children. Because of what we do, we also have the anonymity to live our lives and be happy. Fiona, this is what, I hope, I have given you today. Now dry your eyes and let's go upstairs."

They tried, Louise and Akio, to keep the shock off their faces as I entered the kitchen. Despite everything, I had kept up both the accent and the tone we had decided on. I did a "TA-DA" and took a slow pirouette before asking if it was time to turn on the television.

It was already on, and there was a sandwich and some soup ready for me on the TV tray in front of the television. I took my first bite as the credits rolled. I had finished the sandwich and half the soup when, just before the commercial break, the man behind the desk who had one too many facelifts attempted to raise an eyebrow and informed his audience, "Cat Connors, our generation's Grace Kelly . . ."

I heard Louise say, "Your generation's Grace Kelly *was* Grace Kelly!" with a snicker.

". . . where has she gone?"

I finished my soup, and before I could get up, Akio whisked it away. Louise sat on the other end of the sofa and said, "Johnson is something, isn't he?"

I wanted to do anything but focus on how *something* he was. I reached over and took her hand. "Watch."

I moved her hand in a circular motion over my swollen belly and watched as she jumped almost entirely off the couch.

"Holy shit!" she squeaked.

"Yeah, I know!"

Before either of us could comment, the smooth-faced man reappeared.

"Cat Connors, who this past Sunday finished filming a remake of *Dark Victory* with her costar George Clooney, has disappeared from the hustle and bustle of Hollywood. Sources say that Cat and her identical twin sister, Esperanza, shown here at a premiere of Cat's megahit two years ago, had reportedly flown off to Spain for a long-overdue family vacation."

As the television anchor spoke, a photo of Esperanza and me, dressed indistinguishable Ralph Lauren gowns except for the color, flashed onto the screen.

I screamed!

All three agents were on their feet with guns drawn, searching for the intruder.

"I am such an awful person!" I cried, and I moved from the couch to the center of the living room. "What kind of person am I? Little Ricky! Oh my god! Little Ricky! Oh! Oh! OR." I crumpled to the floor and sobbed, horrified at what I had or hadn't done. Who I had become!

"Who is Little Ricky?" Akio asked.

"OR?" Louise's voice struggled to reach me through my sobs.

Akio shook my shoulder and got me to look up through the tears. "Fiona, what is going on? Who are Little Ricky and OR?"

I laughed, but it was not a laugh of joy but scorn. "We were separated, Esperanza and I, when we were two. She went with my mom to Spain, and I stayed with my dad. When she would visit, oh, shit, I was so mean! I called her Little Ricky because she reminded me of Ricky Ricardo,

Desi Arnez. I really have never called her anything but Little Ricky."

I went on to tell them that even one year we dressed her up as Ricky Ricardo. She hated it but won the best costume at the country club.

"OR?" Louise asked again, impatience in her voice.

I explained that when I was five, my father was making a WW II movie about the Big Red One, the Army at Fort Riley Kansas. It was filmed in and around Fort Riley in the small town of Ogden. My dad's character was a grease-monkey, and most of the film was shot in and around Bergstrom's Auto. Mr. Bergstrom had a daughter, and the rest, as they say, was history. My dad never married Rosemarie Bergstrom but did take financial responsibility for his daughter. "The last time I saw her," I admitted shamefaced, "was when my father died eight years ago. I never even told Esperanza about her."

There was a pause.

Agent Johnson was the one who spoke. He used my name, Teresa, pulling me out of my daze. "We are fully aware of your sisters. The HPB offices in Miami and in Kansas City are already on this. We haven't heard, but both Esperanza and Olli Rose, if not already, will soon be in protective custody."

Of course, the HPB would have known about them. Weren't they connected to the FBI?

"We planted the story of your vacation. Tickets from LA to Miami and then to Madrid, Spain, were purchased. Your passport has been scanned at each location. As far as anyone is concerned, Cat Connors and Esperanza O'Connor are in Spain," Akio told me.

I sat on the sofa staring at the television. The three agents got up and left the room.

"She really is a fucking ice and drama queen. She's just now thinking about her sisters. What a bitch!" I heard Louise comment from the other room.

The words stung. The situation called for a little drama. Didn't it?

I wanted to confront her, yet before I got up from the sofa, the same three men that had brought all the boxes and documents this morning showed up in the doorway.

"The helicopter will be here at four," the agent who had delivered the papers only a few hours before informed the room.

I held my tongue, deciding not to confront Louise. I spent the rest of my time going over the dossier that had been provided for my new persona. I was to know it in and out before I got in the helicopter. Akio and Louise left within thirty minutes of each other, leaving me alone with Agent Johnson.

He took half an hour refreshing me regarding the application of color to my head. "One more thing," he said as he pulled me to my feet and headed with me out to wait for the helicopter, "of the twenty-seven apartments, there are six that IFB Tech has under contract. You and Mason, Akio and Louise have three, and there will be other agents whom you will not know. Of the remaining twenty-one units, seventeen are occupied. The HPB knows who each and every one of the residents is. You are safe inside the walls, remember that." He repeated what Akio and Louise had already told me.

"Teresa, remember, you are safe!" He kissed my cheek as a different helicopter landed.

I dozed on the helicopter ride. The worry I felt for the sisters I had never been a sister to had worn me out. I would do what I was supposed to do . . . be who I was supposed to be. Like any role I had ever taken, I would become Fiona Reid Park. Whoever Mason Park was, I would be such a good wife no one would believe otherwise.

When we began to descend, I glanced at the watch I had been given to see that it was already after six. I focused my attention outside. The sun was already setting in the late March sky. It would be dark before we landed.

It was just barely an airport. There were two small hangars. From what I could see of the landing strip, it was not even paved. The pilot, whom I was never introduced to, put the small craft down by one of the hangars. With only a nod to me as the engine died down, he helped me out of my seat and reached into the small space and pulled out a suitcase and a small carry-on that had been waiting inside when I had left the compound.

I could see the light under the threshold of a door in the front. The pilot opened the door, sat the two cases down, and motioned for me to go in. Once inside, he closed the door behind me. I looked at the closed door, and it was only a few seconds before I heard the engine roar back to life.

"If I didn't know it was you, I would have never guessed," the now familiar voice of Agent Soto spoke from several feet behind me.

I turned to face the agent, who was dressed in khakis and pullover with the HPB logo. She looked almost as tired as I felt. I told her so.

"Where the hell are we?" I asked as she led me to a sofa in the far corner of the hangar. As I took the twelve-foot journey, I realized there were five other agents posted through the small space.

"Flamingo Heights. We're just out of Palm Springs. We will wait here for the agent who will be your husband for the duration, Mason Park. He is on his way now. We pulled him from another assignment because the higher-ups thought he would be the best agent to assign to you." Soto patted the sofa next to her, and I sat down.

I filed that information before asking about my sisters.

"I can tell you what I know, but I don't have a lot the information," she told me as we were both handed a bottle of water from one of the other agents.

What she knew was that the FBI and HPB offices in Miami and the Kansas City were doing their best to secure my sisters. It seemed that both Esperanza and Olli Rose were not at their homes or places of work. However, she told me when I started to get panicky that HPB knew they both were safe.

It seemed that Esperanza was on a date and Olli Rose was in Kansas City for a fund-raiser and to visit with friends.

"Their exact whereabouts have not been established, but we know where they are, generally speaking, and we have teams on the ground to acquire them as soon as possible." She absently had reached over, caressed my stomach, and, like Louise, jumped off the sofa when "the baby" kicked.

"Whoa!" she yelled. "Johnson is a genius!"

From the corner of my eye, I noticed several of the agents move in our direction only to be waved off by Soto before they could get closer.

We sat there making idle conversation for a few more minutes before a thought popped into my head. "Does Mason know who I am?"

"No." She looked over to the far side of the hangar and lifted a finger for me to wait, got up, and walked over to the agent standing there.

A moment later, she was back. "They are sending someone out for a hamburger run. You want something?"

After deciding on what I wanted, Soto went back to the agent and returned.

"OK, where were we? Oh, right. No, he doesn't know only because he was pulled from another assignment only a few hours ago. The helicopter should arrive soon. When he gets here, and you, or Fiona, will be introduced. Rosenbaum has a dossier ready for him to read when you two get to the apartment Palm Springs."

"Are we getting into the apartment tonight?" I inquired.

"Agent Rosenbaum, I mean, Dr. Akio Kajiya has the key to your apartment. Most of your luggage has already been delivered. The apartment is furnished with everything you need, including a stocked refrigerator. So, tonight, all you have to do is get there and settle in."

I nodded as if I understood, while in fact, I was beginning to feel overwhelmed again. I told Soto I was going to rest until my food came and closed my eyes.

Before she walked away, she echoed Johnson's sentiments. "Fiona, love the accent, by the way. You are going to be OK. And so are your sisters."

I hoped she was right!

I stretched out on the old sofa and closed my eyes.

It was the sound of a helicopter outside the hangar that woke me as I must have dozed off.

I decided to stay put. If I pretended I was still sleeping, perhaps I would learn more about the agent assigned to me.

The voice raised in anger was a familiar voice. It was a voice I remembered and dreamed about. The man whom it belonged to, Haneul Palan Song, his Korean name or its English equivalent, Blue Sky Song. He had been my first crush, my first love, and my first heartbreak. Why was he here?

"Soto, what the hell! Who gave you the authority to yank me from an assignment I have been working on for over six fucking months?" I had never heard him use that type of language before. It was shocking. "First, you pull me without even asking. Put my ass in a helicopter with no information. I'm supposed to go into this thing cold."

Soto offered him a name, telling the agent Rosenbaum had all the information for him once he arrived in Palm Springs. She apologized for keeping him out of the loop, saying that Director Christopher had thought it best.

"She better be as important as he thinks, because I had busted my ass on that case," Song said, his tone lowering, although still angry. "Is that her?"

"Yes," Soto's replied, "it's been a rough few days for her." Then I heard her add, "Dinner is here. I got an extra hamburger and fries, just in case you were hungry."

"Thanks."

I opened my eyes and looked over to where the two, presumably three, HPB agents stood. The one returning from the food run was handing Soto two of the four bags he was carrying. He walked away in the direction of the other agents, and Soto and Blue Sky headed toward the sofa.

Because I had heard his voice, I was able to ready myself. *This was a part*, I told myself. *I have won every award there was for my acting skills. This was no different, and I was not going to fall apart!* I was ready and sitting up when they arrived. I was an actress, and this was a part I was going to enjoy!

"Fiona Reid Park, I would like to introduce you to your husband, Mason Park." I nodded and cumbersomely rose to my feet.

"Well, then," I said, my voice a pitch higher and thick with my accent, "Agent Soto, you didn't tell me he was going to be so handsome. I hope his real wife isn't the jealous sort!"

He had no wife. I had kept tabs on him. I knew after leaving the show at twenty-one, Haneul Palan Song had changed his name to Nathan Paul Song, finished his degree in criminal justice, and applied and was accepted to the FBI. He also had been married and divorced in the twelve years since I had last seen him. His mother and father, San Franciscan hippies from the late '60s and early '70s, treated me like family. Therefore, Jangmi Song, Jackie to her friends and family, and Jin-Ho, a.k.a. Donald, had kept me informed whether I wanted the information.

He looked startled as I moved to him and touched my lips to his, leaning in so that the "baby" kicked him in the stomach.

"She's pregnant!" He looked horrified and a little green.

"She's not. Johnson!" Soto said his name as if the one-word moniker explained it all. It seemed that it did as he relaxed.

"Fiona, nice to meet you." He was a little stiff in his greeting.

We were almost eye to eye, and as I took the bag from his hand, there was no recognition of who I was.

"I'm hungry. Do we have time to eat before we head out?" I asked my husband of three years.

He looked at Soto, who nodded, and the three of us sat down at a folding table.

Soto, around bites of hamburger and french fries, informed "Mason" that his coworker from IFB Technologies would have his key and some documentation for him when we arrived. She gave him the address of the Desert Sky Apartments and the apartment number for Akio Kajiya.

I listened, quietly taking in what was being said without comment. However, I had a few of my own questions, and this was as good a time as any.

"I have a few questions. Do you mind?" I asked not really caring if they minded or not. I didn't wait for them to answer.

"I understand I am under protection. But I also was made to understand that within the complex itself, I was more or less free to muck about. Is that correct?"

"It is, Fiona," Soto answered, "but I would appreciate it if you let Mason know before you leave the apartment."

That was reasonable. With a smile on my face, I looked at Soto and asked innocently, "My marriage to this handsome man, does it come will all the perks of a real marriage? Or do I have to do all the cooking and cleaning and not enjoy a roll in the sack?"

Nathan/Mason, as I expected, choked on his bite of burger, while Soto guffawed!

"Fiona, I . . . this is an assignment. My goal is to keep you safe. I wouldn't jeopardize that in any way . . . !"

"Touchy sort, isn't he!" I laughed as Soto slapped his back, informing him I was joking.

I wasn't, though!

"We have to make it look as if we're a happy couple when we are out in public. As far as cooking and cleaning, that is all negotiable. I am happy to cook, although my cooking skills are very limited."

Soto interrupted to inform me my husband was an excellent cook.

"Good. I happen to be partial to bulgogi. I figure with the last name of Park, if that is your real last name, you would know how to cook it."

"I do," he replied and gave me a crooked smiled.

It was a smile that I remember. It was this smile, along with Nathan's charm, good nature, and handsome face, that had left me no option but to fall in love with him.

I had dated and even been close to marriage, but nothing and no one had had my heart like Blue Sky Song!

I let the two agents catch up as I finished half of the hamburger and fries I had ordered. I had eaten more junk in the last several days than I do in a year. Having Nathan be the agent I would be spending every day and night with had me stumped.

Was this going to be a complication to an already horrible situation, or could I be able to consider it, despite the circumstances, more of a time off?

I allowed my mind to ponder this as Soto and Song finished up and moved away from the table to talk about the trip from Flamingo Heights to the apartment in Palm Springs. I knew that most of the clothes that had been chosen for me would have already been delivered. Except for the two bags that had arrived with me to the hangar, I had nothing. Johnson had given me a small purse, but aside from a pack of gum, it was empty.

That, at least, was taken care of when my husband separated from Agent Soto. He was carrying a small box, which had been the topic of their conversation across the room.

He returned to the table and set the box before me.

"Fiona," he said my name with a lift of an eyebrow, indicating he wanted my attention, "I have a wallet with some cash and your new ID. Also, inside are two credit cards issued to Fiona R. Park. I also have,"—he pulled out a small file box—"our marriage license and your Scottish birth certificate and our passports."

Soto came up behind him and placed two simple golden bands on the table.

Without a word, Mason took my hand and slid the ring onto the ring finger of my left hand before adding the duplicate to his left hand.

He smiled at me as he handed me the wallet with my ID and credit cards and then put the small file box on my bags. Two of the other agents took my bags and loaded them into a midsize car that had been parked inside the hangar.

I futzed around with my ring before asking, "Do I get to drive the car?"

"No, Fiona. No." He gave me a sad smile and moved to take my hand. "Let's head to the apartment. It's been a long day for both of us."

It took a moment for Agent Soto to give me last-minute instructions, which basically was a regurgitation of what I had already been told to by Agents Johnson, Little Feather, and Rosenbaum. I listened dutifully nonetheless, nodding my understanding as I was lead to the passenger side of the car and deposited into the seat.

"I will be keeping in touch. Your friend and neighbor Akio Kajiya has a cell phone for you. Everyone has a cell phone these days, and it would look weird for you not to. However, you will be able to only dial programmed phone numbers to those agents around you. They and I are the only ones that have your number and will be the only ones to contact you. If any of the residents ask for or want to give you their numbers, that will be OK. That phone will be activated through HPB. Any questions?" she asked as she closed the door.

Even though the window was down, I only shook my head. What would I ask?

We were on the highway before either of us spoke. It was Mason who broke the silence. "How long have you been in the States?"

I looked over at his profile in the light of the dashboard instruments, trying to see if he was serious. Since I couldn't tell, I answered, "I moved back with you when you finished your PhD at the University of Glasgow. So let's see,"—I paused as if I was thinking about it—"a little over two years now."

He glanced at me for a second before turning his attention back to the dark road. "Do we have a good marriage?"

This time, I could hear the laughter in his voice. "Well, since the sex is absolutely the best, I would say yeah! The good thing, Mason, is I heard from the ob-gyn, and now that I am in my seventh month, sex is back on the table . . . or the floor . . . or the countertop . . . or . . ." I left it there and watched as he squirmed a bit in his seat.

There were about ten minutes of silence before he said, "I can't sleep with you, you know. Totally against the rules."

I sighed and laughed, "Yeah, a bit of a bloody downer!"

We were silent. It was a full moon, and the desert was beautiful. I hadn't been in the desert for many years—LA didn't count—and I had forgotten the stark beauty of it.

As we approached the edge of the city, Mason reached for his cell in the cup holder and instructed, "Call Kajiya."

Over the speakers of the car, I heard Akio answer, "Mason, thought you would be here by now. Hello, Fiona!"

"Cheers!" I answered.

"I was late getting out of, um, arriving in Flamingo Heights."

"I have your keys. I'm in number 214."

"Soto told me."

"Oh, OK. Then I will see you two when you get here. Ms. Grayson already stopped by and asked that the two of you drop by the office tomorrow at about ten to sign in."

I interrupted Akio. "I thought the IFB handled the leasing."

Akio laughed on the other end. "Quick, isn't she? IFB does, but Mrs. Grayson likes to meet the tenants, and when she heard you were pregnant, she was excited. There is another expectant resident, and she wanted to introduce the two of you."

Mason jumped in at the pause. "We will be happy to meet with her. According to the nav system, we are about twenty minutes out."

"I'll meet you by the parking garage to give you your gate key. See ya soon!"

He disconnected before Mason or I could comment further.

"How long have you and Akio been working for IFB?" I asked not expecting an answer and was surprised when he gave one.

"I have known Akio," he said, giving a one-handed air quote, "for maybe ten years. We met in college. Had most of the same classes. We were just lucky that IFB hired us both and we had worked together on many. different projects."

I didn't say anything but nodded. I didn't know what to say to this man whom I hadn't seen for six years. We had attended a Disney Channel Special, a *"where are they now?"* sort of thing. He had been at Quantico, finishing up his training, and his wife of sixteen months was also in attendance. We were polite. He was actually happy to see me and introduced me to his wife, Bethany.

I had attended solo, but according to *TMZ*, I had been at the time in a torrid relationship with Gaspard Ulliel, the French actor. Although I had just finished a movie with Ulliel, we had not been involved. Nathan inquired about him. I had told him Gaspard was doing fine. After the filming shoot and dinner, we both went our separate ways.

I had learned from Nathan's mom, Jackie, about the divorce a year later.

I was both miffed and thankful he had not recognized me under the guise Johnson had created. As soon as Akio handed him the dossier, the gig was up, and I would have to deal with it.

Until that time, I would do a little digging.

"Honey," I began, "what's your least favorite food?"

Without hesitation, "Peas!"

I knew that already, so no new information.

"Favorite?"

"Anything Tex-Mex."

I twisted in my seat, wondering where he would have eaten Tex-Mex. "Are you from Texas?" I inquired, knowing he wasn't.

"No, but I lived in Houston for six months, got addicted to this little place in Rosenberg, just west of Houston, called La Casona."

That *was* new information. Before I could come up with another question, Mason asked, "Your least and most favorite?"

"Haggis, without a doubt."

"Least or most?"

"Most. There is nothing better than a properly cooked haggis." This was true. I had developed a taste for it when I was working in Scotland. "I have to agree with you about peas. Can't stand them unless they're hidden in something."

We were silent again until we entered the city limits as Mason became focused on the nav system in the car.

"What street are we looking for?"

He explained that from Highway 62, we had gotten on N. Indian Canyon Drive. N. Indian Canyon Drive was the street the apartment was on once we got into the city. The apartment was on the south side of Interstate 10, past Highway 111. We would be there in just a few minutes.

I took the rest of the drive to calm my heart. I was about to pay the piper, as they say, and I wasn't ready for that yet.

As promised, Akio was waiting for us at the entrance to the parking garage. Mason pulled up to the curb, and Akio poured his long, lanky body into the backseat.

"Here is the apartment key and the punch code to the garage." He handed the key and paper to Mason and reached between the seats to plant a kiss on my unmarked cheek. "Hey, beautiful. How's the baby?" he said to me as if we indeed had a solid friendship. He informed Mason, "Your parking spot matches your apartment number, which is 106."

Mason punched in the five-digit code, and we pulled into the garage. We found our spot and parked. Akio crawled out of the backseat and opened my door and helped me out of the car. Despite not really being pregnant, the baby bodysuit shifted my center of gravity as promised, so getting up was much more difficult than it would have usually been.

Together, the two men carried the luggage, my two and Mason's larger one, through the garage. The same code to get us into the parking garage allowed us entrance through the gate into the secure courtyard of the Desert Sky Apartments. Akio let us know that the gate code changed every week, and the manager, Mandy Davidson, would text the info to our cell phone.

The courtyard was subtly lit, so it was cozy and homey. The light from inside the gated pool reflected on the palm trees inside the enclosure. As we passed to the right, following Akio, outside the door and to the left of apartment

108 was a small comfortable sitting area complete with two lounges and several tables. A wide-eyed ceramic monkey holding a coffee cup watched us as we passed the area it guarded to arrive at apartment 106.

My home for the next . . . I had no idea.

Mason unlocked the apartment, and he and Akio carried in the bags. I followed and entered the well-appointed living room/dining room and kitchen. The concept was open and airy. It would be a comfortable place to live.

The bedrooms were off the sizeable rectangular room to the right as you walked in the door. One bedroom would have a view of the courtyard; the other had a view of the side of the building next door. I explored, letting the men talk, discovering the front bedroom had access to a bathroom that had an entry from the hall and the bedroom. The larger bedroom, although not by much, at the back of the apartment had a nice size bathroom and an almost walk-in closet. This must be intended to be the master suite.

I heard the door close and the lock being engaged as I returned to the living room. I noticed a thick blue legal binder tucked under Mason's arm. He looked at me and smiled. Again, my heart skipped a beat, not only partly because his smile always did that to me but also because that folder would tell him who I was.

"I want you in the back bedroom. The windows back there are high and almost impossible to get to through the narrow space between this building and the one adjacent." Walking over to the dining table, he put the folder down and walked into the kitchen.

"Are there groceries?" I asked, trying to think of something to say. I wanted to ask where would he be sleeping, but I already knew the answer to that question.

"Yes, the kitchen is stocked." His voice echoed from inside the refrigerator.

While he was looking for whatever, I rolled my two bags to the back bedroom and began to unpack and put away. It took no time. The makeup and other accessories that Agent Johnson had given me, I placed on the countertop of the bathroom.

"Doin' OK?" his voice asked me.

"Yes, just tired. I think I am going to call it a night. It's been a couple of crazy days."

"OK, then . . . um, I'm going to go into the living room and watch some TV. Tomorrow, I need to unpack my things. They have to be in here as well. We have to look like a real couple."

I nodded my understanding. Mason turned to leave, and I followed. He went to the couch, and I to the kitchen, hoping to find a bottle of water in the refrigerator. Seeing the bottom shelf full, I pulled one out.

Taking a deep breath and saying silently the mantra I used before a performance, I went back into the living room and toward the couch. Mason, always being the gentleman, stood.

"Do you need something?"

"I just wanted to say good night and thank you for doing what you are doing."

He smiled again, and I stepped in and up to him, not giving him time to think or pull away. I kissed him. To my surprise, but only for a second, he kissed me back.

I pulled away, enjoying the look on his face. "Good night, baby!"

WEEK I + ONE DAY

It was only eight after six when I looked at the watch on my wrist. Despite having slept all night, I was stiff. I had learned the night before I could remove the mouth prosthetic and contacts just fine, but the baby bodysuit was impossible to get out of by myself. After I kissed my "husband" and left him standing in the living room with his chin to the floor, I couldn't very well go in and ask, "Hey, honey, can you help me take off the baby?"

Johnson had assured me that it would take me a few days to figure it out, so I would be patient.

I quietly got up and opened the door to the bedroom. All I had to do is step into the tiny hallway that connected the two bedrooms and the hall bath to find Mason had sprawled out on the bed in the smaller bedroom, entirely dressed and on top of the covers.

As quietly as possible, I pulled his door closed and returned to my bathroom to empty my bladder, wash my hands and face, and brush my teeth. I also popped in the contacts and the prosthetic before dressing in a light long-sleeved pullover and capris. I opted for the Crocs that had been in the suitcase and, as stealthy as possible, went out to explore the courtyard.

The small setting area in front of apartment 108 was already occupied. The waiflike woman raised a hand and motioned me to come her way. She didn't speak, but her wrinkled face was alight with curiosity and humor.

"Heard ya come in last night. Must have been exhausted traveling and being *so* pregnant. Sit!" she ordered. "I'm Sally Fishman, but everyone just calls me Sally." Her voice was as small as she was, but it was clear and easy to understand.

I smiled warmly at Sally and took a seat in the lounge chair next to her. It was nice not having her freak out because Cat Connors had walked out the door. I liked that.

I didn't get to say anything before she started up again.

"First thing first, what's your name, and how do you like your coffee?" She looked over her shoulder at the table under the living room window of her apartment. A large coffeepot, as well as a smaller pot, stood with an assortment of different types of creamers and sweeteners, several large ceramic mugs, and a dozen or so paper coffee cups with matching lids.

"Good morning to you, Sally. I'm Fiona," I greeted her. My heavily accented voice was high and still odd to my own ears, but Sally's face lit up even more than I thought was possible.

"Well, damn!" She slapped her hand on her thigh and chortled, "Never thought to have a pot of tea ready before."

"No, that's fine," I interrupted. "Coffee is great. I'll get it." I started to get up.

"No!" She was already up before I could even scoot to the edge of the chair. "A bit of a ritual. I serve the first cup as a welcome. The rest you have to get yourself."

"That's fair," I conceded and added that a big splash of cream would be great.

I watched as she poured the coffee into one of the large ceramic mugs, adding more cream than I would have, and handed me the mug before settling back into her chair.

"That's a hell of a port-wine stain on your face," she said as if we were talking about my polished toenails.

I reached up and touched my face. I wouldn't be able to put on the "special" makeup Johnson had given me for another day. I hadn't considered someone would be out so early, so I hadn't paid much attention, but, honestly, I had forgotten about it.

She was observing me. "Here now, Fiona. Don't give a damn about that sort of thing. Sure you have heard it all before. My sweet Morty—may he rest in peace—had one from his Adam's apple to his belly button. Looked like someone drew a crimson line with a wide old brush. It was almost an arrow pointing down to his . . ."—she gave me a wicked lopsided grin—"pecker!"

I just stared at this tiny woman! She had shocked me. Something not easy to do. She had to be in her late seventies or maybe early eighties. Yet her mind was sharp and her wit quick. I liked her. This time in exile might not be too bad after all.

"Lord, I miss that man," she said softly and reached over to squeeze my hand.

I fell in love.

"Fiona, you are just in time to watch the monkeys come and go from this wonderful zoo. I have been here for a long time. I was here when our wonderful Mrs. Grayson bought this dump and cleaned it up. I know everyone and everything! I'm a nosey old thing, and nobody can seem to refuse to answer my questions. Oh,"—she eyed me again— "except those 'temporary' people from that company. What's it called—HPB? No IFB. Them suckers are a tight- lipped bunch."

I nodded, not knowing how to respond to that.

"Well, for example, look over to your left, the far corner, second floor."

I followed the instruction.

"He appeared several days ago. Nice boy but doesn't say much. Each morning, he comes out and sits in that chair up there. He drinks his coffee and reads a newspaper . . ."—the man currently under discussion waved a good morning in our direction and went back to his newspaper—"and waves good morning to me."

"Then at about eleven thirty, he goes in, and a woman from 231 . . ."—she indicated with a nod the direction on the opposite side of the courtyard about the middle of the building—"she basically does the exact same thing. Always has a paperback book. She always says hello."

I thought I saw the man laughing at Sally's last comment before I replied, "That's nice that he is friendly enough to acknowledge you." I knew the two were probably two of the agents assigned to keep an eye on me.

Before Sally could comment, the front gate opened, and a tall, athletic-built woman walked into the courtyard. She waved and headed in our direction.

"That's Pearl Hullingberg. She is a detective with the Palm Springs Police Department. I am not sure, but I think she works homicide. Damn, couldn't do that type of work."

I watched the woman with a cap of short-cropped white hair. Her traditional name, Pearl, didn't seem to match her trim, athletic body. She reminded me of some of the stunt women I had worked with in the past, long and lean.

As she got closer, I could see Pearl was in her midfifties but looked still as if she could run you down if you were unfortunate enough to think she couldn't catch you.

She looked as if she had worked a very long and challenging shift. Her loafers looked comfortable and were almost the same color of charcoal as her pants. She didn't have a jacket, and the badge and gun were clearly visible on her hip. I glanced up at the man who I was sure was watching us. He didn't seem to be worried at all that the gun-packing Pearl Hullingberg, with her long-legged gait, headed toward me.

I relaxed.

"Morning, ladies!" she chirped, another one with a voice that was unexpectedly lyrical. I wondered how she questioned murder suspects with that voice that belied the sharp striking features of her face.

"Morning, Pearl. This here's Fiona. She and her husband come in late last night," Sally introduced.

Pearl reached out and offered her hand, which I took and shook it.

"Nice to meet you," I returned her greeting.

"Wow, that's some accent. Irish, no Scottish or Welsh?" she said still holding my hand as if she had forgotten.

"Scottish, Glasgow."

"Sorry." She let go of my hand and reached down to rub my stomach. Right on cue, Mason Jr. kicked like crazy. Even I felt it.

I watched Pearl's eyes grew huge with amusement. "Gotta soccer team in there?" She laughed.

"Just one, and he is a puncher and a kicker!"

"Let me feel." Sally scrambled over and put her tiny face on my stomach. Again, there was a kick, but as if the machine knew, it was just a soft blow from the inside.

"Damn, can never get enough of that. Even with the seven I had, I just love the feel of a baby even before it's born." She returned to her chair as Pearl wandered to the coffeepot and poured her a cup from the smaller of the two coffeepots. She wanted a bit of coffee before she turned in.

I watched, and Pearl mouthed "decaf."

"Busy night?" Sally asked winking at me as if to say, "Watch her spill the beans."

Pearl sighed and told us that it had actually been a quiet night, but she had worked eighteen hours on a case from last week. "We finally got the suspect! It's up to the DA now. So I am off for two days. If I'm lucky, I will sleep them away. How is Master Sergeant this morning?"

"He's good. I checked in on him last night before bedtime, and Maggie—she left early today—took him out to the roof before she left to the airport this morning. I went in to see about his breakfast. Feisty ol' thing this morning. Wanted to give me a hard time about his favorite chew toy!"

Chew toy? Apparently, the master sergeant wasn't a retired officer, or maybe he was!

"Yeah, I know. The older Bentley has gotten more attached to that old thing he's become. I have a supply in the linen closet in the hall for when the one he has gets too nasty to look at. He don't care, though! He loves that damn thing."

She saluted Sally with a raise of her coffee cup and wished me hello and good night before turning to walk into her apartment, 121.

"Master Sergeant Bentley?" I inquired.

"He is Pearl's Min Pin? He really is a sweet old thing. Quite the charmer when he wants to be. We take turns with the little man when Pearl has to work. I have a key, as does Maggie and Jessie. Oh, I can't wait for you to meet him. Foreign exchange student from France, I think. He is put together very fine, not big and brawny, but small and compact. His ass is so tight I bet you could bounce a quarter off of it. I've been dying to give it a try." She laughed again. "Got off track, but that boy does it. If I were in my seventies, I would be all over him!"

I had a feeling she was dead serious and didn't interrupt her as she continued. "Sandi and Mandy,"—she chuckled at the rhyming names—"they have keys too. I'm sure we can add you to doggie detail if you want. Since your husband will be working and by the looks of you, you won't be doing too much."

I would like that. I had never had a dog before, and this might be an excellent way to see if I wanted to take that on later. I told her that would be fun and got another cup of coffee, this time decaf as I was *pregnant* and too much caffeine wasn't healthy for the baby, Mason Jr.

A door opened across from the apartment that Pearl had just entered.

"Oy, this will be Maj. Brock Willingham, retired," she informed me as I watched the short but solid block of a man head our way. "He is the sweetest thing . . . tells the worst jokes."

As he got closer, I watched as he smiled at Sally and after a second of appraising me included me in his smiling gaze.

"He's a cutie," I commented. "He is close to your age."

"Hell, no," she quipped. "Just barely seventy!"

For a seventy-year-old, he was well muscled, and as he got closer, he looked like he could, if necessary, kick your butt.

"Morning, ladies," he said, pausing to kiss Sally on the cheek before taking my hand and, with as much gallantry as a knight, kissed it. "Madam."

"Brock, this is Fiona Park. She and her husband just arrived last night. Thought I would introduce her to the animals in the zoo."

He nodded as if this was normal and headed for the coffee. After a moment to craft his to-go cup, he returned and stood before us.

"Sally, speaking of the zoo, what happened when the lion ate the comedian?"

Sally groaned and shook her head. "Brock, I have no idea!"

He started the punch line but began laughing so hard he had to wipe tears from his handsome face. After a moment he said, "He felt funny!"

I had to laugh; there was no way not to laugh. Maj. Brock Willingham, retired, was in full hysterics at his own joke. It was absolutely endearing.

After a beat, giving time for Brock to catch his breath, she inquired about his day. It was Thursday, and Thursdays were always the same. He had a workout first and had three karate classes to teach throughout the day.

"Maybe"—he wiggled a bushy eyebrow at Sally—"you can join me for a late dinner?"

"Brock," Sally said in a surprisingly sultry voice for a woman in her eighties, "Maggie would be devastated."

Brock's demeanor changed. He looked like a lovestruck seventeen-year-old. "Do you think? Did she say something?"

I watched as Sally scolded Brock for not speaking with Maggie himself. She liked him, Sally confessed, but Maggie was old fashioned and was waiting for him to get the nerve to ask her out.

"I did!"

"Nonsense! Dammit, Brock, you know she is a deaf as a post even with those implant thingies. You have to be looking at her when you talk to her and not from four feet behind her. The entire place"—she raised a hand to encompass the apartment complex—"knows this, Brock. Stop being a chicken shit and ask her out to her face."

He puffed up like an old rooster, and then his shoulders sagged. "I got to go kick a punching bag. Thanks for the coffee, Sally. Fiona, welcome to Desert Sky Apartments, and don't let this old hen peck at you too!"

I thought Sally had really insulted the major, but he kissed her again on the cheek, and I heard him whisper, "I know . . . scared old dog!"

I waited until he had rounded the corner before I asked.

Maggie Gershon, the same Maggie who had taken Master Sergeant to the roof, was a retired teacher who had gone back to teaching in the Palm Springs school district for homebound kids.

I interrupted her for clarification.

It seemed as if homebound kids were kids who were too sick to come to school. Maggie would go to their homes and make sure they understood the work, instruct the kids what needed to be taught, and help them get ready for when they were able to return to school.

Maggie Gershon was perhaps in her late sixties and was a tall, willowy woman. Both Maggie and the major had been widowed for a decade or so, and the major never could get the courage to ask her out face-to-face. Maggie had two cochlear implants, and while they helped her hear some noise and voices, she depended on speechreading together with what she heard to understand what was being said.

When Brock spoke to her, he always seemed to be behind her back.

It was sweet and sad at the same time. Sweet because Maj. Brock Willingham, retired, was a major, which meant he was a doer. At his age, he had perhaps been in Vietnam, and it was unimaginable the things he had seen, but he was like a teenager awed by the cheerleader in high school. Sad because, as I was learning, life could be very short.

"Will I get to meet Maggie today?" I asked.

Maggie had taken a week off to visit her sons in Houston, Texas, and would be back sometime this weekend. Monday evening, I would be invited to their weekly mah-jongg game.

Before I could tell her I didn't know anything about mah-jongg, Louise Little Feather came round the corner from the garage, and my *husband* stepped out of the apartment.

I caught Louise glance up at Newspaper Man in the corner before turning my attention to Nathan . . . Mason. There was no anger on his handsome face. He seemed to have recently woken. He was still in the clothes he had fallen asleep across the bed in. He touched his ear, a gesture I had begun to recognize as listening to someone, and like Louise, he gave a quick look at the far corner of the complex.

"Hey, sweetie,"—I all but drooled the pet name—"come over and meet our neighbor. She has coffee!"

He smiled and, catching sight of Louise heading in our direction, came over.

"Sally Fishman, this is my husband, Dr. Mason Park."
He reached down and shook her proffered hand.

I got up and got his coffee, knowing how he liked it and
also knowing that this was something that would put a red
flag up.

"Good morning, Louise. Still got some decaf left this
morning. I suppose you already know Dr. Park and his
wife, so I won't do any introductions." She leaned back and
watched. She was indeed a crafty little thing.

"Hey, Louise, when did you get in?" Mason asked after
getting up and giving her a hug.

"I've been in Palm Springs for several months already.
I left a few days for a meeting. Got back early yesterday
afternoon. You two?" She squeezed my shoulder on the way
to the coffee.

I answered before Mason did. "Late last night. We
basically just put down our bags and crawled into bed. He
didn't even do any work before we called it a night."

Mason had sat in the lounge chair, and I sat between
his legs, letting my back and head rest on his chest. It was
something that a loving couple would do, and as he had
not read that damn file yet, it would probably be the last
couple-like thing I would get to do. I relished the feel of his
body under mine. I turned my head and kissed him good
morning. "Did you sleep well?"

I felt him tense for just a second and watched as Louise
stifled a laugh.

Still doing what I could to keep him off balance, I asked,
"Do you two have to go into the office today, or can I have
my husband all to myself for one more day?"

"No. Today is a free day. Have a meeting tomorrow
morning, but then nothing significant until Monday,"
Louise chimed in, smiling too broadly at Mason.

"Are you meeting at the office?" I asked, trying to
clarify what she was doing.

"Yes and no. I meet with the nerd brothers—sorry, your husband and Dr. Kajiya—Monday morning in the office but head off to the college in the afternoon to do my guest lecturing. Did you get a chance to go over the files Akio gave you last night?"

"No. By the time we got settled, we just wanted to get some sleep," Mason replied.

"I think you're going to find it a very interesting reading."

What was she playing at? I wondered.

"I get to it after I finish my coffee."

So I had until then to relax. I wasn't sure how Nathan would feel about the information in the dossier.

I caught in my peripheral Sally taking in the exchange between Louise, Mason, and myself. She turned her attention from Louise to me and asked, "You said you were seven months, right?"

I nodded.

"Hot damn!" She laughed and slapped her leg again. "I expect you two will be going at it like bunnies." She looked over at Louise, adding, "If the door is a rockin'. . . . don't you go a knockin'!"

I was seriously in love with this woman. She reminded me of my gran only bawdier.

Again, Mason stiffened before relaxing. I felt him swallow a large gulp of coffee. "Well, I need to get in the house to do a few things before *bunny* here takes up the rest of the day!"

Louise clutched her coffee in one hand and waved good-bye with the other. Mason got up, told Sally it had been a pleasure meeting her, and leaned over to kiss me. "See you soon, bunny!"

Mason was in character, playing the part of a passionate and loving husband. Did I imagine the tip of his tongue glide over my lips? Certainly not! My body ached, and I understood that this little game was going to come with a price. Hopefully, I wouldn't be the only one to pay.

My attention was pulled back to Sally as a young African American man walked across the courtyard in our direction. As he got closer, I noticed the color of his eyes, a light blue, almost like blue ice. He had a uniform and a badge that communicated to me he worked at Palm Springs International Airport.

He walked up and stopped at the end of the lounge chairs and looked down at my stomach and smiled a brilliant smile. He leaned in to kiss Sally, who pulled up her short legs and patted the fabric of the empty space.

His hands started to move, communicating in a relaxed manner, which was totally lost on me. I knew it was American Sign Language, but I didn't know anything other than a few gestures that I was sure wasn't really part of the language.

To my surprise, Sally signed something back to the young man. He nodded yes, I assume, and Sally turned to me.

She introduced us. "This is Sandy Haley. He and his wife, also Sandi, but with an *i,* live in apartment 201. I asked him if it was all right if I voiced, spoke out loud, and signed, so you were not excluded in the conversation. He said yes."

"I don't know any sign language," I confessed and watched as Sally signed.

Sandy, who was perhaps in his early twenties, laughed and signed back.

Sally laughed and said, "He said, 'I don't speak English well, but I still do fine. Don't worry."

I smiled at the man and nodded.

As he signed, Sally's voice spoke.

"Sandi has a doctor's appointment today at ten." He looked at me and smiled again. "She is pregnant like you.

Sally, can you ride the bus with her to the appointment? She is almost there, and she is afraid to go herself on the bus."

"You know I would love to," Sally spoke and signed simultaneously. "She still has a month, and you both have all of us keeping an eye out, so don't you worry."

He leaned in a kissed her on the cheek and bowed his good-bye to me and left back to his apartment.

"Wow," I gushed, "that was cool!"

From my apartment door, I heard the strained voice of Mason. "Goyang-I Saekki, can you come in? I have breakfast ready."

"That's so sweet," Sally purred.

I swallowed a hard lump down and looked over at my husband. *Goyang-I Saekki* is Korean for "kitten." This is what my old Disney coworker and first love called Cat Connors when we were working together. It had been a sweet pet name, but just now, there was a threat that hung in the word.

"Go have some breakfast, dear. I'm sure that wonderful husband made you a superb meal. Go enjoy!" Sally encouraged with a tap of my hand.

I walked to the door, and Mason stepped back to let me in. He closed it behind me, and I heard the click of the deadbolt.

In a low controlled voice, he hissed, "What the fuck are you playing at, Teresa?"

I noticed he used my name, not my stage name. I could play this. "Blue Sky, I am not playing at anything!" I calmly replied.

"Why are you here? Why am I here?"

This was really the last two things he should have asked me. Using all of my weight, I caught him off guard and shoved him onto the overstuffed sofa. Still in the accented voice of Fiona, my voice low and commanding from years of training, I began to rage. "Did you not read the fucking dossier?"

I knew he hadn't, or he wouldn't have started this conversation with those two questions. I didn't give him the opportunity to answer.

"Apparently, I witnessed a hit by a drug cartel higher-up. The police were able to get me out of the apartment and to safety. From my apartment, I was taken to a building where I was introduced to Soto and Rosenbaum." He opened his mouth to speak, and I warned him not to say a word or get off that couch. He knew me, or he had known me well enough to know not to push me.

"I had no fucking idea what was going to happen or who was going to protect me. I didn't even know you were assigned to me until you walked in the door of the hangar." The tears started to slide down my cheeks. This pissed me off even more.

"When I heard your voice, I thought, *Someone who knows me, who cares about me. I **am** going to be safe. Everything is going to be all right.* But then I remembered how you blew me off all those years ago." I moved to the kitchen and got two bottles of water out of the refrigerator. When I returned to the living room, I threw one at Mr. HPB or FBI, hitting him square in the chest.

"Then I thought, well, you don't give a shit about me. You made that perfectly clear when I told you I was in love with you."

"Teresa, you were seventeen." He got in before I cut him off again.

"So a seventeen-year-old doesn't know anything? My grandparents were sixteen and seventeen when they married. It lasted for almost sixty years. Despite having selfish, self-centered parents, I had two sets of strong, loving grandparents. I knew what love, real love, was even at seventeen!" He tried to say something, but I cut him off again. "And if this wasn't enough,"—I was losing control now—"I think I might have gotten my sisters killed because I am a selfish, cold-hearted bitch."

I sat on the coffee table and began to sob.

He moved to me and pulled me to the sofa and into his arms. "Teresa. Cat. Fiona,"—Mason stumbled over the monikers as he kissed my cheek and wiped away the tears—"I am sorry. It was stupid and unprofessional of me to lash out at you without knowing what was going on. I just froze when I saw your name. It was . . . I don't know. I have wanted to call you. Mom always tells me she has your number. But I was such a dick twelve years ago. Couldn't get up the courage to."

Maj. Brock Willingham popped into my thoughts for a second. Just a second.

He kissed me. It wasn't the passion I had always wanted from him, but it wasn't a friendly peck on the lips. There was heat behind it. I stopped crying and, leaning into him, took what he was offering.

He pulled away from me, and with the crooked smile I had fallen in love with as a teenager, he took my face into his large hands. "Fiona, my wife, we are going to get through this. I am sorry again. Let me get on the phone and see what I can find out about your sister . . ."

"Sisters!" He was so cute when he was confused. "Long story short. There is Esperanza, whom you know, and my dad had another daughter. Her name is Olli Rose, and she lives in Kansas."

"Sisters it is, then."

He kissed me one more time, on the tip of my nose. This is something he could only do if we are sitting or lying down, as I am six feet tall, and my beloved Haneul Palan Song, Blue Sky Song, a.k.a. Nathan Song, currently Mason Park, is five ten.

He asked me to start some breakfast while he went into the front bedroom with his cell attached to his ear.

I needed the distraction, so I went into the kitchen and started breakfast. Everything was ready to be put on the table when Mason came into the kitchen and started pulling down plates.

I didn't say anything. Just waited.

"Agent Soto wanted me to relay to you that both Esperanza and Olli Rose are safe and in HPB custody. That's all she could tell me as they will be placing both into protective custody, and the less we know, the better, safer, it is for everyone."

I was clutching the side of the countertop to keep me from falling to the floor with relief. Mason's arms came around me, and he kissed my neck. "Fiona," he whispered into my ear, "you and both of your sisters are going to be just fine. We just have to follow the rules, the roles we have set, and this will all be over before we know it."

I stood there with the man whom I loved, had never stopped loving, his arms around me and his breath on my neck, and the selfish creature that I am hoped that the "over before we know it" would be a longer time than the HPB was expecting.

We cleaned the kitchen together after breakfast, and with his help, I was able to get the baby body off and take a shower. Akio had called as we were finishing the meal to remind us Mrs. Grayson wanted to meet with us at ten in her office.

While I had been in the shower, Mason finished reading the dossier. As I towel dried my hair in only a camisole and panties, he stood in the doorway. "Damn, Teresa," he whispered. "When you get into trouble, you don't mess around!"

"When have I ever been in trouble?" I asked his reflection in the mirror, watching him try not to check out my butt.

He looked up into my reflection, his dark eyes surrounded by thick black lashes. He hadn't shaved yet, and his beard was dark and heavy as the hair on his head. He was handsome, of course. Nathan was talented too. Disney doesn't build a show around you that runs for five years if you aren't. That he left acting had not been a surprise to me, while it had been to almost everyone else. Nathan had told me all those years ago he had hated it. He didn't like the attention.

I was enough of my parents to not crave it exactly but appreciate it. I had understood him, though. Even then. I had encouraged him to finish the show's run and then follow his dreams. I had at the time mistakenly assumed I would be part of those dreams.

Oh, the mind of a seventeen-year-old.

My daydreaming over, I looked back up to see his brows creased. "I can't ever remember," he said, stepping into the bathroom after a moment, "you being in trouble. You were one of the hardest working kids on the set. We all hated you a little because you were so serious. We loved you too because you were a really nice person."

I felt the heat of a blush travel up my neck to my cheeks.

"Wait! Weren't you in a bar fight in London? I remember seeing some headlines."

I rolled my eyes and turned to kiss his nose before stepping back into the bedroom to put on the baby body. "It was a publicity stunt for a movie. You can't believe everything you read in the *Inquirer!*"

He laughed. "It was the *London Times!*"

With Mason's help, I layered the prosthetics back on and was about to put on some makeup when I noticed the time. It had still not been forty-eight hours. So I was to meet with one of the most beautiful women of her generation or any generation with no makeup on and seven months pregnant. Anything for the role of a lifetime or my life.

I grimaced before I smiled at his reflection, and together we set the stage for Cat Connors, the role that would change her life.

We were almost to the front door when I stopped dead in my tracks. My husband looked quizzically at me. "What?"

"There might be a problem," I confessed. "I've met Renée Grayson before. She might recognize me."

"I doubt it!" His confidence did little to relax me. "Tell me?"

Back in the '70s and the earliest part of the '80s, Renée Grayson had been on the cover of almost every fashion magazine in the world. She began her meteoric climb in the fashion world at the same time as Beverly Johnson, another woman of color, had. There had been a rivalry between the two glamorous women only on the pages of the magazines. The women, however, had actually become great friends and role models to the generations that followed them.

Not only was she beautiful and graceful, but she was also brilliant. While gracing the covers of every magazine in the free world, she quietly worked first on her bachelor's and then her master's and, finally, her PhD in actuarial science from Harvard.

If that wasn't enough, she met and married the man of her dreams, although he was entirely out of her sphere of existence. Her husband, James Waller, was a mechanic who owned his own shop in Palm Springs. Together, they had built, by all accounts, a solid, stable marriage.

They went on to have to equally beautiful and talented children—a daughter, Dianna, who was working in the fashion industry in New York, and Michael, their son, who was finishing his residency at MD Anderson Cancer Hospital in Houston's impressive medical center.

"I was twenty-two and had just signed on with Chanel. Chanel was throwing a benefit and was honoring both Grayson and Johnson for their work in the industry, their philanthropic and charity work. As the new face of Chanel, I was there. I was actually at her table for the evening. I was absolutely terrified. I needn't be. She was as sweet and nice a person as she is beautiful. We had a very long conversation about growing up in front of the camera."

"That was seven years ago, Fiona, and I can guarantee you she will not recognize you. I had worked with you for five years, almost nonstop. You were constantly underfoot, and I had no idea it was you until I read that damn dossier." He took my hand and opened the door.

We stepped out, and he turned to me. "Mrs. Park,"—he kissed my cheek with the alarming port-wine stain—"you don't have to worry about this."

I nodded my agreement not really feeling it as we headed to the front of the complex and our meeting with *The Woman* herself.

I was clutching his hand so tight he whispered in my ear that that hand was his shooting hand and it would be unwise to break it. I let out a nervous laugh and loosed my death grip. As we didn't know exactly where to meet Ms. Grayson, we headed to the office.

Like the rest of the property, the office was welcoming. A woman, tall and full figured, stood behind the desk with the phone receiver pressed to her ear. The man standing several feet from her reminded me of someone who would be cast as the giant and deadly Viking in a Hollywood epic. His smile, though his beard and mustache were so dense you couldn't really see his mouth, lights his face up, and then he looked like a huggable grizzly.

"She'll be right with you," he informed us, indicating for us to have a seat on the small sofa.

After a few minutes, the woman hung up the phone and turned her attention to us. "Dr. and Mrs. Park, welcome. I'm Mandy Davidson, and this"—she pointed to the man who had moved a foot closer to her—"is Johan, my husband. We are the apartment management team. I run the office for Mrs. Grayson, and Johan does the maintenance."

As she moved around the desk, we stood and accepted her extended hand in welcome.

Johan followed his wife's actions, welcoming us as well. "Miss Sally told me you would be taking turns with Master Sergeant."

I hadn't had time to tell Mason about this, so his look of worry was apparent when he looked at me.

"Oh, don't worry, Dr. Park, Master Sergeant can be a little beast, but for the most part, he just wants some affection. A rubbed belly or a scratch behind the ear!" Mandy offered.

I laughed when I saw his face. It was priceless. I am sure Dr. Mason Park was not often left totally confused.

"It's a dog, sweetheart! Master Sergeant Bentley." I kissed his cheek and rubbed his arm. "He belongs to Pearl Hullingberg. She is a detective, and I guess she works crazy hours, and some of the residents take turns caring for him."

"Good." He kissed me lightly on the lips. "I don't want my wife rubbing any man's belly but mine."

"When you're ready,"—Johan drew us back to him—"I'll show you to the roof. He likes it up there, and it is well protected." He added looking pointedly at Mason before clearing his throat, "From the sun, I mean."

Ah, so here were the last of those here to protect me. There were seven in all, maybe more, but seven I had counted: Newspaper Man and Paperback Woman; Agent Rosenbaum, a.k.a. Akio Kajiya; Louise Little Feather; Johan and Mandy Davidson; and, of course, Blue Sky Song, Nathan Song, a.k.a. Mason Park, my husband. What made me want to sit down and cry, or hide under the desk is I knew that these seven people were here to protect me, not because of who I was but because of who Gabriel Planz was.

"It's almost ten, and Mrs. Grayson asked I bring you to her office." Mandy's voice snapped me back to reality.

I was having too much reality.

"Is that far?" Mason asked. He either didn't read the full dossier or hadn't been given all the information about the complex that I had.

Mandy explained that when Mrs. Grayson bought and remodeled the apartment complex, she had turned the front of the complex, which had contained six two-bedrooms and four studios, into her home. All of their living quarters were on the second level. There was a private entrance to the apartment from both the office and from inside the foyer of the complex. The apartment on the opposite end of the entryway to the courtyard was her office.

She stepped out of the office, bidding us to follow.

Renée Grayson at sixty-two was as beautiful and graceful as she had been at seventeen and fifty-five, the last time I saw her. As I had been in awe of her for as long as I remember, this meeting, like the one all those years ago, I was just doing my best to keep from sounding like an idiot.

Albeit an idiot with a very heavy accent.

She was dressed in an off-white linen paint suit that was as classic as she. She rose from an ornate table, already set with coffee and cakes, to greet us.

"Mrs. Grayson, this is Dr. and Mrs. Park. Mason and Fiona." Mandy introduced us, taking only a moment to usher us in before leaving and pulling the door behind her.

The Glaswegian accent was so thick, even I didn't understand myself.

"Honey?" Mason looked at me as if I had lost my mind, which I had.

Mrs. Grayson laughed in a way I understood she was aware I was nervous and walked around to take my hand. "Sweet child, I don't bite! Especially not an expectant mother!" As I remembered, she was as warm and welcoming as anyone possibly could be.

I cleared my thought and started again. My accent was as thick as it had been the first time I had used it with Rosenbaum and Little Feather. "Oh, aye, Mrs. Grayson, I am a big fan of yours. Sorry, but my makeup didn't arrive.

I must be a fright to look at!" When both Mason and our lovely hostess looked confused, I took a deep breath and repeated myself for the third time. This time, I got it correct.

She laughed. "Makeup does do wonders." She indicated her flawless ebony complexion.

I knew for a fact she hadn't needed makeup to cover any flaws on her face.

"Mrs. Grayson, we don't want to take up much of your time," Mason said, stepping forward to take her hand.

"Nonsense, Dr. Park. When I heard that IFB was sending a married couple who was expecting, a first I might add, I wanted to meet you both." She directed us to have a seat at the table and offered us decaf coffee, ever the perfect hostess. "Also," she continued as she slid a plate of petits fours my way, "we have another mother-to-be on the property."

I jumped at the chance to get her attention off me. "Yes, I met Sandy this morning while I was having coffee with Mrs. Fishman."

"Coffee with Sally. She didn't wait, did she?" she commented with a smile in her voice.

"I went out early this morning before Mason woke, and there she was."

"Our Sally is the heart of the community. Also the pulse and the information center. If you need to know anything, Sally is your gal!" She moved the plate a little closer when I hadn't taken one of the bite-size cakes.

I took two, popping one in my mouth and keeping the other near. Oh my lord, it had been such a long time since I had eaten pastries. I actually moaned in pleasure.

Mason laughed. "She loves her sweets."

I glanced over at him, and what I saw on his face made me catch my breath. There were affection and a hint of something else, perhaps desire, in his eyes. I could barely swallow.

"I don't want to keep you too long, just wanted to introduce myself. If there is anything you need, just let Mandy know, and I will see what I can do." She rose, and we followed suit.

"It was a pleasure to meet you." Mason offered his hand again.

"Ay, it was!" I said around the second pastry.

She walked us to the door. "The pleasure is all mine. It is always nice to meet someone as tall as me, Fiona."

"Yes, ma'am!" I turned and faced her, nervous again.

"I look forward to spending some time with you on Monday at our mah-jongg game. Dr. Little Feather will be there as well. I am sure your handsome husband won't mind." She smiled. The look she gave me said more than her words.

The beautiful and graceful Renée Grayson was as observant as I had remembered.

Mason, for his part, replied, "I'm sure that would be fun, honey. What do you think?"

How could he have not heard what I had? Or perhaps, maybe I was seeing and hearing too much.

We returned back to the apartment. Something was said; I wasn't sure what had been floating around in my mind so that when Mason had pulled the door closed behind us, I was ready.

I stalled.

I pulled the drapes open in the living room window and then went to the front bedroom to open those as well.

On my way to the kitchen, I asked, "Do you want some more coffee? I am going to make myself one last cup."

His "That would be great" echoed from the hall bathroom.

Using the Keurig, I made myself a decaf and Mason a French roast. I remembered how he liked his coffee. I took it to him at the small dining room table where he was setting up to do some work.

I put the coffee down in front of him and cleared my throat. "Can I ask Nathan Song, HPB agent, a question?"

He looked up, leaning back in his chair. "Even when I am Mason, I am,"—he added in air quotes—"Nathan Song, HPB agent. Fiona." He took my hand and pulled me down to the chair next to him. "We are in this together. My job is to keep you safe, comfortable, and relaxed. We don't know how long this is going to take, but we will make the best of it."

He raised an eyebrow as if to say, "Ask your question."

"OK, got it." I took a breath. "Louise told me, or maybe it was Abr . . . Akio, that as long as I stayed inside the apartment complex, I could roam about. Visit with Sally or maybe walk Detective Hullingberg's dog. Is that right?"

He nodded.

"OK, here's what I'm thinking. This is going to be my home for the next,"—I waved a hand in the air, trying to think of a time limit—"however long this takes. But it's just not my home. It's the home of Dr. Mason and Fiona Park. So if I have someone over, say, Sally, for lunch one day when you're working, this has to look like a married couple lives here.

"That means our bedroom has to look like we"—I pointed to him and me—"live in that space." I paused and took a sip of my coffee.

"I've already unpacked my three bags. You need to come when you can and unpack your things. The bathrooms are small, so I get the en suite, and you can set up your stuff in the hall bath. That's rather normal."

"You're right." He agreed. "I said that last night. I just didn't want to keep you up. You looked exhausted."

"OK." I remembered now him say exactly that. "We just need to make sure the front bed is always made up and never looks as if you are sleeping in there." *Maybe I can get your sweet ass to sleep in the bed with me,* I said to myself.

"I think that's smart. Let's go do that now."

In less than an hour, everything was set. Some of the stuff, the things Agent Johnson had given me to help with my secret identity, we stashed in one of Mason's smaller suitcases that would fit on top of the shelf in the closet.

We laughed when we fought over which side of the bed we were going to sleep on. Mason won when he brought to my attention Little Mason Jr. would wake me up several times a night, as he was punching my bladder, so the side nearest the bathroom was the best side for me. As he wasn't sleeping with me, it really didn't matter.

That was done, and I was exhausted. I decided even though it was only noon, I was going to lie down and take a short nap.

"Do you want me to help you out of the baby body?" Mason asked as he sat down on the edge of the bed.

"No, I am good for a nap." I reached out and took his hand. He kissed it again and asked me when I wanted to get my wake-up call.

An hour and a half later, Mason woke me. Even though I had slept, my mind had been busy. I had dreamed about spaghetti and meatballs and several glasses of my favorite wine, Banshee Mordecai Proprietary Red Blend. In the bathroom to wash my face and teeth and pee—too much coffee—I noticed the time. My forty-eight hours were up, and I could put on some makeup.

I can only cook three things. My best dish is breakfast: eggs, bacon, hash browns, toast, sometimes French toast. The second recipe is spaghetti and meatballs with a superb red sauce. The third is corned beef and cabbage.

Gran and Pa being Irish immigrants never left the Emerald Isle behind. They brought it with them. Gran would always tell me when she looked into my jade-green eyes that it was like looking out over the green fields in Country Galway. She made sure I could cook at least this one traditional Irish meal.

The breakfast was Dad. When he was home, this is what we made together. I mostly lived with Gran and Pa. They were the stable, always present parents in my life. When I worked on the show *Blue Sky Hawai'i*, they moved, and we lived on Maui. After that show ended, they moved to Glasgow for the entire time I was working on the drama. Later, I bought them a modest home in Santa Rosa, California. I also purchased a small two-bedroom apartment in Oranmore, Ireland. When they passed, Ireland was where I buried them. The cottage was still one of the several homes I kept.

Esperanza and I owned a small island in the Caribbean. It had been one of Dad's investments. He had owed taxes on it when he passed. So after paying them off, we improved the property by building a boutique hotel with thirty rooms and suites, a four-star restaurant, and daily shuttle services to St. Thomas and St. John for both guests and residents of the island.

There also had been an old sugar plantation house, which we had converted into our getaway. With four master suites, each en suite, four double bedrooms, and an additional five bathrooms, it was hardly an island bungalow. It was often leased out, having a staff and within walking distance to the hotel's amenities.

Our island, Isla Tortuga, was located north between the two U.S. territories. We employed most of the 180 residents of the small town on the island. Additionally, the joint venture cooperation provided a free clinic for the residents even if they didn't work at the hotel.

Finally, spaghetti and meatballs with a superb red sauce was something my housekeeper and friend taught me to make. Linda had informed me I needed at least one meal I could prepare for myself to have when I invited friends or family over. Yes, I could afford to cater, she had glowered at me, but everyone appreciates a home-cooked meal including the person who makes it. She was right, of course. I have never thanked her enough for her patience in teaching me.

I thought about all this as I put on the makeup as Agent Johnson had instructed me. I thought it would be heavy, the foundation covering the bright burgundy mark on my face, but it wasn't. It took only a few minutes to apply the foundation, sheer powder, blush, mascara, and, finally, some lip gloss. I felt like a real person again as I stared back at the dark-haired woman in the mirror.

It was Mason's. "Whoa! You look great." That added the twinkle to my eyes.

"I want to have Louise and Akio over for dinner tonight," I told him over my shoulder as I went into the kitchen to see if the makings for my meal were available. They were, and I turned to Mason.

"I don't think that is a problem," he said, placing his hands on my hips.

Mason Jr. kicked.

"I'll call." He reached for his cell.

"No, I want to go and ask them. Do you think they're home?" I paused between the kitchen and the front door.

He looked at his watch. "They should be. We're supposed to let the team know if we leave the compound."

I confirmed their apartment numbers and headed out the door. It was quiet and peaceful in the courtyard. If you really strained your ears, you could hear the sound of cars on N. Indian Canyon Drive. I didn't, and it was the birds chirping in the trees I focused on as I went to Akio's apartment first.

He was surprised when he opened the door. "Fiona, good afternoon. You look radiant by the way." He stood back and motioned me to come into the privacy of his small studio apartment.

It was tiny.

"What can I do for you?" he asked.

"I am inviting you and Louise to a spaghetti dinner tonight at about seven. All you need to bring is a bottle of wine! Maybe two!" I finished hopefully giving him the name of my favorite red wine.

"Mason is a lousy cook!" he warned me, shaking his head.

"He's not really, and I'm sure you know that. However, lucky for us all, I am going to make one of the three meals I excel at. Bring the wine!" I added just to make sure he heard me.

"I'll be there with wine!" He shooed me out the door.

Louise was my next stop. I wanted to get Louise on my good side. She was the reason behind the big meal.

Her face showed surprise when she opened the door. I smiled and repeated almost verbatim to her, including the wine request, and left with her assurance she would be there at about six thirty to help.

When I left Louise's, I heard someone call my name. Sally was waving at me from across the pool, motioning me to come to her. She stood at the bottom of the stairs that led to Pearl's apartment, and I noticed a small cinnamon-colored creature running about at her feet.

I followed the fence line that surrounded the pool, and when I was almost to Sally, Paperback Woman, who took the place of Newspaper Man in the afternoon, moved. Her attention focused on me as I walked.

"I am going take Master Sergeant up to the roof. Wanna come?" Sally asked, pulling my attention away from the woman on the second floor.

We hadn't even gone four steps before Johan, the maintenance man, stepped out of one of the first-floor apartments. "Good afternoon, ladies." He greeted us as if this was purely coincidental.

"Hello to you, handsome," Sally chirped.

"Mr. Davidson," I said.

"Now, just call me Johan. Everyone does." He looked to Sally for confirmation, which she gave.

"Ladies, headed up to the roof with Bentley?" he asked.

I was sure he knew already. The HPB had everything set up rather smoothly. I wondered if Akio and Louise had to explain to someone why I had come to their apartments. I would have to ask Mason about that!

"Yeah. Pearl had to go in even though it was her day off. Asked me to take him up for a little bit to tire him out. A tired dog is a good dog!" She looked at the small dog, who was looking back at her as if to say, "What's the problem? Why are we still here?"

I laughed. "Bentley doesn't look like he appreciates us chatting here."

It was Johan that replied, "No! For seven pounds of fuzz, he is a bossy cuss! Let's get him up on the roof before he reports us!"

The roof was on the third floor of the parking structure nearest the apartment building. It was a high-walled fenced area that was covered to keep the sun off the grass. There were two benches located across from each other, a small pool filled with water, a pole with a sign saying "Please pick up after your pet" over a box containing little bags, and an enclosed trash bin.

"It's a little bit of doggy heaven," Sally informed me as she unhooked the leash from the dog's harness. "Even in the summer, there are the fans." She pointed to two large ceiling fans that would provide quite a breeze.

"See you found your makeup." Sally patted a spot next to her on the bench nearest the door. "Look like a movie star."

I looked up and caught Johan's look of shock before he pretended to tighten something on the gate.

"Oh, aye," I agreed. "Famous as I can be!"

We watched as the dog splashed about in the pool for a moment before running to Johan, who had produced a squeaky ball from somewhere and was tossing it, really rolling it, to the delight of Master Sergeant.

"That'll tire him out. He is old, maybe fourteen. But like most of us who get to be that ancient, we forget sometimes. He'll get back home, eat a biscuit, and sleep for hours. He will be ready for a second go-around at about eight. There are lights up here,"—she pointed them out—"so even at night, this is a good, safe place to bring him."

We sat there watching as the four-legged gentleman slowed down.

"Take care of your doggie business," Sally ordered from her seat.

As if he understood every word, he looked for the exact perfect spot to take care of his business. When Sally was getting up, Johan stated he would do it. Do what, I wasn't sure of until I watched him get a small bag from the box on the pole and, sticking his hand in like a glove, pick up the little pile of poo Master Sergeant had deposited before placing the bag in the enclosed trash bin.

I had never had a dog; this was all new to me. Damn, I had a sheltered life.

"Come on, old man!" Sally told the dog, and he came up to her and waited good-naturedly as she reattached his leash.

I followed her back to Pearl's apartment, Johan leaving us once we were safe inside the compound with the warm "ladies."

Sally showed me where Pearl kept his cookies, as Sally called them, as well as his food, both dry and wet. She took a cookie out and called him over. "You were a good boy today. Showing Fiona your good side, were you? Smart move. Butter her up before you turn into the beast." She patted the small dog bed and placed the cookie on the edge as Bentley sniffed the treat, did a short half circle, and settled into the bed, his paw resting possessively on the wafer.

"Oh, I forgot to ask." I remembered when we were back outside the apartment walking toward our doors. "How was the baby appointment with Sandi this morning?"

"Fine, fine." Sally paused at her door. "First time is scary, you know that!" She patted my stomach, and Mason Jr. seemed to roll over much to Sally's delight. "Dad and Mom just want to make sure everything is going to plan. It is."

"It's sweet they have you." I was growing more smitten with this small woman. "My parents are gone. It's just Mason and me. He has wonderful parents, so I do have a family." I wanted to say more, but a knot stuck in my throat. I wasn't really pregnant, but the thought of me actually being pregnant and alone suddenly struck me.

Sally took my hands and pulled me into her arms. I had to lean over to rest my head on hers. "It'll be OK, my sweet girl." She reached up and wiped the tears. "Hormones are a bitch! Now, go in and get off your feet for a while. I'm going to take a nap." She rubbed my stomach again and shooed me toward my apartment door.

I didn't rest but went into my full-fledged chef's mode. There were only four hours to get dinner ready, and by god, I would serve the best meal I could.

"Oh my god! That was delicious," Akio said as he took a sip of his wine.

Both he and Louise had nursed one glass of Banshee Mordecai throughout dinner.

I looked over my third glass of wine, smiled, and said, "My one of three I can do well."

Mason looked down at his empty plate. I looked at his untouched glass of wine.

"I promise I didn't poison the wine, husband." Like Mrs. Grayson had done to me, I slipped the glass closer to him.

"He is a teetotaler!" Akio added and then went on to finish the story he was telling of their, Mason/Nathan and his, time early in their career. "So we were supposed to be getting drunk with this informant. I don't know how he did it, but your husband here acted like he was four, not three, but four sheets to the wind. I was so drunk, I couldn't even see straight."

"It was a good thing one of us stayed sober!" Mason interjected but took a swallow of the wine.

Louise took a swig of hers and emptied the glass. "Yeah, yeah . . . and you saved the day! We all have had to listen to that story . . . again and again!"

Akio threw up his arms in surrender. "But it's such a damn good story!"

I didn't want this to end. The four of us had eaten, talked, and enjoyed ourselves. I didn't remember the last time I did that when I didn't feel the need to be "on."

The three agents chatted and laughed for a few more minutes before I refilled my glass and stood. "Boys, I cooked. You clean! Louise, let's adjourn to the parlor!"

They all laughed. Louise got up and followed me to the living room. The men's laughter waned as they realized I wasn't joking. Yet with good nature, they started their choir.

"Well, the first day of 'The Life of Fiona Reid Park' hasn't been too bad," I said, toasting Louise with my glass.

"I know." She lifted an air toast in my direction and, with same friendly demeanor she had first been at the cabin, said, "This is how they all will go."

I took another sip. "Are my sisters all right?" Despite what Mason had told me early in the day, I wanted to ask again.

"Yes. They're safe and in the process of going into protection like you. Don't worry about them. I know you're going to, but what I mean is your sisters *are* safe. The teams we have on them are top notch. Just like you have here."

I reached over and squeezed her hand in gratitude. I was buzzed and was enjoying the relaxed feeling I was experiencing. It had been too long.

After about ten minutes of idle chatter, the men joined us in the living room. Mason sat next to me, and Akio took the one large recliner in the place.

"Whoever stocked the kitchen, send them my gratitude. They did a hell of a job," I said before remembering a thought I had had before. "When I went to your apartment,"—I indicated to Louise and Akio—"do you have to report that? I mean, why I was there?"

"No." It was Mason who answered. "If there had been a concern or a problem, yes, but a visit to invite someone for a meal. No."

"I was just curious how closely I am being watched." This seemed like a reasonable question if this situation had been reasonable. Did Mason have to keep a record of our conversations? When the Monday mah-jongg game rolled around, would Agent Little Feather be recording the talk of the woman? They had no clue that they were being recorded.

It was Louise that answered this time. "As I am sure Agent Soto explained, as long as you are within the walls of the apartment complex, you are free to do as you please."

Akio interrupted. "Fiona, we aren't trying to get information from you, only keep you safe. You're not a prisoner."

Louise continued, "Every person that lives at the Desert Sky Apartments has been thoroughly vetted."

I laughed at this.

Mason looked at me over what I assumed was a cup of coffee. "Why are you laughing?"

"Sally Fishman is the least dangerous person in the world. Sandy and Sandi Haley, the deaf couple in the corner, shit, they're barely in their twenties. How dangerous can they be? It seems funny to me, that's all." I tried to justify my skewered sense of humor.

"For your information," Louise began, "Sally Fishman has a higher security clearance than the three of us. Sort of like, if she told you why, 'she'd have to kill you!'"

I felt my jaw drop. Mason reached over to gently close my mouth shut.

The conversation shifted to what the three agents would be doing tomorrow, Friday. Louise Little Feather, PhD, indeed a guest lecturer at the College of the Desert, would be resuming her class in Native American spiritualism.

My husband and his coworker had a meeting at 11:00 a.m. at the IFB office to discuss logistics of their project. I would be free to do as I pleased within the confines of the apartment or courtyard. There would be eyes on me the entire time.

"Wait!" I wasn't happy with this. "You mean this apartment is bugged? That's bullshit. I thought you said I wasn't a prisoner here!"

"Fiona,"—Mason patted my leg—"there are no bugs, no cameras in the apartment. Outside, yes, but we have complete privacy here. You need to calm down."

Too much wine, I knew. I was not much of a drinker. Despite the sizable meal in the short time between each glass, I calculated, with a somewhat fuzzy brain, I had maybe four or five glasses of wine.

Akio and Louise were getting up and thanking me for the meal and the excellent company. They each bid me good night and headed out the door. Mason locked the door behind them and returned to me.

"Honey, let's get you to bed."

"Oh," I purred, "that sounds like a superb idea!"

He ignored me as he led me to the master bedroom and, with a kiss to the corner of my mouth, pulled the door close. *Well*, I thought to myself as I began removing Fiona, starting with the mouth prosthetics, *I should be happy with the kiss.*

It took me about twenty minutes to remove the makeup, the contacts, and the baby body. I took a hot shower to relax me even more before I poured myself into the empty king-size bed.

Whoever had packed my clothes, I assumed it was Agent Johnson, had included several nightshirts with cartoon characters. I pulled out the first I touched. A none-too-happy rabbit warned that without her coffee, she was not a good hare.

I would have laughed. I was too tired.

I tossed and turned. The damn bunny shirt, however, did not. I sat up and pulled it over my head and threw it into the far corner of the room. Sleeping nude was better for you anyway. I snuggled back into the surprisingly comfortable bed and drifted off.

"They did a decent job hiding you, Cat Connors." Gabriel Planz's voice was as smooth and warm as the night he shot and then shoved the body of Hasset off the eighth-floor balcony.

I sat bolt up in the bed, not worried the blankets did not cover my naked torso. "How did you find me?" I croaked.

He stood in the corner. I could see the face of the none-too-happy rabbit under his feet. The gun in his hand was the same as the one he had shot Hasset with. I was surprised I even noticed the silencer was still attached to the end of the gun.

"Easy, really," he said as relaxed as if he had just spent several hours at a spa. "Your sister Esperanza didn't know anything. She died trying to protect you."

A moan of horror at what this man would have done to my beautiful sweet sister. "You sick fucker!" I yelled. I attempted to get up but could not.

I screamed, cursing him with every word I could think of as he stood there smiling.

"I see you will die the same way." He lifted the gun.

The howl came from my soul. It was for my sister. It was for Hasset. It was for me.

Nathan stood in the room looking at me. He was in nothing but a pair of boxer briefs. He had no gun.

I had killed him as well. If I had kept my mouth shut, Planz would have killed me and left. Now the man I had loved all my life would die.

"Fiona? Baby, what's wrong?"

"Planz!" I screamed, pointed to the corner where he still stood smiling and now pointing the gun at Mason.

To my horror, Mason acted as if he didn't see him.

I was sobbing now!

"Say good-bye to your lover. Oh, right!" His smile was a cruel twist on his face. "He was never your lover. So sad."

It was the same slight "Pop! Pop! Pop!"

I jumped out of bed and ran, my hands reaching out to hold back in the blood that was oozing from Mason's stomach.

"I'm sorry! I'm sorry!" I told him as I searched his chest and stomach for the wound.

His voice was calm. "Cat . . . Teresa . . . look at me! You're dreaming! Look at me."

I felt his arms on mine as he gave me a slight shake.

"No," I heard myself say as I looked at the corner. Planz was fading into the off-white of the bedroom walls.

His voice, Nathan's, not Planz's, was a soothing monologue in my ears as he brought me from the depths of the nightmare back into reality.

What I became aware of first was that I was pressing up against him. My nipples ached. My hands had moved from his chest, and, of their own accord, one moved to his lower back, and the other cupped his firm cheek.

"We can't do this," he whispered. It was a lie. His body, hard and erect, was saying something different.

"Nathan, please," I begged and sought his mouth.

There was resistance but only for a second.

"Are you awake?"

I smiled into my kiss and bit his lower lip gently. "What do you think?"

My hand moved from the back of his briefs to the front, and he moaned as I stroked.

"Cat. Teresa. Goyang-I Saekki." His kiss was demanding, punishing. It did not promise slow passion but a ravishing "If I am going to do this, I am going to do this right!"

He turned me around and shoved me onto the bed. I had crooked my head to look at him as he peeled out of his confining briefs.

Oh, he was magnificent.

His mouth found the base of my spine and worked its way up. With each inch, he bit, kissed, sucked until he reached my neck. As his mouth moved up my body, so did his body. By the time he had reached my neck, I could feel the throbbing of his cock against my butt. He rubbed against me as he kissed my neck.

I had never been this aroused before.

I moaned his name.

"Nathan!"

"Yes?" he answered into my ear before rolling me over to my back. "Do you want something?" His eyes were dark and hooded, his lips swollen with their constant attention to my body. "Do you want something?" he asked again around a kiss.

"This perhaps?" he filled me, and I arched, wanting him to stop, praying he would not.

He did stop. It was only a tease.

"Not yet, *nae ma-eum*." The words were a gentle caress. He began working his way down, paying anguishing attention to each of my swollen breasts. With teeth, tongue, and lips, he destroyed my brain. I couldn't think, only feel.

When he reached my center, I gasped. I begged! I writhed!

Finally, I yelled his name . . . a blessing, a curse as an orgasm rocked me.

It was his lips again that brought me back to earth. Slowly, tenderly, he was moving back to my mouth. I was still struggling to breathe.

His words were in Korean, the cadence slow and rhythmic as he entered me again.

I was on fire, and with each stroke, he banked the flames higher.

"Nathan!" I begged or perhaps only imagined I said his name.

The words stopped. The rhythm increased until he matched my frenzied moans.

"Nae ma-eum! Nae ma-eum!" he growled out the words and then yelled, "Now!"

Together, we climaxed.

I could feel the tears on my face as the exquisite convulsions rocked our bodies.

I love you! I thought to him as he relaxed and, with his arms carrying his weight, lay atop of my spent body.

After a time, I wasn't sure how long, his voice still raspy with exhaustion asked, "Did I hurt you?"

"Yes. And it was wonderful!" I sighed. "Kiss me again!"

He did. This was the lazy kiss of a lover, thorough and exploring.

To my surprise and delight, he became hard again.

I smiled, lifting his head so I could look into his deep chocolate eyes, and teased, "Aren't you a little old to be ready again?"

"I'll show you old." He rumbled into my mouth and indeed did show me.

This time was as intense, but he was at his leisure, gently making me feel as if I was the only thing in his world.

I now understood what feeling smug really felt like. I had rested in the arms of my husband, Mason Park, and watched the clock as it approached six thirty in the morning. I wondered if this was the kind of lover he was. Why the hell did his wife divorce him? I would have to ask his mother, Jackie, if I had the chance.

Nathan's arms—I just couldn't think of him as Mason inside this apartment—had been wrapped around me when I had woken. One of his legs had intertwined with mine. There was no way to get up without waking him, and that was fine with me.

At six twenty-seven, he gave a big sigh and disentangled his limbs and rolled over. I took this chance to get up and go to the hall bathroom, closing both the bedroom and bathroom doors. There were several new toothbrushes in the vanity, and I took one to brush my teeth before washing my face and other parts with a warm cloth.

This was going to be a great day!

That thought left me as soon as I walked into the bedroom to find Mason sitting up in the bed. On his face was not an expression of "Wow! That was the best sex ever!" but one of "We have to talk!"

I was a thespian, and so when I straddled his lap and greeted him with "Good morning! I hope you slept a well as I did," it was as cheerful as it could possibly be.

"Fiona, we need to have a conversation."

A "conversation" was always worse than a "talk."

Playing the part of naïve Cat Connors, a voice taunted in my head.

"This will not happen again!" With strong arms, he pulled me off his lap and gently moved me to the other side of the bed.

"Why?"

"It's unprofessional!" he told me as if I was that seventeen-year-old he had patted on the head twelve years ago.

I was hurt, and I couldn't help myself. "I don't know about that," I jabbed. "I would say you could make a ton of money as a professional!"

This, of course, didn't make him happy.

"Look, I don't know what kind of game you're playing at, but I don't want to be one of your boy toys! This is my job. I am good at it. It was a stupid moment of weakness . . . which I regret!" His jab was barbed and directly to the heart.

"OK, asshole!" I started. He headed for the door. I moved faster than he anticipated and blocked his way.

"I have one thing I am going to say, and you will fucking listen. Then we will forget this 'moment of weakness.'" I felt the cold, aloof persona slip over me. "This is between you and me, and I will never discuss it outside this room. You need to understand that. No matter what else you think of me!"

He took several steps back. I tried not to laugh as he looked around for his briefs. We both stood there naked. Good, that was perfect.

I began with "I have seen you naked, so don't worry. Your briefs were behind the headboard. I don't want to see you crawl under the bed to get them.

"If it will make you more comfortable,"—I reached into the bathroom and yanked the towel off the hook and threw it at him—"wrap this around you!

"You, you arrogant bastard, are the third man in my life I have ever slept with."

He started to say something, but I cut him off. "Rag mags and publicity. Not me!"

He nodded his understanding.

"The first time was after I went to Scotland. One of the actors was happy to defile a seventeen-year-old who was heartbroken. Having been told I was too innocent and jailbait, I felt like I needed to remedy that. It was four minutes of, what I don't know. Wham bam! I am sure you are aware of that phrase."

I raised a finger in warning when he looked as if he was going to say something.

"He didn't do well after the drama ended. Booze and drugs. But his one continuing claim to fame is that he was the first to fuck Cat Connors."

"I'm sorry." He shook his head. I could see I had hurt him, and I smiled a little. Good!

"The second time was with an up-and-coming actor, Malcolm Ramsey. I should have known something was up. Anyway, we dated for about six months. We were in all the papers, entertainment shows." I watched as he understood whom I was speaking about. "He was a nice man. A wonderful lover, or at least I thought until last night."

"Teresa," Mason said.

"You don't get to say anything," I whispered before continuing. "What Ramsey was after was Cat Connors, not me but the image of Cat Connors and what it would do for him. He had a lover on the side, actually, a husband. But I was so naïve, I just thought it was me, something wrong with me. Perhaps I was right after all." I stepped away from the bedroom door and moved toward the bathroom.

"Teresa, I never meant it like that," he pleaded.

I shook my head, not allowing him to say anything. "Nathan, few people in the world know who Catálan Orlando Teresa O'Connor is. I thought you were one, but I guess I was wrong. Go away, Mason. The baby is making me feel ill this morning." I turned and stepped into the bathroom, locking the door on his words.

I turned on the water to the shower, masking his words, before I stepped into the hot water and drowned out my heartbreak. I would play the role that was assigned; the lives of my sisters and me depended on it. It was all an act for the audience of the HPB and the Desert Palm Apartments to watch. I didn't have to play a role in this room, and I wouldn't.

At ten thirty, I heard him test the lock on the bedroom door and, after a pause, inform me he had a meeting to go to. He would be back at about three, he had said to the other side of the door. I said nothing.

I applied my contacts, mouth appliance, and baby body. The nose ring things were still in place, and as Agent Johnson had promised, I was not aware they were there unless I thought about them.

I had debated what to wear. Palm Springs on the third week of March was warm during the day and cool at night, like some parts of LA. I dressed in capris and a light sweater. I had wanted to wear the cute sandals that were in the bag, but I needed a good pedicure and opted for soft-sided Keds.

I knew I couldn't go out for a pedicure, so I had added that to my list of stuff to do my own. I would ask Louise to pick them up for me. Other things on my list were groceries I didn't have in the well-stocked pantry but wanted. This included a bottle or two of Banshee Mordecai as well as Barefoot White Zinfandel. I didn't really want to drink, but at least, with it in the apartment, I could if I wanted to. Also tampons.

I had looked through all that was packed for me by Agent Johnson and his team; I supposed he had a team. There were none. My period would begin any day now, and the last thing I needed was to have to ask Mason to go and get them for me. I stuck the small list in my pocket.

I wanted to know if I could use a laptop if one could be provided for me. I wanted to learn about mah-jongg. I needed to get some recipes so I could learn to cook more than the three things I knew how. I wanted to learn more about Min Pins.

I also wanted to tell Jackie Song that her son was an asshole. She would agree with me, I was sure. I knew I couldn't contact her, but still, I smiled at the thought of the mini tirade I knew she would have.

I gave Mason—I would not use his real name—thirty minutes before leaving the bedroom. At eleven, I headed to the kitchen to scramble me an egg and cook some bacon. Oh, and coffee. I needed some coffee. Maybe I would ask for Bailey's instead of the vodka.

Before I had cleaned up the kitchen, I fixed a small salad and put it in a sealed container. That would be my dinner.

After that, I turned on the television and watched about ten minutes of daytime TV before searching and locating an entrainment show.

I was still in the news. It seemed as if we, Esperanza and I, had been seen sunning ourselves on one of the beaches north of Valencia, Spain.

Now, had the HPB pulled that one off?

I turned off the show after a few minutes. I would try to catch this show or *Entertainment Tonight* every day or so to see if news about me was continuing or waning. Until then, I was going to need some books.

What to do? What to do?

Sally was my first stop.

"Afternoon," she greeted me and ushered me into her apartment. It was the same floor plan as ours, but this was homey. Someone lived here.

"When does Master Sergeant go out again?" I asked after some initial small talk.

"At about two. Do you want to take him?"

I was hesitant. "He doesn't really know me."

"That's the thing about the old man. Once you've nuzzled him, he owns you!" She laughed. "I'll give you the key. If you have any problems, come let me know. Just repeat what we did yesterday, and you'll do fine."

"Do you know where I could borrow some books? Don't really want to leave the complex. Haven't mastered driving on the wrong side of the road yet." I lied. It was as good as any lie I could come up with.

"Sure. Mandy." Her cell phone interrupted her.

I listened respectfully. "Hey, son, how are you?"

"Yes, sure, just give me a sec!" She put the phone down on the bar and went to the hallway, pulling a key with a photo of Master Sergeant himself.

"Mandy has a lending library in the office. Go by. She never locks the door, and her apartment is attached to the office. If she isn't in the office, she'll pop right out. Take Bentley at twoish. Just do the same thing we did yesterday." And with that, she ushered me out the door.

There was an entire bookcase full of books tucked in the corner of the office. Everything from paperbacks to hard covers. Some of the authors I had never heard of. Others I knew. If it wasn't a screenplay, I most often didn't have time to read. I saw someone had left the complete *Twilight Saga* in paperback. Several people I knew had worked one or more of the movies, and so these were the first to come off the shelf.

Mandy told me to just return them as I finished. I casually said to her I was going to start the first lounging by the pool until it was time to walk Pearl's Bentley at two. Didn't want to give the HPB any surprises.

I honestly tried to begin the first of Stephanie Meyer's books, *Twilight*. I wanted to read them as Linda Arnold and my hair and makeup team, Robert and Valerie, had gushed at how much they had enjoyed the books. I sat in the comfortable lounge chair inside the enclosed area of the pool, soaking up some sun, and stared at the page.

I had an undetermined number of days or weeks, perhaps months, that I might have to be Mrs. Fiona Reid Park to Dr. Mason Park. I didn't want to make this so uncomfortable that it became an issue.

Nathan had been wrong, and what he had said to me earlier this morning had hurt me. But how was I going to behave around Mason? Naturally, in public, I would be the loving wife. There was no way around this. This wasn't the problem. I had worked with actors I didn't really care for before. "The show must go on," as they say. I am a professional. Also, this was my life, not someone in a ninety-minute movie.

It was what I would do once the apartment door was closed and it was the two of us that was my concern. I puzzled this out until I had a strategy.

First, I no longer needed his help with the baby body. I had figured this out over the last few days. Hair could be done by myself using the color and tools Johnson had provided. I knew well how to tend to mouth prosthetics and contacts, so this wasn't a problem either.

The problem was despite the lapse of twelve years, I was still in love with him. I had resigned myself to a life without him. But on the many first dates I have taken, I always compared their smiles to his. His sense of humor. His good looks. The color of his eyes. His crooked smile when he was genuinely laughing or amused.

I had my pick of handsome, well-to-do, talented men from LA to Cannes and everywhere in between. None compared to him. None made me feel as if they could be the center of my life, as my gran has said a husband should be. I had known one incredible night of his passion. He again had broken my heart, yet it was still his.

I was a damn fool. I shrugged my shoulders. What did it matter?

Before two, I put the books inside the apartment on my nightstand and went to Pearl's.

He stood three feet from the door, his stub of a tail wagging and the leash miraculously at his feet. I swear he lifted an eyebrow at me when I walked in, appraising me in such a way; I had to laugh. Oh, he was going to be a balm to my heart.

"Are you ready to go up to the roof?" I asked as he sat down on his leash. "You are going to make me work for this, aren't you, my furry little friend?"

He barked his answer and allowed me to pick him up, retrieve his leash, and fasten it to his harness like I had seen Sally do the day before.

I was somewhat surprised we didn't have an entourage as we left the apartment and took the stairs to the roof. However, Johan was working on a portion of the fence when we arrived.

"Good afternoon, Fiona." His faux surprise was laughable.

I smiled back and returned the greeting.

"You are a busy man," I finally said after setting Master Sergeant free of his leash and throwing the small squeaky toy Sally told me was his favorite outdoor companion.

"Mrs. Grayson runs a tight ship." This comparison was odd considering we were in the desert and the complex was called the Desert Sky Apartments. "I do what I can to make her happy."

"How long have you and Mandy worked for Mrs. Grayson?" I wondered where his story would lead.

He lifted a finger and went back to the repair he was supposed to be doing. After a few minutes, he turned his attention back to me. "I think about seven years. Mandy and I married young, and our two kids grew up fast and left the nest about nine years ago. We needed something to do, so we sold our big home in Phoenix and, through a friend of mine, got this job. We love Palm Springs. We love Mrs. Grayson and her husband, James."

He put his tools away and came and sat on the bench next to me. "How's the baby? The first ones are always the scariest!"

You have no idea! "We're good." I rubbed my belly for good points and smiled when Mason Jr. went on a kicking spree!

"I'm gonna take a breather, and when Master Bentley has had enough, I'll walk you down."

"No, that's OK. I think I can handle it." Let's see what his response will be.

"Not a problem. I have been going full steam since early this morning. Even had a sandwich on the go," he confessed.

He was good. If I didn't know better, I would have never guessed he was out here with the express purpose of keeping an eye on me.

We sat for a few more minutes, the dog exhausting himself out keeping the squeaky toy in check.

Sally was waiting for me when I arrived back at Pearl's. "How'd it go?"

"He is a charmer." I picked him up and kissed his silky head.

"And he knows it too! OK, if you want the two o'clock time, I will tell Pearl. Most everyone else works, so it's just you and me during the day. Sandi used to help early in her pregnancy, but the doctor doesn't want her to climb too many steps, so . . ."

"I'll do it. It gives me a chance to get out and about, and I have no restrictions yet from my doctor." I hoped all these fabrications I was adding to Fiona's story wouldn't come back to haunt me.

She took the key from me. She would text Pearl, and Pearl would have Mandy get me a key for the apartment. Also, if there needs to be a sub dog-sitter, they would let me know.

I was surprised it was after three when I got back to the apartment. Remembering Louise say she would be home about that time, I left the apartment again with my list and request for a laptop.

We exchanged chitchat. I asked Louise how her lecture went, and she asked me how my day was. I told her I had taken it easy but had spent the last hour on doggy duty, which I loved.

"I want a laptop that I can surf the Net with. Is that possible?" I said like a teenager asking for the car.

"Don't know. Will have to ask and see. There would be a lot of restriction on the use."

"I know. I figured as much." I understood there would be conditions.

"OK, will get with Soto and see. She's good about getting back, so possibly you might have your answer before bedtime."

I thanked her and then gave her the list. She looked it over and said she would have it for me tomorrow.

A thought occurred to me. Who was paying for all this—the apartment, the food, my security? "I don't have any money. How do I pay for this?"

"Right now, the federal government is footing the bill. When we catch Planz, every penny we spend on protecting you, Esperanza, and Olli Rose will be worth it. You're safe. All three of you are safe! That's all you need to worry about. All right?" Louise assured before promising me that she would contact Soto as soon as I left and would get with me the moment she had an answer regarding the laptop.

Mason was waiting for me on the sofa when I got back. "You OK?" His smile and concern were genuine.

"I'm good," I told him and headed to the kitchen and pulled out a bottle of water. "Do you want anything while I'm in here?" I asked as an afterthought.

"No, I'm good."

I took my water and headed for the bedroom door. "I didn't have a very good night last night. I'm going to go lie down for a bit. No need to worry about dinner for me. I'll have something later if I get hungry."

I saw his look of concern, perhaps even hurt, as I finished my way to the bedroom.

There. This would be my routine. There was a small flat-screen in the bedroom. There was a lock on the door to ensure I wouldn't be bothered. I would be pleasant—I didn't need to be rude—but distant.

At seven, Louise knocked on the bedroom door.

"Mason said you were tired and in here relaxing." She entered and pulled the door closed.

"Yep, being seven months pregnant sure zaps out all your energy." My humor was believable. I hadn't won a Tony, Oscar, an Emmy for nothing.

She laughed, as was expected. "Soto said OK on the laptop. A technician will deliver it tomorrow morning."

"It's Saturday," I interrupted.

"We're here to please." She sat on the edge of the bed. "It will have some filters on it. You won't be able to e-mail, but surfing the web won't be a problem. I also asked for them to get us an *Idiots Guide to Mahjongg*. That should come when the laptop arrives. As far as the things on your list, I'll have them tomorrow morning. I gotta go out anyway, so that's perfect."

"I really appreciate all this, Louise," I told her without adding I would not discuss anything personal with her again.

She wished me good night and left.

I hadn't eaten, and I really wasn't hungry. This day had been both ideal and awful. I honestly was exhausted. I opted for a shower and bed. I turned on the TV and let it hum as I went about readying for bed.

I had turned off the lights and the television when there was a soft knock on the door. Mason tested the knob and found it locked.

"Good night, Fiona," he wished me.

I could hear the tone of his voice. I knew him too well. I was hurt by what he had said and done. I struggled a few seconds before opting not to say anything. I rolled over, my back to the door, and slept.

If I dreamed, I didn't remember. If there had been a nightmare, I hadn't cried out in my sleep. I woke rested yet was shocked to see it was only six thirty in the morning.

I got up and, as quietly as possible, readied myself for the day. It had only been three days since I had left the compound where I had been introduced to Akio, Louise, and Johnson. It seemed like a lifetime ago. It took me only thirty minutes to use the WC, shower, reapply contacts, brush my teeth, fasten the baby body, and apply my makeup.

I opened the door leading to the hall. Mason's bedroom door was open. I peeked in. He was spread eagle under the covers on his stomach. His right hand was four inches from the nightstand where his gun was resting.

I pulled the door closed.

I was usually a breakfast person. Sometimes, breakfast was the only meal I would have for most of the day, and I tended to have a substantial one. I was always hydrated and able to grab a banana or other fruit to keep the hunger at bay, but a meal sometimes didn't happen until late in the afternoon or evening.

I opted for a banana and walked to the living room window to see if my neighbor was out on a Saturday morning. She was, so I unlocked the door and joined her.

"Madainn mhath." I greeted her in Scots Gaelic, and then, "Good morning."

"Boker tov!" she replied back and, with confusion obviously on my face, added, "Hebrew. Good day."

I went to the coffeepot and poured half caffeinated and half decaffeinated into a mug, added my milk, and returned to the chaise lounge next to Sally.

I also noticed movement from the top corner of the courtyard. Newspaper Man was up and looking as if he had rushed out of bed and threw on some clothes to get outside as soon as possible. If my apartment wasn't bugged and there were no cameras, I wondered how he knew I was out already.

I wasn't going to worry about it.

I would ask Akio or Louise at some point but now turned my attention to Sally. "Did you sleep well?" I inquired before taking my first sip.

"Not too bad. Your hubby still asleep?"

"Yeah, I think he was working on something late last night. I was too tired to wait up for him. I slept very well, and he was still out." I hadn't any idea if he went to bed early or late and didn't care. I smiled at her comment about my hardworking husband.

"Are you out here every day?" I asked.

"No, Sunday I stay in. The animals typically don't come and go on Sundays. Pearl is the exception, but most often, they go out to church or brunch. Maggie, Dave Hackman—you haven't met him yet—the major,"—she paused as if to see if she was missing anyone—"they go to the Temple Sinai on Friday nights and sometimes Saturday mornings. But for the most part, its quiet on Sundays, and I sleep in."

"Can I give you some money to help pay for the coffee?" I asked, suddenly feeling sorry for drinking her coffee without even asking for a cup.

She moved closer to me and turned to smile and wave at Newspaper Man. He lifted a mug in greeting before looking back at his paper. "That sweet child Renée has Mandy buy the coffee and supplies. I'm not supposed to say anything. She does her mama and dad proud at every turn." The affection in her voice for Mrs. Grayson was evident. I had to remember that Sally was in her eighties, while, perhaps if I remember correctly, Renée Grayson had just turned sixty-one.

"I don't know if you got the monthly schedule." Sally went on only pausing to sip from her mug. "Every Wednesday evening, there is a movie in the courtyard. The office supplies the meat. This Wednesday, it's hamburgers and hot dogs, and we provide the sides or drinks. Depending on your apartment number, you will bring a specific thing."

That sounded fun.

"I think Mandy will have a key for Pearl's apartment ready for you, so ask about the schedule."

We were interrupted when an apartment door opened. The man with flaming red hair, a tall ginger, who departed reminded me of a linebacker for a football team or another Viking come to life.

There seem to be Vikings everywhere in Palm Springs. Johan Davidson and now this man.

"Interesting! You just never know about that one." Sally reached over and shook my arm. "This will be good. Watch!"

I brought my mug up to my lips, focusing my attention on the hot buff man coming out of the apartment. Was "that one" this man or some happy woman who lived in the apartment?

In a deep bass, the man said, "Je me suis amusé! Nous y retournerons certainement! Vous étiez la meilleure!" He looked over our way, his face dazed and lovestruck. I tried and squelched a giggle.

Ah! I thought it was a good thing I had to take a foreign language, and French was it. So he had had fun and would definitely come back for more, and his lover, whoever she was, had been the best! My interest was piqued.

The coffee mug froze at my lower lip when I heard, "Je te l'ai dit! Une fois que je vous avais, vous ne voudriez pas une autre. Ce n'est pas de la vanité, c'était une promesse."

Oh my god, the voice was a man's, a rich tenor, and had stated to the ginger, "I told you! Once I had you, you wouldn't want another. It isn't bragging, it was a promise."

Sally whispered, "Jesse Fournier. I think he is a foreign student at the university. Maybe a nursing student. Sometimes I see him in scrubs. I was talking about him yesterday. *Wait* until you see him." She finished a little breathless.

Jesse Fournier stepped out of his apartment, took the man by his massive arm, and walked with him to the front of the courtyard. "Bonne journée mon cher!" He patted the man's butt and shoved him out the gate.

"Oh my!" was all I could get out.

"I know. When he is dressed, he looks like he should be on the cover of *GQ* or some such magazine. If you didn't see him next to anyone, you wouldn't know he was small."

I looked toward the gate. Jesse was headed our way. I had noticed he had been more than a head shorter than the Viking. Jesse was indeed small in stature, perhaps five six or seven. What he lacked in height he made up in looks. Jesse had the body of a Hollywood stuntman and the face of an Abercrombie model. When he smiled at Sally, I understood what she meant about if she was in her seventies. I was thinking, I wasn't in my seventies, but from the Viking's appearance, it wouldn't have mattered.

"Cher!" he leaned over and kissed Sally on the mouth, and there was nothing chaste about it. "You see my ginger? He was something let me tell you." His English with its strong French accent was just a sexy as the rest of him.

"Oui," she answered back in unaccented French. "Where did you find him?"

"I cannot tell you." He moved to pour himself a mug of coffee and returned to sit at Sally's feet. "You would go and find one for yourself. I know you, Sally!"

They both laughed at his comment, Sally's surprisingly robust guffaw matching his smooth tenor. He turned his attention to me, and I froze.

"Sally, you have been keeping secrets. Where did this beautiful mother come from?" He moved from Sally's lounge to mine and took my hand to kiss it lightly on the knuckles.

"She's new. She and her doctor husband just arrived two days ago, well, three. He and two others work for IFB."

"A physician?" He returned to his place on Sally's lounge but angled his body, so he was facing both her and me.

"No, actually he has a PhD in computer engineering. Just a big nerd!" I corrected the misconception.

"*Oui*, I like the nerds." He smiled at me again.

Damn! He was something.

"My ginger,"—he turned back to Sally—"we met at my job. We are forced to work the same project. Lucky me!"

"Lucky ginger!" Sally said the words I was thinking.

"I must go. It is good to see you again, my love." This time, the kiss was one a boy would give to his mother or grandmother. "As always, I am happy to see that G-D, He does listen to my prayers. Every day I see your face, I am happy!"

I waited until he was back inside his apartment before, "*Wow!*"

"I told you!"

The rest of my day was a great one. I had gone into make breakfast. Mason was up, and while I didn't cook him for him, I did tell him I was leaving things out so if he wanted a meal, he could prepare it himself.

True to Sally's word, when I went to the office at around ten, Mandy had not only a key to Pearl and Master Sergeant Bentley's apartment but also the schedule of what was happening for the month of March. With just a week left in the month, there wasn't a lot left.

Monday, as there was every Monday, there was a mah-jongg game. There was a name next to each mah-jongg game on the calendar. Mandy explained to me that was who would be hosting the game night. Typically, she informed me, there were five to ten people. If the person hosting the game had a small studio, the game would be moved to the office. This coming Monday, it would be at Maggie Gershon's.

The Wednesday movies for March were listed:

Screwball comedy—*Raising Arizona*—pizza

Film noir—*Gaslight*—brisket

Family drama—*The Way Back*—potluck (check with Mandy for suggestions)

Rom-com—*The 40-Year-Old Virgin*—hamburgers and hot dogs

"We vote at the last movie of the month what we want to see the following month. Already we have decided April will be Oscar month. I have a list of twenty Oscar winners we will choose from. If you have any questions, let me know. On the back of your list is what each apartment should bring for each Monday movie night."

I thanked her and was going to return to the pool and read when I heard Louise call my name.

"I got the things from your list." She handed me a bag and headed to my apartment.

I followed. Once inside, I took the bags from Louise and headed into the kitchen. Unpacking and putting away things in there, I went into my bedroom to see what she got for me to do my toes.

I could hear from the en suite Mason and Louise's voices. I tuned them out, but it reminded me of something I wanted to ask Louise. I stuck my head out the hallway and asked if, when she was finished with Mason, she could come into the bedroom.

I asked about Newspaper Man. She laughed, saying the courtyard, the parking garage, the outside of the complex, and the entryway were discreetly monitored by small high-tech cameras.

"When you walked out the door this morning, an alarm went to whoever was on duty to monitor your whereabouts in the courtyard. Newspaper Man was on duty, and so he had to check to make sure who had left the apartment. If it had been Nathan—"

"Mason," I reminded. "His name is Mason."

"Mason," she continued, "would have announced it through his earbud."

I thanked her for her information and told her it was time to walk the Pearl Hullingberg's dog.

I was out with Master Sergeant Bentley for almost an hour. It was fun to watch him as much as it was to watch Johan trying to "fix" something that wasn't broken.

When I returned to the apartment, Akio was there. I chatted with him for a few minutes, not really ignoring Mason but not bringing him into the conversation. If he asked me something, I answered, but that was it.

I told the men I was going to go paint my toes. Stopping in the hallway, I turned to Mason. "I am just going to have leftover spaghetti for dinner. So don't wait for me if you get hungry."

I heard Akio ask, "What's wrong with her? Did you have a lovers' quarrel?"

He had no idea!

Sunday, I got up and made breakfast for myself. After clearing the kitchen and saying good morning and good-bye to Mason, I gathered *Twilight, Strangers* by Dean Koontz and a bag I packed with water and snacks, and headed to the center of the courtyard near the pool to spend the day.

Today, it was the Paperback Woman, across from Newspaper Man, who was out on her balcony. I smiled and lifted a hand. She nodded and raised a large metal thermos-type mug.

When I went to walk Master Sergeant, there had been a note from Pearl letting me know that she and Bentley would not be home and I needn't worry about him. She thanked me for my attention to her furry baby. I literally had nothing to do today but relax.

At five o'clock, having almost finished the first of the *Twilight Saga*, I returned to the apartment. The aroma of something delicious seduced my senses when I walked in the front door. I sort of expected this. Mason was not one to hurt feelings. I remember when we were kids, he had made a remark about my boobs. At eleven, they were already developing.

He didn't think I was there when he said it, but the expression on the gaffer he was speaking to let him know I was. He spent two weeks making it up to me, and even went to my gran and apologized to her and promised never to say rude things about me again. Until Friday morning, I assumed he had kept his promise.

I would accept his meal. I would assent to his conversations. However, I would channel one of the characters that I had won a Tony for. Allyson Grandville, the antagonist, based on Dickens's Miss Havisham. Grandville was not old yet was very cold and aloof might someone break her heart. Pleasant to a fault, but no one could break through the icy exterior she presented. I knew her well.

In the play, she finds love and redemption but in the eleventh hour of her life. For me, I wasn't sure if I would find what she had.

It was a classic pot roast. The table was set, and I noticed one of Banshee Mordecai Proprietary Red Blend had been placed on the table.

"Did you get a lot of reading done?" Mason said, drying his hands on a dishcloth as he came from the kitchen.

"Yes, I did. Thank you." I paused only long enough to tell him I was going to go freshen up.

In the bedroom, I took a moment to stare at myself in the mirror and give myself a stern pep talk. *Nathan basically called you a slut,* I reminded myself. That was enough. All I needed.

I returned to the living room/dining room and offered to help. Mason assured me everything was done.

The meal was delicious.

I was cordial, keeping my answers short and to the point. I complimented Mason on the meal. Wondered out loud when he found the time to prepare everything. I inquired if I could expect to be alone tomorrow, as I was sure he and Akio had work to do. I smiled inwardly, and I could see this was not what he had expected. He wanted forgiveness. I was not ready to give it.

Reminding him about the mah-jongg tomorrow night, I suggested that he would have ample leftovers for his meal.

"Dammit, Teresa!"

"Fiona! We all have our parts to play." I warned him.

"Within the apartment, we can be ourselves," he countered.

"You," I began, sipping my wine and smiling wanly at him, "made abundantly clear two days ago that was not the case. Even within these walls, I am just your job. Something valuable to protect, nothing more."

"Dammit, Tere . . . Fiona. That is not what I meant at all. You have to give me a break. First, I was just as shocked at seeing you Wednesday night as you were at seeing me. Second, Thursday night was absolutely wonderful. Something I had wanted to do since I was twenty-one. But this isn't a game."

"Fuck you! I never thought it was." I spit the words at him. "I saw a man kill another man. He was begging for his life. How can you think I thought it was a game?"

He sighed. "What I meant was our lovemaking was not a game."

I interrupted again. "You seemed to think I was playing a game!"

"I can't be distracted. Teresa, if I am distracted, it is your life. I can't be distracted!" he repeated.

"Thank you for dinner." I stood up and kissed his forehead. "I, Fiona Reid Park, will not distract you in anyway."

Sometime later that night, I thought I heard him in my room. Hadn't I locked the door? Perhaps it was a dream. In my dream, he kissed my lips and whispered those words he had said when he made love to me. Nae ma·eum!

Maggie Gershon's apartment was one of the six two-bedrooms in the complex. Furniture had been moved against the wall, and two card tables had been placed as far apart as possible. On opposite corners of the card tables were small TV trays, each with two coasters and water bottles already in wait. Each card table was already set for the four players to begin the game.

On the pass-through between the kitchen and living room lay a spread of dips, chips, fruit, cheeses, and pastries.

There was a total of ten people, including myself, in the small space. I was introduced to Dave Hackman, a handsome man in his late fifties or early sixties. Mandy had also introduced Andrea Miller, a nurse; Steph Robbins, a kindergarten teacher; and Anna Ball, who, although retired as a librarian, kept herself busy as a volunteer at the Palm Springs Public library and several of the elementary schools. Louise, Mandy, Sally, and Renée were also there.

Our hostess for tonight's games was Maggie Gershon. She was tall, although not as tall as I, stately woman with designer glasses and zebra-striped hearing aids in both ears. As I was introduced to her, I remembered they were not hearing aids but cochlear implants. Remembering Sally's admonishment to the major, I made sure she was looking at me when I spoke.

She stared at me with confusion and regret on her face before speaking. "Fiona, it is a pleasure to meet you. Hello, Sally." She leaned down and kissed the older woman on the cheek. "I was going to have Fiona sit with me tonight and answer her questions, but her accent is so thick I can't understand a word she is saying. Sorry, my dear!"

I apologized to which she told me not to worry; I was going to have a great time.

It worked out so Louise would sit at the table with Maggie and me with Sally.

"Where's Pearl?" I asked, settling into my place with my mah-jongg card opened.

"Work." She turned to look at me. "Ever played before?"

I shook my head. I explained I had spent several hours on the laptop learning about how to play, using the mah-jongg card to make the hands. Also, I confided I was upset and shocked to learn that the mah-jongg tile matching game I played on my smartphone had nothing whatsoever to do with the game of mah-jongg. "I thought for sure it would be easy, you know, matching the tiles. Boy, was I wrong!"

She laughed. "First, it's never easy but always fun. We play to have fun and schmooze and eat. Some groups are deadly serious and don't welcome any laughing or cutting up. Here, you'll see for yourself, anything can happen, and, mostly, we are all laughing."

As if responding to a cue, Dave Hackman roared, "They changed the damn card again!"

The room, except for Louise and I, jeered and booed and laughed at his comment.

"Good lord, Dave." Maggie walked behind him and patted his head. "They change the cards every year. How many years have you been playing with us?"

"Too many!" someone shouted.

There was another chorus of laughter and some agreement.

"I see." I leaned over and smiled at Sally.

"Who wants wine?" Steph asked from the dining room table, where several open bottles and glasses stood.

I started to lift my hand, but a subtle shake of Louise's head stopped me.

There were another ten minutes of getting drinks and plates of food. Mandy walked around with a Sharpie putting initials on the white caps of the water bottles.

Maggie seemed to be explaining the mah-jongg card to Louise.

"Just watch. When this hand is over, ask questions." She opened her small pocketbook and pulled out a three-by-five notepad and handed it and a pen to me. "Take notes."

If someone yelled, "Mahj!" the hand ended, and that person won. If after all the tiles were taken and none were left to make a "hand," the game was declared a wall game.

Mandy, who was at our table, explained that if there are only five or six people, the person who was east would get up, and the person who sat out would take that place.

I had memorized pages and pages of lines, remembered, and followed set directions and movements. This was almost scary in its complexity.

"It only takes a few times to watch, and then it became easier," Anna consoled me.

"She is a liar!" Dave shrieked from across the room.

"Don't make me come over there and put you in time out!" she threatened.

"I'm not afraid of you!"

Andrea, who was sitting next to Dave, warned him, "You should be very afraid. I have seen her in action in the library. It's not pretty!"

Sally added, "You're scaring the newbies!"

Dave countered, "They should get out while they can!" before he slapped the table and triumphantly declared, "*Mahj!*"

Again, there was a reprise of boos but from his table.

We had a wall game a few moments later, and everyone got up and refreshed their food and drinks.

I learned, ate, and laughed for over two and a half hours. I didn't recall ever having this much fun. Most parties I went to were required PR junkets. I needed to be seen here or there. I needed to be "on." But tonight, I was just a woman having fun with her neighbors.

After thanking Maggie and telling everyone good night, I returned to the apartment. Mason was watching television but turned his attention to me when I walked in. "Did you have fun?"

In spite of myself, I sat on the sofa not next to him but near him. "Oh, wow! I really did."

"I'm happy you were able to enjoy yourself. Want to have a glass of wine with me?" The hopefulness in his voice made it hard for me to say no.

"No, but thanks. I think I am going to take off the baby body and take a long hot bath. Good night."

I got up and headed to the bedroom.

"Hey, Fiona!" He called from his place on the sofa.

I stopped and turned to face him.

"Are we ever going to be good again?"

I looked at him trying to find the words that would express my true feelings without being bitchy. When I found the words I wanted, I smiled to take the sting out of them. "Mason, as long as I am nothing more than a job to you, that anything more than that puts your professionalism at risk, no, I don't think we will, and that is very sad to me, Nathan. I would have given almost anything to have what we had a few nights ago. I had hoped it wasn't just a fling or a cold calculation on your part. You proved me wrong. Again."

The long hot bath didn't relax me. I couldn't soak away the look on his face. Mason understood he had hurt me.

Yet I couldn't allow myself to let him get too close to me. I had offered my heart before, and he had handed it back. I refused to do it for a third time.

I didn't think that "third time's the charm" was going to apply to us.

By Tuesday, I had established a routine. Early up, shower, dress, and makeup before breakfast. Coffee with Sally. Greeting the returning animals, as Sally called the residents. After coffee, I helped, as I had done on Monday, carry things into her apartment and put them away.

After that, I would return to my apartment. Monday, Mason had been up and working on his laptop. Today, he was dressed and getting ready to leave the apartment.

Akio and Mason were going to check in at the local office and meet Louise after her class. I had asked Sally if there were any good places to eat Mexican food near the apartment and if some of them delivered.

The ears who listened in the courtyard had relayed my request to Mason, who, along with Akio and Louise, would be reconnoitering the local restaurants near the apartment complex for a possible night out. He let me know we didn't need to have anything delivered.

I spent the day as I had done on Sunday and Monday, reading at the pool with my bag of water and fresh veggies to snack on. I had finished *Twilight* and was now on Dean Koontz's *Strangers*. I would be finished with it most likely by the time I went to bed and would begin with *New Moon* on Wednesday.

I also had decided to warm up the leftovers from Sunday and add some fresh veggies for dinner tonight. I left a note to that effect on the table so Mason would know not to cook anything.

At four thirty, I forced myself to put *Strangers* down and return to the apartment. I took time to freshen up, not because I wanted to look my best for Mason but because my gran would have expected me to.

He came in while I was in the bedroom. Knocking on the door, he said my name.

"I'll be out in a sec," I called back.

"Saw your note. Is there anything I can do to help?" he asked through the closed door.

"No. Just reheating, so there isn't much to do. Thanks, though." My reply was through the closed door as well.

"OK, let me know if there is."

When I came out, the table was set. There was a centerpiece of fresh flowers, daisies. Mason knew they were my favorite. I could hear the shower running in the hall bath, so I would wait until dinner to thank him.

The meal was simple and filling.

"Since you cooked, I'll clean," Mason said, gathering up the empty plates and heading to the kitchen.

"Mason, it was just leftovers, so I will help." I was behind him with a stack of dishes.

He didn't argue, and, together, we cleaned the table and kitchen.

"Did you get everything done you wanted to do today?" I stood next to the refrigerator and watched him put the last of the dishes in the dishwasher.

He waited until the dishwasher was loaded and closed. "Yeah, we did. Also, we found a Mexican place, El Mirasol Cocina Mexicana, just around the corner that is supposed to be really good. Akio, Louise, and I are trying to see how we all can go out one night soon for dinner and drinks. Would you be up for that?"

I realized he was looking at me, waiting for an answer. I had been watching him move but had zoned out. "Uh, yeah. I think that would be fun."

Genuinely excited, he pulled out his cell. "I'll tell Akio, and he can let Louise know."

"Not tomorrow, though," I called out as he began to dial.

"Why not?"

He was watching me puzzle out what I was going to do. Reluctantly, I told him about the movies the complex hosted weekly on Wednesday. It was going to ne hamburgers and hot dogs, and we would need to bring a side dish. Already I had found two large cans of baked beans that I had decided I would bring.

He walked to the sofa and turned on the television. "I think I can do the hamburgers, but I am not sure about the movie. I have a conference call at eight."

I took the overstuffed chair and gazed at the show.

After about five minutes, careful to keep my voice light, I said, "Well, that's OK. It is a romantic comedy. Probably not your thing."

He shrugged his shoulders. "Depends. Some of them are really well done. I really liked *Love Actually,* and I even remember enjoying Shakespeare's *Twelfth Night* with Helena Bonham Carter. Laughed my ass off. I never knew Shakespeare was funny."

I had seen and enjoyed both. I actually had played in a summer stock production of Shakespeare's *Twelfth Night* as Viola. I loved the theater and adored doing Shakespeare.

We chatted about nothing in particular and watched several hours of television including an entertainment gossip show. After seeing my flight from Hollywood was still on the news, I called it a night.

Wednesday arrived in the same manner as the previous days. If I were honest, I would have to admit that I loved this. First and foremost, I was eating anything and everything I wanted, trying to keep the portions small, which I was finding difficult. I knew I would have to get back on track when this was all over, but for now, what a luxury!

I wondered if I was a little twisted. Who in their right mind would enjoy being placed into witness protection because a psycho drug kingpin wanted to keep me quiet? At twenty-nine, I had been working almost steady for nineteen years without a break.

Even when my parents and grandparents passed away, I only got a few weeks to mourn. "The show must go on!" is actually more than just a saying if you worked in the theater, movie, television, or music business.

So, although I was a prisoner in this situation, I was relaxed and enjoying myself. Except for my beloved jailer, Mason.

I hope my sisters were fairing as well as I.

MS Bentley, as I had started calling Pearl's sweet dog, had discovered a sunny spot in the covered roof, which he had taken up napping in. He would do his business, play with whatever squeaky toy I brought with us, and after a time lie in the sun, squeaky toy nearby just in case he or it wanted to play!

How could I not enjoy this time as well? I had asked Johan to bring a lounge chair from the pool. While MS Bentley was snoozing, I would either read—was currently reading *The Host*, another Stephanie Meyer book—or follow his lead and take a nap. There was always someone, most often Johan but occasionally Akio, hanging around in the background.

Mason was out of the apartment when I returned from napping with MS Bentley. I poured a glass of wine and relaxed on the sofa. I turned on TMC, which was showing *Blythe Spirit* with Rex Harrison and Kay Hammond, and watched until it was time to warm up the baked beans for movie night.

Mason arrived as I was headed to the kitchen. He was going to take a shower and then help. He let me know he had checked the weather and was opting for blue jeans and a sweater.

"You may want to change as well," he added, giving me the once-over.

I was in capris and a short-sleeved blouse, so after putting the beans in the oven, I went to change and freshen up my makeup.

When we arrived, the pool area was already packed. I recognized the people from the mah-jongg game and the people I had been introduced to by Sally. There were about eight more whom I didn't know, including Newspaper Man.

"Who is this handsome man?" Pearl asked from behind me.

"I am the lucky husband of this beautiful woman," Mason said, pulling me into his arms and kissing me soundly before offering his hand to Pearl.

"Dr. Park, I presume?" Her husky laugh reverberated around the words.

"Detective Hullingberg!" He shook her hand and took my hand. "Fiona is very good at describing people. She pegged you perfectly. I would know a 'police detective who looks like an older version of Jane Rizzoli with a great short hairstyle' who also is the mother of Master Sergeant Bentley anywhere."

I was embarrassed and shocked he remembered and repeated verbatim every word I used to describe Pearl. I didn't get the chance to respond as Mandy announced the hamburgers and hot dogs were ready.

Before we turned to get in line, Pearl let me know she would be out all day tomorrow. Sally, Maggie, and Sandi, all three will not be able to take MS Bentley out. "Could you look after him all day for me?"

"I would love to! He is the best little thing I have ever been round. If he comes up missing, all you have to do is come to my apartment. I would have stolen him!" I laughed.

"I am a detective, Fiona." She warned with a smile.

"I know, but I am saving you all the legwork. There will be no ransom!"

"I'll keep her honest, detective," Mason interjected.

"Good!" Pearl laughed. "You do that!" She left to get in line.

Everyone took their turns preparing their plates and finding a place to sit at the six tables that had been set up. We found a seat at the table with Sally, Maggie, and Major Willingham. I was surprised when Newspaper Man and Jesse joined us.

Newspaper Man was relatively quiet but pleasant. He never introduced himself. Sally, being Sally, was goading him in her way. She actually got him to blush, which I assumed was impossible; he was so stone-faced.

Jesse added to the conversation when Major Willingham asked about the ginger. We all blushed at his comments until Sally reminded him this was a PG-13 audience.

"You are no fun, *cher!*" he moaned, getting up to kiss Sally on the lips and went for more food.

The conversation moved around and across the tables for another thirty minutes. As it grew darker, I checked my watch, noticing it was seven forty-five.

"Hey, babe," I said, reaching over and touching Mason's arm affectionately, "don't you have a conference call soon?"

I knew his answer the moment his crooked smile spread across his face. "No. I wanted to spend the evening with my favorite woman, so I took care of it this afternoon at the office." He leaned over and kissed me again. "I love a woman who's not afraid of onions."

He kissed me again. The table burst into applause.

His kiss sent electricity all the way down to my toes, returning to my center to start a fire I didn't want to have. To my horror, I had kissed him back.

"Everyone, if you can finish up and we will start the movie in ten minutes." Johan's booming voice spurred on a mass movement to the large trash cans. Also, people were taking the lounge chairs from the pool and moving them to have the best possible view of the large screen hanging in the front of the courtyard. Some people had gone to their apartments and returned with their own chairs.

When I looked around, I noticed there was only one lounge chair left, and Mason was motioning me to come over. As I knew people were watching, I did and reluctantly sat between Mason's legs, my back against his chest. He wrapped his arms around me and kissed my head.

This was going to be a long two hours.

"OK, before we start the movie, I just want to let everyone know we couldn't get a copy of *The 40-Year-Old Virgin*. We tried three different Redboxes, and they were all out. So we opted for *Goodness Sake.* If you haven't seen it—"

"You were living in a cave!" someone yelled out.

Everyone laughed but me! I was thinking, *You have got to be kidding me!*

"Well, yes, Dave. I think you are right," Mandy continued. "It stars Cat Connors and Sam Rockwell. It was nominated for two Golden Globes, one for best comedy and one for original song. It won for original song, which Cat Connors cowrote and performed. I hope you all enjoy!"

"It's OK," Mason whispered into my ear.

I typically never watched myself in anything. I also didn't own any of my records. I had my sister's, who went by the name of Esperanza Teresa. I even had one of Olli Rose's landscapes hanging in my home. It always felt weird watching myself.

For Goodness Sake was about a single woman in her twenties, Karen Miller, who becomes pregnant after a drunken one-night stand with the brother of a coworker. At four months, when she calls her estranged mother to let her know, she discovers that her mother and the stepfather, the reason for the estrangement, had been killed the night before. Karen suddenly becomes the legal guardian of her ten-year-old step bother Byron Goodson, a.k.a. Goodness, whom she had never met. She moved to the house she inherits determined to do right by her brother, who had down syndrome.

One night in desperation, she calls the person listed on the contacts for her brother. When the handsome man arrives at the door, she pulls him into the house and falls into his arms crying; she has no idea what she is doing.

The man, Sam Rockwell's character, is the principal of St. Luke's Lutheran School. Not only is he the principal but he is the priest as well.

It works out for them all by the end of the movie. Several reviewers said the plot was formulaic, but it did well at the box office.

For almost two hours, I watched Karen Miller laugh, worry, and fall in love. For the first time, I joined in on the fantasy of one of my own movies and enjoyed myself.

Mason rubbed my belly and made comments about the movie or the characters. He took my hand. He kissed the top of my head. Had I not allowed myself to fall into the film, I would have returned all his attention with a vengeance.

After the movie was over, everyone pitched in to clean up the pool area. There were comments about the move and even more about Cat Connors.

"She is such a wonderful actress," a woman said.

"I bet she is a raging bitch!" another unfamiliar voice said.

I tensed up at the comment.

"No, not a bitch," another voice said. "I was told she was a cold fish. My cousin works with her doctor. She said Connors's charm was all for the camera."

"Doesn't matter, we aren't ever going to meet her!" I recognized the voice of Andrea Miller.

"Fiona,"—Mason pulled me close so he wouldn't be heard—"they don't mean anything."

"I know," I said, but I knew the truth in their words. That stung!

"Let's go home." Keeping my hand in his, Mason called out a good night, and we headed for the apartment.

Home! It sounded nice, but it wasn't my home. It wasn't our home.

After we were in and the door secured behind us, I kissed him on the cheek, thanked him for a fun night, and stepped away so he couldn't pull me in.

I had had another nightmare. Mason came in and lay with me until I fell back asleep. Later, I wondered how he had gotten into the room. I was sure I had locked the door. He was HPB, so I knew he would be able to access a locked bedroom door. I wondered if I would say anything.

Despite the nightmare, I had a wonderful day. MS Bentley and I spent almost the entire day on the roof. After a long and detailed conversation with a sleepy Bentley, I decided I wouldn't say anything to Mason about how he got into my bedroom unless I woke up and he was sitting in the corner staring at me.

WEEK II

He wasn't sitting in the corner staring at me. He was in my bed with his arms wrapped around me.

I remember the nightmare. I remember the dream that came directly at the end of it. Mason had come into the bedroom assuring me it was just a bad dream. He was here to protect me. I had been crying and shaking from the visions of Planz with the head of Hasset dangling over me.

Mason crawled under the covers and wrapped his arms around me, kissed the back of my head, and told me, "It's OK, nae ma-eum. I am here."

I had thought it was all part of the dream. It wasn't. I felt warm and safe and conflicted to wake up in the arms of the man I loved.

I snuggled deeper into him and cursed myself for being both foolish and weak.

His hand, which was resting on my stomach, tightened and pulled me even closer. I could feel his morning arousal, yet from his breathing, I knew he was still asleep. So I enjoyed this intimacy before he woke and pulled away.

I fell back asleep.

His movement woke me, and I rolled over, filling the spot he had been just moments ago. We were face-to-face. His sleepy eyes hooded and attempting to focus.

I noticed he was between the sheet and the comforter, his idea of a barrier between our bodies.

I pulled the sheet up, covering my mouth so I wouldn't melt his face off with my morning breath. "Thanks again."

"All part of our friendly service, ma'am." He smiled and responded in a surprisingly thick Southern twang. "I didn't mean to fall asleep in here. Sorry!"

Here we go again! I thought.

"Mason, it's no problem. I enjoy waking up in the arms of a strong man." I moved the sheet back so he could see my wicked smile. "Exactly what would you be wearing this morning?"

"Hmm, let me see." He made a great production of putting his head under the covers. He muttered under his breath. He poked his head out and then back under again.

"I wasn't sure. Had to double-check. I am decent. Boxer briefs and a University of Hawai'i, Hilo, T-shirt. I am hoping that is enough for you." He smiled at me, and my heart skipped.

Damn! I was going to regret what I was about to say. "I think it is too much." I could hear a pleading tone in my voice.

I was not happy.

"I want to talk to you about that," he said, sitting up and looking down at me. "I need to go to the bathroom, and I will be right back. Don't go anywhere. I want to have this conversation in bed with you."

What did he want to talk about? I knew what I wanted him to talk about, but was it what he wanted to talk about? I jumped out of bed and ran into my own bathroom. Mason had gone out into the hall bathroom. After washing my hands and then my face, I brushed my teeth.

I could hear the water running in the other bathroom and wondered if he was doing the same thing. If so, that was promising.

As soon as I was finished, I ran like a kid trying not to get caught out of bed and jumped across the bed to resume my spot under the covers.

Mason came in, somewhat shyly and crawled back into bed.

"Come here." He opened his arms. The way he was positioned, I was able to lay my head on his chest, just under his chin.

"I want you to just listen. OK, I know you will want to say something, but I have to say what I want to say first." His chest rattled with his words.

I was too nervous to speak. I nodded.

"First, I didn't mean to imply you were a Hollywood slut. I know you, and I knew better. To be honest, I was just overwhelmed with the night we had. Bad reaction on my part, I know." He kissed the top of my head and continued.

"I hate that I hurt you. I am sorry for that and that alone. You don't know how long I have dreamed of having a night like that with you."

I wanted to interrupt him, remind him I had offered all those years ago.

He had already anticipated that and responded before I could say anything. "I know you told me you loved me all those years ago. I was a naïve, stupid kid, and you had scared the hell out of me. When I came to my senses, you had already left for Scotland. You should have heard my mom . . ."

"I did! She wasn't happy with you." I laughed, feeling the tension ebb away.

"Anyway, I just thought, well, you were seventeen, and I was just a crush. I know I was incredibly off base with that assumption."

I nodded.

"No side comments, not yet!" He pulled me tighter. "This week has been terrible. I couldn't get you and last Friday out of my head. It was magic! It was what I didn't know I was wanting. Teresa,"—he used my real name—"I want this to work. I know my job, and your job is totally opposite, but I think it can work."

Nathan, my Nathan, sat up and pulled me, so I was up and facing him. "We have to be discreet while you are in

131

protective custody. It's exceptionally unethical for me to be intimate with you. After this is put behind us, we can try it for real. I am based out of San Francisco . . ."

I knew this because his mother and I had talked about him moving closer to home.

"I don't have to live there. I can move to LA if you need me to." He took my face in his hands and moved toward me. "I have always been enamored with you." He kissed me on the lips. "I didn't realize until last week I have always been in love with you."

It was all I had ever wanted to hear. Haneul Palan Song, Nathan, telling me he loved me. I was speechless but not frozen into inaction. I returned his kiss, teasing open his lips with my tongue. When the barrier of his lips opened and the wall of his reluctance tumbled down, I pulled his long hard body down onto mine.

Like the week before, the first time was frenzied and uncontrollable. Again, Nathan brought me several orgasms before he entered me. The third time I crested, Nathan joined me.

"Damn! Shit! Fuck!" he cursed trying to sit up.

I wrapped my legs and arms around him, not letting him move. "What?"

"I forgot the condom! I am so sorry! Are you on the pill?" He wiggled free of my arm and propped himself up on his elbows.

"No, had no reason to be." I saw the concern on his face and kissed it away.

"Wait!" He pulled away, and I got a view of his spectacular backside as he ran out into the master bedroom. I heard him rummage through a dresser drawer or something wooden before he returned, giving me an equally panoramic view of his wonderfully talented cock.

I smiled; I just couldn't help myself.

"Do you want to do this?" He offered me the condom and his newly erect penis.

I hadn't ever done this before, and I told him.

He leaned down and kissed me before stepping back. "You know what to do? Teresa, hurry, just looking at you makes me want to come."

My shyness left me as I tore the packet. Taking only a second to see if there was a correct way to do it, I slid it on and over his shaft. When I looked up, I was surprised by the dark passion on his face.

He lowered himself over me again, and before his mouth descended on mine in a heavy voice, he asked, "Where were we?"

He took his time.

My heart opened up and closed again. I would never love another. Nathan Song was it.

We spent Friday and most of Saturday in bed making up for lost time. I left the apartment at noon each day to check with Sally to see if I needed to spend time with MS Bentley.

On Friday, Mason—we had agreed we would stick to our married names as we didn't want to slip up—joined me, and the three of us spent an hour on the roof. Since Mason was with me, we had no other person checking on broken fences or acting as if they were relaxing on the bench.

On Saturday, I had already been told that Pearl would be home and I didn't need to visit with the small dog.

Mason had brought his cell into the bedroom. Once, after I had recently discovered a ticklish spot, I tormented him while he was on the phone with Akio.

Mason ordered pizza, and we ate it in bed. He had had to dress to pick the pizza up at the front gate, but it was well worth it to have the opportunity to undress him again.

On Sunday, we came up for air.

Mason had to go to the "office," and I needed to get out of the apartment. Additionally, while we had spent so much time in the bedroom, we did more than making love. We watched TV. I learned Esperanza and I were currently in Monte Carlo. I asked Mason how people would believe this without actually seeing us. He told me it was all due to the power of the press.

"I like Monte Carlo," I commented as we searched the Internet for easy recipes that we could try together. We had made a list of the staples we had run out of and added to it the ingredients to several new foods we wanted to try. Also on the list were the ingredients for bulgogi, a Korean dish I was fond of.

We each went to our bathrooms and got ready for the day before breakfast. I put on the baby body, something I hadn't done in two days, as well as the other prosthetics. Last Wednesday, I had begrudgingly asked Mason for help with the touch-up on my hair and port-wine stain. So with that done, I was set until this coming Wednesday.

Breakfast was bacon, eggs, and toast. We lingered over our second cups, neither wanting to leave.

"Hey," I thought to ask, "remember Louise, Akio, and you looked at the Mexican restaurant last week? Can we go there tonight? You have been out of the complex, but I haven't. I would love to get out, even if it requires an HPB entourage. Please!" I leaned across the table and kissed him playfully on the chin.

"Let me check with everyone and see. It shouldn't be a problem. It sounds fun." Mason drained his coffee and got up and disappeared into the hall bath.

A few minutes later, he kissed me good-bye and headed out the door. I noticed as he pulled the door closed behind him his cell on the table.

With it in my hand, I opened the door and called, "Hey, sweetie! You forgot something!" I lifted the cell up and shook it.

Newspaper Man was looking over his ever-present newspaper in our direction. From experience, I knew he could hear what we said, so . . .

"No sexting until after lunch!" I teased. "And here's a good-bye kiss in case Sally is snooping." I kissed him soundly.

Mason walked away shaking his head. His shoulders were moving in a way I knew he was laughing.

I stood a moment outside the apartment's open door and cast my glance up to the HPB agent. In a low voice, I asked, "I hope you are having a good day, Newspaper Man. I'm Fiona by the way. Sorry, I can't kiss you good morning. I would guarantee it would get your juices running. Oh, well!" I sighed. "My husband wouldn't like it."

I gave him a nod and noticed he was laughing as well. He lifted his coffee cup to me in a salute and went back to his paper.

Those were damn sensitive microphones, I thought as I closed the door behind me.

I checked in with Sally at about eleven. She had a mischievous smile when she opened the door.

"Afternoon!" she quipped. "Come on in. Have a seat if you can sit!" I followed her laughter into the apartment.

"I have had a lazy few days," I said as she walked to the kitchen.

"Coffee or iced tea?"

"Iced tea would be great, thanks. So, Sally, tell me all the latest gossip." I leaned back into the sofa and waited for her to return.

"Where to start?" she mused, handing me the glass of tea. "Before I begin with that, how are you doing? Now, I'm not going to ask you about all the sex you've been having. I can see that plainly on your face. It's nice you two kids are so much in love. And, anyway, when Mason Jr. comes, you won't be having so much sex or sleep or anything for a time."

"Yeah! It's been nice." I could feel the smug blissfulness radiate from me.

"That, my dear, I can see for myself!" She leaned over and squeezed my hand.

Sally didn't press as she had promised and started with what I had missed in my two days of bliss with my "husband."

Nothing really had happened. The one thing Sally had noticed was the ginger from Jesse Fournier's apartment last week had been seen exiting his apartment every morning since.

"I swear that boy is absolutely besotted." She shook her head in what looked like disbelief.

"I would be too," I admitted, "if I had that red-headed hunk fawning over me."

"Hell, girl! I'm not talking about Jesse. I am talking about that red-headed hunk. He is so gone it is absolutely hilarious. I half expect him to—remember the cartoons? Oh never mind, you're too damn young. I half expect him to go floating a foot off the ground with little cupids flying over his head." She shook her head incredulity.

"Remember you told me Jesse was one hot little number? I guess you hit that one on the head!" I agreed.

Changing the subject of the French Casanova, I asked about Sandi and the baby.

"Oh, they are both doing well. I was over at their apartment yesterday, and I think we need to have a baby shower for her. I don't think her parents, or his, for that matter, do anything for those two sweet kids."

"What does she need?" I interrupted.

"Everything, really. Sandy had bought a nice crib at a resale shop. But other than that, I don't think they have anything. They are going to need a car seat, a changing table, diaper bags . . . well, everything."

"Let's do that next week. You tell me what I need to do, and I will do it. We can do it at my apartment. Sandi will never suspect that!" I was on a roll, having never been in the process of throwing a shower. I had been to a few before, but they were events organized by an event planner. I was one of a hundred guests. This was personal.

Sally was watching me, analyzing me in a way that was uncomfortable.

"I will do some checking around with Sandy and see what they don't have," her attention shifting back to the shower and away from me.

"Also, I will see when people are free and let you know. Oh, this will be fun! Don't you think? Maybe we will have one for you too!" she said.

"Oh, no, don't do that!" I smiled through my panic. "I don't think Mason and I will be here long, and we will be going to San Francisco where his parents live to look for a house. I am sure my mother-in-law has something huge already planned. Let's just keep focused on Sandi. OK?"

Sally didn't even raise an eyebrow. "You're right, of course. Let's take care of the Haleys."

I ran into Pearl after leaving Sally's. She was standing at her door when I called her name.

"Good morning, Pearl. Are you coming or going?"

Pearl looked down at the keys in her hand and gave a soft laugh. "Sometimes, I'm just not sure. But for now, I'm going to the store. Bentley and I have a day of relaxing in front of the television planned."

"That sounds fun. How is he doing today?" I had closed the gap between us so that we were standing side by side.

"He's a little slow this morning but doing well. What are you up to?" Pearl motioned for me to follow her toward the garage.

"It's such a great day today, and Mason is working, so I think I will sit in the sun and read." I would do that until Mason returned.

"OK, well, have fun, and I'll talk to you later. Oh,"—Pearl paused at the gate to the parking garage—"tomorrow, can you take care of Bentley in the morning and at two? I think Sally is taking Sandi somewhere, and Mandy is going to be working on the end-of-the-month reports, so she will be busy."

"It would be my pleasure," I told her and let her head off to do her errands.

I returned to the apartment, taking the time to pull back the curtains and open the windows in the living room and front bedroom to let in some fresh air. I stood in the living room and looked about. The apartment was cluttered, and I was in the mood to clean.

Weird!

As nothing was filthy, it only took me an hour to go from room to room picking up and putting away. The dishes in the dishwasher were clean. I unloaded it and placed the few plates, glasses, and cutlery that had been in the sink into the empty machine.

Anticipating I might have a Mexican food date night with Mason, I returned to the bedroom and looked into the closet. Agent Johnson had packed for me two knee-length sundresses with lightweight jackets. Finding two pairs of sandals, one with a two-inch heel and the other a pair of flats, I pulled a soft floral dress from the closet and placed it, the jacket, and the flats together. To my surprise, when I initially unpacked my two cases, there was a small jewelry box with a dozen or so pairs of earrings. I picked two pairs of loops, a medium size and a smaller size, to add to my stack of wishful preparing for tonight.

I looked at the clock in the kitchen as I gathered my books and tumbler full of water. It was almost one. I took a moment to decide if I should pull out something to defrost for dinner and thought not. I really wanted the night out.

Maggie Gershon was out by the pool working on what looked to be a Sudoku puzzle. When she saw me, she waved and pointed to the chaise next to her.

"Hello, Fiona! Come sit with me. I didn't get a chance to speak with you last Monday. It was too noisy, and your accent is *so* heavy I would have never understood what you said." Her voice was welcoming as I lowered myself onto the companion chaise.

"Did you have a good time?" she asked.

I nodded.

"Good. Are we going to see you this coming Monday?"

I nodded again. The cadence of her speech was unusual as if she was taking pains to articulate each word correctly. It flowed naturally as if she had taken great care all her life with her speech. I had seen it before with foreign actors who struggled to get rid of or lessen accents, and it gave me an idea.

Taking a deep breath, playing up the struggle, I held up a finger as if pooling all of my resources together. I nodded and smiled.

"I had a wonderful time last Monday and am looking forward to this coming Monday. I have been studying my mah-jongg card." My voice held just a touch of an accent, the pitch the same as before. I spoke, however, as if it took everything I had to lessen my brogue.

It was worth it to see her relax and smile at me.

"Oh, that is amazing." She crowed. "I can see you struggle, but it's so quiet here, and it is just us, so I don't think you need to work so hard. I really appreciate it, though. That was very sweet."

I added back some to the brogue, and we talked for a while. I asked Maggie about her job and her two sons. I explained that Sally told me she had gone to visit.

She laughed and said that if anyone knew everything, it was Miss Sally.

She took her time to tell me about her job and her sons. I was an eager listener and asked many questions. Later, our conversation turned to the book I was reading. I had told her I hadn't until recently had time to just sit and read but was enjoying it immensely. I confessed I had never been able to work a Sudoku puzzle. They were a confusing conundrum to me.

Maggie laughed at this. She loved them, and her grandkids had bought her a thick book of nothing but Sudoku, which they presented to her when she disembarked the plane.

It was a pleasant few hours. I didn't do any reading. It was something rare and unusual to have a conversation that wasn't related to work or people in the business. Except for Linda, there were few people I spent hours with talking about nothing in general.

Maggie, after checking her watch, began gathering her things.

Before she could leave, I called out, "Maggie, can I tell you something?"

She turned her attention back to me with a smile. "Sure, Fiona. What's up?"

I took a deep breath hoping I wasn't sticking my nose into something it had no business being stuck in. "Did you know that Major Willingham has a serious crush on you? He wants to ask you out but is so nervous when he is around you. He can't get up the nerve."

"Well, I'll be!" she sighed. "I always thought Brock had something to say to me, but every time I was near, he just told one of his awful jokes."

I laughed. I could see that happening. "Do yourself a favor. If you are interested, ask the major out for coffee or something! I would hate for you two to miss out on something because of fear."

"You're a sweet girl, Fiona. I can see why your husband looks at you as if you hung the moon." She stood up and put her hand on my shoulder. "I think I just might take you up on your advice."

I hoped she would.

My excitement was palpable. When Mason arrived back to the apartment at around four, he let me know it had all been cleared and we, Akio, and Louise would be going to El Mirasol Cocina Mexicana Restaurant for dinner tonight. I did a little dance, kissed him soundly, and convinced him there needed to be some sexual celebration.

I took my time with a hot bath and gave myself a mini facial before the daunting task of reapplying Fiona.

I applied lotion from face to toes and worked on my hair, checking for strawberry blond roots. Before layering on my makeup, I put in the hazel contacts and the mouth prosthetic.

The sundress, light jacket, and the sandals I had chosen made a very casual but attractive ensemble. I was rewarded with a "wow" when I stepped out of the hall into the living room.

"Even with all that makes *Fiona* Fiona, you will still be the most beautiful woman in the place." He nibbled my ear around each word.

"To you maybe." I stepped back and patted my belly.

His answer was another reason I would always love him. Again, a whisper in my ear, he told me, "Teresa, you were and are always more beautiful than Cat Connors."

To my surprise, we drove even though the restaurant was literally across the street. I asked Mason about this and was told those were the rules Soto has set.

"We are going to make an evening of this," Louise said, clapping her hands together like a happy fifth grader given extra recess.

At seven, the place was already packed. We were told we would have a thirty-minute wait when we had asked for one of the large corner booths in the back. The night was clear and warm, and El Mirasol had many tables outside open to the night air, but I understood why they would have requested a booth in the back.

We were told we could wait at the bar.

"I would like"—I had glanced at the bar menu—"a frozen mango margarita."

The bartender looked at me and then at Mason. I was thrilled with his response to his—the barkeep's—raised an eyebrow. "The doctor told her she could have one"—he looked at me and held up one finger—"glass of wine, beer, or alcoholic drink a month. This is it for March."

"April is in a few days!" I mentioned.

"One margarita, babe. I don't want Mason Jr. swimming in tequila."

Louise's laughter was strained.

Akio informed Louise she couldn't have more than one either, as someone had to stay sober.

She punched him playfully in the arm. He hammed it up, and the bartender got our drinks and ignored our behavior.

We would have stood and waited for our table, but several older men chivalrously gave the pregnant woman and her group their bar table. I thanked them graciously, letting them know my husband, pointing to Mason, would have made me sit on the floor if the wait had been too long.

"She is lying!" he informed them.

"Really?" one of the men inquired.

"Really!" confirmed Louise.

"No way," countered Akio.

I leaned over toward the other man who hadn't spoken. "I am pregnant, not incapacitated! They treat me as if I was the first woman in the entire world to become pregnant."

Conspiratorially, he leaned even closer but spoke so that everyone could hear. "I understand this happens sometimes. He does know how you got"—he ran his blue eyes over my protruding stomach—"this way, doesn't he? Sometimes I think we forget."

There was a bust of laughter not only from the four older gentlemen who had given us the table but also from several people standing around.

Akio gave Mason a poke in the side and made a few off-color comments that sent the group into fits of laughter again.

"He is going to make a good daddy, I can tell," the man at my side said. He squeezed my hand and told us to have a good night when their name was called for a table.

As I knew I was only going to have one of the margaritas, I sipped mine between sips of water. We arrived at our table at around seven forty and ordered appetizers.

As the conversation moved around the table, I was surprised that we, or should I say they, were able to hold a conversation that had nothing to do with their jobs, except Louise's classes she was lecturing. It was apparent they had known each other for a long time.

There was a part of me that was jealous. I had a tiny group of close friends, maybe four. Misty Dawn Song-Myeong, Nathan's little sister who, like her older brother, went by her American name. Dawn and I had been close since we were preteens. There was Linda. Astrid Bergès-Frisbey, a French actress whom I had met when I was fourteen at a summer school program in Paris, was also a close friend. Even as close as we were, Astrid was most often an ocean away. Almost everyone I knew were business associates, nothing more. I had acquaintances but few friends.

I took a swallow of my tequila-infused drink and used it to swallow the lump in my throat.

"Hey, hon, what's wrong? You OK?" It was Mason's voice that brought me back to the noise of the place.

I could play this two different ways. The first and less desirable was to tell these three people, two almost complete strangers, I had no life and no friends.

Wasn't going to happen.

Instead, I chose the second. I allowed my eyes to well up with tears before looking at each of my tablemates. "I am not." I was overdramatic. I wanted to make sure this was not serious.

"I canna only have one wee margarita. Tis a sad state of affairs." I dapped my eye and looked at Mason. "This babe in my belly is going to be a big strong Scots like his mother. Not some Yank who canna drink more than a ladyfinger pint"—I spaced my thumb and forefinger about three inches indicating the size of the glass—"before he is out on the floor."

I was on. This is what I did. I entertained. I could deliver lines or a melody, but I was also the granddaughter of good Irish storytellers. I could weave a yarn to put most to shame.

Akio guffawed and admitted as a fellow Yank that this was true.

"I didn't know that!" was Louise's comment.

And from Mason was an insulted "Hey! This is slander!"

"Oh, aye! Tis no such thing!" The waiter arrived, and I promised all a good tale of how I met the Yank and how I got him to marry me after we ordered our dinners.

"Well, ya know . . ." I began my tale.

I started with how he had come into the pub where I worked near the university. He was a studious Yank and always had a stack of books with him. He ordered the same thing, mince and tatties, and a wee ladyfinger pint that he could never finish."

"Mince and tatties?" Louise asked.

I told that by the end of the story she would know what they were.

"Now, here is where the saga gets personal. Until this, he was just some bloke in a pub. Cute, but there are many a cute men in Glasgow. So now, working at a pub so near to the university, I worked hard to make my living." I took a pause to sip my margarita.

"The girls"—I placed both hands under my breasts to indicate these were the girls I was speaking of—"were set up and displayed in a conservative but altogether slutty way. Gotta do what I must. Anyway, this here Yank,"—I leaned over and kissed his cheek—"one fine afternoon, he sat at the bar instead of his customary corner booth. After serving a plate to the man two stools down, I leaned over so he would have a full view of the 'girls' to loosen his wallet. Something miraculous happened!"

"A miracle! Doesn't happen every day," Louise commented.

"I wanna see the girls if they inspire a miracle." Akio leered at my boobs.

"Hey, they are not yours to see," Mason growled.

"Hello,"—Louise interrupted the boy's potential fisticuffs—"I want to hear about the 'miracle'!"

"Well, naturally, he fell under their spell, all but drooling!"

"Lies! All lies." Mason played along. "I was drooling over the meat and potatoes and not your boobs!"

"Miracle!" Louise prompted.

"Yes, well, as I was saying, he indeed was taken in by the 'girls,' but his dark brown eyes moved to me face and stayed. He gave me his winning smile, and I was a goner!"

Louise sighed and used her napkin to fan her face.

"It is some face. But I don't know if it's better than your boobs." This from Akio as Mason reached around me to punch him in the arm.

I continued my saga through dinner and dessert. I had the entire table, myself included, almost falling out of the booth with laughter. I felt good, and I enjoyed the fact they seemed as relaxed as me.

I had noticed midway through the meal that Jesse Fournier and his ginger giant were at a table not far away from us. He had saluted us at one point but focused his attention on the handsome man across from him.

I glanced at my watch. I was astonished we had been at the table for over two hours. "We need to make sure we leave a good tip for this poor waiter. He isn't going to get to have too many here after us." I hope my companions weren't cheapskates.

Akio and Louise were finishing up their second overlarge margarita. I noticed Mason had switched to iced tea after one drink. A dark-haired man in his late forties walked up to the table with a wide grin on his freckled face.

I perceived several things happen as he approached. All three of the agents' attention focused on the man, and there was a hint of threat in their postures. Jesse, who hadn't paid us any heed except to acknowledge our presence, was suddenly at the opposite end of the table from where the newcomer stood.

"Good evening." His Scot Gaelic was a thick as his beard. "I can't tell you how nice it was to hear a fellow Scots. I'm Bothain Robertson." He reached across the table to offer his hand.

I smiled, taking his hand, hoping to relax the agents around me. "It is nice, isn't it?" I replied back.

It was Mason who asked, "Babe, there are three others here who have no idea what is going on? Four . . ." he indicated to Jesse.

"I would like to introduce you to my husband, Mason Park, and our friends Louise Little Feather and Akio Kajiya. Oh, and Jesse Fournier." I included him. "Everyone, this is Bothain."

Bothain shook everyone's hand. "My girlfriend and I,"— he turned and pointed to the attractive brunette still seated at the table—"we couldn't help but hear your voice. Once I heard the accent, I have to admit I paid more attention to it than to her. Luckily, she will forgive me." The woman at Bothain's indication came to the table and was introduced to us as Sabrina.

Love Behind the Lies

We chatted for a few minutes before Bothain and Sabrina wished us, "Oidhche mhath" (Good night).

The ginger had come up behind Jesse, towering over him. "Tell them good night, and we are leaving now," he said in French.

"Don't be rude, speak English!" Jesse scolded him back in French.

Feeling a bit of a show-off, I said back with equally fluent French, "Ce n'est pas grossier, ma chère. Il est très sexy et j'aime toujours entendre la langue" (It is not rude, my dear. It is very sexy, and I always love to hear the language), I had said.

Everyone but Mason, who knew I spoke French, was staring at me.

"I am European." I countered at their stares. "We do speak more than one language."

"Naturellement," Jesse and the Viking agreed in unison.

At Akio's suggestion, the waiter was paid including a hefty tip, and we, Mason, Louise, Akio, Jesse, and his ginger left the restaurant together. The Frenchmen followed us to our car, letting us know they were going for a *promenade* before returning to the apartments.

When we returned to the apartment, Mason asked, "Are you tired? I had a great time. You were hysterical!"

"No. Full but not tired. I do"—I said over my shoulder as I headed for the bedroom—"want to get out of the baby body and take out these damn contacts and dentures."

He followed me into the bedroom and began to undress as I stepped into the bathroom to start removing my contacts.

After a minute, Mason stood at the door in his boxer briefs and asked if I was ready to remove the baby body.

After leaving to place it in the closet, he returned.

147

"What you thinking?" I asked through a mouthful of toothpaste.

"I have known you a long time. What had you down at the restaurant? I know it had nothing to do with that damn margarita!" he warned.

I turned to face him in just my panties. This was a part of a relationship I had never had. Here we were in our underwear having a serious conversation. How wonderful was that?

"You're right. It had nothing to do with the drink. Do you know the last time I sat in a restaurant with friends and was not surrounded by paparazzi? How about when I was ten and with my grandparents? Not my *abuelo* and *abuela*. They were famous in their own right, and, most often, if I was there, so was my mother. But with Gran and Pa, I was only just their granddaughter, but that changed when I started working on *Blue Sky Hawai'i* with you. How long ago was that?"

He moved to me, enfolding me into his arms and kissed me.

Together, we moved to the bed, but I wasn't finished.

"I understood being famous like I am comes with the loss of privacy. I have my privacy in my homes. That's it. But tonight, I was out with my lover," I said, kissing him, "and two people whom I might just be able to call friends. This is something I don't have. You don't know my friend Linda Arnold. I've known her since just after we left Hawai'i. You may or may not know about Astrid Bergès-Frisbey. We met during my breaks with Disney. I went to school in Paris, and she was in my class."

I crawled into bed and laid my head on his chest. He was silent, listening.

"I don't regret my life . . . well most of it. But I do regret I haven't made time to have a real life, and I didn't even know I wanted that until now. How twisted is that?"

"I understand, I truly do." He scooted down, repositioning himself, so we were face-to-face. "That's why I got out of the business. You're not twisted, but I think sometimes you have to get thrown out of the situation you are in before you can realize there are other possibilities. Do you know what I mean?"

Damn, I loved this man.

I snuggled closer feeling the length of his body against mine. "Do you know the first time I fell in love with you?"

"When you showed me your boobs in Glasgow?" He laughed and gently tweaked a nipple.

"No, but it had to do with my boobs. I was eleven, and you had said something about my boobs and how big they were for an eleven-year-old. I wasn't mad when I think about it, but I was eleven, and even though I was thrilled you noticed me, I was hurt. But you spent two weeks doing nice things for me and even went to Gran to apologize. She told me a boy like that would grow up to be a fine young man. You did grow up to be fine!"

"Can I show you how fine I can be?" The kiss that followed was what I needed.

His lovemaking was slow and attentive. There wasn't a part of my body that didn't receive his attention. After the first orgasm, it was my turn to reciprocate.

Later in the darkness of the bedroom, as I drifted off to sleep, I felt a small flutter low in my belly. It wasn't unpleasant, but underneath the awareness was something trying to push its way into my conscience.

Before I had gone to sleep the night before, I had set the alarm for six thirty. I had a busy day. I wanted to have my breakfast before I headed out to sit with Sally. However, when I hit the snooze and rolled back onto my back, I was a little queasy.

I must have moaned as Mason rolled over and questioned if there was something wrong.

I admitted I had eaten like a pig since the first day I had been in HPB custody, and perhaps it was catching up with me. After a minute, though, it passed, and I rolled out of bed as Mason covered his head and went back to sleep.

I showered and dressed as quietly as I could before leaving the bedroom, closing the door behind me.

In the kitchen, I scrambled me an egg and ate a piece of dry toast. I had made coffee, but the taste made me gag, so I took a few extra minutes to make some herbal tea to take out with me.

Sally was in her usual good humor but frowned as I got closer. "My dear, you look a little green this morning." She patted the chaise next to her, and I gratefully lowered myself.

"You OK?"

I told her without going into too much detail that I had been eating like a crazed woman the last few weeks and, last night, had not only eaten Mexican food but also eaten a lot!

She shook her head but added, "That happens. I had seven wonderful children. With each, I gorged on something different. The worst was my fourth. It was sauerkraut. I can't even smell the stuff now without making myself gag! The best was the first, caramel ice cream. I still love that stuff!"

"I've always been careful about what I ate. Not crazy health food. I'm not now nor ever have been a vegetarian, but I was always careful." Now I was going to be a bit creative in my story. "When I first found out I was pregnant, I wanted to do everything just right. Mason's mom, Jackie, laughed at me but told me I was a good daughter. She wanted me to eat lots of kimchi, rice, and wheatgrass. I tried, but she said with every meal . . ." I made a gagging sound to illustrate my reaction to this.

Maggie showed up for her coffee to go.

"I did it," she announced after she had prepared her mug she had brought with her.

"You did?" I scooted to the edge of my chair and motioned for her to sit.

"You did what?" Sally asked looking from Maggie to me and back.

"I asked Maj. Brock Willingham, retired, to go out for brunch sometime this week. I thought the poor man was going to pass out. But"—she smiled a huge smile—"he said yes, although he let me know he was going to ask me the same thing. I just beat him to the punch."

"That's a lie but sweet anyway," Sally said.

Maggie took a sip of her coffee before continuing. "I haven't been out on a date since the late '60s. I am nervous and excited both."

"But you know him. It's not like he is a complete stranger to you. You know enough to go out and have a good time and be relaxed about it," I suggested.

"Just don't sleep with him on the first date!" Sally caught both of us off guard.

Maggie turned a deep shade of red. I just shook my head, as this was entirely something Sally would say.

"Oh, crap!" Maggie gasped. "I haven't had sex with anyone except my husband, and he's been gone ten years. We were married thirty-five years!" This time, the color drained from her face.

"Listen to an old woman, Maggie, my dear. It ain't like riding a bicycle. It's more like remembering how to swim. Just keep your wits about you, and remember it's not like you will end up like our sweet Fiona here." Sally patted my belly, sending Mason Jr. off into a kicking frenzy. At this rate, the lithium batteries would be dead within a month. "If it happens, it happens. Don't worry about it until you need to. You might go out with the major and find out he isn't worth your time. But if he is, don't be afraid. One of you has to have some spunk. If you're both little chickens, nothing is ever going to happen."

Maggie nodded, accepting the sage advice. "I've got to go. Don't want to be late." She patted my knee and stood up to lean over and give Sally a hug.

"Tell me how you got that to happen." Sally's attention had turned to me.

I told her about yesterday and our time at the pool.

"Damn! That was easy."

"I just thought she ought to know," I remarked.

Steph Robbins, the kindergarten teacher I had met at the mah-jongg night, was the next to stop by. She let us know she would be playing tonight and wanted to see if we were as well.

Both Sally and I informed her we would be there. After that, she headed off toward the garage.

Mason was next. He leaned down and gave me a kiss before greeting Sally. He noticed the tea bag string hanging out of my cup and asked if I was still queasy.

"No, not really, but the smell of coffee this morning made me gag. I opted for tea instead."

Sally got after him for letting me eat like a pig, and maybe it was the tequila in the margarita that was turning in my stomach.

"I don't think the bartender put enough in there. He hadn't wanted to make the drink for me to begin with. He asked Mason if it was all right for me to have a drink." I sounded a little horrified at this.

"Welcome to the nineteenth century," Sally sarcastically noted.

"I thought it was gentlemanly," my husband added, leaning over to kiss me again before moving out of arm's reach.

Sally huffed and ordered him to return to the cave he crawled out of until he could behave. He nodded, blew her a kiss, and headed back to the apartment. I noticed his look at the corner and the slight nod from Newspaper Man before he entered the apartment.

Our fourth visitor was Louise. I inquired how she was feeling. Maybe since she had eaten the same thing I had, she was queasy as well. But she was OK, she explained. She declined coffee when Sally asked if she cared for a cup, saying she had already had two before she had left the apartment.

"Are you coming tonight to the game?" I thought she almost had to be there but wanted to ask.

"Yes, I got the same book you got and have been studying. Don't know if it will help. We'll see." As she turned to go, I called out.

Getting up and walking over to her, I asked what her schedule was this coming Wednesday.

"Why, do you need something?"

I would need to have my roots and my "birthmark" touched up, I explained and wanted her to help me.

"I have to check, but I think I will be back on the property at about two. Will that work?"

It would, and I thanked her.

When I returned to Sally, she wanted to let me know that Pearl had left later than expected, so MS Bentley would be OK until ten. "Why don't you go check on your husband? Make sure I didn't ruffle his tail feathers."

I had two hours to kill before ten, so I kissed her on the cheek and said I would check with her later. She let me know that she and Sandi would be out most of the day so didn't need to stop by and she would see me at the game tonight.

Mason was getting ready to leave when I walked into the apartment. He had showered and shaved and looked handsome as ever.

I pulled him to me and kissed him, rubbing my hand up and down his back to squeeze his butt.

"If you keep that up, I won't be able to leave the apartment," he said.

"That's fine with me," I said, nibbling on his neck.

He pulled me away and kissed the tip of my nose.

"I have a meeting at the office, and I cannot miss it. The last thing I need is to walk into the office with my fellow agents looking I had just enjoyed an epic roll in the sack!"

I looked down at the slight bulge in trousers and told him we were going to have to do something about that. He informed me as he walked back to the table to get his briefcase and cell phone that he would be fine by the time he made it out of the apartment. Mason warned me, however, that I needed to keep my hands and lips to myself until he was out the door.

I gloated a little as he pulled the door closed.

At two the next day, Pearl's Bentley wanted to stay on the roof and nap in the sun. I had brought the fourth and final book of the *Twilight Saga* to the roof and stretched out on the chaise that had remained since I had asked Johan to move it last week.

It was Newspaper Man who took his position up in the enclosure near the gate.

He had nodded his greeting but had not said a word the entire hour and a half we were there.

Bentley had done due diligence in regard to inspecting the man's shoes and cuffs of his pants. I had to chuckle that Newspaper Man did well as Bentley worked overtime to get the man to play with him. To his credit, the four-legged Master Sergeant was able to get him to throw his squeaky toy for almost ten minutes before he—Bentley, not Newspaper Man—grew tired and looked for a place for his nap.

When we returned back to Pearl's, Mandy had posted a note on the door with my name written in an immaculate script.

Fiona,

Pearl called and asked me if you could check
on him one more time this afternoon. She
said it would be late before she would be able
to get home. She said you know where his
food is.

Mandy

I would have time before the mah-jongg game started
to swing by take him up for his business and return to feed
him and tuck him in. I pondered whether to go and tell
Mandy that it was no problem just in case Pearl called and
checked. She didn't have my number, so I decided that was
best.

Mandy wasn't alone when I came into the office. Renée
Grayson was in there as well.

"Oh, sorry, I didn't know you were busy. I can come
back," I offered as I began to step back out of the office.

In unison, both women told me no and to come back in.

"We're just talking about Sandi's baby shower." Mrs.
Grayson waved me over to sit in the vacant chair across
from Mandy's desk.

"It's such a great idea. Sally said it was your idea."
Mandy smiled at me over her desk.

"No, not really. I just thought it would be nice, and I
offered to help." I didn't want the credit for this. Really,
Sally was a mini troublemaker.

"We think next week Monday would be a great time to
have it. Instead of the mah-jongg game, we will have the
shower," Grayson said, shifting in her chair to include me
more into their circle. "Mandy has been asking around, and
you were next on her list to see if next Monday is good."

"I don't seem to have a lot to do, so, absolutely!"

"Great!" This was Mandy. "You were the last person on my list. I have contacted a local baker, and they have agreed to do the pastries."

"I contacted the local American Sign Language interpreting agency," Mrs. Grayson said. "I will provide the interpreters for the party. Sally knows the language, but I want her to enjoy herself and not have to interpret for everyone."

I waited for a beat and then added, "I know that Sally said the Haleys really don't have a lot. Is she registered somewhere, or do we need to do that?"

"That's a good question. Mandy, can you get with Sally and ask her? I know she is really close to them and she would know more than any of us what is best to do."

"I agree," Mrs. Grayson said. "I have a meeting, so I will let you two girls take it from here. Mandy, if you need anything, just let me know." With a grace still as stunning as it had been decades ago, Renée Grayson stood and left the office.

"I am completely gobsmacked by her," I confessed.

Mandy laughed and said, "I think I know what that means, and I agree. We, Johan and I, have been working for her for some time now, and, still, I feel as if she is the nicest queen in the world. Almost want to bow!"

I agreed completely.

We took a half hour for planning before I left the office. Remembering why I had come there in the first place, I paused at the door.

"Oh, Mandy, I almost forgot. If Pearl calls, let her know I will take care of Master Sergeant today. She needn't worry." I thanked again and closed the door behind me.

I already knew what I wanted to get for the shower. I would have to have it delivered anonymously, but I would still do it. As for something to bring to the shower itself, I would wait and see what Sally had to say. If anything, gift cards are always welcome.

Mason wasn't home when I arrived back at the apartment. That gave me time to do some Internet research. I wanted to get a stroller–car seat combo. I knew they were expensive, but I was shocked when I actually saw the cost.

Money!

I had more money than most people could dream of. Having wealthy parents and being successful myself, I had never wanted for anything money could buy. I also was fortunate enough to have grandparents who taught me the importance of hard work and the value of a dollar. I wasn't frugal, yet I wasn't a spendthrift either.

It occurred to me that Mason had given me, at the hangar in Flamingo Heights, a wallet with ID, cash, and two credit cards. I wondered if the credit cards were for show or if there was an actual credit limit on either credit card.

I went into the bedroom and opened the bottom drawer of the dresser to pull out the small purse I had yet to carry. Inside was the pocketbook, which I removed and sat on the bed to examine.

Fiona's driver's license was issued in New York. There was also a medical insurance card, a car insurance card, a Visa, and an American Express card. Also, inside was $200. This made me laugh. They would never let me out to go to the corner market for ice cream or any reason whatsoever. Why, then, did I need cash?

It wasn't a life-shattering question, just a curiosity.

I glanced at my watch and went back to the living room to find my cell. Once I had it, I texted Mason. "Hello, sweetie! How is your day going? Can you stop and get something for dinner for yourself? I didn't set out anything, and tonight is my mah-jongg game. Love, Fiona."

That done, I returned to the master bath to check on my makeup and put in new contacts. Having not been a contact wearer, they were starting to bother me.

Mason arrived with a pizza. I declined a slice, having already had a bowl of chicken noodle soup.

"What did you do today?" he asked as he went to put his briefcase away in the smaller bedroom.

I stood in the dining room and waited for his return. "Oh, you know, the usual! First, I went shopping at the mall, spent thousands of your hard-earned dollars, and then came home to watch my soaps and eat bonbons," I answered, kissing him on the cheek.

I followed as he went into the kitchen.

Mason swatted my butt playfully, commenting, "I thought as much!"

"Your day was longer than you thought. What's up?"

"Nothing really" was all he said.

Perhaps he couldn't say anything, but if it was about me, I wanted to know, and I told him after we had sat at the table.

"No, it had nothing to do with you. It was regarding the case they pulled me off to come to Palm Springs. That's all."

I accepted his explanation. Mason moved to the table, and I followed, taking a seat next to him.

I talked about the furry neighbor who had stolen my heart. Then I moved on to the baby shower and the question I had.

"I want to get a stroller—car seat combo for Sandi, but they're expensive. Almost $2,000. Can I pay for it with the credit cards in my pocketbook or do something else? I also want to get a hundred-dollar gift card to actually give her at the shower.

"The stroller, I want to have it delivered, but I don't want my name on it. It's too much money for Fiona and Mason to spend. You understand where I'm coming from, don't you?" I was sure he did.

He had been quiet as we cleaned up the table. He had waited until he had my attention before saying, "There is a credit line on each of the cards. They are issued to Dr. and

Mrs. Park. I will check with Soto and make sure, but I don't think it will be a problem."

I thought of something else. "Whose money is it?"

He smiled and pulled me to the sofa and down next to him.

"Yours."

"Mine! How the hell is it mine?"

Mason explained that the cost of living, the rent, groceries, etc., was provided for by the government. However, for things such as the stroller, they would bill that to me after I was out from under protection.

"This should have been explained to you already." He was concerned that someone dropped the ball.

"Well, hell! They could have told me anything the first two days and I wouldn't remember. I was in a fog and scared out of my wits. I was certain I had gotten my sisters killed and I was going to be next. So if they told me, and I am sure they did, it wasn't something I recalled."

I gave myself an hour to tend to Master Sergeant Bentley before I had to be at the mah-jongg game. He was sleeping when I entered the apartment and wasn't too happy when I woke him up. I decided to carry him instead of using the harness and the leash. This was for an entirely selfish reason. I wanted to cuddle him.

Once he realized I was going to do this, he was putty in my arms.

"So how was your afternoon?" I asked him.

He looked up at me and twitched an ear.

"Really! That sounds very nice. Did you keep the mice in line, or did they cause problems?"

He barked. Not an all-out bark but just a small woof.

"Well, I wouldn't have let them play with my squeaky toy either," I confided, approving of his desire not to share his toys. "I will give them a stern talking to when we go back down."

At this, he gave me the cold shoulder, squirming as we reached the gate to the dog park. I let him down, and he ran a few steps away before lifting his leg.

I noticed Johan standing in the corner at the stairwell and called out my greeting. He nodded hello and went back to playing on his cell, or at least pretended.

Bentley seemed to be ready to leave after about thirty minutes. I was quiet until we returned to Pearl's apartment. As promised, I called out to the nonexistent mice and warned them about trying to play with MS Bentley's toys as I prepared his dinner.

After making sure there were water and a few cookies, I locked up with a good night to my fuzzy friend and headed to my second mah-jongg get-together.

Everyone was there that had been at the game last Monday except Dave. In his place was a woman in her late forties or early fifties who was introduced as Marcie Gutierrez. She, like Andrea Miller, was a nurse.

Louise took a spot at Maggie's table while I again sat at the four top with Sally.

"Are you ready to sit in for a hand?" she asked me as we stood near the card table.

I wasn't really sure, and I told her so.

"OK, then." She turned to address the other three players. "Why don't you let me be east, and the next hand, I will get up and let Fiona take my place."

There was a general concession that was a good idea, so I sat at Sally's side while the first hand was played.

I remembered much of what I had read and learned the week before. I realized last week, and it was reaffirmed tonight, that the game did take skill and knowledge. However, a lot was merely the luck of the draw.

It was Maggie who screamed, "Mahj!" from the other table. At our table, there had been an ongoing discussion regarding the major and Maggie's coffee date, so we were playing a bit slow. Marcie won the first hand, and after a break to freshen up drinks or to get a snack, I took Sally's place.

Whether it was beginner's luck or just dumb luck, I won the fourth hand. We had had two consecutive wall games, and I was giddy.

"This is so much fun," I told Mandy, who was sitting to my left.

Before she could respond, someone, I think it was Anna Ball, snorted, "What is it with these damn hot flashes?" She apparently wasn't as old as I thought.

"Power surges, I used to call them," commented Renée from the table where an assortment of sweets was sitting.

"Power surges, my ass!" This from Anna Ball. "Mine were like a nuclear meltdown. It was awful!"

Marcie leaned over and said to me. "That is one of the many wonderful things about pregnancy. No periods! I know you aren't missing them at all."

Mandy agreed that was one of the best things, and she wasn't thrilled when, after each of her children, her monthly friend returned.

Had I been drinking or eating something, I would have choked.

I must have looked ill because Sally asked if I was going to be sick.

My mind raced for a plausible answer, and I heard Linda say her son Cameron used to push up on her diaphragm and take her breath away. This was the excuse I used.

"They do that sometimes. My Deborah used to do jumping jacks on my bladder." Sally laughed, kissed my forehead, and walked to refill her coffee.

The rest of the night, I was on autopilot. I won another game, surprisingly. I was more focused on what was happening within each round as I had been prior. I needed the distraction until I could get back to the apartment and do some calculations.

Mason was on the sofa watching TV when I returned at nine forty-five.

"Have fun?" he asked, patting the spot next to him.

I put on my acting face and smiled. "You bet. Won two hands. I wasn't too bad. I think I just got lucky, but all in all, I had a great time. What did you do?"

He took my hand and kissed my palm before answering. "Not much. I watched a few shows I hadn't seen in a while. Of course, I had no idea what was happening because I had missed so much."

"You are such a workaholic." I leaned into him, pulled his face to mine, and kissed him.

"I know something I would like to work on right now." His grin was impish.

"You do?"

"Can I show you?"

I needed the distraction. I wasn't ready to face what I needed to. And to be honest, anytime I could make love with Nathan, I wasn't going to miss the opportunity.

"I think"—I reached down and rubbed his erection through his jeans—"you need to be very thorough in your presentation."

He was very thorough.

I woke up to the same feeling of queasiness I had been experiencing for the last few days. Mason had rolled to the edge of his side of the bed, allowing me to get out of bed without having to untangle myself from his limbs.

Instead of going into the master bath, I went into the hall bath, pulling the bedroom door quietly shut behind me. After emptying my bladder and washing my hands, I went to the kitchen table where my laptop was resting.

I had searched for a calendar the other day only to find there was not one in the apartment. My phone, while it looked like a smartphone, just had access to the few limited phone numbers, Mason's, Louise's, and Akio's, and nothing else.

However, I knew I could find a calendar on the laptop. As I waited for it to boot up, I made me some hot tea.

The laptop had a calendar on its desktop, and I pulled it up and found the month of March. I found the Monday, that early morning when I had gone to my apartment in Burbank. I began my count. One, Monday, I was at the HPB office somewhere in LA. Two, Tuesday, at the compound. Three, Wednesday, I was still at the compound. Four, Palm Springs. Five . . . I took a sip of my tea and counted back to the beginning of my last period. Then calculated forward.

I should have started that Tuesday or Wednesday after I had arrived in Palm Springs. You could time my cycle like clockwork. If it weren't for the nausea every morning the past three days, I would have chalked it up to stress. Yet when I thought about it, I wasn't actually stressed.

Once I realized the HPB had my sisters and they were safe, I had relaxed and found myself enjoying this unusual experience. It wasn't just the great sex I was having for the first time in my life. Also as Agent Johnson had foretold, I was delighting with the anonymity of being Fiona Park.

There still could be enough stress to have thrown off my cycle, yet deep down, I felt this wasn't the case.

If I were pregnant, it would have happened the first night Mason and I had sex. That was eleven days ago, and I wasn't sure if a pregnancy test would show up this early. I decided to wait it out, and if I still hadn't started my period next week on Tuesday—that would be nineteen days since our first unprotected sex—I would approach Louise about the test. In the meantime, I would try not to freak-out. Also, I would eat right and lay off the booze.

It was still early.

I peeked out the front window to find it was raining. I looked at the area where Sally and her coffee tables were ordinarily set and found an empty space. I wasn't ready to venture out, which would require me to put on all of Fiona, so I quietly snuck into the bedroom and crawled back into bed.

I wasn't sure for how long I dozed off, but when I awoke, Mason was not in bed. I glanced at the bedside clock and was shocked to see it was almost ten. I dragged myself out of bed. Mason was in running shorts and a sweatshirt on the sofa watching TV.

"Good afternoon," he teased as I made my way to snuggle up next to him. "You were sleeping so soundly I didn't have the heart to wake you. It's raining outside, and I don't have to be anywhere today, so I thought we could just lounge around."

That sounded wonderful to me. I had to ask if I would be required to layer Fiona on or could I have a day off?

I could tell what his answer was before he even spoke the words. "You have two choices. Number one is to hide in the bedroom if anyone knocks on the door. If I have to let them in and they want to see you—Akio or Louise might do that as part of a check-in—you need to present yourself as Fiona. The higher-ups might frown on you not in full Fiona mode."

I groaned my disappointment. I knew Mason was correct, and people *were* putting their lives on the line for me, so the least I could do is my part.

"OK," I concurred sulkily. "I'll see you in about twenty minutes."

It wasn't Akio or Louise who knocked but Sally and Mandy.

It was Mason who opened the door and welcomed the woman in.

"We hope we aren't interrupting anything!" Sally said hopefully.

"Nope," I replied from the sofa, "just lounging about and watching TV. What brings you ladies out in the rain?"

I saw Mandy had a small notebook tucked under her arm. Seeing it, I stood up and suggested we move to the small dining room table.

"This is a list of things that Sandy and Sandi need for the baby." She showed me the two-page handwritten list.

"Wow!" I exclaimed. "They don't have anything, do they?"

Sally almost snarled. "Hell, no. Both their parents are just scum. Those two kids met way back in elementary school at the California School for the Deaf in Freemont. They got married right after graduation. They both attended community college. Sandy has that wonderful job at the airport. Sandi works there too, but the doctor put her on rest last month."

It was easy to see that even if their own parents weren't in their lives, Sally was. They were two lucky people. She continued, "They didn't get pregnant! They were too young maybe, but they have been married for almost five years, and they waited until they both had good jobs before they started a family.

"Their parents refuse to help because they married so young."

I could see this angered her, and I reached over to squeeze her hand. "They have you! I think they're pretty damn lucky. I am sure they know it too."

Her expression softened.

"They do know," Mandy said, "and it's not just Sally. But, anyway, we wanted to ask you if you thought we should draw gift suggestions or set a dollar limit? What do you think?"

It was Mason from the sofa who answered, "Why don't you give a copy of the list to everyone who might be coming?

Tell them to let you or Sally or Fiona know what they can bring and tick off the list that way."

"I was also thinking," I said, "you can't go wrong with gift cards. They're going to need a truckload of diapers, formula, and miscellaneous things, so that might be an option added to the list."

Sally nodded her agreement as Mandy wrote down "gift card" at the end of the list.

We talked a few more minutes before they got ready to leave.

"Oh, I forgot," Mandy said, pulling a sheet of paper from the back of her notebook. "Here is the list of Wednesday movies for this coming month. If you have any suggestions, let me know. However, we decided on these the beginning of March." She handed me the paper, and together they left.

The Wednesday movies for April were listed:
Space flicks—*Star Wars: The Force Awakens*—pizza
Film noir—*Casablanca*—brisket (provided by office)
Comedy/animation—*The Secret Life of Pets*—potluck (check with Mandy for suggestions)
Drama—*My Time Away*—hamburgers and hot dogs

"You have got to be kidding me!" I shook my head and brought the paper to Mason. "Look!" I pointed accusingly at the list. *My Time Away* was a film I had done three years ago. "This is another one of my movies. For God's sake, I am not the only actress in the world. Sandra Bullock just released a new move. She was staggering!"

He kissed me and then laughed, shaking his head. "You really don't see yourself very well."

"What the hell does that mean?"

"Do you not know how famous you are?"

What a stupid question! I am a working actor, that's it. OK, I had to admit I was an award-winning actor, but still.

I told him precisely that.

He looked dumbfounded.

I looked back at him, confused at his expression.

"Look,"—I paused—"yes, I have won many awards, the top of the list. That is only because I worked with great directors, producers, actors, writers, and coaches. They gave me great scripts. I simply followed directions. Same goes for the stage or music. I am lucky to get great material to work with, that's all!"

"Do you really believe that?" Mason pulled me into his arms and gave me the longest bear hug I had ever had as an adult. "This is exactly why you are where you are as a performer. Great performers got where they did because, like you, they were given great material to work from. But they also have talent. Do you know why?"

I shrugged my shoulders.

"Because you do not have a *star* complex. You are a humble, hardworking woman who appreciates those around you. I can guarantee if you became a megabitch and hard to work with, all the accolades in the world wouldn't keep you in front of the camera or on the stage."

Is that how he saw me? I was embarrassed. I could feel the scarlet travel up my neck to my face. I wasn't that person he described. Once maybe, but Louise had called it right at the cabin.

I had become an ice queen. My agent had strongly suggested I take off six months or more. I knew she had begun getting pressure from the Hollywood executives about my cold, often off-putting demeanor.

Away from it all, I could clearly see I had become what I had been accused of being.

"OK, well, maybe. But that's not my point. I am not the only actor in the movies, and already my movies are featured twice." I was sharp.

"Fiona," he said, pulling me to him again and not letting go when I tried to get away, "why are you so touchy about this? Can't you just enjoy the fact you have some popularity?"

Still in his arms, I took a deep breath and relaxed.

167

"Gran warned me against getting 'too big for my britches.' I was to work and work hard, take no advantage of anyone, always be grateful for all that I had. She told me it all could come to an end at the snap of a finger." I could feel the tears on my cheeks as I listened to my grandmother's voice in my head.

I had forgotten her advice. How did following her advice make me anything special? I had talents, I knew that. I had gotten them from my parents, who were talented as well. But I had watched my dad struggle to find work, as he was known for being temperamental. I knew my mother had a reputation for being hard to work with, but she excelled so well it hadn't seemed to matter.

Gran had been right. I had forgotten to be grateful, and I was about to learn my lesson before I had witnessed Hasset's murder.

"Teresa," Nathan whispered in my ear, "you are special not because you are beautiful, which you are. Not because you are exceptionally talented, which you are. Not because you can light up the screen or the stage or the airwaves. It is because people see that, despite all these things, you are a really caring individual. That can't be hidden."

Once maybe, I thought to myself.

One would think just because I was in the public eye so often, I enjoyed the attention. While I usually did publicity for the movies, plays, and CDs I was connected with, it was work. Most often it was great. However, I valued my privacy. This experience of how people viewed me was unsettling. It was surreal, and I wasn't sure how I felt about it.

I wanted to sit down, and we did. I lay with my head in his lap as we watched television. I felt safe and loved, and . . . I didn't want it to end.

Over breakfast on Wednesday morning, I asked Mason if the *Star Wars* movie was any good.

His mug hung in the air as he glared at me with disbelief. "You didn't see it?"

Unaware that somehow I was being compared to a Neanderthal crawling out of her cave to throw rocks at the moon, I shrugged my shoulder and shook my head as I bit into my toast.

He lowered his mug slowly to the table. He leaned near me as if seeing the Neanderthal version of myself for the first time. "Please," he begged, "tell me you just missed this one. Tell me you have seen the others and just haven't had the time to catch *The Force Awakens*. Please!"

I gulped down my bite of toast and, with more hesitation than I thought I should have, shook my head. "No," I disclosed, "I have never seen any of the *Star Wars* movies."

Mason contacted Akio, who shared his bewilderment at me never having seen the movies.

The three of us spent the rest of the day until it was time for the community movie night watching each of the movies Akio had acquired from the corner Redbox.

The information I was a *Star Wars* virgin had apparently spread through the complex like wildfire, thanks to my husband. The teasing was all in fun and good-natured. I hadn't remembered laughing so much or that long in a very long time.

Of course, it was the major who was on fire with the snide comments and off-color jokes at my expense.

"Dr. Park," he said loud enough for all the tables to hear.

"Yes, Major Willingham?" Mason was equally serious, although he couldn't quite get the smirk off his face.

"Did you know?" the major sounded horrified.

"I didn't. I knew Fiona wasn't a nerd, but I didn't realize the depth of her nonnerdness!"

There was a chorus of laughter for the tables.

In his profoundly French-accented English, Jesse inquired, "Monsieur, if you had known about this monstrous flaw, could you have married the *belle fille?*"

Mason didn't say anything but impersonated Auguste Rodin's *The Thinker*. He held the pose long enough and serious enough there were hoots and whistles.

"Hey,"—I let my brogue thicken—"ye canna sit there an' no look at ye àlainn bhean. Tis an awful pain in me heart." I hammed it up for all I was worth, even allowing my eyes to fill with tears. Always loved to have an audience.

"Give the girl a break!" shouted Maggie.

More calls for agreement filled the air until Mason undid his pose. "I've been thinking." That caused a round of boos and hisses. "I think I would have married her."

I moved from Mason and walked over to the major, wrapping my arm around his waist and kissing him on the cheek. "Tis too late, husband. I am marrying the major. He is mature enough to overlook this one small flaw."

"You lose!" the major informed Mason with a smug tone.

"That old man is mine!" It was Maggie's voice from across the table. It was loud enough for all to hear, and the major—God love him—kissed my cheek before stepping out of my arms and into Maggie's.

"Sorry, darling." He smiled at me.

"Mason?" I whispered low so that if he were asleep, I wouldn't wake him. We had gotten to bed late.

"Yes, *nae ma-eum?*"

"Will you tell me what that means?"

"One day but not tonight." I felt his lips on my neck.

"Do you have to work tomorrow?"

"Yes, have a meeting at eleven."

"OK, then. Good night." I hesitated for a heartbeat. "I love you."

He kissed me again on my neck and pulled me tighter. "I know" was his reply.

Mason must have set his alarm when I had gone to the bathroom to remove the baby body, contacts, and mouth prosthetics. Its shrill cadence jolted me awake. I opened an eye in time to see Mason slap the snooze button and curse under his breath to return to gently snoring. I followed his lead only to have the damn thing go off again ten minutes later.

"I will kill it if it goes off again!" I snarled at it or to Mason, I was not sure which.

"Me too!" I felt the bed shake as he moved to turn off the alarm and slowly sat up on the edge of the bed.

He kissed my forehead and pushed me back down, so my head was resting on his pillow and headed off to shower.

I fell back asleep.

"You look exhausted," Sally commented as she handed me a mug of coffee. It was ten thirty. I had knocked on her door after I kissed and waved my husband good-bye.

"I am! We didn't get to bed until after three."

"Why the hell did you stay up so late? That doctor of a husband should know better than that," Sally scolded me and then Mason in absentia.

Coming to his rescue only after several long gulps of my coffee, I told her, "His PhD is in computer science. He can hardly open a bottle of aspirin if he needed one."

"That a girl. Throw him under that train!" Sally patted my tummy, and on cue, Mason Jr. kicked like crazy. The motion of the machine knocked me a little off balance, causing me to sink smartly into a dining room chair.

"Mason Jr. doesn't seem too happy with his daddy," Sally said, pulling out a companion chair at the table.

"He can get in line behind his mama!" I agreed.

"Did you at least enjoy the movies?"

I had, and I told her so. I couldn't believe I had missed them. "Mason said there was another move, *Rogue One,* he would get this weekend for us to watch."

I wanted to say more, but I felt green all of the sudden, and I placed my hand on my belly and over my mouth.

"Floor plan's the same." Sally helped me to my feet as I moved quickly to the small hall bathroom to throw up.

Sally stood in the doorway while I emptied my stomach and waved her away. She merely shook her head, ignoring me and wetting a facecloth with cold water to wipe my face when I was finished.

After a few minutes, Sally walked me out of her apartment and to mine. She opened the door and dragged me in.

The bed was still unmade as she ordered me to take off my shoes and crawl back into bed. I didn't dare disagree. She tucked me in and left with a warning she was going to give Mason an earful.

I hoped I would remember to tell him before Sally got to him.

I hadn't gotten to Mason before Sally, so when he woke me on Thursday after returning home, he was amused and worried.

I didn't have a fever, yet I was exhausted. Mason had inquired if I had eaten, and I had told him I had not. He returned sometime later with a bowl of soup and a piece of dry toast. Along with a can of ginger ale, it seemed to settle my stomach, and I fell back asleep.

WEEK III

Although I had been queasy again, I felt much better on Friday morning. I got out of bed before Mason and went into the kitchen for tea and toast before returning to the bedroom.

Mason was awake and patted the bed next to him. I crawled in, wrapping my arms around his waist and laying my head on his shoulder.

"How you feeling this morning?"

"Better." I lied.

"You looked better. I am really sorry about that. I just didn't think." He apologized.

"No, it wasn't you. I honestly think the events of the last several weeks finally caught up with me." *That, and I think I'm pregnant!*

"That's possible," he agreed.

We lay in bed for perhaps a half hour. I asked about the meeting.

It was a briefing on Planz, he told me.

Planz had gone underground. The law enforcement agencies could not locate him. They felt confident he was still in the States and currently in California. Yet with his connection, he had disappeared without as much as a blip on the radar. However, the FBI, HPB, and the California law agencies were aware that Planz had begun an international search for not only me but also Esperanza and Olli Rose. Mason assured me the three of us were safe and there was virtually no way for them to find us.

Today was the third Friday I had been at the Desert Sky Apartments. With all the resources protecting us, there was no indication whatsoever we were on the Planz's radar.

The meeting at ten was a conference call that would take place in Louise's apartment. After that, we were going to go and spend time outside today. It was supposed to be sunny and warm. A day relaxing at the pool might do us both good, Mason suggested, and I agreed.

I opted to not put on makeup. I packed a picnic lunch, adding books and a chess set to the basket, and headed to the pool when Mason returned for his conference call.

Cleaning up the kitchen after dinner, I told Mason I was going to take a hot bath, put on my PJs, and curl up to watch TV until it was time to go to bed.

As had become my habit, I watched *TMZ* and *Entertainment Tonight*. There were sightings of Esperanza and myself all over Europe. Though the news magazines were attempting to get our photographs, they had not been successful. It seemed odd to me that just by leaving the country, I was still news.

Saturday, even with the morning nausea, I felt great. Mason and I woke and spent the first half hour or so, after brushing our teeth, "freshening up" with surprisingly rambunctious sex. It was indeed an excellent way to start the day.

Pearl had stopped by on Friday night to ask if I could tend to MS Bentley tomorrow. Luckily, at Mason's suggestion, I had put the baby body on before putting on my nightshirt after my relaxing bath.

Even with the early morning romp, showering, and dressing, I was at Pearl's at seven.

He was not his usual feisty self when we went to the roof. He took care of his business and returned to sit at my feet and glared at me until I picked him up and returned him to his bed.

At ten, I headed to the office as Mandy and I had a planning session for the baby shower. Sally met us there, having returned from a doctor's appointment. Together, we made the final arrangements for the evening. Already, many of the gifts had been purchased and brought to the office, where Mandy had stored them in the maintenance office. Johan would deliver all the presents to my apartment before everyone showed up. I would have the stroller already there and wouldn't have to worry about having it delivered to the office.

"We still good for your apartment for the shower?" Mandy caught me off guard with her questions as I had completely forgotten to say anything to Mason.

"Not a problem," I said. "I will kick Mason out, and he can go hang with Akio." I would have to go speak with Mason as soon as I was finished here.

"I think"—Sally spoke from her place on the sofa—"everyone from the mah-jongg game will be there and a few others who don't come. All in all, I think there is going to be about fifteen. So let's plan for twenty just to be safe with regard to the pastries and drinks."

That brought up the subject of different games that we could play, and we spent another hour deciding which would be the best and make a list for one of us to go shopping.

When I returned to the apartment, Mason wasn't there. A note letting me know that he had to run to the store and would be back shortly was taped to the corner of the television.

I called him on his cell phone telling him about the baby-shower at our apartment and also the things we needed for the games and asked if he could pick up the items on my list.

I then called Louise and asked her if she could go to Babies R Us and pick up the stroller–car seat combo I had ordered online and paid for, explaining it was going to be an anonymously donated gift for the Haleys. She agreed to this errand to which I promised I would return the favor someday.

At two, I returned to Pearl's to find her furry baby in a better mood.

"So not always a morning puppy, are you?" I asked as we walked from his apartment toward the parking garage.

His reply was a soft growl, which I interpreted to mean, "No, I sure the hell am not!"

We spent almost an hour on the roof, most of it spent with Bentley taking a nap in a sliver of sunlight.

Dinner was relaxed and straightforward, having opted for something else I hadn't eaten in many years, Frito pie.

Sunday was a repeat of Saturday except for spending time with MS Bentley.

Monday was a whirlwind of activities.

Starting with me in the bathroom trying to keep my dinner from the night before down. I was fortunate, as Mason didn't come around to see if I was all right.

I showered and got dressed before heading to the kitchen for tea and toast. I had learned that if I had the tea and dry toast when I got out of bed, I was able to have a real breakfast later.

After breakfast with Mason, I headed out for coffee and my morning with Sally. Catching up on the latest from the Desert Sky community, I learned that Pearl was home today and tomorrow. No one needed to tend to Master Sergeant Bentley for the next few days.

Jesse and his ginger had come out—I suppose to get some air and maybe breakfast—stopping by to wish us "Bonjour" before disappearing into the parking garage.

Louise, who hadn't been seen for several days, stopped for a cup of coffee and a visit as well.

"Haven't seen you in a month of Sundays," Sally commented as Louise sat at the end of my chaise and sipped at her mug.

"Now, Ms. Sally, I saw you yesterday." Louise shook her finger at the older woman.

"Yes, but you didn't stop for coffee, so it doesn't count."

I laughed and added, "I haven't seen you. You abandoned me to the nerd herd last week. It took me two days to recover."

Louise chuckled and apologized as Sally angrily informed her I was indeed ill for two days and my knucklehead of a husband ought to be knocked in the head with a frying pan for letting me get so exhausted.

This seemed to catch Louise by surprise, and she eyed me suspiciously for a moment before asking if I wanted to join her for a late lunch on Wednesday. I knew it had to do with my roots, but I also had decided I would ask her to get me a pregnancy test on that day as well.

I wasn't sure what my story would be. I had a few more days to come up with a plausible one.

After a bit more conversation, Louise left with a reminder about Wednesday, and I reminded her about the shower tonight at my apartment.

"Oh," I said from the coffee table as she walked off, "you don't need to pick up that parcel at the post for me. It's being delivered."

"Got it," she called over her shoulder.

At three, I threw Mason out as Sally and Mandy arrived to help set up. Before leaving, Mason and I had rearranged the furniture, so there was ample empty space in the center of the living room. Mrs. Grayson had sent over two folding tables and ten folding chairs. With the existing furniture and the folding chairs, we would have plenty seating for all.

Before we got started, I asked Mandy, "Did you remember to get me the copies from the printer?"

"Yes. Two like you asked. What are you going to do with them?" Mandy asked, handing me the two sheets of paper.

"One of the things I bought, other than the gift card, is the complete collection of *Winnie the Pooh* books. My gran and pa used to read them to me when I was little, and I love the old Pooh. I thought it might be nice for her to have that as well." That was part of the truth, about the books anyway. I had other plans.

Once we had finished the arranging, with Mandy's help, we moved all of the decorations and party favors from the guest room into the living room. Another forty-five minutes to arrange and hang everything. Just as we finished, Johan arrived at the door with a cartful of wrapped gifts, gift bags, and envelopes as well as a Nuna MIXX Travel System, each component with a bow and a card.

"Oh, wow!" Mandy chimed as she moved over to the stroller and pulled out the card. "This is a very expensive stroller."

"Who's it from?" I asked innocently, relying on my acting skills to sound convincing.

Sally wasn't fooled for a second. She stared straight at me and mouthed, "I wonder!"

"The card just says from 'Your Desert Sky Family.'" Mandy turned to Sally with concern written on her face. "Were we supposed to take up a collection? Damn, I didn't remember if we were. I didn't. Those things are really expensive!"

Sally gave me one glance before she moved to Mandy. "Honey, this was not something we discussed. Whoever did this was sweet and didn't want it to be a big fuss. And . . ."—a look at me again—"since it says from 'Your Desert Sky Family,' we all can take credit for it. What you think, Fiona?"

"I completely agree. Obviously, that is what was intended in the first place." I hoped Sally would let it go, and for now, it seemed she would. I was sure I would hear about it later when we were alone.

Sandi was supposed to arrive at five thirty under the guidance of Sally. Sandi didn't play mah-jongg and couldn't understand why Sally insisted she come. Sally had told Mandy and me that she had informed Sandi she hadn't been feeling well, hopefully, a lie, and if she needed to leave early, she didn't want to walk to her apartment alone.

"Naturally, the girl's not dumb. She let me know my door and your door were less than ten feet apart. Anyone would be happy to see me home. I gave her my best hurt granny look. That did it! She said she would be here at five forty-five, as Sandy was coming home at five and she wanted to sit down and have dinner first." Sally added that Sandy was in on everything, and as promised, he would have her out the door on time.

People started arriving at five fifteen. Fifteen minutes later, at five thirty, the team of American Sign Language interpreters showed up. I cornered them, asking them my favor, to which they agreed.

Mrs. Grayson arrived with her husband in tow to help deliver all the petits fours. He graciously submitted himself to everyone hellos and introductions to those of us he didn't know before hastily excusing himself.

We all snickered as the door behind him closed. "Looked as if he got out by the skin of his teeth!" Mrs. Grayson chuckled.

Sally, who had been flirting with him, commented, "I think he was afraid that his manly reputation would be besmirched if he stayed much longer."

Mrs. Grayson and most of the women agreed with this assessment and went about making final adjustments. Five minutes before Sandi was to arrive, we quieted down as not to be heard only to have Sally shake her head and remind us all, "My darlings, she's deaf. Make all the noise you want. She won't hear. Just remember that this . . ."—she lifted her hands and shook them in the air—"is the deaf equivalent of applause, so if you want her to 'hear' the applause, do that."

The conversation picked up until there was a knock on the door.

Poor Sandi was overwhelmed and in tears the first thirty minutes. My heart broke a little for her. It was apparent she didn't think anyone would do this for her. One look around the room, and you could see I was not the only one that felt that way.

Not only did the interpreters interpret what was announced, but also one sat next to Sandi, so she was able to have conversations with each of the sixteen women who showed up.

We were able, thanks to the interpreters, to understand precisely how Sandi felt and how much she appreciated everything. Also, we learned she was going to hurt her husband for keeping this a secret. She had thought he was a lousy secret keeper. This had forced her to rethink that. The joking tone of her language was conveyed perfectly by the interpreter, and we all laughed.

After an hour of eating and conversation, we started with a few party games. That took us another hour before we made time for a break to start opening gifts.

Thanks to Sally and Mandy, we were able to provide everything the young family would need including about $600 in gift cards so they would be able to keep their new addition in diapers and formula, at least for the first month or two.

Sandi cried again when the stroller, car seat, and bassinette were brought out of the bedroom. She read the card and, as I had hoped, thanked everyone present for the gift.

I had asked Anna, who had volunteered to coordinate the gift presentations, to make sure the book collection was last.

She handed me the box set.

"Sandi, I am going to ask you a question. Did you ever read or hear the stories about Winnie the Pooh?"

She laughed. "When I was a little girl, my dad tried to sign the books for me. His sign was awful, but that he tried was more important than this signing. That was when I knew my dad really loved me."

This was followed by many "aahs" and "that is so sweet" along with some wiping at tears.

"OK. I can't tell you how glad I am to hear that. I wanted to give the baby this," I said, handing her the set, "and I wanted to give you something as well."

I looked at the interpreter, who had agreed to interpret for me, and she nodded she was ready. I lifted a finger and found the Boise speakers I had hooked up to my cell after downloading the musical score for Kenny Loggins's *Return to Pooh Corner.*

I faced Sandi again. "I know you can't hear me, and maybe this is a bad idea. However, Amanda here"—I indicated the young interpreter—"agreed, and she said she had some experience interpreting music. So I hope you like this." I moved to turn on the music but turned back to the women. "I haven't sung in a while, so if it's too terrible, forgive me."

The music was lyrical and the words heartfelt. Amanda, even without any practice with me, seemed to paint the story in the air. I watched Sandi's face, hoping to see she was enjoying it. What I noticed as I sang the refrain for the second time was tears on almost everyone's faces. Amanda was moving to the rhythm of the music, and Sandi was slightly swaying in time . . .

However, what I caught out of the corner of my eye was the expression on Louise's face. She was not pleased, and for the life of me, I couldn't understand why.

There was a round of applause both from the hearing and the deaf as I ended the song. "It was beautiful. Thank you." Sandi had gotten up and hugged me, her words from the voice of Rita, the other interpreter, in my ears.

"I hope you enjoy reading those books to your baby as much as your dad did reading to you."

She kissed my cheek and thanked me again.

After about fifteen minutes, people were coming up to me and telling me I should have a singing career. That I should be on one of the shows that help bring new talent to the public. That I sounded a lot like someone, they just couldn't remember. I understood what Louise was upset about.

Mason, Johan, and James, Mrs. Grayson's husband, helped Sandy relocate all of the gifts to their apartment when the shower ended. It was some time before he returned, and I could tell from Mason's expression I was in trouble.

I waited, but he didn't say anything even after we had crawled into bed.

Neither of us slept well.

I woke with the same queasy feeling as I had the last several mornings. By the time Mason was up, I was already in the kitchen having finished my tea and toast.

Mason mumbled, "Good morning," as he accepted the mug of coffee I had ready for him. With a peck on the cheek, he headed into the hall bathroom.

I waited until I heard the water stop running in the shower before I headed to the master bath to ready myself for the day.

When I returned to the living room thirty minutes later, Agent Soto was sitting on the sofa. One look at the two agents let me know that this wasn't a social call.

"Good morning, Fiona. Come have a seat. We need to have a conversation." Soto's voice was brisk and to the point.

Mason mouthed, "Sorry," before looking at the end of the sofa further away from him.

In a preemptive move, I argued. "I didn't think about it. I was just doing something nice for a friend."

I could tell this comment didn't help.

"I get the feeling"—Soto turned to face me—"that you were grandstanding the baby shower."

I would have objected, but Soto pulled out her iPad and pulled up my performance. I watched as Cat Connors's voice and manner poured from every pore of Fiona Park.

Soto was visibly upset. "You can't do that, Fiona. How many Grammys has Cat Connors won?" she asked.

I wasn't sure if she wanted an answer or if it was rhetorical.

Her silence made me realize it wasn't rhetorical, so I answered, "Four."

"Louise said when you sang, you had no accent."

"Most people don't have an accent when they sing," I countered on the offensive.

I should have kept my mouth shut. I didn't think of myself as an attention hound, but Soto seemed to think I was.

It was Mason who asked if anyone, other than Louise, had recorded the party. I thought a moment and let him know that Mrs. Grayson had filmed everything including my song for Sandi.

There was a sidebar between Soto and Mason. The agreement was that particular situation was an easy fix. Finding his cell, he dialed a number. Whoever was on the other end of the line, Mason explained the situation. Mrs. Grayson had filmed the shower including me. The tape would have to be confiscated until this was all over.

"That was entirely unfair for Sandi," I commented under my breath and then added in a louder voice that perhaps we could find someone to caption it so Sandy and Sandi could know what was being said.

This time, Soto pulled out her cell again and after a few more minutes with the person got them to agree to that.

That would also make a plausible reason for the tape to be confiscated without causing any suspicion. I was happy with this outcome.

Soto left after a stern reminder of the rules I must follow for my own and everyone else's safety and a promise from me of *no* singing and *no* filming.

The next morning, I prepared Mason breakfast in bed. It was still early, but I knew he had to be out when I left to have my coffee with Sally.

"Oh god!" Mason groaned as he accepted the tray of food. "Let me have a sip of coffee before you ask."

I put on a hurt expression. "I just wanted to do something nice for you."

He rolled his eyes, lifted a finger, and took a deep drink of his coffee.

"What do you want, my love?"

"That really hurts, you know! I just wanted . . ."

He interrupted me and again lifted a finger for me to wait while he swallowed a bit of bacon and egg.

Leaning toward me and whispering in a conspiratorial voice, he said, "Teresa, I remember when you were a kid and you wanted something from anyone, you buttered them up first."

"I want sex!" I hoped that distracted him.

"We can arrange that after I finish my wonderful breakfast. But I know that isn't what the meal and coffee are for."

Damn! He knew me too well.

"I am about to go bat-shit-crazy. I need to get out from these four walls." I waved my hand above my head in a big circle.

"You get out of the apartment every day!" Mason was confused.

"*No,* not the stupid apartment. I mean the complex. Can't we go to a movie or a drive to the desert or the mall? Anything for a few hours. Please!" I begged.

His mouth formed an O, and he understood my meaning. He didn't know, but while he and Akio were guarding the pool and lounge chairs, they would try to think of something; it would have to be the four of us again. He'd have to talk to the office to get approval.

Sally caught me up on everything when I joined her. Pearl was still off. I had missed Major Willingham. He was apparently floating about a foot off the ground.

"Must've gotten laid!" Again, this little woman surprised me with her candor.

I choked on my mouthful of coffee and, after I could breathe again, said, "You think so?"

"We'll know when Maggie comes out. She should be leaving her apartment anytime now."

"Sally, don't say anything to her. I think she is very naive for a woman her age. I think she would be mortified." I was hoping Sally would agree with me.

We didn't have to wait long, and I kept my fingers crossed when Maggie showed up for coffee on her way to the garage.

"You're looking radiant, my dear." Sally welcomed Maggie.

"Oh, I feel radiant!" I watched the blush spread across her face. It was if she was a twenty-year-old again.

"Oh? Do tell."

I knew Sally couldn't leave it. I was just thankful she was tactful.

Maggie looked around to see if anyone other than the two of us was near. I knew Newspaper Man would hear her confession. I just hope he wouldn't be an ass about it.

She cleared her throat. "Brock spent the night last night!" She covered her face with her hands, peeking between her fingers at us.

Maybe she thought we were going to judge her.

"'Bout damn time!" Sally said, of course.

"I am happy for you," I said. I took one of Maggie's hands from her face and squeezed it.

"Me too!" She giggled like a schoolgirl and stood up. "Have a busy day. Gotta go. Later, ladies!"

With nothing to do today, I spent time on the computer looking at songs that I might want to sing for my upcoming album. Lori Liebman, my agent, wanted me to have decided on a total of twenty songs for recording. Most albums had ten to twelve songs, so they would edit the live recording and keep the best. The rest might be released as singles or in some other way. I kept going back and forth on ten of the songs. Ten I had already committed to having on the album. The others I wasn't sure about.

I knew as soon as this was all over that Lori would want me to get on the production and rehearsing as quickly as possible. I could already hear her bitching about this protective custody business being a waste of her time. HBO just didn't wait around for everyone. She was an excellent agent and, despite her brash and thorny exterior, was a sweet as anyone could be.

At around noon, I went to check on Mason and Akio. They were playing chess and eating sandwiches from one of the local sandwich shops.

"I thought you poor boys would be starving," I said before taking a bite of Mason's sandwich.

"It's been really rough out here today," Akio said, wiping his brow in mock exhaustion.

"I can see that! If you don't need anything, I'll go back in. I am working on a project I have to do when Mason and I are transferred from here." I thought that was a respectable way of stating my release from protective custody.

"Before you leave . . ." Akio's voice caused me to turn around and return to the table.

"Yes?"

It was Mason how spoke. "We are going to go for a desert drive to look at the stars tonight. Would you like to come?"

Hell, yes! I kissed Mason on the lips and Akio on the cheek before heading back to the apartment.

We bundled up for the chilly desert night. Louise had rented a convertible, which we all piled into. I was put in the backseat with Mason. Louise and Akio sat in the front with Akio driving. Mason sat in the back. I relaxed as we headed out of Palm Springs into the night.

"Where are we going?" I asked.

It was Louise who answered, "The Mesa-Yucca Valley. They say you can see the Milky Way the best there."

From the driver's seat, Akio asked, "It's about an hour's drive. As soon as we are out of the city limits, I'll pull over and drop the top!"

"It's past the airport where I picked you up." Mason stroked my hair and tweaked my earlobe as we drove in the dark.

As promised, Akio pulled over and lowered the top of the Buick Cascada Louise had rented. There would be a full moon, but it would be early morning before it crested the horizon.

I had seen the Milky Way from our Caribbean Island, but not like this. It was so bright and crisp. I felt as I could reach up and pluck a star from the sky.

I didn't know tears were rolling down my cheek until Mason asked me if I was all right. Akio expressed their concern as well. Louise was silent.

"It's just so awesome. Not like 'totally awesome, dude,' but the real meaning of the word. I am so awestruck. It's so beautiful I can hardly breathe."

As Mason wiped my tears, I leaned in and whispered, "This is a great spot to make love. I want to do that with you under the stars."

"Someday very soon," he promised.

"Louise, is there a Native American story about the Milky Way?" I asked, turning my attention to Louise.

There was. It was a Cherokee legend, and she told us the story. ". . . And so the giant dog turned and began to run. The people chased him, making the loudest noise they could. The dog ran to the top of a hill and jumped into the sky. The cornmeal he still had in his mouth spilled from the side. The giant dog ran across the black sky until he disappeared. The cornmeal that had spilled made a path across the sky, each cereal of cornmeal becoming a star."

It was a beautiful story. I looked around us as the moon began its ascent. In the starkness of the landscape, I could imagine a giant dog leaping into the sky.

As we folded up the blanket, I thanked them all for such a great night.

On the ride back to the apartment, I laid my head on the lap of my lover and fell asleep under the stars and the full moon.

It was almost two when we crawled into bed.

"Thank you, Nathan." I used his real name, hoping he would understand the depth of my gratitude.

"Anything, *nae ma-eum.*" He kissed me good night.

I wasn't just nausea when I woke. I was ill. I made it to the bathroom just in time, with Mason trailing behind me.

"I'm gonna be sick. Get out!" I shouted, trying to close the door behind me.

To my horror, he stood there with a cold, wet facecloth at the ready while I emptied my stomach.

"What did you eat?" he asked after wiping my face.

I couldn't come up with a lie, but I couldn't tell him the truth. Not just yet. It must still be the stress and all the greasy food I have been eating, I suggested to him.

Whether he believed me, I was not sure. He didn't bring it back up and nodded as if that made perfect sense to him.

When I finally came out of the bathroom, he called me into the kitchen for tea and toast. "I think it's time we start eating a little bit healthier."

"Good idea," I agreed. "Are you going anywhere today?"

"Yeah, back to the office for a briefing. How about you?"

I snorted and threw a corner of my toast at him.

He popped the tidbit into his mouth. "I meant, don't you have plans to go over to Louise's this afternoon for some touch-ups?" He gently tugged on a lock of curls to illustrate his point.

"Yeah, at two for a late lunch," I replied.

"Is that what you are calling it?" Mason chuckled, knowing it was for touch-up on my roots and face.

"I was with Sally when we discussed it, so I think that is what we're calling it this week anyway."

"When are you leaving?" I needed to call Louise before she left and ask her to get the pregnancy test before she came back to the complex. I didn't want to seem as if I was rushing Mason out the door, but I needed to build up my nerves before I spoke with Louise.

"About ten."

"I think I'm going to head over to Louise's to make sure she has everything we need or if I need to bring some of my stash over." I decided a face-to-face was better. "Do you think she's still here?"

Mason checked his watch. "She shouldn't have left yet. Let me call her and tell her you are on your way. If she doesn't answer, I'll stick out my head and call you back."

That was perfect. I headed out the door. Louise was waiting for me when I arrived at her apartment standing in the doorway.

She was dressed except for shoes as she ushered me into her small apartment. "Mason said you were sick this morning. Overeating junk food, he'd said."

I gave a half laugh and said under my breath, "Wishful thinking!" She heard me stopped and faced me.

"What's going on, Fiona?"

"I think I'm pregnant, and I want you to stop and bring me a pregnancy test when you come back home."

"That son of a bitch!" Louise slapped her hand on the small eating table. "I knew this was a bad idea. I even told Soto your history would work against you. He shouldn't be screwing his charge!"

This was bad. I was ready. "Whoa! Whoa!" I threw up my arm to get her attention. "You think this is Nathan's? If we were sleeping together, I wouldn't come to you for help. That would be stupid. Anyway, he wouldn't do anything to jeopardize my safety or his career. You know him better than that!"

She forced all of her attention onto me. I could sense she was trying to catch me in a lie, but I knew that wouldn't happen. This was too important to muck up.

"We had a cast party two weeks before this whole stupid thing got started. I got a little too drunk and ended up sleeping with some guy from the editing department. Shit, I barely remember his name." Let her think I was a Hollywood slut, I didn't give a shit. I just wanted her to not be suspicious of Nathan.

I was rewarded as she took a cleansing breath. I saw she accepted my story.

"Can you get a test for me? If I am pregnant, it's just under two months, and I am good. We can go from there if need be."

"Sure." Her answer was already distracted. "I have to get going! Have a morning class. I will see you at two."

She steered me to the door and left me standing there with a wave good-bye.

I returned to the apartment. Mason was already gone. I had three hours to kill before two, and I hadn't a clue as to what to do. I decided to fill the time with trying to figure out how and when to tell Nathan I was pregnant so he wouldn't freak out. Did I wait until this was all over? Did I tell him now? If I told him now, would he do something to get himself in trouble? I could see him going to Soto, telling her he had crossed the line with me. He had been unprofessional. Would she fire him or relocate him? Either way would not be acceptable to me.

If I was pregnant, I knew the baby was Nathan's. He did deserve to know. Let this be over, and I was sure I was pregnant before I hit him with this.

At two, I showed up at Louise's. She had lunch ready, and as we ate our chicken Caesar salad, we made small talk. I did everything I could to focus the attention away from me and on her.

I had her tell me about the class she was teaching, about the students and the curriculum. She was happy to talk about her class and what she hoped the students would learn about Native American people and their religious beliefs. Her goal, she had informed me, was to remove the concept of the Native American from what had been portrayed in movies and on television with the reality that they were a deeply spiritual and civilized people. Perhaps not by Western European standards but by the ideals of what made a culture thrive and last.

After our lunch, we took the time to do the touch-up on my roots and eyebrows. We waited ten minutes before we applied the dye to my face to keep the port-wine stain from fading out. During this time, Louise asked if I wanted to take the test.

I had told her I wasn't in any real hurry. I was somewhat sure I was not pregnant. It had to be all the stress and poor eating.

Elaborating on this concept, I discussed my regular exercise and diet regimen I had followed for over a decade. Except for the time I had to gain weight for the Broadway play, I was relatively strict in following my routine.

"From the first hours," I confessed, "I was in HPB care, I have eaten and drank more than I have in forever. Also, I hadn't exercised since the day before I had witnessed the murder. To say I have fallen off the wagon would be an understatement."

I laughed at this, and Louise followed my lead.

"When I get in the shower to wash this out of my hair," I said, pointing to the dye on my head and face, "I will take the test."

"Were you regular?" she inquired.

I lied through my teeth. "No, not really. Both Esperanza and I always have had problems with our cycles."

I took the test in with me when I went into the bathroom to shower. I was so nervous I could barely hold the test stick steady as I peed on it. After that was done, I stepped into the shower and took my time lathering and rinsing my hair and face. It was a full ten minutes before I got the courage to step out of the shower. Still avoiding the test, I dried myself off, blow-dried my hair, and dressed before I looked at the stick.

I sat on the toilet seat and, finally, after some deep breathing, looked at the small window. The blue plus sign was like a slap in the face with ice cold water. Part of me was ecstatic, part terrified. The last thing I wanted to do was scare Nathan away or get him into trouble with the HPB.

I pulled myself together enough to let out a loud and pleased "Oh, thank you, God!" I was sure Louise was somewhere close to the bathroom door waiting for some type of response from me.

I tucked the test into the pocket of my capris and opened the bathroom door.

As I expected, she was there.

"I heard that!" she offered me a hug.

"That would have been the last thing I needed. I just need to stop eating like I have been and get back on track. Linda, my friend who keeps me in-line, is going to freak out when I get back home!"

Louise seemed to take my relaxed and relieved demeanor at face value. She didn't press me or ask to see the test stick. Had she, I wasn't sure what I would have done.

I let the conversation go on for another half hour before heading back to the apartment. I needed some time alone, and I wasn't sure when Mason would return.

Also, I needed to dispose of the evidence in a place neither Louise nor Mason would find it.

It was the voice of Renée Grayson that stopped me in my path toward the apartment.

"Fiona!" she hailed. There was no other option than to turn around and go to her.

"How are you today, Mrs. Grayson?" I asked, keeping my voice light.

"Oh, have been busy today. I wanted to thank you, however."

"Thank me for what?"

"Yesterday, your sweet husband stopped by my office and asked if they could have the tape I recorded of Sandi's baby shower. He told me you had suggested it be captioned so they could enjoy it without trying to figure out what was being said or asking someone to interpret it for them," she explained, sitting down at the end of one of the pool lounges and patting it so I would follow.

"Well, I just thought it would be nice." I had suggested this as a way to keep the tape out of everyone's hands until the thing with Planz was finished.

"I also wanted to tell you I really enjoyed the song you did for Sandi. That and working with the interpreters to make sure she could follow along."

I wanted some way to deflect this away from me but didn't have the opportunity, as Grayson wasn't finished.

"You sound a lot like an actress I know. You have that same look about you, almost, as her as well. Do you know who Cat Connors is?"

I admitted I knew of her, as we had just watched one of her movies two weeks prior. I also caught Paperback Woman's expression as she focused all her attention on our conversation.

"That's right. I remember. She was such a sweet and down-to-earth woman. I was lucky to meet her when she was very young, and I am happy to say she doesn't seem to have changed. That's a rarity in her industry."

I didn't know what to say to this and agreed that was probably true.

She continued, "I never forget a beautiful bone structure, and you seem to have an almost exact face. Oh, it's different here and there. Funny how that is."

Funny, I agreed silently.

"Well, I must be off." She stood and helped me stand with a gentle tug and squeeze of my hand. "You take care, Fiona. Tell that handsome husband of yours hello for me."

"Yes, ma'am, I will." I stood there and watched her leave. Johan was already at the large barbeque pit tending to the brisket for tonight's movie. I turned to call out to Mrs. Grayson's retreating back. "Will you be coming to the movie tonight?"

She laughed and let me know she had a "date night" with her husband and would be missing the movie. I told her to have fun.

As I headed back to my apartment, Paperback Woman has resumed reading her book. I noticed her lips were moving as if she was mouthing the words on the page. I knew better. She was reporting Mrs. Grayson's and my conversation.

Soto was not going to be happy.

It was one of the four poolside garbage cans that caught my attention. This would be a perfect place to put the test stick. I had watched Johan empty them before, and he paid absolutely no attention to the contents. He just took off the lid, pulled the full garbage bag out, placed it in his cart, and replaced it with a new bag. No one would look there. Johan focusing on the brisket and the agent keeping an eye out on the courtyard seemed to be ignoring me. Feigning picking up something off the ground and throwing it into the can, I included the pregnancy test.

Casablanca was and will always be a great movie. Mason had made baked beans, and this was our potluck to add to the massive perfectly smoked brisket.

As the time before, I sat with my back to Mason, my head resting on his shoulder. I was comfortable and relaxed.

Later that night, when we were in bed, I was tempted to let Mason know he was going to be a daddy but held on to my resolve to wait.

Despite the fact I had only the day before found out I was pregnant, I woke feeling wonderful. Oh, the queasiness was there, but I was walking on air.

Mason was waking when I returned to bed after a quick trip to the bathroom.

"Morning, beautiful." He kissed my cheek. "You look like you rested well. Any morning sickness this morning?" He laughed at his own joke.

I rolled my eyes and groaned, telling him that I thought morning sickness happened at the first part of pregnancy, not the last.

He got out of bed, went out to the hall bathroom, and returned after a few minutes. Sitting up against the headboard, he pulled me to his side, wrapping his arm around me.

"What is your day like today?"

"I have MS Bentley at ten and again at about twoish. Other than that, nothing really. I have been working on a project, finding songs for an HBO Concert, the last few weeks, and I want to finalize the list. My agent wants a total of twenty songs. You?"

He kissed me before he answered. "Just keeping an eye and taking care of the beautiful woman in my bed!"

He took excellent care of me to start my day.

Over breakfast, he said, "I spoke with my folks a few days ago. Mom told me you spent a week at their place several months ago? I remember she had said she had seen you, but I didn't know you stayed."

"I was really there to spend time with Dawn. She had taken a week off from Richard and the kids and had invited me to come and stay with your parents. We actually had a slumber party with a few of her friends from high school."

"A slumber party at your age!"

"It was fun. We watched *Dirty Dancing* and *Notting Hill*, ate popcorn, and drank wine. I think we crashed at about midnight."

"Must have been wild . . . midnight!" He shook his head acknowledging his sister, her friends, and I were not teens anymore.

Many times, when I am working on a project, midnight is often passed by many hours before I get to bed. Just to be with friends was wonderful.

"Both Mom and Dad talk about you all the time. When did you get so close?"

I stared at him as if he had grown an extra head. "What rock have you been living under?"

"Not fair!" He threw up his hands in mock surrender.

"When we were kids and living in Hawai'i, your sister and I became best friends. She still is my best friend. If I wasn't at home with Gran and Pa, I was at your place. Your parents have always been good to me, and I have loved them forever."

I turned so I could look at him. "When Gran passed—remember she had outlived Dad and Pa—your parents flew to Ireland to be with me for the wake and funeral. I don't think I would have made it without their love and support."

He was dumbfounded.

"I didn't know. I mean, I knew you and Dawn were friends, and I knew Mom and Dad talked about you a lot, but I didn't realize how much you were a part of their lives. You really are a part of the family."

I turned so we were face-to-face. "Does that make you uncomfortable?" I couldn't tell from his expression.

He didn't answer right away, and I was getting nervous. I could tell he was thinking about it, and that was worse than a flat-out answer.

"You know . . ." He pulled me back to his side, kissing my cheek in the process. He paused and started again. "How old were you when we started filming for Disney?"

"I was eleven when I got the contract and moved to Hawai'i. We were there for rehearsal and to get acquainted with the other cast members for two months. I had my birthday before we started filming, so, technically, twelve."

"We grew up too fast, I think," Mason said, shaking his head sadly.

"Yeah, probably so." I agreed.

After a beat, Mason continued. "OK, I had turned seventeen six months before. We have known each other now for almost eighteen years. I think that is rare. I'm happy to have you as part of my family. Just don't expect me to have brotherly feelings for you because . . ."

He reached under my T-shirt and cupped my beast.

I followed suit and slid my hand into the front of his briefs, giving him a squeeze and a gentle tug.

Around a kiss, he whispered, "At least I know Mom won't freak if I bring home a white girl."

"Anyone I know?"

"Can't say . . ." The rest of his comment was lost in the kiss.

When we came up for air, Mason took a quick shower and went to make us breakfast and coffee while I showered and put on Fiona.

I cleaned up the kitchen before leaving the apartment. "I'm going to stop by Sally's first," I told Mason, who had already gotten onto his laptop, "and then take Master Sergeant Bentley up to the roof. I am sure someone will follow me up."

"Count on it," he commented absently before standing and giving me a kiss. "Have fun!"

I always had fun on the roof. Maybe I need to include Gerry Goffin and Carole King's classic song "Up on the Roof" in my twenty for the upcoming show and album. I would have to think about it.

Sally had been out with some of her friends for a ladies' night out. They had stayed out scandalously late, returning home at ten thirty. She was still tired and promised she would be better company after she had her after-lunch nap.

Kissing her good-bye on the forehead, I headed to Pearl's apartment.

Bentley barked and growled as I let myself in and asked about his morning.

"Really? That good?" I queried.

He was running around in a large circle as if running the bases on a baseball field. First, his bed and then his squeaky toy, a mongoose, under the dining room table, and then, finally, over the top of my feet. I laughed, and he responded with another round of barks and growls.

As I looked for his leash, I said, "Are you ready to go up to the roof?"

He replied by coming to a dead stop at my feet, running back to get his toy, and then back to wait uncharacteristically quiet at my feet.

Opting to carry the leash, the dog, and the toy, we headed out of the complex to the parking garage.

I didn't check to see who would follow. As Mason assured me, someone would.

Bentley was a fuzz ball of energy. He raced around chasing something I could not see. After fifteen minutes of this, he tended to his toilet before settling down in the sun with his pet mongoose.

I'd brought a book to read, something new from the borrowing library in the office. I didn't start it, as I was thoroughly entertained by Pearl's fuzzy baby. When he napped, I moved the chaise to a spot in the sun and lay back to rest as well. There were things I could have contemplated: my album, how I was going to deal with my pregnancy, if and when I was going to get out of the situation I found myself in. I let all these worries evaporate into the sunny morning.

Perhaps twenty minutes later, I woke with Bentley in my lap sleeping. I cast my attention around to notice there were only the two of us on the roof. I wasn't worried. I knew someone had eyes on me. It was nice, however, for it not to be so overt.

Sometime later, Bentley woke and, after an obligatory kiss on the cheek, requested to be put down on the grass with a side glare in my direction. I obliged and watched as he inspected, first, the mongoose and then the entirety of the roof.

He circled around back to the mongoose, which was resting a yard from the foot of the chaise. He snuggled up to it as if to reassure it, it was not alone before barking and smartly biting the mongoose's neck.

I couldn't help myself and start into a rendition of "It's Only a Paper Moon" by Billy Rose, E. Y. Harburg, and Harold Arlen. Almost at the end, Bentley joined in, howling and barking his way into a raucous duet. Tears rolled down my cheeks as I laughed at him. He had worked his way into my heart. He would be one of the many things I would be sad to leave when it was time to go.

After our duet, I gathered him and his things up and started to head toward the gate. Jesse Fournier stood leaning against the entrance to the stairwell.

"C'était une belle chanson." His presence and his French took me off guard.

I thanked him in French for the compliment of the song. Before I could move, he stilled my approach of the stairs with "You were told not to sing in public. Too many ears to hear a familiar voice!"

The chastisement, even in French, pulled me up short. I had underestimated this handsome young man, taking his small stature and Gallic charm as a modern gadabout.

He smiled at my stunted expression and reached over to rub Bentley between the ears before kissing me on both cheeks, wishing me, "Bonjour," and gently maneuvering me down the stairs.

I was still in a daze as I entered the apartment. Mason was not around. A note was taped to the refrigerator letting me know he had to go out but would be back sometime around two thirty.

As there was no one but me in the house, I set the alarm clock on the bedside table and took a nap.

I must have hit the snooze button more than once, as it was almost two thirty when I woke. I took a few minutes to freshen up before heading out to the courtyard and to Pearl's. I noticed Maggie and the major hand in hand and yelled for them. While Maggie didn't hear me, the major did, and we met halfway between my apartment and the front entrance to the complex.

"What are you kids up to?" I questioned, watching a blush spread across Maggie's face.

"We're walking to the movies. They have a double feature for Seniors' Thursday. We're going to see *Dark Victory* with Bette Davis. It's before your time, but . . ."

I interrupted her. "I actually know both the movie and who Bette Davis is."

"Of course. She was very famous."

"After that," the major began with much enthusiasm, "is *Key Largo* with Bogart and Bacall. That's a great movie!"

I informed them I had seen both of those movies. I was a bit of a classic movie buff, I admitted.

I watched them as they waved good-bye and headed for the front gate. Newspaper Man was not at his post, but Paperback Woman was.

I was about to turn to head to Pearl's apartment when I heard Mandy call my name.

She was standing in the doorway of the office and motioning me to come her way. She had returned to behind her desk when I entered the room.

"How are you today?" Her smile was warm and friendly, and she motioned me to sit at one of the two chairs near the desk.

Indicating to a small stack of envelopes, she began. "Sandi wanted me to mail or hand these out for her.

"I wanted to give you yours and also . . ." She hesitated just a second before pulling another envelope out of her desk drawer. "This is a thank-you card for the stroller, car seat, and bassinette. She asked me to give it to whoever had the idea for them. Mrs. Grayson, Sally, and I discussed it, and we decided to give it to you."

I was shaking my head, denying any involvement. It was to no avail.

"Sally said it was you, and we believe her. We collectively wanted to thank you for including us in the gift."

"I received the same thing from my in-laws, and I wanted Sandi and Sandy to have something as wonderful as I had gotten." This was the first thing that popped into my head, and it sounded plausible.

"Can we give you something . . . ?"

I didn't let her finish. "Absolutely not! That gift was from the entire community. I don't want or need a penny from anyone, and please keep this between us!"

There was a touch of a grin on Mandy's lips as she agreed. "It will be just between you and me and Mrs. Grayson and Sally."

I groaned but knew there was no winning with these particular women. So I asked and got a promise from Mandy it would not be shared with the other women who attended the shower.

I tucked the small thank-you card into my back pocket and, finally, thirty minutes after I had left my apartment, was at the door of Pearl's.

I smiled to myself when, after closing the door behind me, I spied Master Sergeant curled up with his mongoose under the dining room table. At first, he appeared to be sleeping, but as I drew near, I could hear plaintive crying from the small dog.

"What's wrong, Bentley?" I used my most soothing voice as I got down on my hands and knees to get closer to him. Perhaps he was dreaming.

He was shaking. His cries sounded more like those of fear. My heart pounded faster as I pulled the quaking

Bentley into my arms. His forepaws were wrapped around the toy, so I nestled both together close to my face.

"Oh, sweet boy! What's wrong?"

His cries broke my heart and scared me. I kissed his head, his nose, the side of his face, each time reassuring him and myself everything was going to be OK.

I rocked him and his mongoose in my arms. With each caress and soothing word, his shaking began to subside.

"I know!" I comforted him. "That must have been an awful doggy-mare!"

For a brief second, he turned his head to look at me. I could tell his eyes were not focused; he was only following the sound of my constant words. I kept talking.

"You're such a good boy. Your mama loves you, and your aunty Fiona loves you . . ."

He licked my chin, nuzzled his mongoose, gave a small sigh, and was still.

I could feel the panic and the heartbreak building inside of my chest like the impending eruption of a volcano.

"Noooo!" I heard the keening, confused from where it came.

I found myself suddenly outside of Pearl's apartment. From somewhere, I heard the screaming, the demanding "Someone help me." I perceived Sally's name being called again and again.

I looked around surprised to see Sally, Jesse's ginger, the woman who had no name from the second floor, and Johan surrounding me.

"Sally," I screamed! "Something's wrong with Bentley! Help me!"

She was speaking, but I could not understand her words as the loud sobs were surrounding me.

"Let me have him," the ginger said.

"No!" I moved to get away from him. "Why are you taking him? Sally, help!"

I felt hands on my face. I pressed Bentley and his mongoose closer but not too tight. I didn't want to hurt them.

"Fiona,"—it was Sally's voice, stable and loving— "Fiona, Bentley is gone."

My heart broke again. How was that possible? I couldn't breathe.

"No. No!" Her hands kept my face from shaking violently in denial. "Pearl, oh, Pearl." This time, I knew it was me who was sobbing uncontrollably.

"Is there a threat?" I heard a woman's voice ask.

"No, the dog died," someone responded.

I shouted, "His name *is* Bentley!"

"Fiona," Sally said, "let me take him."

"No, he is going to be OK. No. Pearl is . . ." I was racked by sobs again.

Sally's voice moved away as another set of hands touched my face. I would know these hands anywhere.

"Sweetheart."

I cried even harder at the sound of his voice and the touch of his lips on my forehead.

"My heart is breaking!" I howled. "My heart is breaking! I can't breathe."

"Fiona! Baby, you need to let me have Bentley. He's gone."

"No . . . are you sure?"

"Yes, he isn't in any pain anymore."

"Do you promise?" I kissed the still-warm head of this small animal that had stolen my heart.

"Yes, Sally will keep him safe until his mama comes home."

"Poor Pearl." Again, I was wracked by uncontrollable sobs. "He was all alone. He was just waiting for someone to come."

I rocked back and forth with the small bundle in my arms, not letting him go.

"Nathan?"

"I'm here."

"Can you take him?" I begged, not wanting to let go. Then I was afraid again. "Don't forget his mongoose. He loved that damn thing. It was his comfort until I got there." As I felt him being lifted away, I collapsed into Nathan's arms.

Panic rose again, and I said, "Are you sure he's gone?"

"Fiona, you did well," Sally said. "He went out with love. Pearl will be happy to know that."

I didn't respond. I didn't think I could.

There was a conversation going on around me, to which I neither cared nor wanted to understand.

Someone lifted me and was carrying me.

It wasn't possible for me to open my eyes.

"Are you sure?" I asked again, not sure who would answer.

"Teresa, I am sure. Can you get the door?" he asked.

Me, get the door? What door?

"No . . ." Mason was speaking, but it wasn't to me. I was tired. I wanted to sleep. This was one of too many terrifying fucking nightmares I had experienced in too short of time.

"Teresa, honey, I need you to look at me."

I felt the bed under Mason and me as he lay next to me. With reluctance, I opened my eyes. His sad, handsome face was close to mine.

"I am sorry." It was everything, and I curled up against him and cried myself to sleep.

WEEK IV

Thursday night was a blur. I had accepted one stiff shot of something before it registered and the next glass was refused. As some point, either I dreamed Pearl come to see me, sitting on the edge of the bed and hugging and thanking me, or perhaps she actually had.

When he brought me a cup of tea on Friday morning, Mason confirmed she had visited at about eight on Thursday evening.

I drank my tea. I was drained from the emotional roller coaster of the day before. I also found I was still in full "Fiona" gear, with the exception of my contacts, which Mason said had come out sometime during the evening.

After my tea, I dragged myself out of bed and into the bathroom. Removing all the gear and stepping into the shower, I washed away some of the pain of the day before.

I took my time redressing. I needed to pull myself together before I left the bathroom. I had spent half the time in the shower quietly crying, unable to control myself. The last thing I needed was to draw more attention to myself.

Mason had a light breakfast ready when I emerged.

"I heard the shower," he said, looking at me as he placed a plate of fruit on the table, "and thought you could use something to eat. You wouldn't eat last night."

His concern was etched on his face. I walked over and took the piece of toast out of his hand and stepped into him. Resting my cheek on his, I whispered, "I love you."

He pulled me into a tight embrace to whisper back into my ear, "Nae ma·eum. It means 'my heart' in Korean. It's my way of telling you I love you." He pulled me away from his body so he could look into my eyes. "Nae ma·eum, Teresa, I love you."

He kissed me, and I knew I would be all right!

Throughout the day, I had visitors. It was sweet and a little awkward, yet I found it a new experience.

I admitted to Mason I was embarrassed and didn't fully understand why I fell apart over a dog, a dog that wasn't even mine. We concluded it was again the result of everything that had happened over the past month. The totality of things I could not control had overwhelmed me with the loss of poor sweet Bentley. It was a rehashing of the conversation we had previously had, but it made me feel better.

Louise dropped by at around lunchtime for a tête-à-tête with Mason. She wondered how I was feeling. There was something off in the way Louise was including me into the general topics they were discussing. It was as if she was angry with me in some way. Perhaps Louise was annoyed I had put her in the position of having to get the pregnancy test. Maybe she thought I had lied to her, which I had, but without the test itself, she had no proof.

I told myself I was just imagining things and let it go. Everyone has an off day, and today was hers.

I got her to stay for lunch, sandwiches, and soup. She seemed to relax a bit around the table.

Mason admitted he was suffering a bit from cabin fever to Louise. I kept my mouth shut but gave a little smile when Louise told us she wasn't because of her gig at the college, but she knew that Akio was about to throw himself off his second-story balcony.

"It's still early in the day. We don't need to get it approved. Just need to inform Soto." This was Mason suddenly excited. He pulled out his cell and dialed a number. "Akio, its Mason. Get your butt over here. We are cooking up plans for a night on the town."

I think Akio must have flown down from his apartment or he had been standing, stalker-like, at our door. Either way, he didn't even knock but let himself in. He kissed me on the forehead as he moved to the table, asking how I was as he sat. I took his hand and gave it a squeeze and then a slap as he took half of my sandwich off my plate and moved my half-eaten bowl of soup in front of him, sipping a spoonful before blowing me a kiss.

"Thanks for the snack." He winked at me before turning his attention to Mason.

"We need to get the hell out of here!" Mason said before stuffing a quarter of his sandwich in his mouth.

There was a choir of "hell yeahs" from Akio and Louise.

"Where?" asked Louise.

"I know a place," Akio offered.

Everyone's attention turned to the tall, lanky HPB agent who was still chewing what was left of my lunch. Once he had our attention, he began. "There is a real honest-to-goodness drive-in in Twentynine Palms. I say we drive up there, find a place to have dinner, and watch a double drive-in feature."

"I'll call the office and let them know." Louise rose from the table, pulling out her cell and dialing as she left the apartment.

While we waited, I took the dishes to the kitchen. Mason and Akio cleaned off the table and put the condiments away as I added the lunch dishes to the dishwasher.

I left them in the living room and went into the bedroom to put on some makeup and decide what to wear just in case we got the say-so.

I was still shaken from yesterday, and this morning, I had to fight not to throw up everything I had eaten the night before. The pattern for my mornings had fallen into a rough routine. When I woke, I was nauseous, sometimes worse than others, but always worried I wouldn't make it to the bathroom in time.

It was the goal every morning to get to the bathroom in an unrushed manner. I had learned to run the faucet as I sat next to the toilet, waiting to see if it would be a morning of only queasiness or worse. I had been lucky, as most mornings consisted of a rolling stomach but no real morning sickness. This was a blessing, as the last thing I needed was for Mason to become suspicious enough to call me to a doctor.

I knew I was ridiculous about not telling Nathan. I was sure he would be happy. Yet, for some unfathomable reason, I just couldn't bring myself to tell him.

As I applied my makeup, Akio called out he was leaving and thanking me for lunch. I laughed at my reflection. It wasn't much of a lunch, thanks to him.

"What are you laughing about?" Mason asked from the bathroom doorway.

"Akio stealing my lunch and then thanking me for it. There has to be some HPB policy forbidding such behavior."

"Nope, can't say that there is." He walked up and put his arms around me, his comment tickling the nape of my neck.

I finished applying mascara before I turned to him. He had moved to the toilet, dropping the seat so he could watch me. I had wanted to have this conversation, and now, I thought, was as good a time as any.

"Nathan." I began using his real name. As anticipated, I had his full attention.

"Teresa?"

"When all this is over,"—I waved one hand around to make the point—"how are we going to let your bosses know we are together?"

"I've been thinking about that actually." He stood up. "When you're done in here, come sit on the sofa with me."

He left, leaving me to the last bit of application on my face. I took the time to change into maternity jeans and a long-sleeved T-shirt before joining him.

"OK." I kissed him and sat in the corner of the sofa so I could face him.

"There's a couple of options. Let me tell you what I think, and we can decide. We don't have to decide now, but I am hoping soon. It's good to have a plan of action ready. I don't want to wake up ever again without you in my bed." He moved to kiss me before relocating to the opposite end of the sofa from me. He also, it seemed, wanted eye contact.

I waited.

"The first, I've been thinking, is after this has ended, you either go to one of your places in LA or go to Mom and Dad's. I will tell my supervisor I had developed or rekindled feelings for you and I want to get with you to see if you share them or not.

"In that scenario, we can act as if we had not acted on our feelings until your protection had ended. This makes me look less like an idiot who can't keep his dick in his pants and more like an agent who did his job."

I didn't like the "dick in his pants" comment and told him so.

"You have to look at it from their perspective. By sleeping with you, I have crossed a huge line. The agency frowns on that!" He shrugged his shoulders.

I understood then that being with me, telling me he loved me, had undoubtedly compromised his sense of doing his job.

I was sorry for that.

"Nathan, this is as much on me as it is on you. I felt as if I threw myself at you. Even when you told me we couldn't be lovers, I didn't—well, not for long—lessen my efforts to change your mind." I was surprised tears began rolling down my cheeks.

He moved to me. "Teresa, don't. I am glad you did. Letting you go all those years ago was the worst thing I ever did. I don't want to take anything away from Bethany. We tired—well, she tried—but my heart wasn't really into the marriage. That's on me. It wasn't fair for her."

"Nathan, don't. We all make mistakes. That's just part of growing up. Bethany was lucky. She was a nice woman." I took his hand and brought it to my lips, kissing his palm.

"Mom called her 'the *shiksa*.'" He laughed.

"When did your mom start speaking Yiddish?"

"That's a long story and for later. Let's just say Mom didn't like her very much. I think secretly she was comparing Bethany to you."

"Oy!" I added for effect. "You said you had two options. What's the second?"

He moved back to his corner of the sofa. "It isn't the one I want, but I might not have a choice. I can go and inform Agent Soto that I need to be replaced as your assigned agent. I have crossed the line. Accept my reprimand, anything that comes my way. I'll inform her that we are a couple. That I intend to spend my life with you if you'll have me and see what happens." He just shrugged his shoulders, a gesture I didn't care for.

"I don't like that one!" I moved to him. "Are you asking me to marry you?" I asked a little out of breath as my mind caught up with his words.

"Hell, no! I just thought we would shack up for a while!"

I punched his arm half-heartedly. "Oh, well, then. That's OK. I never shacked up with anyone before . . . oh, wait! There was that sexy Frenchman I drooled over for a few weeks."

Nathan moved me away and sat up, so he was face to stomach with Mason Jr.

"Don't believe a word your mother is saying!" He warned the apparatus inside the faux stomach.

His gesture caught me off guard. This was the perfect time to tell him about the baby. I opened my mouth, but the words didn't come out. I wasn't ready just yet. I wanted to get to my ob-gyn before I confessed to Nathan I was pregnant.

He reached down to rub the belly, making Mason Jr. throw a kicking fit.

Instead, I huffed, "I really have to tell Agent Johnson his mechanical baby is too rowdy at times."

"I agree. I think my hand is bruised."

"Oh, poor, strong HPB agent, let me kiss it and make it better."

"I have something else you can kiss." He wiggled his eyebrows suggestively.

I know he wasn't speaking of his mouth, but I started there.

It took little time for things to escalate. We were struggling out of our pants when there was a bang on the door.

"Mason! Fiona! It's me. Open up!" Akio's voice boomed from the other side of the locked door.

"Shit!" I laughed, pulling up my jeans. I looked over at Mason, his rock-hard erection obvious through the fabric of his boxer briefs. "You!" I pointed to the bathroom.

He understood, tugging at his jeans enough for him to hurry into the master bedroom, closing the door behind him.

I took a second to make sure I was all together before unlocking the door and stepping aside to let Akio in.

"Where's Mason?" He looked around the small living room.

"He's taking a shower." I tossed out over my shoulder as I headed for the kitchen to get a bottle of water from the refrigerator.

His glance fell to the open door of the hall bathroom.

"He likes the showerhead in the master bath. I let him use it if he promised to rub my feet in the evening. This baby weight is killing my poor toes." I laughed. Being an actress had its advantages.

"Oh, well, then." He conceded.

"You want some water?" I held up my unopened bottle. He took it with a "Thanks," and I got myself another.

We moved to the living room.

"So?" I asked.

"I got some news, but I'll wait until Louise gets here and Mason is out of the . . ." He paused.

We both looked into the small hall as Mason, with a towel wrapped around his waist, walked from the master bedroom to the smaller bedroom, calling, "Sorry, forgot my clean clothes!"

I huffed, "Gross!"

Akio added, "Hmmm, I don't know," with a leering lilt in his voice.

I slapped his arm. "Don't be rude. You're married, and I happen to know your wonderful husband."

"I ain't dead, though!" he countered.

Further conversation was halted as Louise walked through the now unlocked front door.

To Akio, she asked, "Where's Mason?"

"Getting dressed," I chimed in, not giving Akio the opportunity to answer.

She looked around the room and after a beat settled into a recliner.

"Hurry up, Mr. Park, the day's a-wastin'!" she yelled from her place.

"Yeah! Yeah!" came muffled through the wall.

We three sat in strained silence. Akio casting side glances between Louise and me.

There was a half a minute of uncomfortable silence, Akio beginning to squirm uncomfortably.

"So, hmm, how are the classes going? I haven't asked in a while." I used my best film actress cheer to pose the question.

Akio leaped on it like a drowning man to a rope. "Yeah, how is it going? You still having problems with that student?"

That was all it took to get the conversation going.

"What's up with that student?" Curious now, I leaned around Akio's lanky frame to look at Louise.

Turned out she had a student in his midthirties who was all about revisionist history. As the class was about Native American religion, culture, and history from their perspective, each act of forced removal, false accusations, and genocide was covered to explain where Native American cultures were today and why. The student couldn't wrap his head around the facts, falling back on the antiquated European opinion that everyone else not from Europe were primitives.

Louise had even gone as far as asking the student to reconsider taking the class. When he refused, she had to go to the dean to see what options she had. He had become a significant distraction to her class, losing precious lecture time trying to counter his arguments.

"Finally, this week, after his wife got involved, he pulled out of the class. I'm really a good teacher. Normally, I can work with any student, but wow! He was in a category all to himself."

"Was he just trying to prove a point about something?" Akio asked.

That seemed reasonable to me, and I seconded his question.

"Hell! I haven't a clue. I understood he is a great student. Working on his master's in IT. Who knows?" was Louise's comment.

Mason rounded the corner dressed in his favorite Berkley sweatshirt, jeans, and sneakers. "What did I miss?"

Louise filled him in on the conversation. I watched the only person of European ancestry in the room and suddenly felt a little sad. Here between the four of us, I had been the one to have benefited from white privilege. It was uncomfortable to see it in this light, the light of having the man I loved, another man I cared about, and Louise,

despite the strain—I really did think of her as a friend—
all having the possibility of not having their cultures
understood and looked down upon.

"I'm sorry, Louise, this happened to you. In your own
class." There was sadness in my voice.

"It's resolved now. Unfortunately, I have a student like
this every other year or so. I just work with what I get."
Louise shook her head and then placed a smile on her face.

We let the subject drop and moved on.

"So are we staying in this comfortable prison, or do we get
out for good behavior?" Akio again the cheerleader of us all.

"It's been cleared." This from Louise, who had moved
back to the recliner. "We are to arrive at the Bistro
Twentynine in Twentynine Palm at six thirty. That gives
us an hour and a half for dinner before the movies start."

Akio chimed in with the name of the movies for the
double feature. They were comedies, one animated and the
other happening in space.

"Have you ever been to a drive-in?" I asked between a
lull.

All three of the HPB agents looked at me as if I had
suddenly sprouted antennae and wings.

"What!" I was unexpectedly embarrassed. I didn't think
the question merited such agog looks.

"You have never been to a drive-in?" Louise looked at
me, disbelieving the possibility.

I looked at Mason. "When would I have gone? I have
been working since forever. You never took me to the one
you used to go to in Hawai'i. I never recalled hearing of a
drive-in in Glasgow."

"You were a kid." He was defensive.

"I'm not blaming. I know you didn't want to hang out
with a kid. I'm just saying. No one ever offered to take me,
and I never thought about it on my own."

"It was a great place to go and hang out with your
friends," Akio said.

"OK, then I am assuming I am the only one of us who has never been to a drive-in." I looked at Louise. She nodded, acknowledging it was true.

"You know," I began, "I have spent a lot of time browsing the Internet, and I thought maybe we could leave now and drive through the Joshua Tree National Park. There is a road through the park that goes straight to Twentynine Palms. It would get us out of the house. Hopefully, one of you has a camera, not on your phone, and we could take pictures."

I looked around seeing the wheels begin to turn with Mason and Akio. Louise was still reticent.

"It would be fun, don't you think?"

When Mason took over the conversation, I knew it was a done deal.

Louise left to see if we could get the car sooner.

Akio left to clear this new addendum to our plans, leaving Mason and me alone.

"Have you noticed anything weird about Louise lately?" I asked from the kitchen.

From the hallway, Mason acknowledged he had but supposed it had to do with the student she had been having trouble with. I didn't think that was it but kept my mouth shut.

When he came out of the bathroom, I snuggled up to him. Thickening up my ongoing Glasgow Patter to the sexiest tone I could do, I leaned into him. "Are you sure we can't mess around under the blanket in the backseat? I'll try to be quiet."

"You might be able to be quiet, but you know me."

I did. Blue Sky Song, a.k.a. Nathan Song, a.k.a. Mason Park, was not a quiet man with his lovemaking. I found it incredibly sexy and one hell of a turn-on. I had to agree that perhaps we should just hold hands in the backseat and nothing more. With our chaperones in the front, I suppose that was the safest thing to do.

He looked at the door before kissing me. "I promise to make it up to you when we get home," he whispered into my ear.

"I'm holding you to it!"

We were in the overlarge, dark tinted SUV, by two twenty. The instructions were as follows:

1. I was to ride in the back with Louise for the entire time we were off the complex. (This might be negotiable when we were out of the city.)
2. I was to stay in character anytime I was out of the car. (This was a no-brainer, as I had yet to break character outside the apartment even when poor Master Sergeant Bentley passed.)
3. One of the agents was to check in with our tag at the Cottonwood Visitor Center. (They were given the names of their contact. I didn't need or want to know.)
4. Finally, if there were any problems or suspicions something was amiss, turn around and head back to Palm Springs after notifying the tags that were following us.

I didn't really need to agree with anything but the first two, and once I had, we were on our way. It was nice being off the compound. I was too excited to hold a conversation, which was a good thing, as Louise didn't seem to be too chatty.

The boys in the front seat were discussing the best way to get to I-10 from the apartment. Louise suggested they use the GPS.

I laughed. Louise snickered, and Mason and Akio booed at us from the front seats.

Once on I-10 heading east, I turned and asked in the softest voice I could manage, "Louise, are you OK? You seemed to be really bothered by that student you were having trouble with."

I didn't really think that was it but was hoping she would either agree it was or tell me what was really going on. She took the proffered suggestion of the student a bit faster than I had anticipated.

I listened attentively as she talked about how he had made her class so much more difficult than it needed to be. Akio chimed in with a question, and for the next twenty minutes or so, until we turned to get into the Park, the four of us discussed the student's attitude.

I had seen and been exposed to bias and some harassment from the time I started acting. Unfortunately, it was part of the business. I had been lucky. I hadn't experienced the "casting couch." There were those, both actresses and even actors, I knew who had. I kept this to myself. Right now, this was about Louise.

The ice princess had done enough melting that I didn't want to take away from Louise.

It was a change. I was hoping it would continue. I hadn't liked the woman I had become.

The attention shifted again once we turned into the Joshua Tree National Park as we entered the park.

The first sign gave us directions to the different trails and visitor centers and Twentynine Palms.

I mustered the courage to ask, "Can I sit up in the front so I can see better?"

Akio pulled over to the shoulder of the two-lane road and put the car in park.

Akio looked from Mason to Louise. "What do you think?"

Louise shrugged her shoulders. "You're the lead on this ride."

"Mason?" Akio turned to Mason.

"I think it would be all right. She has all the prosthetics on, her teeth, her contacts, and the baby body. With her accent, which she never drops, and those sunglasses, who would ever recognize her? Louise, do you agree?"

She nodded agreement.

We shuffled in and out of the car. Mason took the driving position, Akio in the back with Louise and me in the passenger seat in the front.

I became "Chatty Kathy." My accent got a hair bit thicker in my excitement. We hadn't even reached the visitor center, yet I felt like I was on the moon. The sixteen-mile drive from I-10 to the center was unexpectedly stark and beautiful.

"Have you ever been to the desert before?" I cast the question out to see who responded.

Joshua Tree National Park contained five different mountain ranges and two different deserts, the Mohave and the Colorado. It encompassed 1,234 square miles and was a relativity new national park being founded on October 31, 1994. According to the website, the Mohave Desert had a higher elevation and was colder than the Colorado Desert. The entrance to the park from I-10 led us through the Colorado Desert.

When we arrived at the visitor center, there were maybe twenty cars already parked. A park ranger, directing traffic, indicated there was a spot further up. Mason expertly maneuvered the SUV into the parking space. We sat there for a moment before getting out.

Mason, my ever-attentive husband, rounded the front of the car to open my door and help me out. An older couple standing at the front of their vehicle—Canadian plates, I had noticed—oohed "how sweet" as I was pulled up and out of the car.

"Oh, my dear. You are rather far along, aren't you?" the woman smiled, moving to rub my protruding stomach.

On cue, as he was wont to do, Mason Jr. kicked up a storm.

The woman snatched her hand away, laughing. "Oh, I remember that!"

I smiled back and said, "He's our first." I leaned in and kissed Mason on the cheek. Like his father, he is a soccer fan."

The woman gaped at me, apparently not understanding my intentionally heavy Glasgow Patter.

Mason translated for me.

"Where you from, dear?"

"Glasgow," I answered. Taking Mason's offered hand and stepping onto the curb. "Sorry, but I have to go the bathroom!"

Mason again interpreted for me. Louise, taking my elbow, walked with me to the restrooms.

I could hear the husband of the woman ask Mason and Akio where they were headed and told them after Akio responded to make sure they check out the Cholla Cactus Garden.

Mason was waiting when I came out of the restroom.

"Where did Louise go?"

"She's inside with Akio. They're paying the parking fee." He took my hand and led me toward the center. Inside was a tight space with a dozen people moving about the displays, the small gift shop, and the ranger's counter.

"Next Friday," I heard the younger female ranger telling one of the park guests, "at the amphitheater, we will be doing a presentation on the night sky as we normally do, but there is actually a meteor shower that will start at about eight thirty. It should be a spectacular show. If you can come, please join us . . ." She went on to give the web address for the park information for the upcoming activities.

I turned to Mason, who was at my side but was distracted by something Akio was telling him. I waited for a break in the conversation before interrupting.

"Did you hear that?"

In unison, they asked, "Hear what?"

I repeated what I had overheard the ranger tell the other guest. "Do you think we could come?"

Louise had joined us at the beginning of the recap and added, "Wow, that would be cool! We can get it planned tomorrow when we have our meeting."

"You have a meeting tomorrow?" I queried.

"Yeah, but it shouldn't be more than a few hours. Do you have something you wanted to do?"

I looked about to see where Akio and Louise had drifted off to before I leaned into Mason and whispered, "Why, yes, I do." For emphasis and clarification, I grabbed his ass and squeezed.

He laughed and took my hand from his backside. With a wiggle of his eyebrows, he kissed my hand.

The woman who had asked about the baby saw the hand kiss and again, and in a louder voice than I thought necessary, commented, "You two are such lovebirds! That is so nice to see."

I smiled at her observation yet caught Louise's narrowing gaze as she looked at our intertwined hands.

I gave her a wink and a smile as if to say, "See, this is all part of the ruse. No one would ever suspect I wasn't Fiona Park, devoted and loving wife of Mason Park, PhD."

Her eyes narrowed even more for the briefest of moments before nodding at me her understanding.

After about twenty minutes exploring the visitor center and the surrounding grounds, we piled back into the SUV and headed north. True to their word, we stopped at each pullout, reading the information and taking pictures, taking our time from one stop to the next.

We stopped. We read. We explored, and we watched the time. Louise had become the official timekeeper. There was a general consensus we would arrive at the diner in Twentynine Palms at around six fifteen. This would give us almost three hours to explore before we had to be out of the park.

The vastness of the area and the differing topography were continually catching my attention and wonder. We had spent some time walking along the Black Eagle Mine Road before getting back into the car. We had developed a rhythm of when to stop and when not to stop, mostly stopping, so we could get in as much sightseeing as possible.

We hadn't been back in the car long when I yelled for Mason to pull the vehicle over and burst into a fit of laughter.

"What the hell!" Louise wondered from the backseat.

"Didn't you see it?"

Akio moved, so his face was between the front seats. "See what?"

"The name on that sign!" I pointed to the back side of a sign perhaps thirty feet behind us.

This time, it was Mason who looked at me as if I had lost my mind. "No, obviously, we didn't."

"Get your camera and come with me. You're going to love it!" I promised as I opened the door, not stepping out until the three agents had followed suit and started to move out of the car.

The signed proclaimed we had entered "Fried Liver Wash."

"What the hell kinda name is that?"

"What were they on when they named it?"

We all enjoyed taking our pictures with the sign. I had to get a promise that after I was no longer under the care of the HPB, I would get copies of the photos we were collecting on this day out.

The Ocotillo Patch was interesting. They were covered in bright red flowers. I thought they were a cactus, but the information board educated the readers, us, that the ocotillo is not, in fact, an actual cactus despite its thorny looks.

It was the Cholla Cactus Garden we spent the most time in. The cholla seemed to reproduce by growing small spiny balls that fall from the parent plant and roll away via wind or other ways to begin a new independent life.

"They remind me of a tribble from the old *Star Trek* series," Akio said.

I hadn't seen the old—well, indeed any of the series. Not that I didn't like science fiction. I just never had time. I wholeheartedly agreed, fearing horrible teasing if I did.

Mason, however, knew I hadn't, as I had admitted as much to him when I had confessed I hadn't seen any of the *Star Wars* movies. He called me out!

The harassment began once we were back in the car.

"For someone who is as wealthy, talented, and famous as our mutual friend Cat Connors, I'm beginning to think she lives under a rock!" Louise wondered behind the headrest of my seat.

"I am sure of it!" Mason confirmed Louise's suspicions.

"I'm staying out of this!" Akio leaned into the corner of the backseat.

I think he wanted to watch and see what happened. I was about to give him a show.

"Louise," I began.

"Uh-oh!" Akio laughed from his corner.

"Yes?" Louise moved to the center of the backseat so she could see me better.

"I have an old friend, ancient. I think you might know him. Do you know a washed-up actor named Blue Sky Song? I think his real name was something like Haneul Palan Song," I asked.

"He's not washed up. He just decided to change careers!" defended Mason.

"Washed up!" I countered.

"Yes, I think I heard of him. Why?"

I slipped into my storytelling mode I had learned from my grandmother.

"Well." I was interrupted by Mason.

"I would be careful if I were you, Fiona Park. I happen to be a very close friend of the man you are about to malign." He poked me in the ribs as a warning, but his tone was full of humor.

I simply smiled.

"Well, it seems this actor had a little sister named Dawn. She happens to be the best friend of this Cat Connors. Anyway, when they were just kids, Haneul Palan Song and Cat Connors were in a Disney series for many years."

Mason remarked, "It was five!"

"Haneul wasn't very pleasant to the poor young Cat or his little sister. Therefore, the two girls did their best to torment the older boy.

"One day, he was on the lanai making out . . ."

"Fiona, my love, where are you going with this story?"

"Just wait! It isn't too bad. Dawn and her sweet friend Cat was hiding behind a mango tree in the yard and watching seventeen-year-old Blue Sky. We—I mean, they were both twelve and doing the best to critique his moves." At this point, I began to giggle remembering what happened next.

"Haneul Palan Song's parents are the best people in the world. Cat loves them like her own, and, best of all, they love her back. Anyway, Blue Sky's dad comes out onto the lanai. Both Blue Sky and the girl—what was her name? Oh, yeah, Cortney Balfour—"

Akio interrupted my story. "I remember her. She was on that show and a few others. There was the one show she was mostly just in her bikini. Nice show!"

"The children in the backseat need to keep their comments to themselves!" Mason warned Akio.

"You're gay." Louise gave him a look.

"Yes, but a hot bod is a hot bod even if you wouldn't *shtup* it!" he commented.

"Oy vey!" Louise laughed.

"I am trying to tell a story here, children."

"Sorry, Mom!"

"It's all right, Akio. OK, where was I? So, Dad, Donald, came out clearing his throat. Both Blue Sky and Cortney shoved each other away so hard they went flying in opposite directions. His dad, bless him, said, 'I've meant to get that chaise fixed. You two kids be careful!'" I had a fit of laughing.

"I don't know how he kept a straight face. Meanwhile, Dawn and Cat were rolling laughing behind the tree."

In the backseat, both passengers were laughing. I noticed when I looked back at Mason, he was smiling at me.

"I remember that," he said softly. "I heard you two laughing but didn't know where you were. If I could have found you, I would have whipped you both."

"Dad wouldn't have let you. Neither would Mom. You know, we could get away with anything. Well, almost! I always hated Cortney Balfour!" It was under my breath, but he heard me. I could tell from the curve of his handsome mouth.

Louise had become strangely quiet again. I glanced back and noticed she was watching us with some speculation. Akio saved the moment.

"You two have known each other for a long time?"

"Yes, but, really, he was always away. It is Dawn and his parents I have always been around. When we finished filming *Blue Sky Hawai'i*, I headed for Scotland, and he headed off to college. I've seen him once since our Disney days."

"You mean Cat has seen him only once since their Disney days?" Louise corrected.

I agreed with her, not wanting to upset her more than she already seemed to be.

We were quiet for some time until we arrived at White Tank campground where the campsites were nestled among huge rocks. There was a bathroom for the campers, so we took the time to use the facilities and do a little exploring. As it was only five o'clock on a Friday, there were just two campers there, so they were able to climb on the rocks.

I did not climb on the rocks, because I was supposed to be seven months pregnant and, with the baby body, looked it. Also, since I was probably really pregnant, I didn't want to take the chance to have anything happen that might put either myself or the baby in jeopardy.

At five thirty, at Louise's instructions, we headed back to the car and made our way out of Joshua Tree National Park to Twentynine Palms and Bistro Twentynine.

It took us another thirty minutes to get out of the park and to locate the restaurant. Before we pulled into the parking lot, we drove around town to see what was in Twentynine Palms.

We had reservations, which I didn't know we needed. Even at six twenty, it was already full. The hostess informed us we would have a five-minute wait before we would be seated and directed us to the bar if we wanted to order drinks while we did so.

I looked around, already knowing I would only be able to have a glass of wine, so I would wait until we had our food on the table. Newspaper Man was with a woman I hadn't seen before. He pointedly ignored us as we moved past him to our table. As we were ordering our drinks, he and his companion sat at a table between ours and the door.

At this point in the game, I assumed, maybe naively so, Planz was not looking or the HPB had done such a bang-up job he hadn't a clue as to where I was. Feeling safe with at least five HPB agents surrounding me, I relaxed as much as possible and enjoyed our dinner.

Mason and Akio each had a steak. I had the crab legs, while Louise had a cup of French onion soup and a Caesar salad. We all gave her a hard time about her healthy choice, which she accepted gracefully and with the promise of reprisal in the not-too-distant future.

The conversation was comfortable and relaxed.

I kept an eye on Newspaper Man and his companion. They seemed to be solely focused on each other, a couple out for a quiet night without the kids. Yet I noticed each time the door to the bistro opened or each time a server or a patron of the bistro moved near or around the corner booth we occupied, there was the slightest shift of attention.

I was looking for it, which is the only reason I noticed. Mason, Louise, and Akio had that quick assessment of a new situation as it happened. I felt terrible for them. I was relaxed and enjoying myself; I wasn't sure they were. It seemed they were always on the job even when feigning a good time.

Smith's Ranch Drive-In was an eight-minute drive from the bistro.

We pulled into the drive-in at seven forty. Akio, who was behind the wheel again, pulled three spaces to the side of the concession and restrooms. He had backed into the spot so we could open the tailgate of the SUV and either sit in the back or pull out the four chaise lawn chairs he had placed in the rear of the SUV to watch the double feature.

A nondescript sedan pulled into the vacant spot two spaces over. Mason gave a subtle nod in the direction of the car. The dark windows were rolled down, and the speaker box was placed on the rim of the driver's side window. I caught the unmistakable profile and color of Jesse Fournier's ginger and wasn't surprised to spy Jesse in the passenger seat.

The four of us optioned for the folding lawn chairs behind the SUV. There were also four light blankets to wrap up with as we were in the high desert, and when the sun settled under the horizon, the temperature would drop.

At eight, the first of three cartoons from the '40s or '50s played, along with a short clip of dancing sodas, popcorn, and candy who all sang and invited everyone to the concession.

"That was a flashback," Louise commented after the singing refreshments danced off the screen.

"How so?" I looked over her direction.

"Remember, she's never been to a drive-in." Mason reminded Louise.

"Didn't you ever go to the movies when you were a kid?" Akio asked.

"No, well, maybe when I was a kid. I will have to ask Dawn. If I went to a movie, it would have been with her. My grandparents didn't go, and my parents had screening rooms in their homes. We got the movies straight from the distributors or the studios." I shrugged as if to say, "Didn't everyone's parents do that?"

"Wow! Big shots!" Louise's tone wasn't very kind.

Out of the corner, I saw Mason stiffen. I reached over and touched his leg before he could say anything. He turned to look at me, and I mouthed for him to "let it go." She wasn't entirely wrong. Having the parents I had, each living on different continents, living mostly with my grandparents, and beginning my career before ten, I didn't really have a normal childhood.

The first movie was an animated movie about a horde of small yellow creatures looking to find a place to belong. It was funny and poignant. I enjoyed it and was surprised this was the third or fourth movie when these lovable misfits were in.

Akio, being the parent of small children, listed the movies by name and stressed they needed to be watched in their release order for maximum enjoyment.

"Really?" inquired Mason.

"This movie"—Akio was as serious as a film critic—"is a prequel."

"Good to know." I nodded.

"Very!" chimed in Louise, this time understandably laughing at her friend.

At intermission, we stood up and stretched. I walked around our small space, knowing I had at least five pairs of watchful eyes on me.

"Hey, Louise, walk with me. Did you see where the restrooms were?" I asked loud enough that my entourage would hear.

"Yeah, around the corner here. Let me show you."

Together, we walked around the SUV and toward the restrooms. I could hear Mason and Akio behind us. There was a debate as to popcorn or not.

The restroom had three stalls behind glossy white-painted doors. Louise stepped to the sink and washed her hands as I stepped into one of the booths. She was still drying her hands when I stepped out a moment later. She moved to the side so I could wash my hands yet was always an arm's length away as we exited the small space.

To my chagrin, there were two large tubs of popcorn and four large drinks waiting for us when we returned to the SUV.

"Can't watch a movie without popcorn," Mason informed us, patting the chair next to him for me to sit.

"I'm still stuffed from dinner," I moaned.

"More for me." Mason moved the bucket from between our chairs to his lap.

"I didn't say that!" I reached over and returned the bucket to the space between us. "What kind of soda did you get me?"

"He was very clear. He seems to think you are some sort of root beer connoisseur." Akio eyed the overlarge Styrofoam cup.

"I love root beer but don't drink it very often. Hey," I said, turning from Akio to Mason, "didn't you buy me three cases of root beer for my thirteenth birthday?"

"Yeah, and you went wild. Might as well been a diamond. It was Dawn's idea. I thought it was crazy, but it worked."

"That's the first time I fell in love with you," I said without thinking.

The second feature began as the last word exited my mouth. I hoped no one heard it but me.

It was already after midnight when we piled into the SUV and headed back to Palm Springs. The movie, a space flick, the sequel to a very successful film, delivered all it was promised to. Great action and humor spurred the flick along too quickly I was surprised when the ending credits rolled.

We were exhausted, or I was. While the three agents seemed to catch a second wind, I was ready to lie down, and I did. Stretching out in the backseat with my head in Mason's lap, I drifted off.

It was the sound of a heated conversation whispered in hisses that roused me. I knew enough to relax even more than I already was and listen.

"Still, I don't know what the hell Christopher and Soto were thinking!" hissed Louise from the front seat.

"I don't see what you are so upset about, Louise. She's a smart woman. An actress. She knows she is playing a role. Just as we are all." Always the voice of reason, Akio tried to placate the angry Louise.

"What set you off? I don't get it." Mason tried to speak without moving his body, thus waking me.

"'The first time I fell in love with you.' We all heard it. She didn't even realize she had said it. When was the next time?"

Mason's hand moved to my arm as if to protect me from her anger. "We were kids. At the end of the show *Blue Sky Hawai'i*, she told me she loved me. Dammit, Louise, she was seventeen, and I was twenty-two. We both went on with our lives."

"She's was still a part of your life. You should have told Soto when she contacted you!"

"For fuck's sake, Louise, you need to back off!" There was anger in his voice, something I hadn't heard in a long time.

Akio again played the peacemaker. "Both of you need to chill. I am sure Christopher and Soto knew about Cat's relationship with his sister and parents. We *are* the HPB! They would have already done intel on her the moment she gave the 911 dispatcher Planz's name.

"We knew she was a professional, and we know we are. So both of you . . ." He let the warning trail off.

When Louise spoke again, there was hurt and sorrow in her voice. "Nathan, I just don't want you to get hurt. She is a Hollywood icon. You're just a working stiff, like us. There is no place in her life for you. That's all!"

I felt his body shift, perhaps to take an offered hand of reassurance. I didn't open my eyes.

Louise was wrong! There had always been a place in my life and in my heart for Nathan Song. That had not nor would that ever change. When this was over, Nathan and I would find a way to make it all work out.

Why had Louise gone from the friendly woman I had met at the compound to this woman who apparently didn't like me?

It was nearly one thirty in the morning when we crawled into bed and fell asleep.

It wasn't the alarm on Mason's cell phone that woke me. Perhaps it had roused me, but it was his voice, still rough with sleep, saying, "Shit, I have to get up!" That woke me.

Without turning over to watch him rise, I asked, "Can't you just call in? What time is it anyway?"

"No, Soto wouldn't care for that, and it's six twenty. I have to be at the office at eight." He kissed my neck and rubbed my hip and left the room.

I went back to sleep.

The bedside clock informed me it was seven eighteen when I forced an eye open. I was awake. I didn't want to be awake, yet I was. I lay there for a moment, knowing the nausea would soon greet me. I crawled out of bed and stumbled to the bathroom, pulled out four saltines from a ziplock bag in the back of my makeup drawer, and took several bites before I gagged.

Being alone in the apartment, I didn't try to be quiet. I allowed the dry heaves to pass before I rinsed my mouth. I pulled on the robe from behind the bathroom door and headed to the kitchen to make a cup of tea.

As I waited for the water to get hot, I thought about the night before. I had enjoyed the trek through Joshua Tree National Park, our dinner, and the double feather at the drive-in. But there was the conversation I had heard between Mason, Louise, and Akio. It worried me to think Louise thought Mason was in over his head. That she thought having him as the official person assigned to me had been a bad idea. It made me wonder if she might say something to Agent Soto.

If so, what was to be done?

I decided not to worry about it and got my day started by showering, getting dressed, and opting out of makeup. I put in a new pair of contacts and realized I would have to let Louise know I would need another supply soon. Before I left the room, I took my bathrobe and casually draped it on the bed before I went out and joined Sally for coffee.

"Well, my dear, I've been a little worried about you." Sally greeted me as I moved to the small coffee station to fix me a mug. "Haven't seen much of you since last Thursday."

"Mason made me take some downtime. But, yesterday, I went to my very first drive-in double feature." I was hoping this information would steer her away from MS Bentley. His passing was still too difficult for me.

"Are you serious?" she said.

I held my comment until I settled myself onto the chaise. I would tell Sally the truth, changing the realities to suit the life of Fiona Park. "I was an only child, raised mostly by my dad's parents. I started working in the family business when I was ten or so. I had a great childhood with lots of love. However, if there was a drive-in near my home, I never heard about it, and no one offered to take me."

I sipped my coffee before continuing, while Sally shifted in her seat to look at me.

"Are your parents gone?" Her small hand bridged the distance between us to land on my arm.

I thought I had told her they were, but maybe she forgot, or I only thought I had. "Yes, both my parents and grandparents."

"So you're alone." There was sadness in her voice I recognized.

I wasn't alone, and I told her, "Mason's parents and sister are my family. They have loved me since the first time we met. Between my husband, his family,"—I laid my hand on the baby body, loving the child already growing inside me, "and with this beautiful baby, I will never be alone again."

I hadn't realized the tears rolling down my face until Sally got up from her chair and moved to me. She wrapped her arms around me, and I cried, letting all the horrors, insecurities, and possibilities go.

"You know," she began, me still in her arms, "love is all around us. Sometimes it's hard to find. We just have to be open to the possibility of it." She pulled away and brushed the tears from my face. "I have seven children, more grandkids, and great-grandkids than I can count, but, my sweet child, there is always room for one more."

She kissed my forehead and then my nose before informing me that was enough boohooing and it was time to make breakfast. Maggie was coming over soon, and I was going to join them.

She gave me the chore of cutting slices from a loaf of homemade bread and readying them for the toaster.

While she expertly supervised two pans on the stove, I set the table, following her instruction as to what dishes to use and where to locate them.

Maggie showed up with a small bouquet of flowers for the table. We greeted each other as we went about our tasks. Maggie headed to the small hutch in the corner of the living room for a vase and carried it and the flowers to the kitchen.

Sally called out for me to put the bread in the toaster, and I set several jars of jelly homemade from her daughter, butter, salt, and pepper on the table.

As the last slices popped up from the toaster, Sally announced our breakfast was ready.

Maggie was radiant. There was an aura about her of joy and excitement I hadn't noticed until we sat down for breakfast.

When I did, I asked, "Maggie, you are glowing! What's up with you?"

Like a sixteen-year-old, she giggled and blushed.

"Go on and tell her! I know you want to. You're embarrassing an old woman with your blushing!" chastised Sally.

"The major and I eloped!" She thrust her left hand out so that the beautiful diamond ring was visible for us to see.

I was stunned!

Sally was up doing a gig around the table!

"When?" I asked when I found my voice.

Maggie seemed to wait for Sally to return to her chair before she answered. "It happened on Thursday. It really is because of Pearl's poor little Bentley."

"How so?" This was Sally asking around a mouthful of toast.

"Well," Maggie said, reaching over and squeezed my hand, "he just made us realize we didn't have forever. I'm seventy, and the major is seventy-two. We got maybe a good decade ahead of us. Why not be happy?"

She was correct. I was leaning this the hard way. Watching Gabriel Planz murder Hasset, who was begging for his life, and then Bentley, I understood more than I had in a long time that life was fleeting.

I had never been close to my mother, so when she died, I mourned, but I didn't feel her loss. Even though I was closer to my dad, it was almost the same as it had been with Mom. It wasn't until my grandparents passed when I felt death really smack me in the face. They had gone so close together that I hadn't finished grieving for Pa before I started grieving for Gran.

It was Sally who spoke. "Oh, hell, you two got more years than that. I'm eighty-three, and I got twenty good years of making my children crazy before I'm done!"

In her usual manner, she slapped her hands on the table and grinned her wicked smile. I didn't doubt for a second she would live to be in her hundreds.

"I am thrilled for you both. Have you told your kids? Does he have kids?" I knew she had boys, if I remember correctly, as she was visiting them when I arrived at Desert Sky Apartments.

She laughed. "Brock has four daughters!"

That must have been hard for the major. He seemed like such a macho man; having been surrounded by women his whole life seemed fitting somehow.

We talked as we finished our breakfast. Both Maggie and the major had told their kids they wanted them to come

235

for a visit in the next few weeks. Maggie was working with her boys and the major with his girls to get the schedule down so all six would be here at the same time.

Maggie looked at me and nodded. "We told them everything was OK, but I wanted them to meet my new boyfriend. I didn't tell them we were already married." She shrugged.

It seemed the major's daughter who lived locally already knew but had promised to keep it a secret. She was the one getting her sibling to come for a visit. She had a large home, enough rooms for each of the sisters and their families, and she had promised them a long weekend of fun.

Maggie's apartment was the same layout as mine. The major had already moved into her larger flat, and when the boys arrived, they could stay in his.

I was very happy for her and let her know. She pulled me over and kissed my cheek. When she leaned in, Mason Jr. began his soccer practice kicks.

"That kid is very active." She laughed, pulling away.

"You have no idea!"

We enjoyed another cup of coffee before getting up and cleaning off the table. The small grandfather clock struck the half hour past eleven when we had finished clearing up. Sally needed to go check on Sandi, and Maggie was out the door, as she and the major were going to the travel agent to plan a twenty-day cruise as a honeymoon.

I was kissed on the cheek by each of the older women as we went our separate ways. I didn't get a chance to return to the apartment before I heard Pearl calling my name.

I made my way to where she was standing outside her apartment and accepted her hug. Everyone seemed to want to hug me today.

"How you doing?" she asked once she let me go.

"I'm doing all right. What about you?" I couldn't imagine how empty her apartment must be now that her sweet companion was no longer in the house. I wondered if she had gotten rid of his things, or were they still lying about as a reminder?

"I'm doing good too! I miss the little monster, but we had a good twelve years together. I am grateful for that." She smiled a little sadly.

"Did you need me to help you with something?" I asked curious to know why she had called me over.

"No, I just wanted to see if you were all right and tell you again how sorry and how grateful I am Bentley was with you when he passed. Knowing he wasn't alone means so much to me." Tears rolled down her cheeks, and I took her hand.

We stood there for a moment before Pearl let me know she had to go to work, yet she was happy she got to see me before she left.

I returned to the empty apartment, wondering what I was going to do with the rest of my day.

I had almost decided on the twenty songs for the HBO Concert and the live album. I wanted to check on the Internet to see who the singers were in the past sixty or so years who had lived in Palm Springs and add their most famous songs to my list. I already had "The Man That Got Away" sung by Judy Garland, who had lived here. I was going to add "When I Love I Love" by the Brazilian actress and singer Carmen Miranda. Peggy Lee also had been a resident of Palm Springs, so I added her to the list I was compiling.

I went to YouTube and browsed the available soundtrack or performances of the songs I was interested in. Some were scratchy recording or clips from films, while other had been remastered. I would, when I returned to LA, have Liebman try and get digital copies of the older songs so I could listen to them. Additionally, once I had the set list and was able to contact my agent, I would be able to have the orchestration and sheet music.

I was focused on what I was doing and was caught by surprise when my cell phone rang. I paused only a moment before recognizing Mason's number.

"Hey. What's up?" I asked.

"I wanted to call and let you know," Mason began, "I'm going to be out for a few days. I can't tell you more other than everything is all right."

I wanted to ask if he was in trouble but didn't. I wasn't sure who was listening to the conversation.

"OK." What else could I say?

"There will be an agent assigned to you. They will spend the nights until I get back. I don't know who. Fiona, are you OK?" he asked again when I didn't say anything.

"Sure." I was going to miss him, but I was OK.

He seemed satisfied with my answer. "I won't be able to call you. Akio and Louise will be off the property as well. You're safe. Don't worry, and I will see you in a couple of days." There was a pause as if he wanted to say more. "Bye, Fiona. See you soon."

Later that evening, Mandy knocked on the door. It seemed she would be the agent spending the night and keeping an eye on me.

I was happy it was someone I knew and was able to spend the rest of the evening watching TV and chatting about what was going on in the complex.

Sunday morning after Mandy left, I did laundry, read, watched television, and listened to playlist I was able to pull off YouTube and several of the artists' websites. I hadn't enjoyed sleeping without Mason next to me. I did, however, enjoy the solitude of being able to do what I wanted all day long.

I had made several ventures out of the apartment, once to Sally's to see if she wanted to join me for lunch, which she did. Another time I went to the office to exchange books before spending several hours reading on a chaise near the pool.

After salad and soup for dinner, I took a hot bath, put on my pajamas, and curled up on the sofa to read. Because I wasn't sure when the agent would arrive or who it would be, I opted to keep the baby body on as well as the contacts and mouth prosthetics in place.

I was almost ready for bed when a different agent knocked. He was not anyone I had seen before. He stood in the doorway, tall and dark, a small duffel bag in one hand, and nodded, saying, "Elizabeth Soto sends her regards. Mason wanted to let you know he would see you soon."

I understood he was confirming who he was, and I stepped aside, letting him in.

Once the door was closed, he introduced himself as Agent Ledbetter. He knew the layout of the apartment and would make himself at home.

"There is food and drink in the kitchen, Agent Ledbetter. I'm going to bed," I said before heading into the bedroom and closing the door.

I didn't lock the door. I knew from experience that, like Mason, if he needed to get in, he could.

I knew the moment I awoke that this was not a dream. Even in the darkness, I could make out the silhouette of a large man hovering over me. A heavy hand held my two together, keeping them in place on my stomach with his body weight. The other hand covered my mouth, leaving my nose uncovered so I could breathe but not scream.

The voice in my face I knew. Yet it didn't eliminate the panic I felt at being restrained.

"Ms. O'Connor, it's Agent Ledbetter. I need you to listen for a moment. There is a situation, and we need to get you off-site. I don't know for how long. I need you to get up and put on that contraption of Johnson's. Put it on and put back on your nightshirt. Hurry, and if you can put on some shoes."

Ledbetter hadn't released his grip on either my hands or remove his from my mouth. "I have Agent Rosenbaum on the phone for you. If I step away, are you going to scream?"

I shook my head as much as possible to let him know I understood and would cooperate.

"Good. I'm going to the bathroom to get your mouthpiece and contacts." He let go of my hands and quickly placed a cell phone on my stomach. He lifted his hand from my mouth and moved silently toward the bathroom.

"Fiona," I heard Akio, Agent Rosenbaum's voice on the phone still sitting on my stomach. I hurriedly brought the phone to my ear.

"Akio?" The panic in my voice was thick.

"Listen, Teresa. Do everything Ledbetter tells you. I should see you soon, but until then, he's in charge of keeping you safe." His calmness did nothing to help.

I squeaked, "Nathan? My sisters?"

"They're fine. Teresa, get going." The line went dead.

This was not a game, and with a deep inhale, I jumped out of bed, stripped out of my nightshirt, and, naked, went to the closet to put on the baby body. Weeks of practice allowed me to have it on and my nightshirt back over my head in less than a minute. I reached into the closet for the nearest pair of shoes and slipped the sandals on.

Ledbetter was behind me. He gently took my elbow and led me into the living room. "We are going out the front of the complex. There is a vehicle waiting. Get in the back and lie down until I tell you otherwise. Do you understand, Ms. O'Connor?"

"Yes."

Without a word, the agent took my hand, and we were out the door. He didn't pull it closed but pulled me quickly across the courtyard and out the front gate. The SUV was parked at the curb, its front and back passenger doors open.

It seemed like only a short time before the SUV slowed, turned, and pulled into a garage. I watched as the garage door closed yet kept my place.

"OK, Ms. O'Connor, let's get you inside," Ledbetter said after getting out of the front and opening the back door. He offered his hand to help me up and out.

The house was small, about the size of our apartment. Besides Ledbetter, there were two other agents. The windows in the small open space that held the dining room, kitchen, and living room were covered with thick blackout curtains.

After a moment to confer with his comrades, Ledbetter motioned for me to follow him into the hall. He opened the door that led into a small bathroom, stepping in to place my contact case and mouth prosthetic case on the vanity.

"There are contact solution, toothbrush, and toothpaste, and other toiletries in the medicine cabinet and drawer." He pointed to the locations as he spoke. "If you would, put on the contacts and the mouthpiece." He lowered his voice. "I am the only one who knows who you actually are, and I want to keep it that way."

I nodded again and waited for him to leave. He didn't.

"If you can or want to, the master bedroom is out the door to the right. You can try and get some sleep, or you can come out and have coffee and watch TV. Either way, it's up to you." With that offer, Ledbetter stepped back into the hall and pulled the door closed.

I sat down on the toilet lid and allowed the trimmers I had been holding back to rack my body. I was terrified, worried, and wanted to know what was going on. After a few moments to get myself together, I put on the contacts and the prosthetic as instructed and stepped out into the living room.

Ledbetter nodded at me and pointed to the kitchen. There were food and drinks. I was to help myself to whatever I wanted.

I didn't want coffee. A brief search provided teabags for hot tea. Also, I was happy to discover saltines in the refrigerator. I glanced at the clock on the 1970s avocado-colored stove. It was only a little after midnight. I had gone to bed at ten twenty, so I must have just been asleep for less than an hour before Ledbetter had roused me from my sleep.

I took my tea into the living room, and one of the two other agents moved out of the recliner and onto the sofa, indicating I should take the vacated chair.

The flat-screen television was oddly out of place with the forty-year-old décor of the house. It caught my attention as soon as I took my first sip of tea.

"This is CNN," a voiceover said as a news anchor I hadn't seen and didn't know filled the screen. "We have more news from Embalse de Pinilla, Spain. Embalse de Pinilla is a community about one hundred kilometers from Madrid. It is also the location of the late Spanish actress and singer Consuela Del Torro's estate. The estate now belongs to Esperanza Teresa and Cat Connors, the twin daughter of Del Torro and American actor Richard O'Connor.

"Ms. Connors and her sister are reportedly vacationing in Europe and had been reported to have returned to the De Pinilla estate. Before dawn, five heavily armed men stormed the estate and critically wounded the caretaker. The caretaker's wife was able to hide and contact local authorities, who were able to respond quickly to the armed siege.

"A gunfight ensued, resulting in the deaths of four of the five gunmen and two local law enforcement officers."

I looked at Ledbetter, who was looking at me as if trying to gauge my reaction to the information. The estate was only mine via a technicality. I have never been there, and although I worried about the caretaker, I didn't know him or his wife.

I turned my attention back to the anchor.

"Local authorities reported neither Ms. Connors nor her sister was at the estate. The caretaker, Mr. Arturo Rubio-Garza, is expected to fully recover from his injuries. Now in Washington DC . . ."

Had there been a breach of information? I had to trust Agent Rosenbaum's words that my sisters were not in danger.

Ledbetter motioned me to come into the kitchen. We took the door from the kitchen into the garage. Telling me to take the passenger seat, he opened the driver's side door and got behind the wheel.

I followed suit, and once the doors were closed, he spoke.

"This is why we moved you. We wanted to make sure this was just a fishing expedition, which we are rather confident it was. Our assets in Spain currently have the survivor and are interrogating him. As it seems now, however, Planz's men were simply trying to ascertain if you were there. He, Planz, still has no idea where you or your sisters are."

I started to cry, the relief overcoming me. Ledbetter reached into the console and handed me several tissues before he continued. "We are going to ride out the night and morning just to be safe. Then Agent Song will probably pick you up and return with you to the Dessert Sky later this afternoon or early evening. It's just a waiting game now."

Had I been paying attention, I wouldn't have stepped on the spray paint can that I had noticed on my way out of the garage. I was so focused on the information I had just received from Ledbetter along with what I had seen on the news.

My foot came down on a small paint can. Agent Ledbetter hadn't been close enough to catch me or stop my fall as my face slammed into the metal storage cabinet against the wall. The collision was loud enough, along with my cry of surprise and then pain, to bring the two agents out of the house and into the garage.

"Jesus, Fiona!" Ledbetter said as he hauled me to my feet.

I could feel the blood running down the side of my temple and also from my nose. I was pretty sure my lip was bleeding as well.

"What happened?" asked the older of the two agents.

The other commented, "Soto isn't going to like this!"

For his part, Ledbetter got me into the house and sitting at the small dining room table so he could look at my face.

"That's going to be a hell of a shiner!" Agent One said.

"Baker! You are not helping the situation. Go get the damn first-aid kit!" Ledbetter growled at the older agent, who turned and went back out into the garage.

"Lopez, can you get me a warm wet cloth? I'm going need to clean this up so I can see what's going on," he asked the second of the two agents.

"Song is going to kick my ass!" Ledbetter said as he shook his head in disbelief.

"How bad is it?" I asked once I found my voice.

"You are going to probably need one butterfly patch over your eye." He pointed to my right temple. "Your nose is or was bleeding, and you cut the right side of your upper lip." He listed the damage. "Either way, it's going to be black and blue."

"I'll make sure Nathan and Agent Soto know it was my clumsiness and not anything to do with you or your guys," I offered.

"I don't think that's going to matter to Song."

Why would Ledbetter think Agent Song would care if I was injured? Honestly, from the perspective of the HPB, I was just an assignment and Nathan just a babysitter. But Ledbetter's reaction to how Nathan might possibly react seemed to indicate it was common knowledge that I might be more to Agent Nathan Song than an assignment.

The two agents, Baker and Lopez, returned before I could ask and Ledbetter began his triage of my face.

I was given two aspirin and asked if I would go lie down and rest. I agreed, hoping I would fall asleep before the throbbing of my face worsened.

The bed had been comfortable enough that I had fallen asleep almost as soon as my head had hit the pillow. It wasn't the pounding of my face that woke me but nausea.

As carefully as I could, I walked out of the bedroom and into the kitchen, pulling a handful of saltines from their sleeve and returning to the bathroom. I ate the crackers and waited for the seasickness to fade.

I wondered as I washed my face and brushed my teeth if Ledbetter had arranged for me to have a change of clothes. I asked as I stepped out into the living room only to be told no.

I asked if there was some way to get a change of clothes. Again, the answer was no.

Was there stuff for breakfast? This, finally, was a yes.

I prepared an egg and toast for myself. Baker had informed me as I was scrambling my egg that they had already had breakfast.

I cleaned up and, with nothing else to do, took two more aspirin and went back to bed.

I spent the day between napping and watching the news. The information hadn't changed since I had first seen it shortly after midnight. Ledbetter let me know that, as expected, the raid was to see if we were actually there. FBI sources had verified Planz still had no idea where I was.

I was sleeping when Nathan crawled onto the bed. "Hey, beautiful! I missed you."

I opened my left eye, my right being swollen shut. "I don't think I look too beautiful just right now," I whispered. "I tripped. No one's fault but my own." I told him, not wanting the three men in the other room to get the blame.

"Ledbetter told me. I am sorry." He kissed the tip of my nose. "You ready to go home?"

"Yes!" I wanted to say more but didn't get the chance as Nathan pulled a bag onto the bed.

"Your devoted husband"—he took a small bow—"stopped by the apartment and got you a change of clothes. You can clean up when you get back to the complex, but for now, change and then come out to the living room."

It took no time for me to join the four HPB agents. I took a few minutes to thank each for their time with me and apologized for the fall.

Ledbetter walked us out and helped me get into the car, before saying, "Ms. Connors, it was a pleasure to meet you. I hope this ends soon for you." He offered my hand. I used it to pull him close enough to kiss his cheek, thanking him again.

"Let's go home," I told Mason as the car door was closed.

We stopped at the local hamburger joint and ordered hamburgers, onion rings, and strawberry milkshakes to bring home.

Once we were back inside the apartment, Mason put the bags on the small table and ushered me to sit.

"Are you OK?" he asked halfway through the meal.

"I am now. Or I am better now. My face hurts like hell, though."

Mason took my chin in his hand and moved my face, so he was able to get a better look at the carnage.

"Ledbetter said it was one hell of a fall. Said you almost kept your feet. He told me you were just too far for him to catch. He was sorry about that," Mason said before popping an onion ring dipped in ketchup into his mouth.

"My mind wasn't focused on what I was doing," I confessed.

"You're gonna have a little scar there, I think." He pointed to my temple. "I suppose you can have it fixed when this is all over."

I shrugged my shoulders. In the scheme of things, I didn't think it was worth worrying about.

We were cleaning up when a thought occurred to me. "What am I going to tell Sally?"

The truth, Mason said. It was easier to tell the truth than to make up a lie. "You did it late last night, and I took you to the emergency room. They kept you there for observation as you wacked your head rather hard."

I could do that. It was an easy enough story and close enough to the truth.

I expected his lovemaking to be urgent, quick. It was the opposite.

His kisses were peppered with his telling me he had missed me. Missed going to bed and waking up with me. Missed having my body against his. Missed the smell and presence of me.

His attention to my body, every inch of it, was erotic and thorough! He was in no hurry!

When he finally entered me, I was almost in a frenzy. Even then, Mason took his time. I crested and yelled his name, begging him to stop and praying he did not.

"Nae ma-eum! Nae ma-eum!" His words exploded like his orgasm.

He allowed his body to go limp, heavy on mine. I knew he would be resting some of his weight on his elbows. I welcome the feel of him on me.

"I missed you!" I kissed his lips, only inches from mine.

"I'm glad to hear it."

He rolled off me and pulled me to him, so my head rested on his chest and our legs were intertwined.

After we both showered, we opted for an early night. I knew he had been exhausted when I saw his face at the small house with Ledbetter, Baker, and Lopez.

Once in bed, I curled up around him, making myself more comfortable, more a part of him before I drifted off to sleep.

Mason was still asleep when I rolled out of bed and hurried to the hall bathroom, securing the bedroom door behind me as I left. There was always the nausea, today a little less than the day before.

I was quiet enough that I didn't wake him as I moved from the bathroom to the kitchen for my morning tea and saltines. I hadn't thought to lay out anything to wear the night before. Therefore, I didn't get dressed.

I did, however, sneak into the master bedroom to get the baby body and the prosthetic for my mouth and to check to make sure my eyes were still hazel, which they were.

I rummaged through his room to find a large sweatshirt and some jogging shorts to wear so I wouldn't have to venture into the bedroom again. He needed the rest. If he hadn't set his alarm to get up for any reason, I wasn't going to be the one to wake him.

With one last look in the mirror to assure I was in full Fiona mode and knowing I could do nothing about my injured face, I quietly opened the front door and joined Sally for morning coffee.

"What the hell happened to your face?" Sally came to her feet, pulling me over to her for inspection.

"Can I get some coffee first?" I asked, pulling away from her and fixing my mug of coffee. I didn't answer right away but took a few sips. "I tripped and fell. Mason took me to the hospital. They kept me from midnight to late yesterday evening before they let me come home."

"Any permanent damage?" she asked, relaxing back into her lounge.

"Just my pride. Mason was beside himself with worry. I just wasn't paying attention." I was embarrassed, and it was clear.

"Shit happens. You need to be more careful. I am sure Mason was sick with worry for you two." Sally leaned over and rubbed my stomach. Mason Jr. gave a half-hearted kick. "He seems tired too."

I agreed we all were still a little tired after the ordeal.

Sally changed the subject. "What does your husband do for IFB? I wondered what you would do if you had a PhD in tech stuff."

"It's all high-tech geek stuff, which I do not understand in the least." My confession was genuine.

"Same as my Morty. He spent so many years in education that sometimes I think he spoke 'principalesse.' I never understood what he did or said. I worked and raised seven kids, and in my day, not understanding or knowing what your husband did wasn't too unusual." Sally looked over at me, giving her wise old owl look.

"I really don't want to know what he does. It hurts my brain."

"Understand," she agreed. Sally paused and looked at me all kidding aside. "Fiona, when that baby comes, what are you going to do? Did you work? I know you said you worked in a pub, but did you have any education?"

To this, I was a little embarrassed. I never had time to go to college; I was always working. Come to think of it, none of us did. Esperanza was an internationally famous musician and singer but had no university education. Olli Rose, as far as I knew, had graduated from high school like the rest of us but hadn't gone to college either. She was an accomplished artist in her own right, a painter, who also ran a family business Ogden, Kansas.

I shook my head. "I suppose one PhD in the family is enough."

"That's bullshit, and you know it, girl!" she scolded me.

I smiled weakly. My grandparents were gentle speaking folk, never heard them use a curse word. Yet, despite her gruffness, Sally Fishman reminded me of my grandmother.

She didn't mince words and spoke her mind, her love for me in every syllable.

"I don't know what I would learn. I . . ." The words drifted as I realized this was true. If I wasn't an actor, who would I be? I had no idea.

"What did your people do?"

I looked at her. How much could I tell her? My grandparents raised me, they looked out for me, and my father paid them for it.

"My mother's parents were restaurateurs," I said after a moment. My dad's father was a tailor, and my grandma was a housewife. They raised me, my dad's parents. My parents divorced . . ." I couldn't seem to keep my mouth shut. I understood I needed to edit, yet the words just seemed to come out on their own. "My mother left to follow her career, and my dad did pretty much the same."

"Don't sound like they were ready to be parents. You were blessed you had grandparents who could take you."

I couldn't have agreed more, and I let her know they were the best parents in the world.

Sally reached over and patted my arm. "As long as you had a good loving and supportive environment, it doesn't matter who they were. It seems to me they did a damn fine job of raising a beautiful granddaughter."

Like the words, the tears flowed on their own.

"Damn! I hate to cry!" I said more to myself. Sally heard me.

"Oh, well, that's just part of being pregnant. With the first two, I cried the entire nine months. 'Oops! I dropped a bean!' twenty minutes of sobbing. It was crazy. With the next three, it was the first three months only. Not as bad as the first two. And the last two, I was a crybaby the last three months of my pregnancy. It was awful, but not as bad the first two. Those two can still bring me to tears. Little bastards!" Sally reached over and squeezed my arm.

I patted her hand, and when her attention shifted, I followed her gaze.

Mason, dressed in his favorite sweatshirt, cargo shorts, and barefooted, headed our way.

"Good morning, beautiful!" He leaned down as if to kiss me yet abruptly turned and kissed Sally on the cheek.

"What a charmer!" she squeaked, clapping her hands.

He turned to me. "Good morning, my lovely wife and soon-to-be son." He leaned down and kissed me on the mouth and then on my fake baby belly. "I am getting some coffee and then going to sit down here with my arms wrapped around my wife. She had a bad fall. I was worried about you."

After bringing his coffee and setting it next to the chaise, I moved forward, allowing him to take my place. Once he was settled, I scooted back against him. Mason took his right arm and rested it on top of my baby belly, just under my breasts. His other hand brought his coffee to his lips.

He wasn't being sexual. His touch was intimate but casual.

I relaxed into the conversation Mason was having with Sally. I had missed the question. However, he was just beginning to answer.

I felt his chest rumble as he spoke. "Dr. Kajiya, Akio, and I have worked together for about a decade. His specialty is in the application of new technology for research, both scientific and data mining. My expertise is in the development of the technology, especially writing programs to accomplish a specific task."

I merely listened as they continued their conversation, awed at what I was hearing. I wondered to myself if Nathan Song actually did what he said he did. I know he had his master's, but in what I wasn't sure. I suppose it could be in code writing or whatever it was called.

Another layer to peel back and learn about this man I loved.

Mason spoke more about his project. I thought it was a bunch BS, yet the more he talked, the more I understood he was actually doing all he said he and Akio were working on.

The baby kicked, and Mason laughed. I took the interruption as an opportunity to refill everyone's coffee before returning to my place against Mason.

Sally was regaling him about her seven children and her hordes of grand- and great-grandchildren. They were entertaining each other, each making the other laugh. I was relaxed and enjoying the morning sun when Dave Hackman came into the courtyard from the parking garage. He was not alone, as he was being trailed by a young woman who looked a great deal like him and a small boy, perhaps four or five.

Dave turned our way and walked over to the three of us.

"Good Morning, Dave," I said, pulling myself up off the chaise and wrapped my arms around him. He was perhaps five inches shorter than I even without shoes, but I didn't care. I whispered into his ear, "I am so sorry about your mother." After a kiss on the cheek, I moved away.

Sally and Mason had stood up, Sally to wrap her arms around him, and Mason, once Dave was free from Sally, to take his hand and pull him forward to gently slap his back.

"Dave Hackman, this is my husband, Mason Park." I introduced the two men.

Dave thanked us all and introduced us to his daughter Susan and his grandson Austin and inquired about my face. After a moment of explanations, hellos, and condolences, Dave said, "Mom was ninety-six and hadn't been in very good health for about four years. It was her time." Tears threatened to spill but didn't.

"It's still always hard to lose a parent. I lost both of mine in my late teens and early twenties. You were blessed to have her for all this time. I know it still hurts." I let him know, a little teary eyed.

Susan took her father's hand and stepped to his side. "Yes, we have all been lucky to have her for so long!"

If she were to say more, we wouldn't know. Sandy Haley came running out of his apartment, headed our way. He was, for lack of a better description, hooting in a high piercing voice.

We all stopped and turned his way. Sally had moved around us and met him halfway. We watched as he frantically informed Sally of something in sign language. Sally reached over and touched his arm. It seemed to calm him. It was her turn to speak.

I hadn't a clue what was being said and felt terrible as I had a deaf sister whom I realized now more than ever I could not communicate with at all.

Sally returned.

"Sandi's water broke."

"Do you need someone to drive you?" asked Dave and Mason at the same time.

Sally cut them both off with a smile and a shake of her head.

"Sandy and Sandi have this all covered. I am going as the official grandmother to these two kids. They don't have a very supportive family, so it's me." She looked at the table with the coffee and turned back to Mason and me. "Can you two put this away for me? Just pull the door closed when you are done. I have to let the doctor know we're coming so they can have an ASL interpreter ready when we arrive at the hospital." She moved to me, pulling my arm down so I would lean over, and she kissed my cheek. "You take good care of your father," she told Susan, "and you take good care of these two." She waved a hand, encompassing me and the "baby" before disappearing into her apartment.

Dave and his family headed to their apartment as Mason and I began to clear up the morning coffee station.

We had just started when Pearl returned from work and blessed us for not having put away the decaf.

"Where's Sally?"

Mason answered, "The Haleys are having a baby. Sally is in getting ready to go with them to the hospital."

"Do they need a ride?" Pearl reached into her pocket as if to ensure her keys were still there.

"We offered! They have it covered," I told her as I handed her a large mug of coffee fixed the way she liked it.

She accepted the mug and laughed. "Those two are such a cute couple. They would do well on their own, but with Sally, they are going to do great."

Mason and I agreed.

Sally came out as Pearl was about to leave. "Let me know if you or the 'Sandies'"—she put the name in air quotes—"need anything. OK?"

"Will do!" Sally didn't even pause as she headed for the front of the complex.

We watched her go. Sandy and Sandi were already at the bottom of the stairs leading from their apartment.

Fifteen minutes later, when all was cleaned and put away, Mason said, "I'm hungry!" as he pulled the door closed behind him.

"Me too. What should we have?"

Once inside the apartment, we explored the kitchen. Mason found a waffle iron, and I located a box of pancake mix. Additional searching gave us two types of syrup, maple and blueberry. We were out of breakfast meat yet had strawberries and bananas—our own brunch of waffles, scrambled eggs, and a strawberry and banana fruit bowl.

I was beginning my second waffle, this time with blueberry syrup, when a question popped into my head.

"I'm curious."

"About what?"

"I was listening to you tell Sally about your job. It sounded to me as if you actually did that. Do you?"

Mason had a mouthful of waffle and eggs, so it took him a moment before he could answer. "Yes and no."

That didn't answer anything.

I waited.

"I have a bachelor's in computer engineering. What I told Sally was something I have done and occasionally still do for FBI." He wiggled his dark eyebrows up and down, our little secret. "Therefore, when I go undercover, such as I am now, this is the story I fall back on, as it is something I can speak of with knowledge."

"Is it the same for Akio?"

"Yes."

"Do your parents know where you are?" This was my real question, and it stumped him, so he almost choked on a mouthful of food. While he caught his breath, I continued, "I mean, when you are on an assignment like this, do you check in? I know your mom and your dad, though they won't say so, worry about you."

He took a sip from his orange juice before pushing away from the table.

"I didn't mean to upset you," I said before he could speak.

"No, you didn't." He moved back to the table and forked a strawberry into his mouth.

"I was wondering, you know. We have been here now for almost a month. This Thursday, it will be a month. I was just wondering if you check in with them when you are out for such a long time." I followed him with a bit of strawberry, waiting.

"I spoke with Mom two days ago. She knows not to ask about what I am doing. I know they worry, so when I can—I can't always, but when I can, I check in every few weeks or so." He took my hand and squeezed. "Mom asked about you."

"She *what?*" I yelled, not really intending to do so.

"In a very general way. She always has. 'Haneul,' she says in that innocently sweet voice of hers."

I laughed because I have seen Jackie use it on not only his father, Donald, but also Dawn and myself.

"Yeah, you know the one. 'Haneul, I heard our sweet Teresa has left the country for a visit with her sister. I hope she is all right. Maybe you should call her and find out if she is OK.' I say, 'Mom, Teresa is a big girl . . .' She interrupts me. 'If you need her phone number, I am sure your sister has it for you.' Meanwhile, I know good damn and well she has it in her hot little hand, just waiting for me to show a chink in the armor."

I was almost on the floor with laughter. I could see Jackie. I could hear her.

He was laughing as well.

"She is still matchmaking?"

"No, just with you." He leaned in and kissed me, the taste of strawberry sweet on his mouth.

He sat back in his chair. I got out of mine, carefully maneuvering my baby body so I could sit in his lap. "I am full from all this food,"—I leaned in and kissed him, nipping his bottom lip—"yet for some reason, I am still hungry . . . for you."

It was almost two hours before we resurfaced. Sated and hungry again, we moved from the bedroom to the living room after making ourselves presentable once more. We cleaned up the remains of our brunch and snacked on cheese, crackers, and the remaining fruit.

At around six thirty, after a half hour of debate, Mason called and ordered a pizza. We had decided together to call and invite Akio and Louise for a meal by the pool, to which they agreed.

Once the pizzas had arrived, I brought out a salad along with plates and utensils, while Mason called the two other agents to let them know dinner was ready.

The conversation was light and general. Throughout the evening, several visitors stopped by, including Sally.

Sally let us know the Haleys were the proud new parents of a healthy baby girl. Mom and baby were doing wonderfully. We all were invited to come and visit tomorrow if possible. She, Sally, was tired after spending the entire time in the delivery room and then the new parent's hospital room. She was going to shower and go to bed. We had offered her pizza and salad, which she gratefully accepted, and she sat with us. She ate and then kissed us each on the cheek and retired for the night.

Akio went upstairs to bring down a beer for the three of them and brought me a red plastic cup he had filled with white wine for me to enjoy. This garnered him a kiss and a hug before I sat back and pretended to enjoy the refreshing "nonalcoholic beverage."

At around nine, we split up and went our separate ways.

"This is what we are going to do tonight," he whispered with a conspiratorial tone in his deep voice. "Watch a bit more TV. I am going to shower. When you are ready for bed . . ."—by this time, he had backed me into the corner of the kitchen, a blind spot from everywhere except the entryway to the kitchen itself, and commenced kissing my neck—"and if you are willing, I want to have my way with you again! I can't get enough of you!"

He left me in the corner against the wall and the refrigerator, trying to keep my knees from buckling. The next few hours could not go by fast enough.

Three and a half hours later, I snuggled into his naked body and passed out exhausted and exceptionally satisfied.

I woke up violently ill. As much as I had tried in the last few weeks to keep my morning sickness hidden from Mason, this morning, I was not able to. I had had to climb over his sleeping body to get to the bathroom fast enough not to throw up in the bedroom.

He was just a few seconds behind me. I fell to my knees, snapping up the toilet lid, and heaved into the toilet. He was right there pulling my hair back.

"Teresa, was it the pizza?" he said, evidently thinking I had some reaction to something I ate.

I shook my head but didn't dare answer as the second wave hit.

He got up to get a cold, wet washcloth for me as I sat against the tub but away from the flushing toilet. He placed it on my forehead, which I, in turn, moved across my face and then to my mouth to wipe it clean.

"Can I get you something?"

Here it was! The moment I had been dreading and hoping for at the same time.

"In the back of the cabinet," I said, pointing to the single door under the bathroom sink, "is a ziplock baggy with saltines. Hand me a couple and sit down here with me."

He followed my instructions. As he sat, he handed my three saltines, concern and something else written over his face.

"Do you need to see a doctor?" was his first question. He was worried.

"Yes, but it's not an emergency. I'm pregnant, or rather sure I am. I'll need to see my ob-gyn soon, but I think we are OK for now."

He just stared at me, his jaw slack.

I waited for him. I didn't want to say anything until he spoke.

"We use condoms!" I wasn't sure if there was an accusation in there.

"Not the first few times." I let that sink before I pulled up something I heard many times from my grandmother. "It only takes once!"

"Or three times!" His answer came with a continual shake of his head.

I wanted to laugh. We were both sitting naked on the bathroom rug, each of us in our own state of shock.

"Dammit, Teresa!" His voice was only just audible. He quickly stood up and moved out of the small room.

"Son of a bitch!" I heard from the other room along with the punch or slap to something solid. His ranting continued as he seemed to move around the apartment.

As it had when I was seventeen, my heart shattered at his words.

I pulled myself up and turned on the shower, adjusting the temperature as hot as I could stand it before stepping in and drawing the shower curtain to seal me into the damp space.

I began to sob. My body shook with the force of it. How could he react in that way? I didn't see his reaction coming. Oh, yes, maybe he would be upset, yet not the cursing and banging around I was sure he was still doing.

I stopped crying as abruptly as I had begun. It didn't matter. This baby was important to me. I had the money and resources to have a child without him. If he didn't want to be a father to his child, I didn't want him. That was a lie, I knew, but I would say it until I had convinced myself it was true.

I opened my eyes when the water suddenly was shut off.

Nathan's hand was drawing back the curtain, and he, still naked, stepped into the shower and sat on the edge of the tub. He didn't look up at me. He placed a hand on each of my hips and pulled me around, so his face was level with my belly button.

I stilled.

He laid his cheek against my wet skin and then pulled just far enough away so he could put several kisses where his cheek had been.

"Hello, baby. I am your *abeoji*, your daddy. I want to let you know I love you already with all my heart. You have made me the happiest man alive.

"We need to talk about your *eomma*, mommy. I know she loves us as much as we love her, but I am just a bit upset with her. It seems as if she has been keeping you all to herself." His fingers gently squeezed my hips before he kissed my stomach again.

"We will forgive her, what do you think?" He turned his head to the side as if to listen to the too small voice that would, should, answer.

"I agree." He laughed, again kissing my stomach. "She is in a very unusual situation. We shouldn't be too hard on her."

His rich brown eyes looked up at mine. The glistening of unshed tears in his eyes and the crooked smile on his face brought tears again to my eyes. This time, they were not for the hurt I had imagined but for the joy I was feeling.

"What?" His attention went back to my stomach. "I don't know, but I will ask. If I do this for you, will you try and stop making your eomma so sick in the morning?" There was a pause. "Deal!"

He stood and moved me so we were both standing in the shower.

"Teresa, I am sorry you didn't feel you could tell me. I understand why. I love you! I love you both!" His kiss was full of promise.

After a moment, Nathan said, "Mason has to go to the office soon. I need to shower and get dressed. If you want, we can have breakfast. Oh, man! I can't wait to tell my folks."

I left him in the shower with his excitement of being a father. I towel dried my hair before heading to the bedroom to dress. I would put on Fiona after we ate.

As we made breakfast, I thought about his outburst before returning to the bathroom. I had thought it was because I was pregnant, yet now I was rather sure it was because I didn't tell him.

If that was the case, he had the right to throw a fit. I think I would have if the roles had been reversed.

Over breakfast, I said, "Tonight's movie is *The Secret Life of Pets* and a potluck. Are you going to be home for that?"

He said he would. Today was only for a few hours. He should return to the complex before three and could help me with our contribution to the potluck.

"I am going to check with Mandy after you leave to make sure I know what to bring. If it is something you can pick up at the market, can I text you?"

He reached over taking my hand. "Yes, eomma you can."

I giggled.

"I'm going to be a mama!" For the first time, it really hit me. "We're going to be a family!"

Mason came out of his chair and pulled me to my feet. His arms wrapped around me, his mouth on my neck. "I can't think of anything I have ever wanted more in my life than to have a family with you!"

His kiss was possessive, a claim on my heart and soul.

I returned it in kind.

"What are we going to tell Soto when the time comes?"

It was like a splash of cold water, but we needed to consider this.

We took back our seats. Mason glanced at his watch, apparently seeing how much time he had before he needed to leave.

"My parents were married seven months when I was born. I have many friends and even cousins, us firstborn sons and daughters, who, when we got into our teenage years and understood about sex and babies, realized our parents were pregnant when they married." He smiled his lopsided grin.

I knew many of the same, however, in my parents' circles, they didn't bother with marrying for the sake of their children. Half of the kids and then adults I worked with had parents who were not married or whose parent had married years after they were born.

"Times changed," I commented.

"Yes, they have. We can say as little or as much as we want."

"Nathan," I said using his name and not his alias, "Soto and those above her are not so unaware that when Mason Jr. is born five months after my protective custody is over, they are going to be rather positive we were screwing around before this all came to an end."

"True."

I put my fork down, the bite of egg still on its tines. "Would they fire you over this?"

He shrugged his shoulders.

Mason pushed his plate away. "I want you both," he said, his gaze moving from my face to my belly, "to listen. We will work this out. If it comes to that, I can always find a job. My record with the bureau is stellar. I don't think they will hold this one thing against me as it was they who set up this situation."

I agreed with his last statement. Soto or Christopher had put this team together. They knew of our history— knew we were or had been close.

Well, that wasn't entirely true. We knew each other. I was a part of Nathan's parents and his sister's lives, but not his. They had reasoned that since we knew each other, this pairing would be more natural to me. It had, but perhaps they hadn't really thought it all out.

"We will work it out one way or another," he admitted. "It will all depend on how long this takes."

I didn't question his last comment.

If I were in this place for another three or four months, we would have to explain why I was "pregnant" and then why I was *pregnant!* I didn't look forward to that. Also, at eight months, Fiona would be due in less than four weeks.

How was I going to procure a baby?

We spent the remaining hour before he had to leave cleaning up. I had also asked him to check with Louise to see if she was available this afternoon to do a touch-up on my roots and birthmark.

We, Louise and I, had agreed, with Mason as the intermediary, we would meet at her apartment at three thirty.

At ten, Mason left for the office.

I returned to the bathroom and put on Fiona. I wanted to check in with Sally to see how the Haleys were doing. I knew I couldn't go to see them in the hospital. Mason and I had already come up with a plausible excuse for me not being able to go. Part of the conversation when he had spoken with Louise was to ensure she was available to take me to a baby appointment whenever and whatever time there was a trip scheduled to the hospital.

Sally wasn't home when I knocked on her door. I went to the office, taking a moment to wave at Newspaper Man and checking to see if his female clone was up and out. She was not. From him, I got an almost unperceivable nod over his newspaper.

I smiled to myself. Not a bad gig if you could get it!

Mandy was behind the desk when I stepped in.

"How're you this morning?" I asked, moving to take a seat in front of the desk.

"Good. Sally told me about your fall. It looks rather bad. Are you OK?" Mandy said as soon as I was in the chair.

I told her it looked worse than it was. I bruised easily, I explained. It would all fade in a few more days.

Satisfied with my explanation, Mandy excitedly said, "Just got back from the hospital. Oh, that baby is gorgeous! Thick black hair and those blue eyes like her daddy. Wait!" she reached under her desk. "I have pictures!"

Moving around and taking the seat next to me, Mandy pulled up the photos she had taken of the baby in her smartphone. The new addition to the family was indeed beautiful. She had her father's steel blue eyes and her mother's freckled complexion. Also, like her father, she had a patch of snow white hair at her temple, which was striking to see on a baby. I was sure some of this would change, but for now, Baby Haley was everything a parent could wish for.

"She's deaf. The hospital already checked," Mandy told me once she had moved back around to her chair.

"Oh, that's so sad!" My heart broke for this young family.

"Good god! Don't let Sally hear you say that. I learned the hard way several months ago. If the parents are deaf, it is a cause for celebration in the deaf community if the children are deaf. They're like royalty. Sally told me. Really, she scolded me." Mandy laughed, and I joined her at her impression of Sally.

"Everyone wants healthy children. Everyone wants children to carry on their culture and legacy. Deaf parents are no different. They want children who are deaf. That don't mean," Mandy said, shaking her finger in a way I had seen Sally do, "they don't love their hearing kids. 'But it ain't no damn tragedy if they are deaf.'"

Well, then, I learned something. At the same time, I felt as if I had been chastised by Mama Sally herself.

"Thanks!" I would have hated to say something when I finally met the baby that would have hurt Sandi and Sandy's feeling. Also, this was something I could put in my file. Olli Rose, my half sister who was deaf, if I remembered correctly, had many deaf family members.

I had almost forgotten why I had come to the office. As I opened the door to leave, I asked about the potluck for tonight. Mandy informed me we were to bring a dessert.

After I closed the door, I pulled out my phone and texted Mason to bring home some sort of sweet.

I returned to the apartment and spent an hour working on the finalization of my song list for the HBO show and live album I would be doing soon—someday, whenever I was free from this mess.

Next, I took a nap.

It was almost two thirty when I woke. My hour nap had been nearly two hours. I put on the baby body, made sure the contacts were still in place, rinsed out my mouth, and took the prosthetics out and rinsed them as well before heading out to the living room and opening the curtains.

I watched television, trying to catch anything regarding the raid on Esperanza's home in Spain. There was some speculation now according to the news that neither Esperanza nor I were actually vacationing together. The media had brought up the murder at my condo in Burbank. The reporter was trying to investigate the possibility I had been involved in some way.

That was all I could stand to listen to, so I turned off the television and told myself I would speak with Nathan after the movie.

I gathered the bag under the bathroom sink, which contained all the things Louise would need to do the touch-up on my hair, eyebrows, and port-wine stain. Setting it by the front door, I returned to Mason's bedroom and opened the window, pulling the drapes back, and then followed suit with the living room windows.

Then I headed out to wait at the pool with a book.

Louise was her old self again. There was none of the tension I had felt from her over the last two weeks. I was glad of that. I had hoped to count her as a friend when all this was over. I had begun to understand she was a close friend of both Akio, Agent Rosenbaum, and Mason, Agent

Song. Her attitude was merely one of concern for friends and colleagues.

We chatted about the movie tonight and the potluck. Louise and Akio were responsible for a side dish. She had let herself get talked into making Akio's as well. She confessed she didn't know how she allowed him do it, but according to her, Akio was a sneaky son of a bitch!

I offered to help, but she declined. She was bringing deviled eggs for Akio and a tomato, cucumber, and onion salad for herself.

"I got it at the store." Louise laughed. "I am going to tell him I spent hours cutting and chopping, though."

I agreed to give him a hard time, telling him I witnessed the struggle she had.

"Why couldn't he cook for himself?"

He, like Mason, was tied up in the office.

"I have some information I can share with you. I just got it before you arrived. Nathan, I mean Mason, wanted me to let you know."

I told her to wait until I had rinsed the color out of my hair, which was due to happen in two minutes before she told me. After I had showered, returning all the prosthetics and new contacts on before leaving the bathroom, I joined Louise, who had set up a plate of cookies and fresh coffee on the small kitchen table.

Instructed to sit, I took a moment to doctor my coffee and add a few of the snickerdoodles to my plate before I turned my attention to her.

It seemed that Gabriel Planz had seriously pissed off the cartel that he was connected to. His murder of Hasset, and then his attempted murder of me had put the higher-ups, with all the HPB's attention to finding Planz, in a position they did not like. The raid on the estate at Embalse de Pinilla had only compounded their resolve to cut their ties with him.

Sources were saying they were trying to set up Planz for a fall.

"The bureau isn't sure exactly what that will entail or when it will happen. Needless to say, we think it will happen soon. If that is the case, depending on how the cartel sets him up, you may not have to do anything more than give a deposition . . . no trial. That would be the best outcome for you and your sisters. If there is no trial and the cartel wants Planz to go away, you three won't be held up for a lengthy trial.

"Additionally, the FBI and CIA are trying to locate him so they can offer him a deal. We would rather use him to curtail the cartel business than have him six feet under."

Louise reached over and took my hand. I hadn't realized it was shaking. The thought of wishing ill on someone was foreign to me, yet I couldn't help hope, even in the smallest of ways, that Planz got what he deserved. Hasset, I was sure, hadn't been an innocent. However, I was sure he didn't deserve to be shot and then thrown off the eighth-floor balcony of the apartment building.

Her voice brought me back to the cookie in one hand and her hand on mine. "It could be several weeks. Don't get discouraged. It will happen when it happens."

I smiled my thanks and ate the cookie.

"You're going to have a scar. You know that, right?" Louise pointed to the butterfly bandage on my temple.

I told her it would add to my mysterious disappearance. Lori Liebman, my agent, would find a way to use it to our advantage.

After we finished our coffees and cleaned up, I asked about the meteor shower this Friday, hoping it was still on. As far as she knew, it was on. All the arrangements had been made. The exact detail wouldn't be finalized until tomorrow afternoon, so we would have to wait to see exactly what we were going to be allowed to do.

Thursday morning, I woke with only the threat of morning sickness but no actual morning sickness. I guess Mason Jr.'s talk with his father worked. Nice!

The movie the night before had been funny and sweet. When we were introduced the sweet-faced Snowball, we gave a collective "aah." As we watched the bunny turn psycho, I leaned back to Mason. I was sitting between his legs on the chaise, and his arms wrapped around my protruding stomach and said loud enough for people around us to here, "That does it, no pet rabbits for Mason Jr."

There was scatter of laughs and several murmurs of agreement.

That rabbit was crazy!

After the movie, as we all got up and gathered our things to return to our apartments, Akio asked me, "Did you decide what you were going to name the bundle of joy?" He indicated to my stomach.

I laughed and informed him and everyone else around me I was going to name him after his father. "Akio, I don't know your middle name!"

There was a roar of laughter from those around us and from Mason, who had punched Akio on the arm and let us know his best friend's middle name was Asshole.

"Akio Asshole doesn't have a very good ring to it! Perhaps I'll just call him Nathan!" I smiled at Mason. From the corner of my eye, I saw Louise's face was frozen in a scowl.

I gathered our things and turned to look at her to ask what the problem was, but she had already made it to her apartment door.

Once back in the apartment, I decided to shower before bed and moved into the master bedroom and bath. I opted to clean the contacts and store them in the small container, as Louise has informed me it would be a few days before a new supply would be available.

Mason was already in bed when I came out of the bathroom.

"Sleepy?" he inquired, looking up from the folder he was reading.

"Kinda." I crawled in next to him. He pulled the folder closed and placed it on the nightstand.

"Secret HPB information?" jokingly I whispered.

"Yes, and it wouldn't be good for you to see it. Might have to punish you if you did." He wiggled his eyebrows at me, suggesting the punishment might be something I would enjoy.

"Keep that thought." I lifted a finger. "Louise told me about Planz. Seems like he got in over his head! Too bad for him," I mused.

He pulled me closer to him. "It's a 'wait and see' game now. We're not sure, but we know from our informants that something is in the works and it won't work out as Planz hopes. I just hope we can keep the body count low."

The last comment was under his breath, but I heard it anyway.

"What do you mean?"

I watched as Mason sorted through what he could tell me or feel comfortable telling me before he spoke. "You've seen enough television to know sometimes that when the mob or a cartel or even a gang 'cleans up,' it can become a bloody mess.

"What I meant is I, we, truly believe you and your sisters are safe. The cartel doesn't have anything against you. They are royally pissed at Planz. He seems to have become a major embarrassment to them. Knowing this, Planz is the one in danger. We just have to wait until the Los Tigres Rugientes' plans for him pan out. What the FBI is trying to do is get with Planz before Los Tigres do. For your safety as well as his, that would be the best option."

I told Mason that this is what Louise had said as well. I didn't know which of the two options I wanted for the outcome.

After a moment, Mason pulled me into his chest, and we drifted off to sleep.

Mason, Louise, and Akio had an early morning meeting, leaving me to have coffee with Sally.

The usual crowd, those coming from or going to work every morning, stopped by to get their coffee and chat for a few minutes before heading on their way. I didn't see Pearl, nor had I seen Maggie or the major.

Sally informed me the newlyweds had gone to Tahoe for the week. "Preparing themselves for their children's arrival in ten days. They still hadn't told any of their kiddos they went and got married. Damn! I wanted to be a fly on the wall for that conversation."

"Do you think it will be a problem?" I asked, knowing Sally knew both Maggie and the major much better than I.

"I'm sure the major's kids, all girls, will be OK. He was pretty messed up when his wife died. I know they worried about him. Those girls are sweet girls, and I know they want their daddy happy. One look at how he looks at Maggie and you can see how happy he is.

"Now, her boys,"—she shook her head—"I don't know them like I know the girls. Met them last year when they come for a visit. Seemed like nice enough kids to me. But I think they will like the major, and that will be good for Maggie. Also, one of the major's daughters, Lacy, is the same age as the youngest boy. I think his name was Luke. They are both single, so maybe I will do a little matchmaking on the side."

Sally laughed her surprisingly bawdy laugh and rubbed her hands together in an attempt to look evil. It failed but was a good attempt.

Pearl, she informed me, was on loan to the neighboring communities on a big case. She would be home maybe this weekend, but she wasn't sure.

When I returned with my second cup of tea, Sally was texting someone. I sat and waited for her to finish.

"They're bringing the baby home. Should be here any second now. Now you get to see the baby."

"Did they pick a name?" I was excited. I wanted to know, and I also asked how to say "beautiful daughter" in sign language.

Sally blushed! Actually blushed. I was shocked.

"Why the hell are you blushing, Sally?" I laughed.

She didn't answer right away but looked away. She wiped tears from her face, and I moved to sit next to her. "Sally, sweetie, what's wrong?" I took her hand and, with my free hand, wiped a tear from her cheek.

"Nothing's wrong, but them sweet kids named their baby after *me!*" She shook her head as if the idea was incomprehensible.

"Sally's a nice name," I offered.

"It is, but it is my English name. I have a Hebrew name, and *that's* the name they use. Oh, the poor little baby."

Whatever it was couldn't be as bad as Sally was making it out to be. I looked at her and realized she was so proud she couldn't keep it contained.

"What is it, Sally?"

She sat up and shooed me back to my own chaise. "You will soon meet Chana Tamar Haley." She smiled over at me and then instructed me on how to sign "You have a beautiful daughter." I practiced, while she went into her apartment to get something, a stuffed porcupine named Kippi Ben Kippod, who was on the Israeli version of Sesame Street.

I eyed the small animal and was informed that three of her seven children lived in Israel. She had asked for her daughter-in-law to send her a stuffed animal from one of her grandchildren's collection. They were all over the age they used them anyway, Sally admitted.

I could see Kippi Ben Kippod was a meaningful gift for her namesake.

Chana Tamar was as beautiful as she was attentive. Her eyes seemed to follow every movement within her limited sight. Sandi and Sandy acknowledged they were a little afraid to be alone with her but were looking forward to the time.

Sandy had three weeks off with pay to spend time with the baby and help get acclimated to the new arrival.

I received a hug and a kiss from Sandi after I awkwardly signed, "Daughter beautiful, you two have."

Sally nodded her approval.

We visited for a few more minutes before, with Sally in tow, the three and a quarter headed to the Haley's apartment.

I made a third cup of Earl Grey before cleaning up the morning coffee station. I straightened up Sally's kitchen before leaving, pulling the door behind me but not locking it.

The rest of the day I spent relaxing with a paperback at the pool. With Mason gone, there was really nothing I wanted to do. The apartment was clean; as small as it was, it was easy for the two of us to keep it in order.

I set out steaks for dinner. Mason could grill them on the community grills located in the common area of the courtyard. It would take no time to throw potatoes in the microwave and put a salad together. Therefore, lounging at the pool with sparkling water and a book seemed just what the doctor—me playing the role of said doctor—ordered.

It was almost five when the three agents returned to Desert Sky Apartments. I was still at the pool engrossed in Stephen King's *The Stand* when they arrived. Akio beat Mason to me, and it was he who gave me a kiss on the mouth and a hug before the other two neared.

I waited to see how Louise's temperament was today and found she was in a good mood, which I found out was due to our impending meteor shower adventure. She left us with a wave and an "I'll see ya later!"

Akio followed shortly after her. Mason took a seat at the foot of the lounge.

"What did you do today?" he asked, laying his hand on my ankle.

"Pretty much what you see here." I waved a hand indicating the pool and the book before adding, "Oh, I set out steaks for dinner. Can you grill them? I'll make a salad and nuke some potatoes."

"Sounds great!" He stood, pulling me to my feet. "We didn't have time to really eat today. Not even something for breakfast, so I'm starving."

We chatted as we made our way back to the apartment.

Once inside, we moved to the kitchen and took a few minutes to make out before Mason pulled the steaks out of the refrigerator and prepped them for the grill.

"So you had a busy day?" I asked. I hoped it had something to do with my situation here, but I also knew he had been pulled from another case.

"Yeah!" He was focused on his task, not really ready to answer.

I didn't push it. It wasn't my business. If Mason wanted or could tell me, he would.

Mason took the plate with the prepared steaks and headed for the door only to turn around and come back to the kitchen where I was working on the salad.

He kissed me again. "I missed you," he whispered into my ear. "How's the baby?"

"We're good. Didn't get too sick this morning. Not like yesterday, but that, I think, is the exception, not the rule."

Mason chuckled and kissed me again. "I'll tell you all about today at work when we sit down for dinner. OK?"

I nodded, letting him go cook the steaks.

As it turned out, Mason's day was mostly about me but not all. There was a general meeting regarding possible assignments when this one had come to its end. I asked him, using his name Nathan, what he had decided if anything. He had told Soto he might want a week or two off, something he hadn't had in several years, to visit with family.

"I didn't elaborate more than that. But I think you and I will have a lot to sit down, talk about, and plan when this is over. I do want to visit with the folks, but maybe, I was thinking, that is something we could do together." There was a hint of hopefulness in his deep voice I found endearing.

I agreed a trip to San Francisco would be in order after we had a week to ourselves. I suggested either my Malibu beach home or possibly Isla Tortuga, the island I owned with my sister off the coast of St. Thomas.

While a week in the Caribbean would be great, Nathan conceded he thought it was best for us to stay close, so perhaps the Malibu house or even just my home in Beverly Hills.

We agreed to think about it, as we had the time.

What was exciting was the approved schedule for tomorrow.

We, the four of us as usual, would first go to the Cottonwood Visitor Center for a presentation by one of the rangers. Then we would drive to Belle Campground. The campground was almost twenty-nine miles from the visitor center and twelve miles from Twentynine Palms. We would not be alone, as there would be at least two other units nearby.

I was happy with this arrangement. We had not been approved for dinner out of the compound. However, Nathan, Louise, and Akio had agreed, if it was all right with me, to pack a picnic basket with some snacks as we watched the meteor shower.

I wholeheartedly agreed to this and would get with the other two in the morning to prepare a list of things we might want or need.

We cleaned up the kitchen and relaxed in front of the television until it was time for bed.

While he did his thing, I did mine, with one small change. I left my makeup on, the bright burgundy of the port-wine stain I wanted to mask. The makeup, however, was the only thing I had on when Mason finally arrived.

Mason had been left in the front part of the house. Nathan came into the bedroom wearing nothing but his smile. It only took a moment for me to get his rigid attention!

"I was hoping to get a raise from you," I said, using my sexiest movie voice, still in full Scottish mode.

He didn't say anything at first but raised an ebony eyebrow almost to his hairline. "Is this"—he pointed to the eyebrow—"what you had in mind?" He moved a few feet closer to me.

I reached out and took his erection into my hand. "No." I gave a gentle tug. "This is what I was thinking about!"

He moved me to the bed and lowered himself over me.

His mouth took mine, and I met his demand.

Nathan was a thorough lover. There was no part of my body, mouth, neck, breasts, stomach, and lower that he ignored. Unlike the few other lovers I had had, Nathan Song made it his mission to please me first before he joined me.

Even when I wanted him inside me, he made sure I was almost there before he slid into me. Once I was pleading for him, only then did he push his way into me.

Here he took his time as well. When I was about to crest again, he said my name.

"Teresa, look at me!"

It was difficult for me to concentrate on his words, yet I forced myself to open my eyes. What I saw filled my heart. The love on his face, the desire, the passion was staggering.

Once he had my attention, he continued his deep rhythm.

"I love you!" His words fell upon me as if they were light from heaven. "I love you!" He repeated.

Surprisingly, I was able to remember—I had Googled it—the same words in Korean, so I echoed them back.

They spurred him on, his thrusts becoming deeper and harder.

I saw it on his face the second before his orgasm ripped through us both, mine swept up in its wake. Our eyes parted until finally, his fluttered closed.

Still inside me yet resting over me, his weight supported on his elbows, he kissed me and whispered, "I want to marry you."

There was no pause, no moment to consider his words.

"Yes."

The word was simple, yet everything I felt was carried on the breath that escaped my lips.

He kissed me again, and together we rolled and faced one another.

"I don't have a ring." His words were embarrassed as if he hadn't followed a planned-out course of action and was only now realizing it.

"Nathan," I said, kissing his worried brow, "I don't need a ring. At least not now. We will work it all out. I think your mother has one she wants to give you." I teased, having seen the ring she had just for that purpose.

He nodded. I was sure he had seen it before also.

We spent a few moments wrapped in each other's arms, discussing our future in vague, nebulous possibilities. We took turns in the bathroom cleaning up and readying ourselves for sleep before returning and curling up around each other.

"I have to leave early in the morning. Another long day, but should be home again about three." His breath rustled my hair as he informed me.

I reminded him about the picnic and asked if they would make the menu and do the shopping before they came home.

"Good night, Teresa."

"Good night, Nathan."

"I am happy I finally found you . . . again." Nathan pulled me even closer.

I didn't say anything. How could I? This was what I had always wanted.

What could go wrong?

WEEK V

I woke violently ill Friday morning. It was more the morning sickness. Nathan tried to comfort me, but I shooed him away after I realized this was more. He wasn't ill, so it wasn't due to our meal the night before. Perhaps it was just stress.

I asked him, as he was getting ready to leave for his meetings, to stop by and tell Sally I wouldn't be joining her. I was going to go back to bed and wait to see if I felt better later in the morning.

Nathan kissed my forehead, telling me to call or text if I needed anything. What I needed yet didn't say was for him to go away so I could go back to sleep.

I peered at the alarm clock on the nightstand. Its green number informed me I had indeed slept an additional four hours, as it was eleven forty-eight. I opened my eyes but didn't move to sit up. When no nausea followed, I cautiously rolled over on my back. After that hurdle was passed, I slowly sat up. Then I moved to the edge of the bed and let my feet touch the floor.

With each step, I waited, testing to see if I would need to make a repeat dash to the bathroom.

After a minute or two, I pulled myself up and went to shower.

The water was hot and seemed to wash away both my fatigue and my uneasiness about this morning. The back of the bathroom door had a mirror. I took a moment, after I had dried off, to appraise my body.

In the last four weeks, I had eaten more on a daily basis than since I was in my early teens. It showed. Perhaps there was some baby weight. Who was I kidding? I had gained probably twenty pounds.

Surprisingly, I looked good. I had always been curvy, but now there were curves to my curves. Since I was six feet tall, the extra weight didn't look too awful. I kind of liked it.

My agent, Lori Liebman, would have a hissy fit. I could hear her already, but things were going to change once this fiasco was over. Lori would have to adjust . . . we all would.

Reluctantly, I redressed in Fiona before heading to the kitchen to further test if my stomach could handle tea and toast.

I took my time eating the two slices of buttered toast and tea, sans cream. Once I had eaten, I cleaned the kitchen, sat on the sofa, and texted Mason that I was alive and well—feeling surprisingly well, considering this morning.

His reply was prompt. He was glad to hear. Also, if I still wanted to go watch the meteor shower.

"Meteor shower is still on! Feeling Better J"

"Great! Home @ 3"

"Don't forget food for snack"

"Done. No worries. Gotta go!"

At one, I went to go let Sally know I was all right. She did not answer when I knocked. I opened the door to say hello but found the apartment door locked. She must be out; otherwise, the door would have been opened.

I went to check in with Mandy yet found a note on the door letting anyone who stopped by that the office was closed until three. If there was an emergency, a phone number was provided.

I walked back to the apartment glancing to up to check on Newspaper Man, who was not there. Nor was the Paperback Woman. Her apartment balcony, opposite his, was empty as well.

"You doing OK?" A deep voice from behind made me yelp and jump to face the speaker. It was Johan. I patted my heart and took a deep breath.

"Wow! You scared the crap out of me!" I laughed, trying to take any sting out of my voice.

"Sorry! Didn't mean to. I saw you. I was working on an empty apartment," he said, pointing to an upstairs apartment three doors down from Newspaper Man's, "and I saw you go to Miss Sally's and then to the office. Did you need anything?" His face was concerned. I also noticed he was tense, as if ready to spring into action if I actually alarmed about something.

"No. No." I reached out and patted his arm. "Just wanted to check in. Wasn't feeling good this morning, and Mason told Sally. So I wanted to let her know I was OK."

He nodded, accepting my explanation. He also let me know Mandy, Sally, Sandi, and the baby, Chana, were at the doctor's for a checkup. Chana was OK, he reassured me when I asked if there was something to worry about. The doctor just wanted to see how mom and baby were doing.

We chatted a few more minutes before I returned to the apartment. I was going to rest until Mason returned. I wanted to enjoy the evening.

They arrived back at the apartment after three. Akio and Louise would be packing the picnic basket, I was informed when Mason walked through the door.

After making sure I was all right, we sat down at the small dining table to discuss the plans for tonight.

There would be four other agents both at the Cottonwood Visitor Center as well as Belle Campground. They would arrive in teams of two, separate cars. He was sure Jesse and his ginger would be one of the teams and thought the two agents who were always keeping an eye out from their second-floor perches would be the other team.

"There may be one more team, but we were not told who, only that it was possible." Mason took my hand. "I'm sorry you were sick this morning. I really hated leaving you." He squeezed my hand gently.

"I was OK. I went back to bed when you left. I didn't wake until almost noon. I felt much better then." I shrugged off the spell not wanting to make a drama of it.

The park rangers would be doing a lecture on star gazing with focus on this particular meteor shower starting at seven thirty. We would leave, the four of us, at around six fifteen to ensure we would be at the visitor center before the lecture began.

The ride was surprisingly upbeat. I never knew how Louise would be at any given time. I still couldn't figure out what her problem was. Unfortunately, I didn't feel as I could ask either Akio or Mason.

Louise had surprised us all with four sets of binoculars for our star and meteor gazing this evening. I took a pair and used them to look out at some of the local landscape as we drove east on I-10 toward the exit and Cottonwood Springs Road.

"Oh, by the way, Fiona, I heard from Agent Johnson. Your contacts will be delivered on Sunday to the local office. Nathan will need to go get them, but you will have a fresh pair on Monday." She seemed happy to share the news with me.

"That's great!" I agreed. What I really wanted to say was "I don't want to wear them—any of Fiona—anymore." Yet I held my tongue. I *was* happy for the new contacts.

Akio was driving. Mason was riding shotgun, so this left Louise and me to chat. Unexpectedly, we had a good conversation. With the new baby, Chana, to ooh and aah over, we filled the time until we pulled up to the visitor center.

As expected, Newspaper Man and Paperback Woman from across the courtyard were already there as a couple, excited to listen to the upcoming lecture. We had been in our seats in the small amphitheater only a few minutes when Jesse and the ginger arrived. Like the other two agents, they didn't acknowledge us other than a friendly nod, as they had with the other twelve people there.

The ranger, Ranger Stephanie Burns, welcomed us all. She informed us she had a master's in astronomy, so she really knew her stuff! Her manner was relaxed and full of humor. She had all twenty of us in her audience at ease, asking questions and enjoying the lecture she was clearly thrilled to share.

I was shocked, and I don't think I was alone when Ranger Burns concluded her lecture. It had been enjoyable and fascinating. She had told us the meteor shower would be in full swing between ten and midnight. And it was only eight thirty.

We loaded up and headed to Belle Campground. It would take us three-quarters of an hour to get there. We figured it would take about another ten minutes to find a spot so we would be in place before ten to begin watching. Ranger Burns had promised a moonless and cloudless night would ensure our viewing pleasure.

Her promise was kept as we spread out our blankets on top of the large protruding rocks within the campground. Already the sky was being painted with long white strokes spaced five minutes or so apart. Some were singles, some multiples, all beautiful.

Akio had brought up the picnic basket, so, soon, we all had a glass of wine. I opted for half a glass. Akio or Louise had also packed four different types of cheese, crackers, and assorted fruits to enjoy as we watched.

I didn't look around for the other two, possibly three teams near us. I didn't care. I knew we were safe.

We watched the light show. Between meteors, I used the binoculars to locate the stars and constellations Ranger Burns had pointed out.

Just before ten, the sky filled with streaks of light as the first large group of meteors burned through the night sky. I had never seen a meteor shower before. I wasn't even born for Halley's Comet 1986 appearance.

I was awed by the beauty of it.

Time flew by, or so it seemed. We had eaten the contents of the basket. They had thought to remember bottled water. I had drunk one already, and I had noticed Nathan, Akio, and Louise all had bottles of water in their hands.

I was not surprised when he excused himself to climb down the rock and head to the facilities one hundred feet or so away from the base of the rocks we were perched on.

I pulled out my cell. Although we had no signal, it let me know we had only been here less than an hour. At ten forty, we had almost an hour and a half left of the most spectacular showers.

I turned to Akio, who was sitting on my left. Louise had moved up to the next ledge of the rock, perhaps eight feet over our heads.

"Can we stay until after midnight? I am really loving this!"

He looked around and touched his ear. I knew he was listening to the other agents, who each had a com or bug or whatever they were called stuck in their ear. Apparently, my question had been heard by whomever.

"Cool!" Akio slapped his leg and nudged me with his shoulder. "We are clear for an after-midnight departure."

We sat a few more minutes in silence and looked out at the vastness.

Suddenly, there was one giant meteor streaking across the sky and then a burst of light, the meteor becoming two glowing orbs zooming in perpendicular lines.

"Twins!" Akio shouted, causing me to start.

"I'm a twin!" I whispered softly.

"I heard that about you!"

Even lower—I was sure no one would hear me—I wished for myself, "Maybe I'll have twins."

"Did you tell him you were pregnant?" Louise's voice came from behind and slightly above me.

I didn't say anything, feigning ignorance to the question.

"Tell who?" Akio turned to look up at Louise, who was descending from her roost.

She dropped her voice. I noticed she was pulling out the bug from her ear and motioning for Akio to follow.

"Guys," Akio spoke to the empty space around him, "we are going to need a minute of radio silence. Just a personal discussion. Is that cool? I am sure it will just take a few minutes. No, not long!" His one-sided conversation ended as he pulled the bug out of his ear and switched it off.

I didn't want to have this discussion. Not now and not with these two people.

I was pissed. "I told you I wasn't pregnant!"

"Well, next time," she sneered, "you need to do a better job of getting rid of the pregnancy test. I saw you throw it away. I knew you had lied to me."

"I didn't think it's any of your damn business, and I don't think it is now!" I quipped.

Even in the dark, I could see Akio's shocked expression at the tone of our voices.

"The hell it isn't. He's my friend. The last thing I'm going to do is let some spoiled Hollywood prima donna use him. I see how he looks at you! I don't know what you have done to him, but he is throwing his career out the window."

"Whoa! That's a little out of order!" Akio stepped up to my side, reaching to touch my arm.

"First of all, not that's it any of your fucking business, but I did tell him."

All three of us turned as Nathan's voice asked, "Tell me what!"

Again with a sneer, Louise spat, "That she's pregnant!"

Clearly confused at the hostility in her voice, Nathan looked at me.

"Yes. We have discussed this. I agree with . . . Teresa . . . Fiona," Nathan said. "It's not any of your business."

Louise growled in my direction. The look in her eyes was frightening. She hissed, "Did she tell you it was yours!"

Now he looked shocked and puzzled.

"She told me she had fucked some guy whose name she didn't even remember at a wrap party two weeks before you even saw her!" She was smugly sharing this information.

"It's not true!" I raised my hands to Nathan, pleading for his attention. "I only told you that because I didn't want Nathan to get into any trouble."

"Right!" She smirked again in my direction, clearly not believing me.

"What?" Nathan moved to me, Akio stepping out of his way.

"I lied to her because I love you. I didn't want you to get in trouble because of me!" Clearly, he could see I was telling him the truth.

"I wouldn't believe her! Nathan, you're going to go down if this is true. You know Soto will fry your ass!" Louise's voice had softened. "You are my friend. I have known the two of you ugly bastards as long as you have known each other. I don't want you to get hurt because of this. I'm trying to . . . " She seemed to search for words.

Her eyes widened for a second. She looked at me again, her expression full of loathing.

As if all the fight had left her, she turned to Nathan and said, "Nathan, please tell me there is no way she could be pregnant by you! Nathan, you worked too hard to fuck up like this."

Nathan took two steps away from me, his face full of doubt. He opened his mouth to speak, but before his answer could be heard, each of their cell phones rang. I could hear others ringing in the distance.

Akio, Agent Rosenbaum, who was closer to me than Nathan, pushed me down on the rock, indicating for me to lie on my back.

I watched as each spoke on their cells, each replacing the bug in their ear.

I pulled my cell out of my hoodie packet. It was ten forty-nine.

We left everything on the flat surface of the rock.

Akio took my arm, helping down the rock.

Louise ran off in the direction of a pair of headlights. I could see the massive silhouette of the ginger and knew Jess would be in that car.

Nathan had sprinted to another set of headlights without a backward glance. I supposed Newspaper Man was in that car.

Akio, still not speaking to me but having a conversation with someone on the other end of the bug, led me to the sedan we had arrived in.

"Get in. Put your seat belt on. Recline the seat all the way back. Understand?"

I nodded and did as he said.

I couldn't find my voice. This couldn't be how it ended with Nathan. Not after all we had promised each other.

"It'll be OK," Akio's soft voice, almost a caress, told me as we pulled onto the road.

At his voice, I realized I was softly sobbing.

"What's going on?" I reached over to lay my hand on Akio's side.

"Not sure yet. We will have more information when we get up in the air."

Up in the air?

Were we headed to an airport?

Where were we going?

I wanted to ask but couldn't find the courage.

I watched the time on the dashboard clock. I wondered why Nathan and Louise went in two separate directions and us in a third.

It was almost a half hour before we arrived at someplace. We pulled up to a brightly lit gate. "Stay down!" I was ordered again.

"State your business!" A gruff voice spoke to Akio through the opened window.

"Agent Rosenbaum, HPB." He flashed his ID to the guard.

"Welcome to Camp Wilson, Agent. Proceed to heliport pad F. Follow the signs. It is clearly marked. There is a chopper waiting. Ma'am, you all right!" he barked at me.

"Yes, sir!" I said to him and then added to Agent Rosenbaum, "Can I sit up now?"

As I sat up, I was able to see the helicopter waiting. It looked almost the same as the one that flew me to the compound where I had met Rosenbaum and Louise, if that was her real name.

We were ushered from the car to the helicopter by two uniformed military personnel. The young man helped me in and secured my harness before helping me with the headphones and mic, which allowed for communication inside the mighty machine.

Once we were up, Rosenbaum cleared his throat. "This is what I have." His voice echoed into the headphones. "At ten forty-eight, local time, there was a raid on the location where your sister Esperanza was being housed. One of the agents and your sister were shot. The agent is in critical condition . . ."

The pain in my chest was as if someone had punched me! I couldn't catch my breath.

His hands reached over and pulled my attention to him. "Fiona . . . Teresa, Esperanza is fine. She had on a Kevlar vest. Take a breath." He shook my arm.

I looked at him.

"Kevlar?" I repeated the word.

He nodded. "Esperanza will be sore, but that's it."

"Olli Rose?"

"Don't know. I know we'll move her like we're moving you."

I nodded. I could process this. Esperanza was going to be so pissed at me. I would do whatever it took to win her forgiveness. I didn't know Olli Rose well enough to assume anything. That was something I needed to remedy as well.

"Where are we going?"

"Back to the HPB headquarters in Los Angeles. That's all I know."

"What about Nathan? Where is he?"

He shrugged his shoulders. "I don't know. My orders were to get you safely back to LA. After that, I don't know!"

I waited for a beat. "What about Louise?"

I was hoping I could preempt anything she did that would negatively impact Nathan. If I didn't know where they were, how could I make a difference?

I received the same negative answer. Rosenbaum didn't know.

I was wide awake the entire flight. Agent Rosenbaum had asked for my cell phone after our brief conversation, so I depended on my watch to check the time as we flew over the outskirts of the sprawling metropolis that is Los Angeles.

It took just a little over an hour to make the flight.

When we landed, Rosenbaum helped me out of the helicopter and ushered me into the enclosed room that provided access to the roof. A fresh-faced agent was waiting for us.

"Agent Rosenbaum, you're requested to go to the debriefing room on the fourteenth floor. Soto is waiting for you." He spoke to Rosenbaum, focusing his attention on him before he looked at me. "Ms. O'Connor, I'm Agent Martinez. I am to accompany you to the twenty-third floor and to see to your needs."

I glanced at Akio, Abraham, who gave me a reassuring nod and a gentle squeeze of my hand.

Two of the four elevators were open and waiting. Martinez indicated for Abraham to enter the one on the right, and I followed him to the one on the left.

I said nothing as he pushed the button for the twenty-third floor. He turned to me and smiled. "Ms. O'Connor, on the twenty-third floor are small suites for visiting agents or for short-term safe accommodations."

The elevator dinged, the door slid aside, and we stepped out. I followed Martinez to a door marked 23R. Martinez pulled out a card from his pocket, placing it against the locking mechanism. There was a flash of green light and a click of the lock before he opened the door, stepped aside, and ushered me into the room.

The room was well appointed. There was a kitchenette with a bar for eating, a postage-stamp-sized living room with a sofa, recliner, large flat-screen television, and a desk. I followed Martinez into the bedroom and was happy to see a queen-size bed already turned down and waiting.

"The bathroom is in there." He indicated to the closed door. "Since we had only a short notice, there wasn't time to shop for you. We did, however, get . . ." He moved to another closed door. Opening it, he indicated to a hanging HPB T-shirt. "It's an extralarge, and it should be OK to sleep in. If you put your clothes, including your undergarments . . ." He looked away embarrassed. He cleared his throat and started again, "If you could put your clothes into the bag in the bathroom and leave it outside the front door, they will be laundered and ready for you in the morning."

He returned to the living room. I followed, as it didn't seem as if he was done.

I was right.

"An agent will arrive for you in the morning at seven. You will have an hour and a half to ready yourself for a hectic day. At eight thirty, Agent Johnson will arrive here to help . . ."—he paused, seeming to look for the correct words, "to help."

Martinez walked to the bar and laid the keycard on the corner.

"You are scheduled from eleven to three for debriefing and to give your deposition. After that, unless something has changed, you will be provided transportation to a location of your choosing."

He started to head for the door but turned around, pulling a small vial out of his pocket, placing it next to the keycard. "One more thing. This is melatonin. It is all natural and will not harm you or the baby. It will help you relax and sleep. Tomorrow is going to be a bitch of a day, pardon the language. You are going to need as much rest as you can get. Good night!"

Had our conversation at the campsite been overheard?

"Thank you," I said to the closing door. It paused, and I heard his "You're welcome" as the door clicked shut.

I stared at the vial for a full minute before going into the kitchen to check if there was water in the refrigerator. As there was, I swallowed the two white tablets before heading off to shower.

I flushed the contacts.

I threw the prosthetic I had had in my mouth in the trash.

I took off the baby body and dropped it onto the closet floor. I pulled out the T-shirt before closing the sliding door.

The shower was hot and fast. There were toothpaste and a new toothbrush as well as face cleanser and moisturizer.

It was almost two before I crawled into bed.

I was glad I had taken the melatonin, as I was sure I would not have slept otherwise.

I was still asleep at 7:00 a.m. It wasn't the fact someone was in the suite with me that woke me. It was the smell of strong coffee that roused me.

"Hello?" I called out.

"Ms. O'Connor, it's me, Agent Turnbull. I have coffee and something for breakfast waiting for you. Also," she said, filling the doorway to the bedroom with her blocklike build. "I have your clothes." She offered up my clothes, clearly washed and pressed for me.

"Thank you! If you could just hang them in the closet, I will be right out. I would love some coffee," I told her over my shoulder as I headed for the bathroom.

The agent was sitting at the bar, drinking her coffee when I emerged.

She didn't say a word yet slid the large Starbucks cup in my direction. I took a sip. It was just as I liked it.

I smiled at her. "You remembered!"

"Yes, ma'am, I did," she acknowledged shyly.

"Can I ask your first name?" I didn't feel like calling her Turnbull.

She blushed a bright red. It was not attractive on her square face. "You're going to laugh."

"I would never!" I teased, preparing myself for something usual.

"OK, but if you do, I'll forgive you," she teased back, her smile as warm and friendly as I remembered.

"It's Daisy."

I tried not to gawk, yet I could feel my bottom jaw drop open in shock.

"Daisy?"

"Yeah, I know. I think my parents wanted to soften me up with a really girly name. As you can see, it didn't work." She shrugged her massive shoulders.

"I think it is absolutely perfect. I love it!" I reached over and kissed her cheek.

I didn't realize a person could turn such a shade of red without requiring the Heimlich maneuver.

"OK, Daisy," I said between sips of coffee, "I need some information."

She interrupted me. "Sit down and eat. I have, I think, what you want to hear."

I followed her instructions. She moved from the chair to the other side of the bar so we could be face-to-face.

"First, you sisters are fine. Olli Rose has been relocated to the HPB office in Seattle. Esperanza, I know you were scared for her, but she has been treated and is awake and alert. There will be no repercussions from being shot. They will be flying her home, back to Florida, tomorrow."

I burst into tears.

She moved around the bar and wrapped me into her thick arms.

I sobbed.

I sobbed for everything.

For my sisters. For Nathan, whom I was worried about and unsure of what was happening with him. I sobbed for Hasset and his family.

Yet right now, I sobbed mostly for myself. I was tired and afraid, and I missed and worried about Nathan.

Daisy patted my back and rocked me as if I were a six-year-old crying over a playground snub. It was so comforting. She smelled like my grandmother, her scent floral, so I cried even harder.

After a moment, she pulled me away from her embrace, giving me a little shake before looking me in the eyes. That smile, the smile that turned her unattractive face into an angel's, was on her face.

"OK, now, Teresa, you need to go in and take a shower. Then get dressed. Agent Johnson will be here in less than an hour. I will be with you all day and will be assigned to you for the next day or so."

She patted my hand, giving it a squeeze. "After you give your deposition, the rest of your personal belongings will be returned." She paused as if to see if there was some detail she had forgotten.

She had. "Your friend Linda Arnold is also safe and will be returning to Los Angeles tomorrow as well. She asked that we let you know she will be going home first and then will be coming to your place."

I smiled at Daisy. "Thanks! I'm glad you're going to be around a little bit longer."

"I have to go to my daughter's Parents' Day Monday, but it will only be for a few hours. Then I will be back. Someone will be stationed at the house, so you won't need to worry. Oh . . . also, when you decided where you want to be taken after today, let me know. I have to let Soto know as well so we can get all our ducks in a row."

I told her I would most likely be going to my Beverly Hills home on Summit Drive.

I left her in the small living room as I went to shower and dress.

It felt wonderful not to have to put on all the layers needed to create Fiona Park. I still had the accent all last night and even this morning when I was speaking with Daisy. I knew from experience that it would take several days, perhaps even a week, before I would shake it altogether.

I smiled at my reflection in the steamed mirror. Right now, I didn't even mind the bright burgundy stain on my face.

Agent Johnson arrived precisely at eight.

"How are you doing this morning?" he asked as he put the small satchel he was carrying on the kitchen island.

"I'm good," I said. "Do you know what happened to Nathan Song? Have you spoken to Abraham? Does he know?"

He didn't answer me right away but turned to Agent Turnbull and said, "Good morning, Daisy. You are looking well. How are Randy and Heather?"

"They're great, thanks. I have to go to Heather's class on Monday for Parents' Day. Heather thinks it's cool I have a gun . . ."

I listened to the two chat, trying not to scream! Was his failure to answer me right away a bad sign? Or perhaps this is just him. Either way, I was freaking out.

"Teresa, Abe was home last night for about five hours. He slept mostly but had an early meeting. He didn't say anything to me about Louise or Nathan, so I can't answer your question." He patted my arm, trying to calm me. "This morning, we are going to give you back your wonderful strawberry blond hair and a good style."

He maneuvered me to the chair at the bar and held it out while I sat.

"I just showered," I moaned after an hour when Johnson instructed me to go rinse out the color treatment currently in my hair. He had styled it first before stripping the color and applying a color close to my natural one. "This will be the third shower this morning."

"At least you'll be clean," Daisy added, trying to lighten my mood.

"That's a good one!" Johnson high-fived the blushing agent.

"I have my moments!"

I just gawked at the two overlarge agents. They seemed to be having the time of their lives, and I wanted to scream at the top of my lungs.

I showered for the third time instead.

It was nice to look like myself again. Well, almost. I would have to use the unique makeup designed to conceal the port-wine stain. Johnson assured me it would take a good fourteen to eighteen days for it to fade. I applied the makeup as he had initially instructed.

Before Agent Johnson left, I asked if he would contact Abraham for me to inquire about Nathan and, if possible, have Abraham let me know what he knows. He assured me he would and left Agent Turnbull and me sitting on the sofa.

At ten fifty, Daisy took me to the fourteenth floor, where I was escorted into a small conference room. There were five different agents and a stenographer.

Agent Turnbull introduced me. I found that funny, as I was somewhat sure they all knew who I was. After the introduction, she leaned over to me and whispered, "I can't be in the room, but I will be back in an hour to make sure you get a break. If you need anything in the meantime, ask Brandt," she said, indicating a young agent sitting closest to the door, "and he will come find me. Are you OK?" she finished, squeezing my arm.

I nodded. Turnbull gave me her beautiful smile and left.

It took three and a half hours for the federal attorneys to be satisfied with my account of what had happened.

Agent Brandt returned me to my suite and let me know Agent Turnbull would return shortly. "I am supposed to inquire as to the location you want to be taken to."

I gave him my Summit Drive address in Beverly Hills. He thanked me and left.

Daisy returned with a case containing all of my personal belongings. She pulled my smartphone from her blazer pocket, letting me know she had charged it while I was in with the attorneys.

I took the time to put on my own jewelry and watch and check the contents of my purse and wallet. Everything was as I had last seen it.

Looking at the time, I noticed it was almost four.

"You know, the traffic is going to be awful at this time of the day," I commented.

When she didn't answer, I looked in her direction, noticing she was reading something on her smartphone. Aware I was looking at her, she lifted a finger indicating I need to give her a moment.

"OK," she said, turning to me, "Planz is in custody. He is willing to make a deal with the federal authorities. Los Tigres Rugientes are after him and not you, so we feel confident you and your sisters are safe."

Sunday morning, I was up early.

I had called Lori Liebman as soon as I walked into the house on Summit Drive. I told her I had my song list ready, I would e-mail her a copy, and I wanted the HBO Special to be filmed in Palm Springs. I would be all set in two weeks if she could make the arrangements for my usual backup singers as well as the small band I typically worked with.

She listened without too many side comments—unusual for Lori—and then after welcoming me home in one piece, she agreed to handle the arrangements, saying she knew of the perfect place, a former Rat Pack hangout. HBO, she knew, would approve.

One more thing I needed from her.

"Lori, can you find a way for me to contact Marlee Matlin?"

"Girl," she hissed in her way, "you are getting to be a lot of trouble." I could hear the laughter under the snide comment.

I agreed. I was sure there would be more to come.

"Why? I need to know why you want to contact her. I know her agent, nice guy. He'll want to know why."

Without going into too much detail, I told her about Olli Rose and how Esperanza and I wanted to talk to our sister.

Before hanging up, she assured me she would have some news on Monday afternoon. She also let me know she was giving me only a few days before she was going to be riding me to use what had happened as publicity, not only for the HBO Special but also for the live album and the movie to be released within the year.

I wasn't going to argue . . . there was no point.

Linda had come by later Saturday night, and we spent hours just catching up. I also had asked her to return with me to Palm Springs and the Desert Sky Apartments, to which she agreed.

Linda returned to her small house in West Hollywood at around two in the morning, promising me she would meet me at the apartment in Palm Springs on Monday evening.

Sunday morning at nine, my cell rang. I looked at the number and inhaled deeply. The call was from Esperanza, my older sister.

"Here goes . . ." I said to the cup of tea I had just doctored and accepted the call.

"Morning, Esperanza."

"Cat," her beautifully accented voice purred calmly into the phone using my stage name, "you owe me big time, and here is what I want you to do."

She explained her situation in Minnesota and the four, really five agents, who had become her friends and how they might have gotten themselves into trouble. She asked me, genuinely begged me, to use whatever connections I had to make sure they didn't get into trouble for keeping her safe and caring for her.

As I had my own situation to clean up, I promised her I would make a few calls to friends in Washington, doing what I could to help those we had come to care for.

After that, we took some time to tell each other what we had experienced while under HPB protection and how our lives had been changed. Esperanza explained to me her plans, and I explained mine.

We wished each other the best.

I had held out the possibility I was pregnant, wanting to wait until I was sure.

She was about to hang up when I blurted out, "Esperanza, there is one other thing I need to tell you."

"Oh?" Her voice was full of dread.

"Remember that WW II movie dad filmed in Kansas twenty-something years ago?"

"Yes?"

"Well . . . he and a little fling."

"¿Y?"

"We have a sister. She is twenty-three, and her name is Olli Rose O'Connor Bergstrom." It was like ripping off a Band-Aid; I didn't know how else to say it.

"A sister?" she repeated.

"Yes, I hear she is a really sweet girl," I offered.

"You've never met her before?"

"Once, when her mother died, when she was three, I went with Dad to the funeral."

"I want to meet her!" she responded. I could tell from her voice she was excited.

"Wait." I was serious again. "Olli Rose has just gone through the same experience as you and me. The HPB has assured me she is fine, but it will be another few weeks before we can meet up with her. Esperanza, take care of what you need to. I have a few things I need to take care of. Then we'll find a way to meet up with our little sister, OK?"

She agreed.

"Esperanza, let me know if you need anything." There was more I wanted to say but just couldn't find the words.

"Love you too!" she told me and hung up.

I was up before six on Monday morning, having had to race to the bathroom. I had not been bothered by my morning bouts of nausea for a few days. I had hoped it had passed.

I had a lot I wanted to do today. Daisy, Agent Turnbull, arrived at six, trading out with the agent who had come at ten the night before to replace her.

I inquired as to what time she would be leaving for her daughter's class. She would go at nine thirty, she informed me.

It was difficult to find something in my closet that fit. I remembered, in the back of my room-sized closet, clothes I had kept from a movie I had done two years ago. I had gained twenty pounds for the character. I wasn't sure why I had kept a third of the wardrobe; however, I was happy that I did.

I opted for a pair of capri slacks, a summer blouse, and sandals with a flat heel. I finished my makeup before joining Daisy in the kitchen.

Getting her attention, I said, "I am about to make a phone call. To my ob-gyn. I don't want you to be uncomfortable."

She shrugged. "No. I'm good. If you want me to leave, I will."

I shook my head and called Dr. Geller on her cell. I had her number because we ran in the same circles when I socialized. Although not a friend, she was an acquaintance.

She answered on the second ring. I apologized for calling her, but after explaining my situation and that I was going to be out of town for the next two to three weeks, she agreed to see me at eight in her office.

I looked at the oven clock and told her I would see her soon.

As for Daisy, her eyes were huge. She straightened her shoulders and informed me she would not say a word to anyone.

I thanked her, not really worried, and asked if she was going to drive me or ride with me. She told me I could drive myself. However, there would be an agent following.

I also let her know I would be returning to Palm Springs after lunch.

She nodded as if she already knew this was in the works.

"I have Agent Rosenbaum's cell number. He asked me to give it to you." She pulled out a yellow sticky note and handed it to me.

"Thanks."

He did not answer when I called. I left him a message, asking him to let me know if he had heard from Nathan.

Although the blood test results would be ready after two, Dr. Geller was sure I was pregnant. She had given me the name of a prenatal nutritionist in Palm Springs, telling me I should meet with her as soon as I could. Also, prenatal vitamins would be ready to pick up at my local pharmacist.

I was thrilled.

I was scared.

I wanted to tell Nathan.

Once back at the house, I called and spoke with Mandy Davidson using my Fiona persona, as my accent had yet to fade, asking if it were possible to meet with Mrs. Grayson this afternoon at around four. I also inquired if I could rent the apartment I had been staying in for the next three weeks. I, of course, would pay whatever rent was required.

She told me she would make the inquiries and call me back as soon as she had the answers.

I took to on my laptop to locate the name of the director of the HPB, jotting down the contact info.

I was packed and on the road by eleven forty-five.

I opted for the Tesla, remembering the parking garage at Desert Sky Apartments had four spots for electric cars. Daisy didn't follow me but returned to her office with the understanding that if I needed anything, all I had to do was call.

I was halfway between Los Angeles and Palm Springs when I received Mandy's call. Mrs. Grayson would love to meet me at four, and the apartment was always available for me until I no longer needed it.

I thanked her, hung up, and spent the rest of the trip planning how I would explain and apologize to the people at the apartment complex who had become my friends.

Almost as soon as I disconnected from Mandy, Dr. Geller called. She confirmed I was pregnant. According to the timetable I gave her, I would be due in about eight months. She suggested I come back in a month unless I had some concerns. As far as the morning sickness went, she assured me I was doing everything possible to lessen the morning spells.

After disconnecting from her, I tried Abraham again. Again, I connected with his voice mail. "Tell Nathan I have to speak with him. Tell him I didn't lie to him." My voice hitched with a sob. "Tell him I went back to the apartment in Palm Springs."

I stopped in Banning for a drink and a bathroom break. Once I was back in the car, I used the Tesla's phone system to dial the HPB office in Washington DC. Once connected, I explained I was a friend of the governor of California, giving the direct phone number to the governor's office, before introducing myself.

Surprisingly, I was put through to the assistant to the director's secretary.

After assuring I was *that* Cat Connors, I went on to explain the situation. I described my intentions, wanting to make sure none of the agents involved would suffer any repercussions for their heroic actions. Having pulled out the list of names Esperanza had given me, I added Nathan's and Abraham Rosenbaum to the list.

I also agreed, for attention to these matters, I would do several PSAs for the HPB at no charge.

I gave the helpful man my cell phone number and asked if he would please forward my request to the director.

I was assured the director would get the message.

I arrived at the apartments at three fifty. The key code worked, letting me into the secured gate of the garage. Pulling my car into one of the places allocated for the electric cars, I sat for a moment. I left everything but my purse in the car when I got out.

Before walking into the compound, I texted Linda the key code and gave her the apartment number, telling her I would see her later.

And, oh, I was pregnant.

"WTF!" said her text. "See you at around 8. Will eat then! Find place. Mexican my favorite."

"DUH," I texted back before placing my phone into my purse.

Mandy's instructions were to go to Renee Grayson's first-floor office and knock. She would be waiting.

The door to Renée Grayson's first-floor office opened, and the grand woman was standing there looking as if Chanel had dressed her herself. It wasn't the fabulous clothes that made this woman who she was. It was the genuine warmth of not only her smile but also her chocolate eyes.

"Right on time. Come in and have a seat." She welcomed me as if I was a weekly visitor. "I have some tea and biscuits in the other room. Just give me a minute."

Without having the opportunity to tell her not to bother, she was out of the small classically decorated room.

She started to speak as soon as she crossed the threshold from the small room into her office, yet I interrupted her.

"Ms. Grayson, I want to apologize to you."

She laughed, lifting a finger after setting down the tray. "Do I call you Cat, Teresa, or Fiona?"

I gawked at her.

"Do you think I would not remember a face like this even if it was camouflaged? Cheekbones like yours do not happen often."

"You knew?" I asked.

She didn't answer me at first, pouring a cup of tea and placing two of the giant sugar cookies on a plate before me.

"Teresa,"—she used my real name even though I never answered her question—"this is my place. Do you think I don't know who IFB really is? My office and maintenance staff, Mandy and Johan, came to me when I signed the contracts. I know a government check when I see one. You have nothing to apologize for."

She took a sip of her tea, raising an eyebrow at me to follow suit.

I used the sip to gather my focus again. "To be honest, I thought you recognized me when Mason and I came to visit that first time."

"I still remember the nineteen-year-old who sat at my table. Despite having already established yourself, you were gracious, polite, and unaffected. I liked that about you. Not many in your shoes are that way."

"My grandparents would have 'taken me to the barn,' as Pa used to warn me. He never did." I laughed at the memory. "the threat was enough."

She smiled at that.

"So, Teresa, why are you here?"

I explained I needed time for my port-wine stain to fade. Grayson didn't buy that. Her look told me she expected honesty. I would give her that.

I told her everything. We ended up on the small sofa, her arms around me, comforting me as I cried.

She gave me time to gather myself, pushed me up, and looked at me. "Teresa, I think it all will work out. Have a little faith. The apartment is yours until you don't need it anymore."

I wiped my face and blew my nose with the tissue she handed me.

"I know Sally was worried when you didn't come back. Also, Maggie and Pearl were asking about you. Being able to speak to them will be good. Tell them the truth or as much of it as you can." She went on to instruct me exactly how much of the truth I could tell. I was to leave out the part of IFB being the HPB/FBI. I also was to leave out the number and identities of the agents with the exception perhaps of Nathan Song.

As he was the real reason, I was back at the apartment. I promised her I would follow her directions to the letter. "Teresa!" She got my attention as my fingers touched the doorknob. "I would like for you to visit now and again. I meant it when I told you I remembered you. I always felt, despite the age difference, we would be good friends."

I turned and wrapped my arms around her before kissing her cheek. "I will see you soon. How many tickets for the dinner and concert?"

I had explained the HBO show. I would start with dinner first, as in the old days, and then do the concert. Everyone at the Desert Sky Apartments would be getting an invitation.

She put up four long fingers.

I smiled and left the beautiful woman in her classical office.

Next, I located Sally. She was not surprised by anything, saying she had lived too long to get really shocked by things. She always liked my movies, except one I did several years ago. "Don't know why you wasted your time!"

I loved her even more after our hour together.

Pearl was not home. I would catch her later. Maggie was. She stood frozen in place as I explained who I was. She took off her cochlear implants and adjusted them as if sure they were malfunctioning before placing them back on her head and asking me to repeat what I had just said.

As I repeated the information, she sank slowly into her recliner. "Well!" She said, "I didn't see that one coming. Oh my! I got love advice from Cat Connors." She started laughing or crying, I wasn't sure. I gave her a hug, and after a moment to get her composure, she calmed down enough for me to explain why I was back. "Fiona! What do I call you?" she asked flustered.

"Teresa," I told her. "That's who I am to my friends."

She puffed up like a proud mother hen.

"Teresa, I want to let you know that Fiona was my friend. I'm going to miss her." She wiped a tear from her cheek.

"I'm right here, Maggie. I'm right here." I took her in my arms.

I went to find Mandy to thank her and Johan for their service. On my way across the courtyard, I saw Newspaper Man sitting in his usual spot. I waved and was rewarded with a wave back.

Mandy and Johan were in the office. They were expecting me. After receiving hugs from them both, I asked about Agents Rosenbaum, Little Feather, and Song.

Rosenbaum, I was informed, was back on duty at the bureau office. Little Feather was still on the property, as she really was teaching a class, as I knew. They were not sure what was going on regarding Agent Song.

I thanked them. I needed to get to my car and also check my cell. I had had several phone calls while I was with Ms. Grayson and Sally.

I saw her near the pool moving in the direction of her apartment.

"Hey, bitch!" I barked.

Louise's head snapped up, and she paused only for a second in her stride.

"I'm surprised to see you!" she commented, her voice a neutral tone.

I didn't move as she headed my way.

Once she was within arm's length, I shoved her hard, forcing her to fly backward and land on one of the lounge chairs. Once she was down, she stayed sitting in the chair.

"Ma'am?" A deep voice came from close behind me. "You just accosted a federal agent."

I turned to find Newspaper Man a foot from me, his hand resting lightly on his service revolver.

"Look, Newspaper Man!" I started, anger still heavy in my words.

"It's Norman, ma'am." Norman's voice was as calm as his face.

"Norman? Really?" The exchange took the fire out of me. I looked at him for a moment and then back at Louise and then back to him. "Norman, I didn't accost a federal agent. I accosted someone whom I thought was my friend and who betrayed me. Hurt me for no reason other than she could!"

"That's not true!" Louise countered. "I am your friend. But I was Nathan's for longer. I didn't want him to be hurt."

"Excuse me, ladies." Norman's soft comment pulled my attention back to him. "I think this is where I leave. You good with that?" The last words were directed at Louise. Her slight nod sent the man away.

"Will you come with me into the apartment?" Louise asked.

We spent almost an hour talking. When we were finished, Louise was convinced I was telling the truth about Nathan being the father. Like Abraham and the Davidsons, Louise did not know where Nathan was. Yet she promised to find out.

Louise helped me get my things out of the car and back into the apartment.

Linda arrived at eight. I remembered the restaurant we had eaten at the first time we went out. El Mirasol Cocina Mexicana was just across the street.

I had had just enough time to listen to my messages before Linda showed up and ordered us to leave. She was hungry. She was upset with me regarding my cryptic text and, after asking me when I ate last, was more upset with me for starving my baby.

She was a powerhouse like my grandma was.

Dinner was going to be a long affair. I couldn't wait to sit down with my best friend and tell her everything.

Tuesday morning, before Linda came into my room and told me to get my lazy butt out of bed, the smell of coffee and bacon woke me from my sleep. I had been lying around trying to gauge if morning sickness was soon to descend upon me.

There had been a slight queasiness but nothing more.

I looked at Linda's back as she left the bedroom. If I didn't get up, she would hound me, so I slid out of bed and, after a trip to the bathroom, stumbled into the central part of the apartment.

"I have tea or coffee. Here is your plate." She put down a plate with two eggs, several slices of bacon, and toast on the table, eyeing me until I sat.

"Lori Liebman has called already three times this morning," she scolded me.

I looked at my watch; it was only seven twenty.

"Wow!" I commented.

"You know how she gets. Tea or coffee?"

"Tea." I waited for her to sit down at her own plate before I said anything.

"What did she say?"

"Not a lot. Sounds like she has been busy and wanted to get with you early this morning." She paused to take a bite of egg and bacon and wash it down with a gulp of coffee before continuing. "Also, you need to call the HPB man in Washington. I'm sure he is waiting for your call."

One of the messages I had received yesterday—well, actually two of them—was from the office of the director of the HPB. The first was the secretary I had spoken with. Then the second was from the actual secretary of the director. I was informed that the director, of course, had already taken care of what I had asked. He, the director, would appreciate a call at my earliest convenience to discuss the PSAs I had offered to do.

I would have to call Lori first to let her know what I had done. I am sure she wouldn't be happy.

"As soon as we're finished with breakfast, I'll call Lori. I have to tell her what I promised the HPB."

"She's gonna rage at that!" Linda, as my assistant and friend, knew how my agent acted.

Being one of the top agents on the West Coast, I allowed her many of her foibles.

I shrugged my shoulders.

I changed the subject, asking Linda how long she could stay.

It depended on how much I needed her. Almost anything I needed could be handled with a call or text.

Linda needed to get back to LA, as she had several appointments of her own. I knew I would be good with Sally, Maggie, Pearl, and the rest nearby.

I tried to help clean up the breakfast dishes. Linda shooed me away and told me to get on the phone with Lori. She didn't want her cell to ring one more time.

Before she left, I asked Linda if she would go to my house and overnight to Esperanza in Naples, Florida, an evening dress I had in my closet. I explained Esperanza's plans, and Linda agreed the dress would be perfect.

Lori had indeed been busy. She had secured the Purple Room, a former Rat Pack hangout that had been restored for the dinner and concert, being recorded by HBO in less than two weeks. HBO had been waiting for the call and was ready. They had liked the theme songs from the '40s and '50s.

Lori told me HBO would arrange for a fitting for me in a week. They wanted ball gowns from those eras as my attire. I let Lori know I would use my stylist team, Robert and Valerie, for hair and makeup.

The ensemble and backup singers would be set to start tomorrow, Wednesday, at a small dinner theater that would be rented out during the day for us to rehearse.

Additionally, she had contacted Marlee Matlin's agent. Ms. Matlin would be happy to meet with me on Wednesday morning at eleven at her house for lunch if that was good for me.

It would be perfect, I let her know. I jotted down the address, thanking Lori for all her hard work.

"It's what I get paid the big bucks for dear!" she roared.

She was worth every penny.

I took a breath and hoped she was in as good a mood as she sounded. I informed her first of my deal with the HPB.

True to her nature, she chastised me and scolded me for not letting her know first. I apologized, letting her know it was a snap decision. Of course, she was right. Blah! Blah! Blah!

"Well, this works out better than I had hoped. This is what I have in mind, and since I have to talk to the HPB director, I will get it all ironed out," Lori said in her most calm voice.

I listened as she told me that I could expect to be on a plane on Sunday to appear on several of the morning news shows to speak about my ordeal. Lori would also be talking to Ellen to line up a time for me in the next week or so to be on her show, as it was local.

I knew better to argue and told her to keep me informed as to what I could and couldn't say when I was being interviewed. Lori promised she would.

Retaking a breath, I hurriedly said between a pause, "Lori, I'm pregnant!"

There was an unusually long silence from her end of the phone. And once again, Lori Liebman, agent extraordinaire, illustrated why I loved her.

"Oh, baby!" Still in her whiny New York accent but full of love and concern. "You all right? Who's the dad? I know you don't sleep around." There was an even longer pause. "The agent in charge of your protection? That son of a bitch?"

"Lori." I tried to interrupt her.

"They need to hang him by his balls, taking advantage of you like that!?" She was actually angry for me.

"It's Haneul Palan Song, Nathan Song!" I blurted.

The silence was longer.

"He was the agent who was assigned as your husband?"

"Yes."

"Does he know?"

"Yes."

"Is he happy or a dick?" Classic Lori.

"He's thrilled." I hoped that was still true.

"Where is he now?

"I don't know. The HPB pulled him back to an old assignment, and no one seems to know where he is." The hurt in my voice surprised even me.

"He's a good man, Teresa! A good man. I don't think you have anything to worry about." She soothed me and then went back to her ol' self. "Now I need to hear from that director about your free . . . I can't believe you did that by the way! *Oy!*"

We talked for a few more minutes before Lori had to go. "I'll call Matlin's agent and let him know you will see her tomorrow. But you gotta get your butt back to Palm Spring for rehearsal!"

I promised I would. Without a word, Lori hung up!

Next, I placed a call the Washington DC.

The man was as excited as a teenager when my call was put through. He gushed at how much he loved my movies.

He had seen me in the play I had won the Tony award for *and* had all my albums.

I told him I was happy to hear that and thanked him for his quick response to my request.

"Not a problem. Not a problem!" He assured me.

We were on the phone for almost a half hour. I gave Lori's information to him, letting him know she would be the one whom the arrangements would need to go through.

Before he hung up, I asked, "Excuse me, I was wondering if you could let me know how I could locate Agent Song."

He apologized, letting me know Agent Song had been pulled back into the case he had been working before he was assigned to me. Of all the agents, he was the only one who had not been contacted directly by their bureau chiefs to get their commendations.

I thanked him, disconnecting the call before I could cry.

Linda made the arrangements for me to take a helicopter from Palm Springs to the studio helipad on early Wednesday morning. From there, I was picked up by a driver and delivered to Ms. Matlin's home for lunch.

I was met at the door and ushered in. Two teenagers were waiting in the large eat-in kitchen. They introduced themselves, asking if they could get a photo with me. Once that was done, Matlin signed something to the two, who signed something back before leaving the kitchen with a wave and good-bye.

Her sign language interpreter, a man I had seen on television with her before, explained I should speak directly to Ms. Matlin. I thanked him.

Over a meal consisting of charred salmon on a bed of an avocado, kale, and tomato salad, I thanked her for seeing me. I explained about having found out I had a half sister, and Esperanza and I wanted to include her as part of the family.

She was deaf and used American Sign Language, which we didn't know yet wanted to learn. My goal for meeting with her, Ms. Matlin, was to see what kind of help or advice she could give us. I gave her Olli Rose's name, and Ms. Matlin was excited to let me know she knew of my sister. She even had met her at an auction, where she had purchased one of Olli Rose's landscapes.

She had several ideas. It would take a day or two to check, but she could call or text me with the information when she had it.

At one, I left. It had been a delightful time. I had wondered why we hadn't ever worked together. Matlin had wondered the same. We decided jointly to look for a project that would suit us and let the other know if we found something. I had also confessed I was pregnant. I would be taking some time off. However, I would genuinely like to do a play or a movie with her.

The drive to the studio and the short flight got me back to Palm Springs at three thirty. I was to meet with the backup singers and the band at five. I stopped for a hamburger, french fries, and a strawberry shake before heading to the address Lori had given me.

By Tuesday the following week, we were ready.

All the invitations had been sent out. RSVPs had been received. Including Linda, Lori, my family from the Desert Sky Apartments, HBO execs, the record company execs, and several of their VIP invitees, there would be a total of sixty-nine for dinner and the concert afterward.

I arrived at the Purple Room at noon. We would have one rehearsal before the actual filming. Additionally, HBO wanted to do an interview with me before the concert, which would be included in the broadcast.

The actual dinner would be from seven thirty to eight forty-five. The concert and filming would begin at around nine.

I had made sure Sally had a beautiful outfit to wear. I also had arranged for four stretch limos to pick up the residents of the apartments. I had included the Haleys, Sandi and Sandy. They declined, letting me know through Sally they were not yet ready to leave Chana with a sitter just yet.

At seven, people started to arrive. Linda had accompanied me when I came at noon. She had changed in my dressing room and used Robert and Valerie's services. Lori had come at around three to listen to the rehearsal and to work with the director who would be shooting the HBO Special. She likewise had used the makeup artist and hairdresser.

Sally, Pearl, Maggie, the major, Andrea Miller, Steph Robbins, and Anna Ball were the first to arrive.

The tables were four tops. The band would be on the stage. The backup singers and I would be on the postage-stamp-sized dance floor. There were three stationary cameras set up as well as one team that would film from body cameras.

I had placed Sally, Pearl, Maggie, and the major at one table close to the dance floor. On another, I had arranged for Louise Little Feather, Agents Rosenbaum, and Johnson, as well as Agent Soto, who hoped she would be able to come. Louise was in the second limo to arrive.

I had one small two top near the corner of the dance floor, out of the way of the cameras, I had reserved for Nathan if he came. Using everyone I knew, I had let him know there was a place for him.

I prayed he would come.

Dinner was a four-course affair. Each course offered two choices. The first course was lobster bisque or gazpacho soup. This was followed by an appetizer of eggplant and hummus pâté with grilled ciabatta or crab cakes. The salad choices were between a classic Caesar salad or a garden salad.

The main course consisted of either a prime rib with sautéed asparagus or petite potato medley or chicken Kiev with grilled green beans and sautéed root vegetables.

Finally, dessert was either crème brûlée or chocolate molten cake.

There were wine and mixed drinks for those who wanted and sparkling water for those who didn't care for a cocktail.

I worked the room as people ate, going from table to table to welcome my friends, the executives in attendance, and those I didn't know but understood the importance of their being at the concert.

Linda made me sit and have a little something to eat before I was ushered into the dressing room for hair, makeup, and the first of three wardrobe changes.

"Ladies and Gentlemen, the Incomparable Cat Connors!" the emcee announced, and I stepped out from behind the curtain to the applause of my guests.

I began with "It's Only a Paper Moon" written by Billy Rose, E. Y. Harburg, and Harold Arlen, made famous by Ella Fitzgerald. The first forty minutes were these types of standards made famous by singers such as Fitzgerald, Clooney, Lee, and Holiday.

I loved performing. I was in my element. Because I knew almost each one of those faces, I paid that much more attention to the audience. I could tell from Lori Liebman's expression that I was on fire.

I took a twenty-minute intermission, while dessert and coffee were served.

The second set would be more substantial. The song list would include "La Vie En Rose" made famous by Edith

Piaf, "Being Good Isn't Good Enough" from the Broadway Musical *Hallelujah, Baby!* "Complainte de la Butte" from the 1955 French move *French Cancan*, also a song by Piaf. I would include "El Fuego en Mi Corazón," this one made famous by my sister Esperanza.

I had loved the song "Say Something" written by Ian Axel and Chad King of the group A Great Big World. I had seen the video with Christina Aguilera; it had taken my breath away.

My final song would be Judy Garland's version of "The Man That Got Away" from the classic *A Star Is Born*.

Each song was a show-stopping, heart-wrenching moment. There were tears in the eyes of those I could see. After I sang "El Fuego en Mi Corazón," I took a small break.

Louise had got up in the middle of the song. I paid little attention, but her movement distracted me for a second.

The band began the introduction. The three backup singers left the stage and moved to the bar. I started "The Man That Got Away."

I poured my heart into the song. I felt every word. I could belt this, perhaps not as Garland had, but close enough.

I looked at the empty space at the back of the room. A camera was there, and I sang to it as if it alone could find Nathan.

A movement caught my eye. Louise was standing in the far corner. There were tears on her copper cheeks. Perhaps she understood now what her careless words had done.

There was silence and then an explosion of applause and cheers from the audience. Lori was wiping tears from her face, something I thought would never happen in my lifetime.

I was spent. I didn't bother to wipe the tears from my face. I was frozen in place. So much so the people at their tables had turned to look where I was fixed.

I had seen Louise pull him from the dark corner of the bar just as I had let the last note fade. He stood there, his face lit with a smile. His clothes were simple, jeans and a T-shirt, as mine were fit for a grand ball.

He walked to me. I heard a laugh as the sound of a waltz from the band filled the air. Sally and her table were applauding, spurring on the rest.

My knees wanted to go out from under me. It was by sheer determination that kept me from falling to the floor.

"Teresa, you are the most beautiful thing I have ever seen. But . . ." he said and took me in his arms and kissed. When I could catch my breath, he continued, "I am not the *man who got away!* If you'll have me, I will be the man you get to keep."

He dropped to his knee and from his pocket pulled out a small velvet box.

I heard "oohs" and "aahs" around me, yet I focused only on him.

Holding his grandmother's diamond ring up, Nathan Song said in a voice that filled the Purple Room, "Catálan Orlando Teresa O'Connor, will you do the honor of marrying me?"

The words would not come out of my mouth. So I shook my head and dropped to my knees, so we were eye to eye.

The crowd was going wild.

As Nathan slid the ring onto my left hand, I promised, "Haneul Palan Song, I will! I love you!" I laughed. "By the way, we're going to have a baby!"

I don't know if the cameras were still running. After a half hour or so, I sang one more song. It took the band a few minutes to see who knew it. The bassist, the drummer, and the pianist all knew the song. One of the backup singers also knew the lyrics. We took another few just to get it all together, the audience enjoying champagne and cake, which had appeared from nowhere.

With their help, with Nathan sitting on a chair at the edge of the dance floor, I belted out a song sung by Trisha Yearwood and written by Jon Ims, "She's In Love with the Boy."

Later, we returned to the apartment, Nathan and I.

"I don't want to wait," he called from the bathroom.

"Me either!"

"We need to call my folks in the morning."

"I want to call Dawn!"

He came out fresh from the shower, water still gleaming of his naked body.

"You look nice." I smiled.

"You'll look better once you get out of the outfit."

I was still in the last ball gown from the concert.

"I might need some help," I teased.

"I will always be happy to help you get out of your clothes!"

And he did!

EPILOGUE

EIGHTEEN MONTHS LATER, ISLA TORTUGA

Nathan and I married two weeks after my Emmy and Grammy award-winning HBO Special filmed. Eight months later, the twins were born. We had opted to name the boys after both our grandfathers. Patrick Jung-hee Song was born first; three minutes later, Gonzalo In-suk Song followed.

We, Nathan, the boys, and I, split our time between the Summit Drive house and a home we purchased in Monterey near Nathan's parents.

Nathan had taken a leave of absence when the boys were born. After much discussion, he then decided to leave the HPB and do consulting work for a few of the major studios.

I had been equally busy.

True to her word, Marlee Matlin had found a play about two sisters, one deaf and the other hearing. The hearing sister was the only member of the family who was not deaf. Although this was part of the theme of the play, it was more about two sisters reconnecting, discovering they had more in common than either had assumed.

The play had been an enormous success at one of the local playhouses in LA. One of the networks was currently in negotiation to bring a limited twelve-episode adaption to the small screen. Both Matlin and I had been tapped to reprise our rolls.

A month after we were married, I started my American Sign Language classes. Marlee had recommended several deaf ASL teachers on both the West and East Coasts, so Esperanza had begun her classes as well.

Three months after we had been released from the protective services of the HPB, Esperanza, Olli Rose, and I had flown to the Plantation on Isla Tortuga. We spent two weeks getting to know each other. Of course, our teachers as well as ASL interpreters accompanied us and had been guests at the hotel.

So much had happened, all wonderful, since that scary night I witnessed Gabriel Planz kill Hasset. As weird as it was to say, having my life turned upside down had been one of the best things to happen to me.

I had learned so much during my time at the Desert Sky Apartments. My teachers had been Renée Grayson, who had reminded me of who I had been. Sally Fishman, who had reminded me so much of Gran and how I was raised. Gran would not have like the woman I had become.

Maggie Gershon and Major Brock Willingham, who helped me remember that love was out there for us.

And, finally, Master Sergeant Bentley, who had captured my heart and taught me to love without expectations.

I was grateful beyond measure.

Now, I stood on the balcony of the Isla Tortuga Plantation marveling how perfect my life had become. It was always great. Now it was perfect!

Collectively, Esperanza, Olli Rose, now a full partner in the businesses on the island and a third owner of the plantation house, and I had decided to close the hotel from the twentieth of December to the third of January. We gave the hotel staff off until the twenty-seventh with pay. This had been our thank-you for their hard work and dedication to the hotel and us.

On the twenty-seventh, Dawn and her family, as well as several from the Desert Palm Apartments, Sally included, would be arriving for a week at the hotel. I knew both Esperanza and Olli Rose would have their own set of visitors as well.

Yet from now until the day after Christmas, it was just us sisters and a few others.

We had arrived yesterday. Esperanza and Olli Rose would be at arriving anytime today. Their lives had changed as well, and I looked forward to our Christmas holiday together. It would be our first. Hopefully, the first of many.

Jackie and Donald, Nathan's parents, had been on the flight with us and would have one of the en suite masters.

I had more news to share with my family. Even Nathan didn't know yet. I was pregnant again.

What a perfect gift to share for the holiday.

I heard the sound of a pontoon plane and watched as it made its descent into the protected lagoon of the island. I didn't know which sister it would be, and I didn't care.

"Nathan! They're here!" I called out, knowing he would hear me in the bedroom.

His arms slid around me as he kissed my neck. "I suppose we should go meet them."

"Are the boys down for their nap?"

"Yep, and *halmeoni* promised to keep an eye on them."

I turned to him and kissed him. "I don't know what we would do without your mother."

Nathan rolled his eyes and laughed. "We aren't going to find out anytime soon, I promise you. Come on!"

We walked hand in hand down the stairs connecting the covered balcony, which ran the entire circumference of the second floor, giving each bedroom and even both end of the hallways access to the beautiful vistas and ocean breezes.

As we loaded into the open air van to head to the lagoon, I leaned over, kissed his cheek, and quietly said, "Nathan, before everyone gets here, I have something to tell you."

List of the songs sung by Cat Connors and suggested **YouTube** versions.

1. "Return to Pooh Corner," by Kenny Loggins
   https://www.youtube.com/watch?v=wQhCNOV5Gnk

2. "The Man That Got Away," performed by Judy Garland from *A Star Is Born*
   https://www.youtube.com/watch?v=UzyPMRo8ZUQ

3. "When I Love I Love," performed by Carmen Miranda from *A Weekend In Havana*
   https://www.youtube.com/watch?v=vPmZ9cdKeOY

4. "It's Only a Paper Moon," written by Billy Rose, E. Y. Harburg, and Harold Arlen, made famous by Ella Fitzgerald
   https://www.youtube.com/watch?v=CHCMWaiG-gI

5. "La Vie En Rose," performed by Edith Piaf
   https://www.youtube.com/watch?v=rzeLynj1GYM

6. "Being Good Isn't Good Enough," from the Broadway Musical *Hallelujah, Baby!* performed by Lea Michele
   https://www.youtube.com/watch?v=ox7WUbaRMXk

7. "Complainte de la Butte," from the 1955 French move *French Cancan*, performed by Rufus Wainwright
   https://www.youtube.com/watch?v=iqUazoCayx0

8. "Say Something," written by Ian Axel and Chad King, performed by A Big World featuring Christina Aguilera
https://www.youtube.com/watch?v=-2U0Ivkn2Ds

9. "She's In Love with the Boy," written by Jon Ims, performed by Trisha Yearwood
https://www.youtube.com/watch?v=mUFObCZtGWQ

10. "Up on the Roof," written by Gerry Goffin and Carole King
https://www.youtube.com/watch?v=ySAmXOy0CuE

The Cherokee legend about the Milky Way:
http://www.powersource.com/cocinc/articles/milkyway.htm